<u>**Praise for Minerva Spencer & S.M. LaViolette's**</u>

"Spencer creates characters worth rooting for. Readers will be eager to see Phoebe's sisters find their own matches next."

-Publishers Weekly on PHOEBE

<u>THE BOXING BARONESS</u>

"Swooningly romantic, sizzling sensual…superbly realized."

–Booklist **STARRED REVIEW**

A *Library Journal* **Best Book of 2022**

A Publishers Marketplace Buzz Books Romance Selection

"Fans of historical romances with strong female characters in non-traditional roles and the men who aren't afraid to love them won't be disappointed by this series starter."

–Library Journal **STARRED REVIEW**

"Spencer (*Notorious*) launches her Wicked Women of Whitechapel Regency series with an outstanding romance based in part on a real historical figure. . . This is sure to wow!"

-Publishers Weekly **STARRED REVIEW**

<u>THE DUELING DUCHESS:</u>

"Another carefully calibrated mix of steamy passion, delectably dry humor, and daringly original characters."

—Booklist **STARRED REVIEW**

VERDICT: Readers who enjoyed *The Boxing Baroness* won't want to miss Spencer's sequel.

–Library Journal STARRED REVIEW

A *Library Journal* Best Book of 2023

"[A] pitch perfect Regency …. Readers will be hooked." (***THE MUSIC OF LOVE)***

★*Publishers Weekly **STARRED REVIEW***

"Lovers of historical romance will be hooked on this twisty story of revenge, redemption, and reversal of fortunes."

This book is dedicated to Jackie.

I miss you every single day.

10

The Shrew

The Hale Saga Series
Americans in London
Book 2

Minerva Spencer

writing as

S.M. LAVIOLETTE

Prologue

London
January 17, 1872
A Wednesday

I hate you!" Lady Io Hale snarled as Corbin Masterson bent her over the back of the settee and gave her bottom three hard slaps.

"I hate you more," Masterson snarled right back, delivering another three swats that were even harder, until Io's body hummed with need for him.

"Lift your skirts. *Now!*" He gave her another hard swat when she didn't move fast enough for his taste.

Io was tempted to tell him to go to the devil, but she wanted him too badly, and so she hastily hiked the heavy velvet gown up to her waist.

Masterson hissed in a harsh breath when he saw that she had worn nothing else today—not even drawers. "You hussy!"

It sounded more like a compliment than an insult and Io smirked at both his accusation and his hungry tone.

Aside from her brother Zeus, the Duke of Hastings, Corbin Masterson was the most conventional, conservative, and repressed man Io had ever met. Most of the time.

But not when he was in the bedchamber.

She knew it must drive him half-mad that his sexual tastes aligned so perfectly with a woman like her.

Io was more than a little dumbfounded herself that she had anything at all in common with Corbin Masterson—aside from their mutual dislike, which had sparked between them since the first moment they met—but the last six weeks they'd spent as lovers had been eye-opening, to say the least.

Somehow this stern, prim, and aloof man had discovered cravings within her that she never would have imagined existed.

Cravings like spankings…

Masterson stroked Io's bare buttock with one large, warm palm. "Your skin marks beautifully," he muttered quietly, as if to himself. He followed his words with a series of flat palmed swats that made Io's eyes water.

And that wasn't all that happened.

Her infuriating lover stroked a bold finger between the folds of her sex. "You get so wet for me." His smug tone was both annoying and arousing, like so much about this man.

Masterson might act like a humorless, moralizing prig toward the rest of the world, but the man knew his way around a female body, and not just to take his own pleasure, either. Who would have guessed?

One of the things he enjoyed most was bringing her right to the edge of her climax and then maddeningly denying her satisfaction.

Which is what he was doing right now, toying with her in a way designed to make her even more desperately needy for him.

But Io had a few tricks of her own.

When Masterson continued to tease Io shifted lower over the settee, canting her hips and thrusting up her bottom in a way that never failed to drive him to distraction.

"My God." His guttural growl told her that it had worked just as well this time.

Even though they had been engaging in these furtive trysts for weeks, their lust for each other showed no sign of abating, which had been their stated intention when they'd agreed to commence these Wednesday assignations.

In fact, the opposite was proving true. Corbin Masterson was like a fever in Io's blood and she was determined to fuck him out of her system. It had to work.

It *had* to.

And why wouldn't it? It had worked so well in the past with Io's other lovers.

Io: The Shrew

***

Corbin Masterson stared down at his hand as he massaged Io's spread, slick sex and felt the same howling, consuming hunger he always did with this blasted, infuriating, intoxicating woman.

He needed Io Hale worse than food or water.

Or at least that was how it felt most days.

Corbin slid his wet finger away from the source of her pleasure, smirking at her groan of frustration. She liked to be the boss in the bedchamber. So did Corbin. He greatly enjoyed proving to her just who was master again and again and again.

To that end, he stroked a finger slowly toward her back hole, spreading her copious arousal over the tight pink furl. They had done many things over the past weeks, but never had he explored this taboo part of her body.

Rather than be outraged or shocked—as any virtuous woman would and should be—Io merely chuckled throatily and thrust her ass higher. "*Mmm*, Masterson… that's so *naughty*."

Corbin's eyes narrowed. The vixen was mocking him, was she?

"I am going to take you back here next time." The words were out of his mouth before his brain had granted permission.

Predictably, Io barked a laugh.

Unpredictably, she said, "Of course you may do that."

Stupefaction, mixed with excitement and almost crippling arousal, caused pre-ejaculate to spurt from Corbin's tormented cock, contributing to the already mortifying stain on the front of his trousers.

And his heart seemed to have relocated to his throat.

"You would allow it?" he asked, surprised he could squeeze even that much around the obstructing organ and relieved that he did not sound a fraction as excited as he felt. Indeed, he sounded almost…bored.

"*Mmm-hmm*," she purred. "Right after I do it to you."

Corbin's jaw dropped and his finger froze. His mouth moved wordlessly for a moment, no doubt making him resemble a landed fish. He was beyond grateful that she could not see his foolish expression.

"I can almost see your face, Masterson," she said in a voice rich with amusement.

Not that she *needed* to see him to know what he looked like, evidently.

How on earth did this woman *do* that to him? He was almost forty years of age! He'd not blushed this much since—Hell! He had no recollection of ever blushing as much as he did in the presence of this twenty-five-year-old temptress.

Corbin scrambled to scavenge a scrap of dignity and retorted, "Fortunately for me you are not physically equipped to carry through with your threat, my lady."

Her lush body shook with mirth beneath his nerveless fingers. "Are you really unaware of how a woman can do such a thing?" She *hooted* at him. "Oh, Masterson! How I look forward to shattering your innocence and giving you *that* lesson. I can just imagine what your expression will be *then.*"

Corbin's jaw sagged when her meaning struck him like a baseball bat to the side of the head.

"You will need to keep using your imagination, my lady, because I am hard pressed to imagine a less likely scenario than *that* one," he shot back.

As retorts went, it was pathetic. But it was better than admitting what was really going on in his mind, which was utter bafflement that any man would submit to such a thing.

"You really are a babe in arms, aren't you, darling? For your information, there is a spot inside the male rectum which yields a considerable amount of pleasure when stimulated. I would love to be the first to—"

Corbin gave her bottom a sharp smack. "Shut up, you obstreperous mantrap."

A peal of laughter filled the room.

He stared down at her beautiful body in wonder. This woman was unlike anyone Corbin had ever met—male *or* female. She was arrogant, crude, self-possessed, and she had absolutely invaded every nook and cranny of his being until he could scarcely think straight.

Not that Corbin would ever let *her* know that.

Io: The Shrew

You poor fool. Don't you think she already knows?

Scowling, Corbin unbuttoned his trousers, freed his aching erection, and used the head of his cock to stroke the soft wet petals of her sex, teasingly nudging her sensitive *clitoris*—the only word he now used in Io's presence since the first time when he had referred to it as her *pleasure button* and she had laughed herself silly.

With each caress he earned soft, encouraging moans, sounds he felt inordinately proud of eliciting from this proud, demanding woman.

"So good, Masterson," she purred, pulsing her lush hips at him. "Put on a condom and fuck me, *now.*"

Corbin's eyelids fluttered and his balls clenched up to his body so hard and fast that he almost spent at her crude command.

Bloody hell but she was a vulgar vixen! And there must be something wrong with him because he simply could not get enough of her.

Fortunately, he had developed iron control since meeting her weekly and enduring her sensual abuse—and reveling in her pleasure—and was able to keep from making a fool of himself.

At least when it came to condoms.

The first time they had made love—or *fucked* as Io insisted upon calling it—Corbin had fumbled so badly that he had torn one of the thin rubber johnnies before managing to pull on the infernal device.

Naturally, Io had mocked him cruelly.

Corbin firmly and viciously pushed the embarrassing memory from his thoughts and took the packet that he'd brought along with him, quickly and deftly sheathing his hard shaft.

He should have known that first time—when his reaction to the nagging harridan's taunting had been arousal rather than strangling her—that he was far more smitten than he had ever believed possible.

He, Corbin Jacob Masterson, a man whose name in the army had been *Sober Sides*, had fallen for a woman who had never seen a rule she didn't want to shatter or a person she didn't want to render speechless. A female who was fond of saying—not only to Corbin's face, but also in the middle of balls and dinners—that there was only one use for men, and most of them were not even good for *that.*

A woman who hated the concept of marriage and all it stood for.

A woman who hated *Corbin* and all *he* stood for.

The only thing Io liked about him was *this*—these illicit, rushed couplings filled with deviant activities like spankings. These once-weekly meetings that only lasted a few brief hours and never happened often enough.

And which always left him *starving* in body and soul for more.

Corbin truly was every bit as stupid as she was always accusing him of being.

"What are you doing back there, Masterson? Composing a sermon?" she demanded, twisting around to look at him.

He grabbed a fistful of her hair and yanked her head back *hard*. "Stay put and don't speak unless I tell you or I will gag you, my lady."

As always, her magnificent body went pliant at his cruel treatment.

And then she whispered, "*Please…sir*," and all but unmanned him.

Corbin snarled like the animal she made him and rammed himself deeply into the wet hot heaven of her body.

"Yes!" She arched her elegant spine and raised her hips to take him even deeper.

"My God," Corbin muttered, thankfully under his breath, trying not to think of where all this would end.

Because end it would.

And he feared the end would come sooner, rather than later.

Beneath him, Io squirmed. "Faster and harder, Masterson!"

Corbin gave her buttock a stinging slap. "Quiet!" he growled, giving her other cheek an even harder swat. "I'll be damned if I take orders from likes of *you*, Lady Io Hale," he said, even as he did as she bade him and sped his thrusts, pumping into her with brutal snaps of his hips.

You will be damned, Corbin Masterson, a grim mental voice agreed Not only your immortal soul but also any chance you might have for future happiness in this life, as well.

The words rang out so loudly in his head that his thrusting stuttered and he was momentarily thrown off his stride.

Yes, he shot back, his hips quickly regaining their rhythm, *I will be damned. And I do not care about that, either.*

The truth was that Corbin had no intention of calling a halt to these weekly Wednesday trysts. Trysts which he now lived for.

He would keep coming to this room—to this woman—for as long as she would meet him.

Because afterward—when she eventually decided that she was finished with him and moved on—Corbin would have the rest of his life to pick up the pieces of his heart and try to forget about Lady Io Hale.

Chapter 1

The carriage slowed and Io gawked at the monstrous Fifth Avenue mansion looming above them. It looked large enough to easily accommodate all the members of the Canoga Community with plenty of room to spare.

"Good Lord," Balthazar, Io's twin, muttered beside her.

Their other three siblings—Apollo, Ares, and Evadne—appeared to be awed into silence.

The moment the carriage drew to a halt a dozen servants erupted from the enormous house and descended on the two luxurious coaches that had collected the five Hale siblings and their scant luggage from the recently completed Grand Central Depot.

The horde of servants put Io in mind of ants—but garbed in expensive livery—working as a single organism, intent on their task.

It was a little unnerving to be the focus of so much domestic service, especially since Io had never had a servant in her life.

A man in a sober black suit followed behind all the others, his clothing declaring his role as butler.

He came to a halt in front of the carriages once the Hales had all scrambled out.

"Good evening, my lords, my ladies. My name is Collins, His Grace's butler."

Io startled at the sound of their ridiculous new titles on his tongue and felt Balthazar jolt beside her. Their younger brothers—yet another set of twins, but identical rather than fraternal—snickered, the sound more than a little scoffing.

Only their little sister Eva—an anglophile through and through—smiled, looking as if she were in heaven.

Io: The Shrew

Collins ignored all their reactions and boomed, "Please, come in. His Grace and Miss Barrymore are expecting you."

Io and Bal looked at each other. *Miss Barrymore?*

Her twin knew what she was thinking without her needing to speak, and he shrugged. So, Bal didn't know who this person was, either.

Ever since they'd discovered a month ago that they had a recently deceased millionaire grandfather and an older brother they'd not known existed—Zeus Constantine Jonathan Hale—and that Zeus had recently inherited an English dukedom, Balthazar had been the one who'd been in charge of communicating with their new sibling.

Not because Bal wanted to, mind, but because Zeus was a product of paternalistic male-dominated New York society and believed that only men were capable of comprehending subjects like their grandfather's last will and testament.

Or complex subjects of any kind, for that matter.

A woman's role was to be decorative, deferential, and obedient. Seen but not heard, just like all the children they were expected to bear for their lords and masters.

Io felt her temperature rising just thinking about the world she was walking into. She reluctantly thrust away her irritation. She would have months and months—two whole years, in fact—to fume and seethe about the injustices rampant in upper class society.

"This way," Collins said, gesturing to the room beyond the double doors.

They all filed into a foyer that was bigger than the dining hall at Canoga and which could probably accommodate at least a hundred people.

"This is phenomenal," Ares said, his admiring gaze fixed on the marquetry floor as one servant took his hat and another helped him from his coat.

The instant her youngest brother was free of his outdoor garments he dropped to his haunches and stroked the intricate woodwork. "This cannot be new work. It is a masterpiece."

"It came from a castle in Florence," a voice above them said,

Io looked up to find Zeus, whom she had only met once, descending the stairs. Beside her oldest brother was a tall, raven-haired woman who would have been beautiful if not for the appalled expression on her face as she looked at Ares petting the foyer floor.

"Welcome to your new home," Zeus said, sounding as if he meant it. "The train was on time, I see. I trust you had a pleasant trip?"

"Yes, thank you. Your private railcar was most, er, commodious," Bal said when the rest of them stood tongue-tied.

Io suspected that her twin had changed the word from *ostentatious* at the last moment.

"I am pleased to hear it," Zeus said. "This is my fiancée, Miss Edith Winston Barrymore."

"Miss Barrymore," Bal said bowing. "I am Balthazar, this is my twin sister, Io, my brothers Apollo and Ares, and my youngest sister, Evadne."

Miss Barrymore did not seem to hear Bal's greeting, her disbelieving gaze moving slowly over the rest of them.

Io had noticed the supercilious and even outraged looks they had attracted when they'd disembarked from her brother's private railcar at the train station. Most of the negative attention had been directed at her and Eva, who wore the short skirts and bloomers common among women at Canoga. Io had expected such reactions from strangers.

She did *not* expect such open censure from his brother's fiancée.

"Why, what quaint clothing," Miss Barrymore murmured as she looked from Io to Eva. "And such interesting hairstyles."

Io sucked in a breath, preparing to give the other woman a *quaint* piece of her mind.

"The garments we wear are purposely designed for comfort and economy rather than fashion," Bal—ever the peacemaker—said before Io could commence her assault. "As for Io and Eva's short hair, not only do they look fetching, but it does not require the services of a maid or a great deal of time spent in front of a looking glass." He paused and then added, "All of us work, Miss Barrymore."

Io was proud of the way her twin managed to impart censure while still smiling.

It was, however, wasted on Miss Barrymore who merely murmured, "Hmm." And then moved her attention from Bal and Io to the twins.

"Ah," she said, her cool blue gaze sliding from Ares to Apollo and then back. "My, you certainly are… similar."

"Identical, in point of fact," Ares said dryly. "I am Ares." He took Miss Barrymore's limp hand and lowered his lips over it, causing their sister-in-law-to-be to wince.

"I am Apollo," Pol said, a dangerously mild expression on his face. He ignored Miss Barrymore's hand—which she had pulled closer to her body, as if afraid he might touch it like his brother had—and bowed so slightly it could scarcely be called one.

Edith blinked at his dismissive attitude; her expression amusingly perplexed.

"Would you like to have tea? Or do you need to rest and freshen up first?" Zeus asked, apparently unaware of the tension in the cavernous room.

Io didn't need to look at her siblings to know what they wanted. All five of them were normally active people who had sat in a luxurious railcar for the entire day, doing nothing but eating and relaxing.

"I don't think we need any more rest," Bal said when the rest of them merely stared.

"Tea, then. Right this way," Zeus said. He and Miss Barrymore headed back up the stairs.

"I've never seen anything like this," Io hissed in Bal's ear as they followed the other pair. "How many people do you think live here?"

Bal shrugged. "I thought it was only Zeus, but perhaps *she* lives here, too."

"You forget we are no longer at Canoga, Brother. She does not live here as they are not yet married," Io pointed out.

Bal just grunted, his eyes darting around as he tried to take everything in.

The room their brother led them to was so opulent that it was even more of an assault on the senses than the foyer had been.

The ceiling was monstrously high—complete with lounging cherubs and gods and other mythical creatures—and the walls held massive landscapes that were bigger than a dining room table at Canoga.

Heavy velvet drapes swathed windows that were twice as tall as Io's twin. The gleaming wood floors, or at least what one could see of them, were covered in thick, jewel toned carpets.

Io resisted the urge to check her battered old black ankle boots for dirt or muck.

"Allow me to introduce you to Miss Barclay, who is Miss Barrymore's cousin and companion." Zeus nodded to a woman who was so tiny and drably dressed that Io had not even noticed her in the midst of so much luxury.

"And this is my friend and secretary, Corbin Masterson," Zeus said, gesturing to the side of the room, where a tall, attractive blond man stood surveying them. For some reason, he put Io in mind of a Viking, his broad, powerfully built shoulders slightly incongruous in his exquisitely tailored suit. His hair was the color of ripe wheat and his eyes were a coldly appraising slate gray. For one moment his flat gaze rested on Io. She lifted an eyebrow at his haughty, measuring look.

He blinked slowly and ignored her challenging expression, turned to her siblings, and said, "It is a pleasure to meet all of you." His voice was cool and clipped and he was obviously a man of Zeus's own class, which made it surprising that he worked for her brother as a secretary.

Or perhaps not. After all, what did Io know of such matters? The new world around her could hardly be more different than the rustic, cozy agrarian home she had left behind.

Far behind.

"Please, have a seat," Zeus said, gesturing to the collection of silk covered settees and chairs clustered together.

Everyone sat.

"I noticed there was not much luggage," Zeus said, "Is the rest still to come?"

"No, we brought everything with us," Io said, deciding poor Bal shouldn't have to bear *all* the burden when it came to communicating.

Io: The Shrew

"But there were only a half dozen bags," Miss Barrymore said, her eyebrows arching high, her tone one of disbelief.

"That is all we are bringing with us," Io replied as politely as she could manage.

Once again, the other woman's eyes flickered over their clothing, lingering on Io and Eva's calf-length skirts. "It is probably for the best that you left most of your…garments behind."

"You misunderstand," Bal said quickly, before Io could speak. "This is everything we own. We do not have a great many personal possessions."

Another silence inserted itself, only broken when the door opened and two servants entered one bearing a tray laden with pastries and cake, the other balancing an enormous tea tray.

Zeus glanced at Io and looked as if he were about to say something.

"Set it right here," Miss Barrymore said to the servants in a cool, confident voice, and then she occupied herself with the business of preparing their tea.

Io had the distinct feeling that her brother had been about to ask *her* to take charge of the tea ritual.

Zeus asked questions about the trip and the weather, and Bal answered them while the others seemed content to gaze around at the spectacular room.

Io found that her gaze kept being pulled to Mr. Masterson, who sat at some remove from the group, as if to emphasize his position as a menial in her brother's household. Although there was nothing menial about the proud set of his broad shoulders or the arrogant tilt of his chin.

He was too well-bred to show his thoughts, unlike Zeus's fiancée, who clearly loathed them all on sight, but Io couldn't help thinking that his gaze was faintly disbelieving. As if he could not countenance that his regal friend and employer was related to this band of rustic yokels.

"When will we leave for England?" Eva asked, the only one of the five of them who was genuinely pleased to be there, although they had all voted on the matter and agreed to come.

It is an opportunity we should not pass up, Balthazar had insisted when they'd discussed leaving their home for two years and going to England under their oldest brother's tutelage.

Io looked at that older brother now.

Zeus was an extremely handsome, if stern, man. Right now, he was looking at Eva and, shockingly, a slight smile curved his lips, making him look almost human.

But then, Io's little sister tended to have that effect on people—making them smile—whereas Io usually made their hackles rise.

"We will leave in just a little shy of three weeks," Zeus said.

"And what ship are we sailing on?" Eva asked.

"*The Petrel.* It is not the fastest Transatlantic ship but we will still arrive in Southampton in less than nine days."

"Nine days," Ares repeated, sounding as awed as Io felt. It was hard to imagine going so far a distance—not just physical, but temporal, as well—in such a brief time.

"It is one of your brother's ships," Miss Barrymore said, sounding as proud as if she already owned it. She met Io's gaze. "How do you take your tea?"

"Black, please," Io said.

"Susan," Miss Barrymore barked.

Miss Barclay sprang from her chair, hurried to her cousin, and brought the teacup and saucer to Io.

"Thank you, Miss Barclay," Io said.

The woman looked flustered, as if nobody had ever thanked her before. Judging by the way her cousin barked orders at her, Io could well believe it.

"I thought you were a banker. I didn't know you owned ships," Apollo said.

"My interests are quite varied," Zeus said, his almost gentle tone making the younger man blush.

Io felt bad for her brother; she had believed the same thing—that Zeus was only involved in banking. It was rather humiliating to realize just how little they seemed to know about life outside the boundaries of the Canoga Community.

Indeed, learning more about the world had been the main reason Io had voted along with her twin to go to England.

"Well then," Miss Barrymore said once she'd handed off the last cup of tea. "I don't wish to rush everyone—"

"*And yet here she goes,*" Io muttered so softly that only her twin could hear her.

"—but we have only three weeks until we depart for England and—"

"Are you going with Zeus and the rest of us?" Ares asked.

Their brother's fiancée frowned, clearly not accustomed to interruptions. "His Grace does not use that name. If you address with his Christian name, then you should call him *John*. As to your question, *yes,* I am going to England."

"Are we supposed to call you *His Grace?*" Io ignored the supercilious woman and addressed her question to her brother.

Zeus looked slightly pained. "No, of course not. You are family."

"But you want us to call you *John.*"

"It is the name I have always used," he said, subtly evading her question.

"Why don't you use the name *Zeus?*" Io persisted.

"John is what my aunt and uncle, who raised me after my mother's death, always called me."

His answer reminded Io that their deceased father had, for reasons unknown to them, abandoned the only child of his first wife and kept his existence a secret from the rest of his children. a fact that made her ashamed of their parent.

Miss Barrymore gave a condescending laugh. "My dear Lady…Io, you must understand where you are *now*. Not in some backwater, but the most sophisticated city in America—perhaps in the world. His Grace is a well-respected man of business and such a frivolous first name would make your brother a figure of ridicule. *John* is far more appropriate."

Io was rendered speechless—a rare occasion—and looked at *Zeus* to see how he took his fiancée's characterization of his name.

But her brother's expression was unreadable as he set his cup back in the saucer and then stepped into the ringing silence. "Edith has been gracious enough to offer her assistance with our transition to England," he began, evidently choosing to ignore the issue of his name. "As the future mistress of Hastings Park and all the other estates that come with the dukedom it seems only sensible that she and her cousin"—he inclined his head slightly toward the tiny, colorless Miss Barclay, who was perched on the edge of her seat and the only one of them without a cup of tea— "will both travel with us to England."

Miss Barrymore gave Zeus an approving look, as if he were a dog that had just adequately performed a trick, and then turned and snapped at her cousin, "Fetch my list, Susan."

Again Io looked at her older brother to see how he viewed such a curt command, but Zeus was busy saying something to his secretary in a low voice and the other man was nodding and jotting something down.

Miss Barclay quickly scurried back to Miss Barrymore, who snatched the paper from her hands without a *thank you* and then turned her gimlet eye on Io and her siblings, her nose wrinkling slightly—as if she smelled something foul.

Io could not recall ever before having taken such a complete and instant dislike to another person.

"I can't help wondering if that is really proper, Miss Barrymore," Io said, employing a tone that was every bit as crisp and abrasive as the other woman's had been. Beside her, Bal shifted in his chair. Io's twin knew her well. Bal would recognize her tone and know she was girding for battle.

"Is *what* really proper?" Miss Barrymore demanded.

"You are an unmarried maiden. Should you be cohabitating with our brother? Or will you be living elsewhere?" *Please, please, please let it be the latter*, Io prayed.

Miss Barrymore's eyes bulged and she opened her mouth, but Zeus beat her to it.

"Edith's reputation is above reproach. And she will have chaperonage in the person of her cousin, Miss Barclay. Admittedly the circumstances are unusual, but we have our reasons—socially acceptable and yes, *proper* reasons—for Edith to be joining me."

So much for Io's prayers.

Io: The Shrew

Miss Barrymore gave Io a brief, scathing, glance and said. "Thank you, John." She gestured to her black gown. "I daresay you've noticed that I am in mourning. My dearest Mama recently went to her eternal reward, and so I am officially in my blacks for another ten months. Of course I shall *always* mourn her in my heart."

Ares snorted.

Both Miss Barrymore and Zeus frowned at her youngest brother.

Io bit her lip to smother a laugh. If they thought dirty looks would be enough to dampen Ares's irrepressible and irreverent sense of humor, they were barking up the wrong tree.

"The wedding will be in England, then?" Eva asked.

"Yes, the ceremony is to take place in St. George's," Miss Barrymore said, a smug, self-satisfied smile curving her lips.

"Oh, that will be so lovely," Eva said dreamily, clearly in seventh heaven imagining such a grand event.

"It *will* be lovely," Miss Barrymore agreed firmly, as if anything having to do with her was, by definition, *lovely*. She looked from Eva to the rest of them, obviously waiting for their congratulations.

She would be waiting a long, long time. Io could already see that all her siblings—except Eva and the man who would be marrying Miss Barrymore—were going to rub Zeus's fiancée the wrong way, and vice versa.

When they remained silent, Miss Barrymore treated them to yet another disapproving moue and then said, "There are a good many matters that must be attended to before we depart."

And off she went.

Io blocked out the other woman's hectoring voice as she sipped her tea and glanced around the room, her gaze again stopping on Mr. Masterson, who was staring at Miss Barrymore as if she were some sort of oracle, jotting down notes on the lap desk that looked laughably small compared to his large body. Could the man really be so rapt about what she was saying?

As if he'd heard her, Mr. Masterson's eyes slid in Io's direction. The change in his expression was barely discernable, but the muscles moved under the skin until they formed a subtle mask of disapproval.

Io bristled. Just what right did he have to exhibit such an unfavorable opinion about her or her siblings? He did not even *know* them!

He did not acknowledge her scowl and his cool gaze slid back to Miss Barrymore, whose droning voice interrupted Io's angry thoughts.

"—however, this will only serve for your most immediate use. Most of the shopping we shall save for London. His Grace will take us all to the capital before the Season officially commences so that you may all be properly outfitted."

Eva made an appreciative noise at the thought of a London shopping excursion and Miss Barrymore gave Io's sister a lofty look of approval—as if Eva were a frolicsome toddler.

Did Zeus really mean to shackle himself to such an overbearing, judgmental woman?

"—but aside from that, the very first thing to be done is to acquire appropriate clothing for your sisters before—"

The word *appropriate* yanked Io from her contemplation of her oldest brother's grim marital future. "Appropriate?" she repeated.

Miss Barrymore expelled the slightest of pained sighs, as if she were being forced to explain a complicated matter to an imbecile. "Yes, dear. Your garments—as quaint as they are—will hardly do for New York and London. And your *hair*…Well, I'm not sure if anything can be done to remedy that right now."

"Is that so, *dear?*" Io asked, her tone causing Bal to nudge her foot under the coffee table.

Her twin cleared his throat loudly. "We all understand that our more relaxed country garments will not do for city entertainments," he interjected. "We have always chosen our own clothing, but I'm sure we would appreciate any guidance you might have to offer."

Miss Barrymore turned her patronizing smile from Io to Balthazar. "I am sure that you've been accustomed to being in charge of your family, my lord. But you may now pass that burden to somebody who is better equipped to bear it."

Bal blinked. "Excuse me?"

"Your siblings are no longer your responsibility, but His Grace's. The duke is the head of your family and will manage any important matters for you and your younger siblings."

"Says whom?" Ares asked.

"I'm sorry, but I'm afraid I don't remember your name," Miss Barrymore said.

She had only met them a quarter of an hour ago and already she'd forgotten their names?

Io opened her mouth.

"Ares," her brother said, beating her to the punch. He smiled brittlely. "The god of war."

"Actually," Miss Barrymore said, completely ignoring Ares's dangerous tone and glancing down at her notebook and making a check mark before looking up again. "You have just raised an important issue."

"I have?" Ares asked.

"Yes: your names."

"What about our names?" Apollo asked.

Io's second youngest brother was also the quietest of the five of them, but that did not mean he was soft and malleable, only that he was inscrutable, even to those who knew him best.

"Clearly you can see that your names are far too odd to be appropriate for the brothers and sisters of a duke." Miss Barrymore suddenly squinted and leaned toward the twins. "Is there something wrong with your eyes?"

"Heterochromia." Apollo enunciated each syllable.

"It means two different colors of irises in the same person," Ares explained in a voice that mimicked Miss Barrymore's tone too closely to be an accident.

"It is quite rare," Apollo said.

"Estimated to occur in less than one percent of the population," Ares said.

Miss Barrymore's head moved back and forth, like a woman watching a tennis match.

"We are proud of our names," Eva chimed in, jerking Miss Barrymore's attention in yet another direction. Eva dimpled at the older woman. "Although it is kind of you to be concerned about the impact they may have on our social success in London."

"We shall not be adopting new names to satisfy anyone, Edith—may I call you by your Christian name, as we are going to be sisters?" Io asked in a syrupy sweet tone that nobody in their right mind would believe genuine.

Edith ignored her question. "I'm sure you are *quite* attached to your names, but they are rather—"

"Quaint?" Io guessed.

Zeus set down his cup with more haste than grace and cleared his throat. "I believe we've discussed more than enough for today. There will be ample time to talk about all these matters and more in the weeks to come." He turned his pale blue gaze toward Miss Barrymore. "You must be exhausted, my dear. I'm sure my siblings will excuse you."

Io smirked at Miss Barrymore's look of fury at being so obviously, if politely, dismissed.

Miss Barrymore smiled at her betrothed in a way that was probably supposed to be biddable but came across as constipated. "Are you sure you don't need my help to get everyone settled in, John?"

"Collins and I shall manage, my dear."

"Oh, but he is just a butler and doesn't have an appreciation for the finer points."

"Corbin is here to help with that and I am not utterly incompetent on the subject of my own house."

"No, no, of course not," Edith said, finally hearing the iron in Zeus's tone and fluttering her eyelashes, all soft compliance. "I'm sure you are correct, John." She then ruined the image of a gentle bride by turning to her cousin and saying sharply, "Fetch my things, Susan."

Miss Barclay scrambled to her feet. "Yes, of course, Edith."

Miss Barrymore was clearly unhappy to leave them all to settle in without her, but even she must have realized that clinging to Zeus's trousers like a burr would hardly be dignified.

Io: The Shrew

"I shall call for Lady Io and Lady Evadne tomorrow at eleven to take them to my dressmaker." She ignored Io's snort and fixed Eva with yet another of her beneficent half-smiles. "Madame Thérèse has kindly made an opening in her schedule to accommodate you both in private so that you do not need to mix with anyone else."

Her meaning was clear: she would make sure that her betrothed's sisters wouldn't outrage New York Society in their rustic clothing.

"And we look forward to considering what Madame Thérèse has to offer, dear *Edith*," Io said, speaking in a tone and volume more appropriate to standing on a Boston wharf and reading the Riot Act to revolting colonists.

Zeus hastily placed his body between Edith and Io and said to his fiancée, "I shall see you and Miss Barclay out, my dear." He ushered the women from the room, leaving the other five Hale siblings alone.

Io glanced at her brothers and sister and smiled grimly. "It would seem that we shall have to do something to earn all those millions grandfather left us, after all."

"Io," Bal said in a low voice, darting a look at Zeus's secretary, who still lurked in the background.

"Why do you look so disapproving, brother?" she asked Bal, her gaze on the stranger in their midst. "We need not mind our tongues in front of Mr. Masterson. As our brother's social, er, secretary, he is no doubt aware of the terms of our maternal grandfather's asinine will." She smiled sweetly. "Is that not true, Mr. Masterson?"

Chapter 2

I f Lady Io Hale believed that Corbin was going to discuss his employer's private business with her—or anyone else—then she was not nearly as clever as she thought she was.

Instead of commenting on her verbal gauntlet, Corbin merely smiled coolly at the Duke of Hasting's siblings. "I cannot discuss my employer's affairs with anyone other than His Grace. But I am sure the duke would be more than happy to answer any questions you might have on that subject or any other, my lady."

Lady Io stared steadily at Corbin for a long moment, as if she could somehow reduce him to a quivering mass of jelly with a look. When it was apparent that her harsh glare was having no effect on him, she gave an unladylike snort that contrasted jarringly with her beautiful, feminine features. And she *was* lovely—quite the most attractive woman Corbin had ever seen—as long as one ignored the combative glint in her gaze and the stories he knew about her sordid past. Of which there were many.

"*His Grace*," Lady Io repeated giving Corbin a look so filled with mockery that his skin actually tingled. He locked eyes with the witch, refusing to look away.

"Yoyo," her twin murmured in a gently chastising tone.

Yoyo? Corbin blinked at the soft, sweet pet name. It was like calling a cobra *Fluffy*.

As if she'd heard him, Lady Io gave Corbin a look that promised she was not finished with him, and turned to her brother.

The two commenced to converse in tones too quiet for him to hear so Corbin ignored their chatter and thought instead about how *these* people— the denizens of a lunatic fringe religious commune that was anathema to everything men like Corbin and the duke stood for—had come to be not only in Hastings's drawing room, but in his *life* for the foreseeable future.

Not to mention that Lord Balthazar—a man who'd been raised to eschew personal wealth and donate every cent he earned to the depraved leadership of the Canoga Community—was in line to inherit *four million dollars.*

The injustice of all that money falling into the hands of religious extremists not only made Corbin feel ill. It also enraged him.

Even though he had learned of the duke's connection to the Canoga Hales almost a month ago, he was still in shock.

He'd been best friends with Zeus Constantine Jonathan Hale since the two had met at boarding school at the age of eight almost three decades earlier. Not until this past month had Corbin learned that the name he had called his friend all these years—John—was preceded by two other names, and outlandish ones, at that. Far too outlandish for the stern, practical man whose nickname in the world of New York finance was the *Puritan of Wall Street.*

Not that it mattered what John Hale's given name was because there would be very few people in the world invited to use it now that he'd inherited the ancient Dukedom of Hastings.

Even if John hadn't become a duke, Corbin still would not be using his Christian name because Hastings was—for the last six months—his employer.

They had been best mates through school and soldiers in the army, saving each other's lives more than a few times.

And then, half-a-year ago John—not yet a duke—had also become Corbin's savior.

For twenty years Corbin had worked alongside James Corbin—the source of his Christian name and also his father—growing their construction business into the largest in New York state.

Only after his father's death did Corbin learn that his name had not been included in his will. Whether it had been an oversight, or on purpose, every bit of James Corbin's considerable estate had gone to his younger— and legitimate—son, Richard.

In the blink of an eye an empire that Corbin had devoted most of his adult life to building now belonged to somebody else.

And somebody who hated and despised him: his own half-brother.

Corbin had been devastated and confused. And also without a source of income.

John Hale had wanted to offer Corbin a partnership in a new construction venture. He had argued that Corbin could contribute his labor and experience and John would provide the capital.

But the last thing Corbin had wanted was to borrow money from his oldest friend, which is essentially what such a partnership would have been.

Instead, Corbin had asked for a different favor. "You are still seeking a secretary?"

A notch of confusion had appeared between John's unusual ice-blue eyes. "Yes."

"I would like to interview for the position."

"*What?*"

"I have the qualifications. In addition to learning every other aspect of my *father's* construction business," he had all but snarled, "I also spent time during the early years familiarizing myself with financial and business matters of the firm." But not enough time, evidently, or he would have been wise enough to insist on formalizing the hand-shake agreement he and his father had formed years before, when Corbin had still been in school.

"Of course you are qualified, Corbin! *Over*qualified," John had said. "And far too intelligent and hard-working and—"

"I will not accept your money in any capacity other than a salary, John. If you don't wish to employ me as your secretary, perhaps there is an opening at one of your banks, or at—"

"Corbin!"

He'd stopped talking at the sight of his friend's obvious distress.

"Any job you want is yours," John had said firmly, hurt glinting in his frosty eyes. "Anything at *all* I can give you is yours."

"I want the position of personal secretary."

"Then you have it."

And so Corbin had begun working as a combined business and social secretary to the most powerful banker in New York state, quite possibly in the entire country.

And over the past six months Corbin's brother Richard drove the construction business into the ground while Corbin could do nothing but watch, powerless to stop him.

All water under the bridge.

Indeed, it was. He pushed the depressing thoughts aside and turned his attention to Hastings' newly discovered siblings.

Corbin, a Presbyterian, had known about the Canoga cult for years—for that is what it was in his opinion: a cult. Indeed, during the year he had spent in seminary, the disbanding of the Canoga commune had been the *raison d'être* of several of the leaders of the Presbyterian community.

Corbin had a less than positive opinion of the place and the ragtag appearance of the five Canoga members currently sitting in front of him had not raised his estimation, any.

Although all the Hales were attractive and well-formed young people, the glint of rebellion in their eyes—even the youngest girl's—was more than a little concerning to him.

And then there was Lady Io Hale, whose willful, independent, and almost masculine behavior made the hairs on Corbin's neck stand on end.

"They are each impressive people, Corbin," the duke had said after returning from his visit to Canoga a month ago—the first time he and his siblings had met. Corbin and the duke had been enjoying brandy and cigars, a pastime the duke's fiancée, Miss Edith Barrymore, despised and had relegated to Hastings's study or the dining room.

"And you think the oldest one—Lord Balthazar—will fall into line with the requirements of his grandfather's will?" Corbin had asked, dubious.

"No. Not without some exertion on my part," the duke had admitted, and then added, "Balthazar has asked me not to inform our younger siblings of the true details of the will."

"What? Why not?"

"He was very upset to learn that their grandfather left everything to him."

"But Balthazar is Horace Sinclair's oldest grandson and heir," Corbin had said. "Why wouldn't Sinclair leave it all to him?"

The duke had smiled faintly at his words. "I'm afraid my brother sees things differently, Corbin. It is Balthazar's intention to split the fortune into equal shares when he inherits."

"Equal shares for his brothers?"

"For *all* his siblings." The duke had paused, his eyes glinting with something that had looked like amusement at Corbin's obvious shock. "You know their commune discourages marriage?" he asked.

Corbin's lips had curled at the question. "Yes. They believe in *group marriage* and *free love*."

"Yes, well, Balthazar fears his siblings' views on marriage would sway them against accepting their share if they found out that he was forced to marry against his principles."

"And you've agreed to keep the terms confidential?"

The duke shrugged. "I am not pleased with his deception, but he asked for no other concessions, so I will grant it. It is my intention to settle money on all of them, regardless if Balthazar inherits. That is something else they don't need to know. I am determined to use the two years they've all agreed to spend in England to wrangle them around to a sensible point of view."

"And by sensible you mean convincing them never to return to Canoga?"

"Just so." His jaw had flexed. "I will never forgive my father for what he did to my siblings. Not only separating us but raising my brothers and sisters as if they were so many chickens in a barnyard." The anger and determination in Hasting's unusual eyes would have chilled his siblings if they had seen it.

Or so Corbin had believed.

But now that he sat looking at the five younger Hales, he had to admit that none of them appeared to be the sort who would cow easily. It was his opinion that the duke would have his hands full breaking them to bridle.

Corbin already knew quite a bit about them thanks to a report prepared by the private investigator Hastings had sent to inquire into his newly discovered siblings.

The investigator's report was interesting, to say the least.

Io: The Shrew

The oldest brother, Lord Balthazar, was as tall as the duke but his build was massive and brawny rather than lean and elegant. Balthazar was a brilliant engineer who was already well-respected for his agricultural inventions.

Unfortunately—thanks to a recent expose written by one of Lord Balthazar's former lovers from the commune—he was now notorious across the entire nation for his unorthodox sexual relations.

Already there were journalists sniffing around the duke's mansion, seeking tidbits about his infamous brother. Corbin could only imagine the circus that would ensue when the press discovered that The Wicked Spare—as they'd dubbed Hastings's heir presumptive—was no longer tucked away in his rural commune but running amok among the female population of New York City.

Next in age was Lord Balthazar's twin, Lady Io.

Corbin's jaw flexed as he examined the older of the two Hale sisters from beneath his lashes. She was tall—all the siblings were—and built upon Junoesque lines.

Her clothing was a disgrace to fashion, but he had to admit the short skirts and bloomers showed her figure to far better advantage than the padding and bustles and other feminine falderal that were now so popular among society women.

She was obviously uncorsetted and her threadbare gown left little to the imagination. High breasts, long legs, and a small waist made for a magnificent body. Lady Io had probably drawn the eyes of every man in Grand Central Depot.

Her hair was shockingly short, the dark glossy curls framing a face as appealing as a mythical siren's. Her high cheekbones and slightly tilted hazel eyes were—and he hated to use the word—bewitching. And her full red lips—even when thinned in anger—had unwanted wicked thoughts springing into his head.

Some of those thoughts were probably due in part to the private investigator's report on Lady Io, which had been extensive and explicit, painting the picture of a woman who was as well-versed in the erotic arts as any Parisian demimondaine twice her age.

But it wasn't only Lady Io who had sexual experience beyond her years. *All* the Hales did, as did every adult member of their commune.

Many of the policies of Canoga offended notions of decency, but none more than their commitment to equality of the sexes when it came to carnal relations.

When a member of the commune turned eighteen, they were encouraged to choose a sexual mentor—usually an older member of the commune—to tutor them in sensual pleasure.

Lady Io had chosen Lamar Jacobsen for her tutor. Jacobsen was the scion of a rich Boston brahmin family. Or at least he had been until he'd donated all his worldly wealth and possessions to the Canoga commune at the tender age of twenty-three.

Jacobsen had been forty-four to Lady Io's eighteen when the two had commenced their *mentoring* relationship, one that had lasted far longer than usual for a collective that disapproved of monogamy. Lady Io had become pregnant at twenty-one but had suffered an early miscarriage.

After her association with Jacobsen ended, she had taken frequent, but casual, lovers.

Lady Io's passion in life was the furtherance of reproductive rights for women. To that end, she had run afoul of the law outside the commune numerous times for distributing radical literature and condoms.

Corbin reluctantly wrenched his gaze from Lady Io and turned to her younger brothers. Lords Apollo and Ares might look identical, but the young men could hardly be more different in nature.

Lord Ares was another in the stamp of his older brother Balthazar. Which was to say he was a rampant womanizer who'd had so many lovers the investigator had simply given up listing them all.

But Lord Ares was not all fluff, he was also a master woodworker on the level of Chippendale and Sheraton. After learning that his brother was a wood worker the duke had purchased one of Lord Ares's pieces from a New York City fine furniture dealer. It was only a small cabinet, but Corbin had never seen such a beautiful piece of woodworking. The man was truly an artist.

As for his twin, Lord Apollo, he was fast on his way to becoming one of the most respected thoroughbred breeders in New York state. The small stud he operated out of Canoga had produced three of the last five winners in faraway New Orleans, at the Fair Grounds Race Course.

Lord Apollo's stud operation was severely limited by Canoga's governing council which disapproved of money derived from gambling-related activity, although it was worth noting that the council had not rejected the earnings Lord Apollo's endeavors brought in.

Lord Apollo was the most circumspect of the Hale brothers and had only taken two lovers and neither union had lasted for more than a few months. An introvert and loner, he was the Hale sibling the investigator had learned the least about.

Corbin turned to the youngest of the Hale progeny, Lady Evadne, who was only twenty.

While Lady Io was a siren who lured men to their deaths, Lady Evadne resembled an angel come to Earth.

She had lovely, even features and huge eyes, blue-violet eyes rather than hazel. Her dark hair and ridiculously thick eyelashes made for a mesmerizing contrast with her peaches and cream skin.

While Lady Evadne looked like an angel, she most certainly was not. The youngest Hale was busily engaged in compiling a volume of street cant. According to the investigator, her lexicon was not the sort that would be published by any reputable publisher.

Lady Evadne's only relationship had been her brief association with a *mentor* at nineteen for half a year.

Eva, as she was called by her siblings, was an ardent anglophile and, aside from Lord Balthazar, had been the Hale sibling who'd argued most vigorously to accept the duke's invitation to live with him in England for two years.

Corbin anticipated there would be little trouble getting the youngest Hale to acculturate to life outside the Canoga colony.

Her older brothers and sister, however…

Corbin certainly could not envision any of the Hales other than Lady Eva embracing the lessons that Miss Barrymore thought to teach them in the coming weeks.

Especially not Lady Io.

Privately, Corbin questioned Balthazar's wisdom when it came to concealing the truth of his grandfather's will. Oh, he understood why Balthazar's communitarian upbringing, not to mention his unconventional belief that women were the equals of men before the law, made him want to share the inheritance with his siblings. But he doubted the younger man had thought about what would happen if he did *not* knuckle under and locate a *suitable*—according to the will—wife to marry.

Had Lord Balthazar considered how vulnerable he and his siblings would be at that point?

Because the truth of the matter was that all the Hales would be dependent on the duke's generosity for the two years they lived outside Canoga, and possibly afterward.

He doubted any of them suspected the will of iron hidden behind the duke's aloof façade. Corbin knew the other man did not want his brothers and sisters to only stay in his life for a few years. Hastings wanted them permanently and would use everything at his disposal to keep them from returning to Canoga. And there was no better persuasive weapon than money.

Had any of them considered that?

Well, it was not Corbin's affair if they hadn't.

He found his gaze sliding back to Lady Io Hale who was animatedly discussing the sights they should all go see while they were in the city. When she lost her antagonistic frown, she was breathtakingly beautiful and far more youthful-looking.

For a moment, Corbin felt sorry for Lady Io. Indeed, he felt sorry for all five of them. There would be no time for sightseeing in Miss Barrymore's stringent schedule of shopping, manners training, dance lessons, and on and on.

Indeed, the siblings would be fortunate to find enough time to eat and sleep in the coming weeks.

Chapter 3

A Week Later…

I o had had enough.

Enough of Edith Barrymore's incessant sniping and carping.

Enough pointless shopping for clothing she had no intention of wearing.

Enough of the endless lectures about manners and vapid social convention.

Just *enough*.

Day after day, Io accompanied her sister and Miss Barrymore shopping, spending hours trying on garments she neither wanted nor needed. She'd had to all but fight physically for the right to choose her own clothing—garments that reflected her belief in the Reform Dress movement—rather than the dangerous crinolines, unhealthy corsets, objectifying bustles, and acres of skirts that Edith tried to force on her.

Last, but not least, Io had had enough of Corbin Masterson's cool, judging gaze on her every night at dinner, not to mention his infuriating presence at the manners and dancing lessons Edith insisted they all endure every minute they were not eating, sleeping, or shopping.

Yesterday had been the last straw.

Io and Eva had spent *three hours* learning how to hold a teacup properly and *sit like a lady* while paying insipid morning calls.

Io had already been on the verge of flinging her cup through the window when Mr. Masterson had arrived early for their wretched dance lessons.

Edith had immediately gestured to Eva and Io—as if they were a pair of trained poodles—and said, "Are they not sitting politely and holding their cups like proper ladies, Mr. Masterson?"

Io's head had become so hot so fast that she thought the top of it would blow off.

But that had been nothing to the fury that had seized her when Masterson had turned his opaque gray gaze on her and opened his mouth—as if he would actually *answer* the demeaning question!

"Oh yes, my dear Mr. Masterson," Io had simpered in a deliberately vapid tone before he could get a word out. "Please *do* share your opinion!" She fluttered her lashes and then added, "The way Edith is all but panting for your judgment makes me believe you are an expert on the critical subject of teacup holding." Io was vaguely aware that Edith had gasped, but not for the world could she have pulled her eyes away from Masterson's inscrutable face.

After a long, pregnant moment, he had turned back to Edith. "Very nice, Miss Barrymore. You have worked miracles in such a short time." And then he'd had the gall to add, "Perhaps you might work next on the proper way to hold a wine glass."

Io had lurched to her feet, spilling hot tea all over herself in the process, her clumsiness only adding to her fury. "And just how is the way I am holding this damned cup any different from the way I did at breakfast this morning, Mr. Masterson?"

His eyebrows had lifted fractionally, the minute shift of his features even more aggravating than an open smirk would have been. "This morning you were holding your cup like a longshoreman gripping a pint glass. Today you are—or you were until a moment ago—making great strides toward behaving like a lady." He paused, and then said, "Your language, however, is another matter entirely. Vulgarity will not endear you to society hostesses in either New York or London, my lady."

At that point, her sister had shot to her feet and forcibly removed the cup from Io's hand before she could throw it at Masterson's head.

Even Edith had not protested when Io had stormed from the room, flinging over her shoulder that they could bloody well practice their dancing without her.

As little as Io had wanted to go down to dinner last night, she'd not wanted to give either Edith or Masterson the satisfaction of thinking that she was sulking in her room.

But she had drawn the line at spending time doing *needlework* in the drawing room after dinner.

Io: The Shrew

As for today?

Today Io planned to get away entirely. If she did not escape her gilded cage and do something worthwhile, she could not be held responsible for her behavior. And Edith, along with her vile henchman Masterson, would be the ones who bore the brunt of her wrath.

If Io lost her temper and attacked Zeus's fiancée—or his best friend and secretary—then she would doubtless be sent packing back to Canoga in disgrace.

While that vision of the future did not bother her, she knew it would upset her twin. For whatever reason, Bal had been as fierce an advocate for giving up two years of their lives to Zeus's plans as their little sister Eva.

Io understood Eva's desire to move in *tonish* circles—she was wild about anything English—but she was utterly baffled as to why Bal was so keen to leave his life in Canoga behind.

In any event, Io was more than willing to risk banishment if it meant she could get away for a day.

To that end, she woke up before first light this morning and dressed not in her old clothing which would be far too conspicuous even in a city as vast as New York, but in a dress that she'd obtained from one of Zeus's maids.

The woman, Mary, had been ecstatic but dubious when Io had offered a straight trade: one of the new gowns Edith had foisted on her for Mary's plain brown worsted.

"But, my lady, this gown is *far* more valuable." Mary had stared lustfully at the putrid peach walking costume that Io wouldn't be caught dead in. "It wouldn't be right," she'd added, with far less conviction.

"Value is a subjective matter, Mary." At the woman's blank look, Io had elaborated. "Your gown is far more valuable to *me* than this peach one. So, from my point of view, I am the one getting the better bargain."

Mary's brow had puckered. "Oh. I would never have thought of that."

"So, you will do me this favor and trade?"

"Well, if you put it that way—"

"Excellent! Just, er, don't wear the outfit anyplace where Miss Barrymore might see you, hmm?"

Mary had even offered up her superior needlework talent to alter the brown gown for Io, bringing in the waist and lengthening the hem.

Once Io was dressed in her new brown gown and her satchel was filled with all the information she needed for the day—as well as enough money to pay for street trams or cabs—she tiptoed down the hall to her twin's room, shocked to find Bal still asleep in his monstrous canopied bed, face down in the pillow.

Io pinched his bare shoulder. Hard.

"*Ow!*" Bal shouted, flipping onto his back, his angry eyes heavy with sleep. "What the hell are you doing, Yoyo?" He glanced at the window and then squinted at the clock. "And why are you bothering me at this ungodly hour?"

"If we were at Canoga, you would have been up and breaking your fast by now."

"We're not at Canoga," he retorted sourly.

"Did you overindulge last night, twin?"

Bal rubbed his shoulder, his look of reproach ruined by the guilt she saw seeping in.

Io clucked her tongue. "My, my. How well you have taken to a life of sloth and indolence, Balthazar. Drinking and gambling and carousing all night and then shopping and lounging all day. Tell me, have you sunk to visiting brothels and foisting yourself on prostitutes, as well?"

Bal glowered. "Oh, leave off, Yoyo! What do you want with me, anyhow?"

"I need you to lie for me today."

He seemed to notice her gown for the first time and sat up. "Why are you dressed like that?" His eyes darted to her heavy black satchel and he groaned. "Oh God. You are going out to get yourself arrested. Again."

"I am doing no such thing."

"Then where are you going and why do I have to lie about it?"

"You cannot tell anyone what you do not know, Balthazar."

He flopped onto his back and stared at the canopy above his head. "Please do not do this, Io."

Io: The Shrew

"I have commitments to fulfill before I leave here, Bal, important ones. Also, I *need* to do something worthwhile. If I don't, I'll scratch Miss Barrymore's eyes out. And Masterson's too," she added for good measure.

When he didn't answer, she felt a pang of remorse and put a hand on his shoulder, but gently this time, until he turned to meet her gaze. "I will drink tea like a lady and dance at their parties and every other manner of vapidity when we reach England. But right now, there are things I must do before I leave everything behind."

"You are still planning to continue your efforts when we reach Britain?"

By *efforts,* he meant Io's commitment to women's reproductive rights. "Yes, Bal."

"Our brother will not be happy about this, Yoyo. He will take action to stop you, you must know that."

"Zeus cannot take action if he does not know, can he?"

Bal snorted. "Because you are *so* subtle in pursuing what you believe in."

"I promise I will be more circumspect in my efforts."

"You had better be, Yoyo. You are the sister of a duke, now. Like it or not, Zeus cares about his reputation. Having a sister in jail is the last thing he will want.

"I will be careful. But please—cover for me today?"

He huffed out a pained sigh. "Fine. What am I to tell them?"

"That I have gone to visit a friend who left the colony and lives here in the city." She grinned and added, "Tell them my friend is now married to a Presbyterian minister."

Bal gave a grudging laugh. Presbyterians were the chief persecutors of the Canoga Colony. It also happened to be the religion of their oldest brother, not to mention his insufferable fiancée and secretary.

"You want them to *believe* me, Yoyo, so I will leave that last part out."

"Thank you, twin." She kissed his forehead and turned to go, but he caught her hand and pulled her back.

The laughter had drained from his green eyes, which were the same shape as hers, but a far lighter and prettier—in Io's opinion—peridot while hers were a boring hazel.

"What is it, Bal?"

"I will cover for you *today*. But this is the last time, Yoyo. We all voted and agreed before leaving Canoga that we would give our brother's plan a chance for the next two years. I know this past week has been difficult— especially for you and Eva—but it won't take two years to—" He broke off, an odd look in his eyes. "Just be patient."

"It won't take two years to what? Is there something you should tell me?"

He gave her a gentle shove. "Go and enjoy your day."

Io was sorely tempted to push the matter, but she was also desperate to embrace her freedom.

And so, she shrugged off her concern and said, "I will be back in time to dress for dinner."

***

Although it was barely after daybreak, Corbin had just returned to his room after his morning bout of boxing with the duke.

This morning, to his surprise, Lords Ares and Apollo had joined the two of them in the basement room where he and the duke were once again, for an hour three mornings a week, just plain Corbin and John as they pummeled each other.

The duke had set up the room so it was just like the boxing saloons that had become so popular in New York among upper-class men over the last few decades.

In addition to the heavy sandbags, dumbbells, and other accoutrements associated with pugilism, there were also comfortable overstuffed chairs made for sitting in, rather than for their appearance, and a small kitchen where the duke's valet—Crombie a man who'd been Hastings's corporal during the war—prepared less delicate fare than Miss Barrymore allowed the cook to make. Food for men, in other words, rather than dainty finger sandwiches and fussy cakes and pastries.

Io: The Shrew

The duke's youngest brothers were pleasant company, and if Corbin regretted the invasion of the hour that he usually jealously guarded, he soon lost the feeling as he watched the twins beat each other with far more vigor than he and Hastings—fifteen years their senior—could manage these days.

Corbin had just indulged in a hot shower—a modern miracle the duke had installed in both his Fifth Avenue home and his country house on Long Island—and finished dressing when he happened to glance out his window and saw a familiar body wearing a very unfamiliar dress, bustling down the street, without a maid or footman to attend her.

"Damnation! And just where are you going so early and so quickly and so alone, my lady?" he muttered under his breath.

Corbin snatched up his coat and hat. And then, on impulse, he yanked open the drawer in his nightstand and removed his service pistol, tucking it away as he sprinted from his room.

He was fortunate that his quarry was walking and not taking a cab, which allowed him to catch up to her a block away.

She'd been easy to spot as it was so early in the morning that the only people moving about were the armies of domestics who served the grand mansions that lined the most prestigious street in the city.

Corbin was not surprised that Lady Io had bolted her brother's house with such stealth. The duke had warned him of the possibility several nights before, when the two of them had enjoyed a glass of whiskey after a grueling day of negotiations regarding an upcoming bank merger.

"Io is like a wolf on a chain, snapping and snarling at her captivity," Hastings had said with a weary sigh. "Watch her for me, will you? And keep her out of trouble if you can." His chiseled jaw had flexed with tension. "I am afraid that my sister does not care for Miss Barrymore's assistance when it comes to preparing for her new life in England."

It had taken all Corbin's self-control not to laugh. *Does not care for* was an understatement of epic proportions. It had only been a few days at that point and already the two women were at each other's throats.

Corbin respected Hastings greatly, but the man had a blind spot as large as a stagecoach when it came to his fiancée and her rather abrasive nature and rigid expectations.

Nobody understood better why his friend was so forgiving of Miss Barrymore's prickly ways, but Corbin thought it was going to prove a huge mistake turning the care and training of his new siblings over to his exacting fiancée.

Hastings could have chosen from a number of female relatives on his mother's side, any of whom would have been able to handle the transformation with more tact and care.

But what Edith wanted, Edith got as far as Hastings was concerned. It had been that way for years, ever since her brother Kelvin—who'd been a very close friend to both Corbin and the duke—had extracted a deathbed promise from Hastings. Corbin didn't know the exact nature of the promise, but he suspected the burden was a heavy one.

Ahead of him, Lady Io suddenly lifted her hand, the action pulling Corbin from his thoughts.

"Hell," he muttered under his breath as a cab rolled to a stop beside her. He glanced around for another one and waved his arm wildly to capture the attention of a driver half a block away, keeping his gaze locked onto Lady Io's rapidly disappearing carriage until his own stopped beside him. "Follow that cab," he told the driver, raising a shiny new dollar coin.

The cab lurched down the street before Corbin had even closed the door.

Luckily, there were few conveyances on the road, so his driver was able to keep up.

Corbin's mood turned darker and darker the farther they went from the respectable part of town.

"Where the devil are you going, my lady?" he muttered to himself as both cabs continued to roll toward a part of the island that was even more dangerous than the Wild West.

By the time the cab finally stopped it was barely a stone's throw from the area that was still infamously known as Five Points, even though the streets that comprised those points were no longer in existence.

It was the most treacherous part of the city, infested by hardened criminals and their powerless prey—the vulnerable immigrants who were too poor to escape to someplace better.

Corbin tossed the driver his coin and followed Lady Io, who'd disembarked and was hurrying along on foot.

Io: The Shrew

He watched in open-mouthed horror as she blithely passed a pack of lads who, while only eleven or twelve in age, were ancient in the ways of crime and fell into step behind her, their intentions nefarious.

Utterly unaware of the danger creeping up behind her, she stopped in front of a building that must have once been quite grand but was now mostly shuttered and dilapidated, the formerly white siding blackish brown from years of smoke and filth.

Corbin waited until she disappeared inside before approaching the obviously disappointed gang of lads.

"What's in that building?" he asked the boy who looked to be the leader.

"What's it to you?" the boy shot back.

Corbin drew a coin from his pocket.

"There's quacks in there—and those do-gooders," the boy obligingly said.

"Aye," another chimed in. "And free rubbers."

The others laughed at the new street cant for what had been called *johnnies* when Corbin had been a boy.

So. Lady Io was here to meet with her radical suffragette associates. Corbin sighed.

"Did you see that lady who just went inside?"

The oldest boy's leer was worrying, even though he could not possibly have hair on his balls. "Aye," he said with a suggestive thrust of his hips. "A real handsome piece o' calico."

Again, the others chuckled.

Corbin drew out his wallet and extracted a bill that made even the jaded young ruffians' eyes widen.

"This is for you if you do what I say."

"Why should I do anything? Why don't I just take it—and all the rest—from you?"

The boys behind him moved a bit closer to their leader, muttering and nodding.

"Why don't you try?" Corbin said, smiling unpleasantly. He would take some licks if the whole gang attacked him like the feral dogs they aped, but his blood was up thanks to Lady Io's thoughtless idiocy, so he was not afraid of a few bruises.

They must have recognized the violent glitter in his gaze because, after a moment, the leader eased back. "Alright. What do we have to do?"

"Is there a back entrance to this building?"

"Aye."

"I want you to keep an eye on it. If she slips out the back, come and tell me. If you stay there until she leaves—whether through the front door or the back—I'll give you the same amount again. And there is one more thing." He held up yet another note. "If one of you will accompany me to that saloon across the street, I will pay you to deliver a message." Corbin would need to let Hastings know that he might be out of commission for a while.

"A message? Where to?"

"I'll tell you when I give it to you."

The little ruffian was so pleased by the prospect of such easy money that, for a moment, he looked his age. But then he remembered to be tough and growled, "Aye, I can do that."

Corbin handed over the money and watched as the boys split into three groups. Two went behind the building to wait while three others headed directly to one of the small carts that sprang up each morning to sell roasted corn.

Corbin was impressed that they went to buy food. If they were beyond redemption, they would have gone into one of the saloons that infected the area like carbuncles on a prostitute.

The leader of the small gang waited patiently beside him, evidently taking the delivery job for himself.

Corbin briefly considered entering the building and bodily dragging Lady Io out of it, but decided discretion was the better part of valor. Besides, the last thing he wanted to do was draw attention to her presence in this part of the city.

10: The Shrew

Instead, Corbin strode across the street into the saloon that afforded him the best view of the building and settled in to wait.

Chapter 4

Seven O'Clock That Same Day

Io was flabbergasted when she stepped out of New York's headquarters for the Ladies Aid Association—a necessarily vague euphemism for the organization given Anthony Comstock's obsession and the current political climate—and discovered that the street outside the filthy building, which had been quiet when Io had entered, was now raucous and crowded.

How in the world had the entire day gotten away from her?

Well, she knew how, because she had crammed two years' worth of her volunteer work for the LAA into one day. Her job was to distill the information the association collected on subjects like nutrition and health, childcare, and contraception, among many other subjects, into pamphlet-length articles.

Today she had spent three and a half hours with a female physician to draft an updated pamphlet that would accompany the condoms Io would distribute under the umbrella of their sister agency of the LAA in England.

After that, she had spoken to a journalist who had spent four hours outlining the current movement spearheaded by Comstock.

Both the doctor and journalist had left hours before, while Io had stayed on, furiously scribbling.

She now wished that she had left with them.

Io backed up to the door as she studied the almost Boschian scene before her.

The cacophony of dozens of saloons, all with pianos playing different melodies, made it difficult to think.

There were people *everywhere*, and apart from a few ladies of the night, all of them were rough-looking men.

Men who were exhibiting more than a little interest in Io's sudden appearance.

Io: The Shrew

Perhaps she should go back inside the building until she could decide how to hail a cab. Not that it looked like one could make its way down the congested street.

Io turned and knocked on the door. She had been the second to last to leave. The last was the woman who cleaned the building and had waited with poorly veiled impatience for Io to clear off so she could finish her work and go home.

When nobody answered, Io knocked again, harder.

"You lookin' for somewhere to stay the night darlin'?" The voice came from so close to her ear that she felt hot breath on her neck as a large hand closed around her shoulder and spun her around.

Io's hand, the one that hadn't been knocking, had already slipped into her satchel and closed around the hat pin she kept for exactly this sort of occasion.

Without pausing to think, she yanked it out of her bag and jabbed it into the man's hand.

He screamed and immediately released her.

Io pressed her back against the door and stared up at her aggressor, who was a mountain of a man dressed in a vulgar plaid suit.

"You *bitch!*" he shouted, clutching his bleeding hand and glaring from it to Io, his expression one of disbelief.

Io raised the hat pin before he could gather his wits. "I'll do it again if you don't go away and leave me be."

The man's eyes narrowed, and he reached behind him. When his hand reappeared, it held a knife as long as Io's forearm. "You'll do what I say, or I'll give you a taste of *this*." he brandished the glittering blade, which looked better cared for than anything else about his person.

Don't show fear—and don't even feel it—because a feral dog can smell it.

"Step away from me right now or I will make a racket to wake the dead," Io snarled.

His eyes widened. And then he laughed. "And who would care, even if they heard you?" He gestured to his right, where a lounging group of young men eyed her with predatory interest. "Do you think those lads will save you?"

"No. But I will."

Io's head whipped around at the familiar voice, her jaw sagging when she saw Corbin Masterson scarcely a foot from her tormentor.

Where had *he* come from?

Not that Io cared. She could not recall a time when she had been so happy to see another human being.

The man in the suit cut Masterson a disparaging glance, his posture shifting subtly when he took in the expensive clothing. "And who might you be?"

"The man who is going to pay for your evening's entertainment." Masterson held out a large denomination bill. "Take it and leave the lady alone."

"Why don't I take it *and* the lady?" he asked, eyeing Mr. Masterson. "And I'll have whatever else you've got in that fine coat o' yours." He leered at Io. "Then I can wet my dick *and* my whistle."

Mr. Masterson's hand came out from inside his coat holding a pistol, which he pointed—Io noted with interest—at the other man's groin, rather than his head. "It will be difficult for you to enjoy anything at all if you do not take my offer and *leave.*"

The bully's hands shot up, his eyes wide. "Hell! Don't shoot, friend. You'll get no trouble offa me."

Masterson crumpled up the bill and threw it into the street. "Go."

The man scowled but turned away just as the boys who'd been lounging pounced on the money.

The fight broke out so quickly Io couldn't have said who threw the first punch. It spread like a keg of gunpowder touched by a match, even as she watched.

A large hand closed around her upper arm. "Come with me. *Now, my lady,*" Masterson added, dragging Io in the opposite direction from the rapidly escalating brawl.

Io wrenched her gaze away from the melee and hurried to keep up with Masterson's far longer stride. All around them, people seemed drawn to the noisy altercation, even though they could not possibly know what it was about.

"Why are they running *toward* a fight?" she demanded breathlessly, needing to run, herself.

Masterson ignored her, his eyes darting around, the hand not holding her arm still in his pocket.

Io wanted to jerk out of his grasp but knew it would be foolish as he was all that stood between her and rape or worse.

And so she shut her mouth and kept up as best she could, almost weeping with relief when he led her down a street, to where several rickety cabs were gathered.

***

Not until they were inside the least reprehensible-looking cab and rolling north did Corbin turn to the woman across from him. "What the *hell* were you thinking?"

Lady Io's face, which had been pinched with fear as she'd trotted after him, rapidly shifted to her characteristic—at least with him—haughty expression. "Why were you following me?"

Corbin could not *believe* this woman! "Do you *want* to get raped?" he demanded coldly. "Is that another experience you'd like to try? Because if I had not been there tonight, rape is probably the best thing that would have happened to you."

Her jaw worked furiously, her eyes incandescent with rage and something else—fear, perhaps. When she opened her mouth, Corbin expected her to tear a strip off his hide.

Instead, she said—in the most grudging tone possible, "Thank you for getting me out of that bind."

Corbin did not trust himself to respond he was so bloody mad.

Calm down, some still rational part of him said. *The way to handle this woman is not with anger.*

"Why were you following me?" she repeated.

The urge to grab her, turn her over his knee, and spank her until she sobbed slammed into him like a fist.

Corbin blinked, horrified by the violent vision.

Where had *that* come from? He had never raised a hand to a woman in his life!

"Did Zeus put you up to this?" she asked.

"What?" he snapped, still dazed from his brief but intemperate fantasy.

"I asked you if Zeus tasked you to follow me."

He couldn't help noticing that she used Hastings's given name even though she knew the duke hated it. Or probably *because* he hated it. Corbin would not put it past the woman.

"Or was it the meddling, superior *Edith* who told you to stalk me?" she went on when he didn't answer her first question.

Corbin gave in to a petty, stupid impulse he knew he should resist and said, "Miss Barrymore is a *lady*. As such, I doubt she could ever conceive of behaving in such a foolish, common, and thoughtless way as you have done today."

Her eyes glittered in the dimness of the cab and when they passed a streetlamp, he saw her cheeks were stained red.

"I'm sorry," Corbin said stiffly, ashamed by his ungentlemanly outburst. "I should not have said that. It was unkind and cruel." He could not lie and say it was untrue, however.

"Please do not apologize. That was the first genuine utterance to come out of your mouth since I met you, Mr. Masterson. I am grateful for your candor."

Corbin kept his mouth shut.

"So," she said when it was obvious he would not reply, "It was Zeus who sent you to follow me."

"Yes."

"I suppose you will run and tattle to him when we arrive at that gothic monstrosity that he calls home?"

Corbin's entire body heated at her scorn, but he refused to be drawn.

"I daresay Zeus will curtail my allowance once you relate the events of today? Or perhaps he will even beat me for my disobedience? Lock me in my room. Starve me until I submit and become a *real lady* like Miss Barrymore."

Corbin had not believed he could get any angrier. He'd been wrong. "I have known your brother for most of my life," he said icily, "and your words do him a grievous disservice. Never have I seen John Hale raise his hand to any woman, child, animal, or subordinate. Nor would he deprive you of food or water or hold you against your will."

Something that looked like contrition flickered across her face but was quickly replaced by a stony glare.

"It was my understanding that you and your siblings took a vote—as is the Canoga way," he added, unable to keep a hint of scorn from his words, "and that you all decided to accompany His Grace to England. Is that not true?"

"It is true," she bit out.

"In return, the duke agreed to provide allowances for the two years you reside with him. Do you think Hastings is the sort of man to go back on his word?"

"I met my brother scarcely a month ago, Mr. Masterson. I hardly know what sort of *person* he is."

Corbin was exasperated but amused by her correction. "I will tell you, then: John Hale has never gone back on his word in his life. He is a ma—a *person*—of integrity and it is of paramount importance to him to honor his promises." He narrowed his eyes. "But what sort of *person* are you, my lady?"

"What do you mean?"

"Didn't you agree, along with your brothers and sister, to give the duke's offer a fair chance? And yet you have done nothing but rail against every proposed change to your life—from clothing to manners to behaving in a way that does not shame your family or jeopardize your own safety. That hardly sounds like a *fair chance* to me."

Her lips twisted and he suspected she was chewing her cheek to ribbons not to lash out.

Corbin took a deep breath and forcibly gentled his tone. "Your brother is about to enter British society at a level that is only one step below royalty, my lady. He is offering you and your siblings an opportunity that only a handful of people in the world will ever have. All he asks in return is that you behave with enough decorum that none of you are excoriated by your peers, the public, or the press."

She suddenly leaned forward until their knees were touching. "Are you saying that providing information about contraception and disease to poor women is a matter for excoriation?"

Corbin had his own opinions about gently bred women penning incendiary literature and handing out johnnies on street corners but kept them to himself.

Instead, he said, "Has your brother forbidden you from supporting any of your causes?"

"No," she said with an annoyed moue. "But I am sure it is only a matter of time."

Corbin ignored that last part and said, "You knew that what you were doing today would draw fire or you would not have crept from the house at dawn. Why didn't you take your maid with you to lend you respectability and a footman to protect you? Why didn't you travel in one of the several carriages His Grace has left at your disposal? Why didn't you—"

"I have already left Canoga, the only place I have ever known," she broke in, her voice shaking with emotion. "In a few weeks we will leave New York and the United States behind. I am abandoning *everything*. Before I go, I just wanted to spend a day reminding myself that life is not only ball gowns and jewels and rich dinners with thirty courses. I wanted some time to remember who I *am* before I am completely and utterly swallowed up by who I am *supposed* to be."

Her voice rang out in the cab, her breathing ragged and her eyes glittering, not only with anger, but also, he suspected, with unshed tears, making him feel like the worst sort of bully.

Corbin opened his mouth to apologize for his harsh candor, but the cab jolted to a stop. He glanced out the window and saw, with no little astonishment, that they had come all the way across town and were home.

Lady Io made no move to exit the cab. Instead, she was staring at him, her eyes huge and her expression pensive, obviously waiting for some response to her heartfelt declaration—and not an apology, either. No, he knew that she wanted some sign that he comprehended her fears about the future. Some acknowledgment from him that he understood what a terrifying change all this was.

Coward that he was, Corbin wrenched his gaze away, opened the door, hopped out of the cab, and held out a hand. "Come, my lady. There is still time for you to dress for dinner."

Chapter 5

Aboard the *Petrel*
Two Weeks Later

Io looked around the luxurious cabin, amazed that such a place existed on board a ship.

On one of Zeus's ships, in point of fact.

In the last three weeks, Io had learned just how wealthy her oldest brother really was. If there was something in the Western world that Zeus Constantine Jonathan Hale did not own at least part of, Io had yet to discover it.

In addition to his immense wealth and power, he was also an English peer. Not just any peer—not a mere baron or viscount, oh no—but a *duke*.

Io hadn't really understood what being a duke meant when she'd come to New York City with her siblings almost a month ago. Eva had tried to explain to all of them, but it had not gained purchase in her brain until she had actually witnessed the way people—Americans!—treated her brother.

She had also learned that Zeus had a hereditary seat in Parliament, four estates scattered about the country, a London house, and dependents in the hundreds, if not thousands.

And that wasn't counting all the property, employees, and wealth he was leaving behind in the United States.

It was obscene and beyond unjust for one person to have so very *much* when so many others had so little.

And it was beyond maddening to think of Edith *at Zeus's side and enjoying all that wealth and privilege*, a sly mental voice suggested.

Yes, that was, Io had to admit, the worst part of it.

The connecting door flew open, and Eva burst into Io's stateroom, her violet-blue eyes sparkling. "Is it not beautiful, Yoyo?"

Io smiled because it was impossible not to smile when a person was near Eva. "It is beautiful," she agreed, keeping her thoughts on the matter of her brother's wealth to herself. Her gaze flickered over her sister's elegant gown. "As are you."

Eva grinned and glanced down at her person. "I am so glad I insisted on this color. I know Edith means well"—Io snorted, and Eva rolled her eyes and clarified. "She means well in the sense she does not want us to bring shame on her and Zeus—that much is true. I know she advised me against deeper colors because she legitimately believes it is unfitting for a woman my age." Eva pulled a face. "But I *so* hate white. And pastel shades make me look insipid." Her magnificent eyes turned dreamy as she stroked the silk gown. "And this shade of mauveine is just *too* delectable for words."

Trust her sister to know the aniline dye name for *purple*. "Too delectable for words, Eva? *Tsk, tsk.* I know you are in a state of bliss when *you* can't come up with a word, my dearest lexicographer."

Eva laughed. "You look lovely, as well. That sort of gown is magnificent on you and shows off your figure to perfection. You really do look like a goddess, Yoyo."

Io's face heated at her sister's compliment. "Are you ready to go to dinner?"

"Will you wait while I fetch my reticule?" Eva asked.

"I will be right here," Io promised. Once her sister had gone, she turned to look out of the small window into the darkness, absently stroking the rich velvet of her gown, which was what many called *artistic dress*, an offshoot of the Reform Dress movement.

Artistic dress followed the natural lines of a woman's body, the style reminiscent of gowns worn during the medieval era. The luxurious fabric had been dyed using ancient methods rather than modern, man-made chemicals. It was elegant and comfortable and something Io felt confident wearing in public.

It had also scandalized Edith.

In fact, she had been so outraged that Io refused to engage in tight lacing—or even wear a corset—that she had taken the matter to Zeus.

When Zeus summoned Io to his study she had been ready to pack her bags if her brother tried to dictate her clothing.

Instead, Zeus had said, "The clothing you wear is your own affair, Io. I have instructed Miss Barrymore to refrain from doing anything other than *suggesting* other fashion choices."

Io had been stunned and momentarily speechless as she'd stared into Zeus's cold blue eyes—the eyes of a stranger who was suddenly not just her brother, but in charge of her future and that of everyone she loved.

Io did not dislike Zeus, but she found him unfathomable and did not entirely trust him, or his judgment. For example, why in the world would her brother marry a woman as unpleasant as Edith? She knew Edith was the heiress to some bank or other, so a marriage would join the two fortunes. That was the only reason Io could see for Zeus's betrothal. Which was no reason at all, in her opinion. How much wealth did her brother need? Did he not have enough already?

Of course, Io had not said any of that to her brother that day. Instead, she had shoved down her natural inclination to freely air her opinions and had said, "Thank you, Zeus. I am sorry to take up your time with something so trifling as my clothing."

He had escorted Io to the door, pausing with his hand on the knob and looking down at her, making her aware of how very tall he was.

She'd been standing close enough that she could not help staring at his eyes, which really were arresting, the color an almost inhumanly pale blue.

"I hope you know that I want you to be happy, Io. It is not my intention to stifle who you are."

Io had been too startled by his pronouncement to do more than nod.

That episode took place only a few days after Io's clash with Masterson. If the stern secretary had told her brother of Io's idiotic journey to Five Points, the duke had given no sign that he knew.

Io hadn't been sure what to make of that. She had been positive that Masterson would *sprint* to tell her brother about her—admittedly—foolish behavior.

She had avoided Masterson like the plague in the weeks that followed that hair-raising event.

The haughty secretary had been right about one thing he'd said that day: Io *had* promised Zeus to at least try to fit into his world.

Io: The Shrew

So here she was, dressed like a fashion plate for dinner, *trying*.

The door opened and Eva entered. "I am ready!"

They were halfway down the corridor when they encountered Bal leaving his room. He smiled at them. "You look beautiful, sisters. I would offer you both an arm, but I'm afraid we'd never squeeze down the corridor."

"Eva will walk with you," Io said, giving her twin a reassuring smile when he shot her a questioning look.

It was true that she had been rather subdued since that near catastrophe in the Five Points Area. Not that she had abandoned her cause. Indeed, Io had gone for a second visit to the Ladies Aid Association. That time, she had done as Masterson all but ordered and took along one of the housemaids, a brawny footman, and two grooms. She had felt silly and conspicuous with such an entourage and had been glad that at least Zeus's carriage was unmarked to avoid advertising Io's ducal connections. The visit had not ended in violence, nor had any of the journalists who haunted her brother's Fifth Avenue mansion published an expose about her activities. That had been miraculous considering how closely journalists watched poor Zeus—and the rest of them by association.

As apprehensive as Io was about leaving the country, she would be glad to escape the rabid fascination the city of New York had with the new Duke of Hastings.

Io had to admit her handsome, austere, and dignified older brother looked just like one of Eva's fairy tale princes.

It wasn't only Zeus's attractive person, but also his behavior—he was a moral, upstanding man in a world that was peopled by plutocrats like Vanderbilt and Morgan—made him even more appealing.

And to top it all off, Zeus had rescued an injured three-legged street cur several years earlier, whom he had named Mr. Clemens. To the city's vast amusement, and Edith's chagrin, Zeus took the ugly but charming hound everywhere with him. Stories about the handsome, wealthy duke's devotion to his dog delighted readers not just in New York, but across the country.

The fact that Zeus kept such an unprepossessing pet gave Io hope that her brother might wake up in time to avoid a truly horrid marriage.

Io pulled her thoughts from Zeus as the three of them entered the dining room, which was just as draw-droppingly elegant as their cabins. The black and white floor appeared to go on forever and the crystal chandeliers that swayed from the gilded and vaulted ceiling were impossibly huge.

The maître d greeted them by name—without them having to tell him who they were—and led them directly to the captain's table.

Io was aware of the eyes of the other guests on her as they crossed the elegant, cavernous dining room. Every single person on this ship knew who they were.

Io hated the attention, but was happy for Eva, who relished it and sparkled, more beautiful than ever. She didn't begrudge her sister her enjoyment. After all, going to England was Eva's dream.

The men stood to greet them when they arrived at the table. In addition to their family and the captain, two other couples joined them. Zeus had told them beforehand that four of the guests at their table would rotate in order to keep the peace with all the other wealthy people who yearned to be in the spotlight and dine not only with the captain, but also the ship's owner.

Io would have much rather eaten in her room but could imagine the trouble such a request would cause.

A servant seated her between Ares and Apollo, both of whom *mooed* quietly at her.

Io snorted. "Oh, that never gets old. One would think the two of you could come up with something new after fifteen years."

"Why fix what isn't broken?" Apollo murmured.

"We just want you to feel at home, Yoyo," Ares added.

Io grunted skeptically and narrowed her eyes at the remaining empty seat. "Where is Masterson?" she asked before she could help herself.

"He is unwell," Apollo said, giving Io a knowing look that made her cheeks heat.

"What?" she demanded sharply.

Pol shrugged. "Nothing."

Io: The Shrew

"I last saw Masterson shooting the cat over the portside railing," Ares said with cruel casualness.

"*Shooting the cat?*" Io repeated. "Let me guess, Eva's contribution?"

"Of course," Ares said. "Hard to believe the indefatigable Masterson is brought low by something so mild as sailing. Especially on a great cow like this where you can barely feel the pitch and roll."

"Yes, how unmanly of him," Io agreed. "Almost as bad as getting carriage sick."

Ares, who *hated* traveling in an enclosed carriage and always became ill, scowled at her.

Apollo chuckled and grinned at his red-faced twin. "Touché, Yoyo."

Why Io had felt the urge to defend Masterson in any way was beyond her.

The chatter around the dinner table flowed much easier than it had at Zeus's Fifth Avenue home and Io could only assume it was the addition of the five strangers at the table. Hopefully, rotating the guests would make it difficult for Edith to dictate acceptable subjects and control the conversation as she was wont to do.

In any case, Io barely listened, her thoughts, for some annoying reason fixing on Masterson and the reason for his absence. Since that day in the Five Points, she had felt guilty about how churlishly she had treated him after he'd rescued her.

And then she had felt furious at *him* for making her so angry that she had not behaved more gratefully.

Yes. Io knew how illogical that was.

A week ago, she had been on the verge of swallowing her pride, seeking out Masterson, and apologizing when Apollo had invited her down to the basement to watch the men spar early one morning.

Physical pursuits and naked bodies were not things to be ashamed of at Canoga. Certainly, a shirtless man would not give any Canoga woman the vapors.

But when Io had walked into that basement—where Zeus and Corbin had been beating on each other, their muscular torsos glistening with sweat and red marks showing they were well matched—one would have thought she had stripped off her own clothing and asked to fight.

It had been Masterson who had noticed her first. He'd dropped his jaw, and then his guard, allowing Zeus to pop in what Eva would call *a proper facer.*

"Hell! I'm sorry, Corbin," Zeus had muttered when he'd noticed what had so distracted his opponent. "Is something wrong, Io?" he'd asked, hastily snatching a shirt off a peg and shrugging into it.

"You mean other than Masterson dropping his left like a debutant dropping a handkerchief?" Io had retorted.

Ares and Apollo had laughed. And for a second Io had thought her stern brother might actually smile.

But she must have imagined it, because the next second he'd said, "What brought you down here this morning?"

"Ares and Pol brought me down here," she'd retorted, even though she knew exactly what he was driving at.

Zeus had looked pained. "I'm afraid this is not a place for a lady."

To say her hackles had gone up would have been an understatement. "Oh? Why is that?" she'd asked sweetly.

It had been fun to see the great duke speechless.

Naturally, Masterson had not been so tongue-tied. "What His Grace is too polite to say is that this is a masculine refuge."

Io's face had scalded and their eyes had locked, the room around them deadly quiet.

In the next instant, Ares and Apollo had closed ranks, one on either side. Surprisingly, it was quiet, reserved Pol who'd spoken first. "If Io isn't welcome here, then Ares and I will—"

"No," Io had said quietly, her gaze finally breaking with her nemesis.

She'd turned to Apollo and forced a smile. "Mr. Masterson is right. All of us deserve a refuge from the outside world. I do not box, hence there is no reason for me to be here." She'd squeezed Pol's arm and turned to leave.

Io: The Shrew

When she got to the door, it was to find Zeus had somehow beaten her there. "Just because we have never had women here before does not mean we cannot now. You are welcome to stay and watch, sister."

Io had appreciated his lie. It had been kind. "Perhaps some other morning."

And *that* day had been the last exchange she'd had with Masterson.

He had avoided her every bit as sedulously as she'd avoided him.

Io wanted to feel vindicated at the thought of him succumbing to weakness and vomiting over the side of the ship. But as sharp and outspoken as she could be, she could not take pleasure in anyone's pain.

Not even Corbin Masterson's.

*****

Corbin wanted to die.

The thought was not hyperbolic. Never in his life had he felt such unrelenting misery.

And he could not even characterize exactly what was causing it. Well, except for the vomiting.

He just felt *awful*, his body, his brain, his skin, his bones, his organs, his *toenails*, for pity's sake.

His misery had started a few moments after the massive ocean liner had set sail. He'd spent the first few hours being sick in his cabin. Then Hastings knocked on his door, observed his condition, and advised him to go up on deck. "The fresh air is better for seasickness. Trust me."

"Has this happened to you?" Corbin had asked, having to puke before he could listen to the other man's answer.

The duke's smile had been wryly embarrassed. "Yes. Once."

"I will go up when you have all gone to dinner." It had been all Corbin could do to get the words out and he'd been relieved when Hastings had not argued.

And so, he'd waited until dark and then slinked out of his cabin like a rodent.

Hastings had been marginally right in that Corbin had stopped puking when he'd reached the deck. But part of him wondered if that was just because he had nothing left to bring up.

He shivered as the wind blew over the unprotected deck. Out here on the open water, it was hard to believe it was summer.

"Ah, here you are." It was the last voice on earth that Corbin wanted to hear. The same one he heard in his nightmares.

Liar. You hear her voice in your dreams. In those dreams.

Corbin shoved away the mortifying thought and turned to stare up at his tormentress. "So, you've come to gloat at my misfortune."

Lady Io's full, shapely lips twitched at the sight of him, which he was sure was pitiful. "Perhaps a little."

Corbin snorted. And then immediately had to hurry to the railing. Nothing but clear bile came up.

"You need to drink something, or you will get dehydrated, Mr. Masterson."

Ignoring her obvious suggestion, he replaced his sodden handkerchief in his pocket, turned, and croaked, "What can I do for you, my lady?"

"I brought you this." She held out a bottle of Vernor's ginger beer. "Ginger will settle your stomach and it is also helpful with seasickness."

Corbin adored ginger beer. But right now…well, he could only imagine how unpleasant the fizzy liquid would be coming back up.

Still…to not accept it would be boorish.

"Thank you," he muttered, awkwardly holding the cold bottle and wondering what the hell she wanted.

"Sit," she ordered.

Corbin sat down before he fell down.

Lady Io lowered herself onto the deckchair beside him. Even in his diminished state he could admire the gown she wore.

Ever the iconoclast, Lady Io Hale had adopted artistic dress and the style flattered her voluptuous curves like no other—not even the shorter gown and bloomers she'd worn almost a month ago when she'd arrived in New York.

Christ. Could it really be less than a month since I met this woman? I feel like she's been tormenting me all my life.

"Drink the ginger beer, Mr. Masterson."

Corbin sighed, too tired to argue, and took a tiny sip from the bottle she'd had the sense to bring uncapped. Encouraged when it didn't make him rush for the railing, he took another, larger, drink.

"I brought you something else, too."

Corbin turned his head slowly toward her, but even that much movement made him clench his teeth. "What?" It was all he could force out.

She reached into the pocket of her pale green velvet cloak and brought out something.

Corbin squinted at the brown lump in her palm and then at her face. "What is that?"

"It is raw ginger and proven to help with seasickness. It is better to take it before you get onboard, but it can still work now." She paused and then said, "My siblings and I all took it."

"The duke ate *that?*" Corbin asked in open disbelief.

She smiled. "I should have said *four* of my siblings."

"Who told you this works against seasickness? Perhaps you are all just good sailors."

"A physician I know from the Ladies Aid Association gave me this information when I told her I would be on a long sea voyage."

"A doctor?"

"Yes, a doctor—a *woman* doctor."

Corbin frowned. "I thought Elizabeth Blackwell opposed the distribution of co-condoms. Why would she join your organization?" Corbin was annoyed at himself for stumbling over the word *condom*, but he felt indecent speaking it aloud in the presence of a gently born female.

"It is true that Doctor Blackwell is not a member of the LAA." She cocked her head, an expression of genuine amusement on her face. "Do you think she is the only female doctor in the nation?"

Blackwell was the only woman doctor Corbin had ever heard of, but he suspected her question was a trap. "I have no idea," he answered, his voice weak and querulous, like that of an old curmudgeon.

"There are over five hundred female physicians in the United States, Mr. Masterson. More than the rest of the world combined."

Corbin gave a huff of disbelief and immediately regretted it, nausea roiling in his stomach like grease mixed with broken glass.

"Breathe, Mr. Masterson. Slowly, deeply. Resist the urge to vomit—it will only weaken you."

He did what she suggested, but only because his legs were too bloody weak to stand and run to the railing.

After a moment, the nausea passed.

"Do you want this?"

He turned and saw she was still holding the vile-looking lump. "No." And then, because courtesy was bred into him, he added, "Thank you."

She snorted and shook her head. "You don't believe what I'm saying because the information came from a woman."

"That's not true." At least not completely.

"Then why?" she demanded.

"Because I resist all quackery, whether it originates from male or female quacks."

Rather than get offended, which is what Corbin had hoped for— maybe a rousing argument would take his mind off his misery for a few minutes—she merely laughed and deposited her offer back in her pocket.

Her easy compliance—which made Corbin feel like a rude, ungrateful idiot—just irked him. "You should not be up here alone," he snapped.

Her expressive eyebrows shot up. "I am not alone. I'm with you."

Corbin ground his teeth. "You know what I mean. It is nighttime. You are an unmarried female and I am an unmarried male who is not related to you. It is unseemly."

"Unseemly?" She laughed. "Why? Am I in danger of ravishment?" The scornful look she gave him told him just how pitiful he looked.

"Because it will cause *talk*, my lady. Talk that will follow you and haunt you after you make your entrée into society." There. *That* should provoke her.

But she only smiled, amused rather than angered. "Who will talk? The fish you've been puking on? The whales I saw in the distance earlier?"

"How about the crew—of which I've seen at least five of since you've been sitting here."

"The crew? So what if they talk, Masterson? Or do you believe the ship's bursar or one of the porters is going to pop up at a *ton* ball and tell everyone how I offered a very stubborn, ill man a solution that he rejected out of hand? Maybe that is what you are worried about—that people will hear what a stubborn *ass* you are." She no longer looked amused by the time she reached the last word. "Have a lovely evening, Masterson." On that note, she pushed up from her chair and left in a swirl of green velvet.

Corbin opened his mouth to shout after her—although he had nothing pithy in mind. Instead, he clamped a hand over his lips, lurched to his feet, and scrambled toward the railing.

Chapter 6

The Following Night

I brought you this," Io said, staring down at the mere shell of her enemy.

Corbin Masterson, a man usually with ramrod posture and so impeccably groomed and garbed that he did not look *real* was currently slumped in a deckchair in a rumpled suit, his unwashed hair sticking up in greasy tufts, and his big hands shaking.

His head slowly turned toward Io, until his blank eyes stared up at her. He blinked and then looked at her hands.

"Crackers and ginger beer?" he croaked, his voice was a mere husk but he still managed to broadcast disbelief.

Io sighed. Really. Was there a more stubborn man in Creation?

She deliberated just leaving him to his misery. But he looked so ill that she feared he'd roll right off the deck and into the ocean as easily as a child's marble if a swell came up.

And so, she tried again. "Can what I'm offering make you feel any worse than you are now, Masterson?"

He pondered her question for a long moment.

And then reached out two shaky hands. "Thank you."

Io lowered herself into the same chair she'd had the evening before and stared up at the night sky, which was clear. The seas were easy, which she was grateful for on Masterson's behalf. She hated to imagine what shape he would be in if they encountered rotten weather.

"Thank you."

Io turned at the sound of his voice and watched as he put the last cracker into his mouth. "Should I fetch you more?"

He shook his head, his cheeks bulging as he swallowed a mouthful of ginger beer to wash down the crackers.

Io turned back to the sky. After a moment, she said, "I was wrong to agitate you last night. Part of the remedy I was going to suggest is that you remain as still as possible and try not to talk, which is just more motion, after all."

Io turned when he made no response. He was staring straight ahead and appeared to be listening, so she continued. "There are two schools of thought about seasickness. Those who say you should try to sleep through it, not talking or moving. And those who believe a distraction will help pull your mind away from the discomfort. I can go away, or I can remain here and—"

"Talk." The word was more of a grunt. "Talk about anything. Just…talk."

After a moment of surprise, she said the first thing that came to mind. "This sky is already slightly different than the one I am used to at Canoga. I am determined to look at it every night so that I do not arrive in Southampton surprised by stars that are strangers to me."

Io slid a glance at him and saw that some of the tension had lessened around his eyes.

And so she continued to talk about the stars.

***

Her voice was like a balm on Corbin's raw nerves. Which was odd because normally Io Hale only made him agitated.

"My father was the one who taught me about the heavens and the various bodies that inhabit them. And, of course, he is the one who named me. It was Simon Marius, a German astronomer who decided the moons of Jupiter—that most libidinous and inconstant of gods—would be named after the most successful of his adulterous unions. Io, Europa, Callista— and let us not forget Ganymede." Again, she laughed, the throaty sound traveling straight to Corbin's balls. How the hell was it possible that his body could manage lust at such a time?

"I have always found Marius's notion of *successful* deeply amusing," she went on. "My own idea of success would have been if one of those poor mortals Jupiter pestered had managed to lay hands on a mythical, god-slaying sword and cut off Jupiter's head." She paused, and then added, "Both his heads, just for good measure."

Corbin choked on his own spit and then fell into a hacking, coughing fit. He hunched over, afraid that he might start puking again.

A hand landed on his back and rubbed in firm circles. "Breathe, Mr. Masterson." Her touch even through a half dozen layers of clothing was electric. Corbin knew he could not possibly feel her warmth—that it must all be in his head—which was somehow even worse.

This woman had wormed her way into his brain—into his very *being*— deeply, like the tiny wood-boring creatures that had brought down the great sailing ships of old.

She would probably love that comparison, a dry voice suggested.

Corbin sat back and was relieved when her hand dropped away.

When he opened his eyes, he saw her palm, holding the same lump out to him.

"It will help you," she said quietly.

Corbin's hand reached out of its own volition.

"What you must do is take it to your cabin and—"

Corbin tossed the root into his mouth and chewed.

"No!" she yelped. "Don't—"

His head burst into flame and he spat the pieces onto the deck, gasping. When he raised the ginger beer bottle to his lips, he discovered it was empty.

Lady Io dropped to her knees, heedless of her finery, and scrabbled around on the deck.

"Are you trying to kill me?" he demanded hoarsely when she pushed up holding the remnants of the devil root in her palm.

"If you had waited and *listened* you would have heard me say that you should use it to make a tea, not gobble down the whole lump. Spitting it out onto the deck was inconsiderate, Mr. Masterson. For your information, this is all I have. What if somebody else were to need it?"

She shoved the pieces into her pocket and stood. "If you want to suffer. Go ahead."

And then she whirled and left him to his misery.

***

The next night...

"Have you seen Masterson?" Bal asked Io as they waltzed around the dance floor, practicing the steps they'd spent hours learning in New York.

"Why?" she snapped.

"Because the man is truly ill. You need to give him ginger and help him, Yoyo."

"I have tried to give it to him." She forced the words through gritted teeth.

Her twin sighed.

"What, Bal?"

"Have you tried doing it *kindly*? He is ill, Yoyo. Zeus is very concerned about him."

"Fine. I will go to him—again—as soon as we finish this waltz. And I will be kind," she added grudgingly.

Bal grinned. "That's my twin," he praised. After a moment, he said, "Er, Yoyo, you are trying to lead again."

Io was relieved to disappear from the grand ballroom before getting roped into any more dancing. It wasn't the dancing itself she hated; it was the vapid conversation she was forced to engage in with anyone other than her brothers.

If one more man asked her if she was excited to go to *ton* parties, she thought she would scream.

It was chilly out tonight, so she made a detour to her cabin first, to collect the ginger and also the fur-lined cloak she'd resisted buying as an unnecessary extravagance and now appreciated.

As she approached her room, she squinted at the pile of dirty linen in front of her door.

And then the linen moved.

"Good God!" Io hastened her steps. "Mr. Masterson?" she said, dropping to her haunches to peer at him.

His striking gray eyes were sunken and rimmed with red, his skin a pasty shade that no living human being should be.

He clutched at her arm with a weak hand. "I'll try it. Please. I will try *anything*."

"Of course, Masterson. Here, let me help you to your cabin and I will bring you your tea."

He moaned when she tried to get him to stand. "s'too far."

Io thought so, too. "Then come into mine—no, don't protest," she said, when he opened his mouth. "Eva is in her room to serve as chaperone," she lied. "And you will only be there a short while." *And you are so sick that a fly could knock you over.*

It was a sign of how ill he was that he did not protest. Nor did he stand. Instead, he crawled when she opened the door. Not until he reached her sitting area did he allow her to help him into a chair.

Io immediately rang for a servant and ordered hot water, requesting that it be brought quickly, adding a generous gratuity to cover any inconvenience.

Mr. Masterson shivered in his chair, unconscious, as far as she could tell.

Io was genuinely worried by the time the water had been delivered and she had a nice strong tea ready.

She poured a cup and let it cool a bit before waking him.

"Mr. Masterson?" Io gently squeezed his shoulder, not wanting to startle him.

His eyes opened a crack and then he did the oddest thing: he smiled. Not his usual superior faint smirk but a huge, genuine grin.

Io's jaw dropped at the sight, her heart pounding, as if she'd just discovered a chest full of buried treasure.

Even in his weakened state, the expression was devastating. Who would have guessed that stern, joyless Mr. Masterson had dimples—two deep, delightful ones? Her sister Eva had a dimple on one side of her mouth, just a bit below her lips, and Io had always coveted it.

"Io," he said, for the first time forgetting her courtesy title, still grinning.

Clearly, he was very ill.

Io raised the cup. "You must drink this, Mr. Masterson."

He blinked a few times and the charming smile slid away. It was like watching a rose wither.

Just as well. You were in danger of falling for dimples. Shame on you.

Io agreed.

"Come now, just a sip," she urged.

***

Corbin woke with a start, his entire body aching as if somebody had beaten him with sticks. He blinked in the near darkness and looked around, his eyes bulging almost out of his head when he saw Lady Io Hale sleeping on the settee across from him, bundled up in a blanket.

Corbin glanced down. He was fully clothed and also wrapped in a blanket.

He sighed with relief. Clearly nothing sexual had occurred.

He immediately sneered at himself for such a stupid thought. He'd been as weak as a kitten for days. He had vague memories of sleeping outside her door. His face heated as he imagined living that down.

Well, he could deal with that later.

Right now, he felt… strange.

It took him a full minute to realize that he no longer had the urge to vomit up his internal organs.

Damnation. Her cure had worked!

And he had resisted it for *days*.

Corbin wanted to slap himself, but it would have taken too much effort to lift his arm. And he needed all the energy he could muster to get the hell out of his employer's sister's room.

He shakily pushed to his feet, standing a moment to make sure he could remain upright. He noticed a piece of paper on the low table between his chair and her sofa.

Clutching the chairback, he leaned low.

Mr. Masterson:

Take this ginger with you. Shave a small amount into a cup and add boiling water. Drink five times a day. Get plenty of sleep and drink lots of water.

There was no signature, just her bold, messy handwriting.

Corbin swallowed and picked up the ginger root, putting it carefully into the inner pocket of his coat as if it were a priceless heirloom. He hesitated, and then took the brief message as well, not thinking too closely about why he would want something Lady Io Hale had written to him.

And then Corbin slinked out of her room.

***

Three days later...

Io was playing whist with Eva and the twins when she next saw Corbin Masterson. He'd not been up on deck for the last few nights. At first, she'd been concerned, but Zeus had mentioned at dinner two nights before that Masterson was on the mend.

"Oh, Mr. Masterson!" Eva said, spotting him first and laying down her cards. "You must be feeling better."

He smiled stiffly and nodded, "Yes, my lady. I feel much better." His gray eyes slid to Io. "I wanted to thank you for helping me. And thank you so much for the ginger root. It effected a miracle."

"You are welcome, Mr. Masterson," she said, speaking just as coolly.

The moment he was out of earshot the twins were *moo*ing and Eva was giggling.

"You two are idiots," Io said, hating that her face was hot, and not from the brutal sun. She glared at her sister. "And you are encouraging their juvenile behavior."

"Oh, Yoyo, you have to admit it is humorous. Mr. Masterson *hated* having to thank you."

"He looked like he was in physical pain," Apollo agreed with a rare grin.

Io just grunted.

"The man is actually not so bad," Ares said.

Pol's eyes widened and scowled at his twin. "Don't you recall how he tossed Yoyo out of the basement?" he demanded, his chastising tone making Ares blush.

"He was right to do so," Io said before Ares could respond.

All three of her siblings looked at her with eyes on stalks.

She shrugged. "Maybe his reasoning wasn't right, but what he wanted was. Can you imagine how much enjoyment you would have down there if you had to comply with the current female requirements for civilized behavior? You would have to box in a full suit of clothing." The twins laughed, but she ignored them and went on, pushing the memory of Mr. Masterson's magnificent naked torso from her mind. "That is true and you know it. Shirtless men are considered as damaging to the female eye as staring directly at the sun. More, probably. Eva and I—and the women from Canoga—might have been able to enjoy watching you spar without getting the vapors, but society women in New York seem eager to embrace a weaker role. They would titter and squeal and soon there would be no sparring. Mr. Masterson was right about deserving a refuge from such foolishness. And neither he nor Zeus said I could *never* come down there. If I decide that I want to watch you two cockerels spar, I can go any time. Right?"

Both twins nodded.

"So, it is not a tragedy," Io finished, her tone indicating this was the end of the subject. "Now. Are you going to make your bid before we reach Southampton, Ares?"

***

Later that night, after dinner, Io was dancing with Zeus and trying to pay attention to the steps rather than stare at Mr. Masterson, who was waltzing with a young woman who didn't appear to have stopped giggling since he'd led her out onto the floor.

Tonight was the first time Masterson had eaten in the ballroom. He'd dined at the captain's table, along with Miss Barclay, Edith's downtrodden cousin, who must have been relegated to eating in her room until this evening.

Io had tried to speak to the shy woman more than a few times, but Miss Barclay seemed to always be running from one place to another, her expression usually one of worry, if not outright terror.

While Masterson had looked far healthier than the last time Io had seen him, it was obvious that he'd lost some weight after his four-day purge.

Io's brothers—*all* of them, including Zeus—had ribbed him mercilessly about being seasick.

Masterson had taken it in good spirits, giving them his polite social smile, which she now knew was nothing like his real smile.

Indeed, Io probably thought about that slow, sensual grin he'd given her at least once an hour.

It was most irksome.

"Io?"

Io blinked and looked up at Zeus. "I'm sorry. Was I trying to lead again?"

Zeus chuckled. "You were dancing perfectly. I was just wondering how you've been enjoying your first voyage at sea?"

"I like it. At the same time, I would not want to live this way forever. I do not understand how the men who crew this ship can bear to always be floating from one destination to another. Don't they miss their homes?"

"For many of them this ship *is* their home." He paused, his gaze suddenly going distant.

Io watched him, feeling a bit guilty that she never bothered to make conversation with him—or get to know him—when he was always so attentive and polite.

Polite. It wasn't what she was accustomed to from her other three brothers.

Give him time. He's known you less than two months, a voice that sounded remarkably like Bal's said.

"Are you happy to be a duke?" Io asked.

He blinked at her question, rapidly returning from wherever he'd gone.

"It does not make me *un*happy, but it is another responsibility. I might enjoy my new position at some point, but right now I find there to be a great deal of…uncertainty."

Uncertain? Zeus?

"I have a hard time imagining you being uncertain about anything," Io said.

He regarded her through his jewel-like eyes for a long moment, the weight of his stare almost palpable. "I am human, Io. Just like everyone else."

For some reason, Io felt a strange tightness in her throat at his quiet declaration.

***

Corbin told himself that he'd gone to the two deckchairs he thought of as *theirs* because he wanted fresh air, not because he hoped to see Lady Io again.

He wasn't sure when he had become such a liar—to himself.

Even now you are lying! You became a liar after meeting Lady Io. You lie to evade your feelings. You lie to avoid the truth. You lie—

"Good evening, Mr. Masterson."

Corbin shot to his feet as the woman who was never far from his thoughts arrived in person. "Good evening, my lady."

"I was impressed to see that you are well enough to be dancing."

"I was roped into it before I could think of an excuse," he said, and then because the words sounded ungallant he added, "I experienced a slight bout of nausea for my efforts."

"Yes. Ginger isn't a magical talisman—there are limits."

An uncomfortable silence inserted itself.

"It is a beautiful night," he said inanely.

"You will be pleased to hear the captain said it should be clear sailing for at least the next few days."

"Yes, that is a relief." Corbin had already decided that he would simply throw himself overboard if the ship were caught in a storm. He kept that pitiful thought to himself.

They both spoke at the same time.

"Do you want to——" he said.

"I should leave you——" she said.

"I'm sorry," Corbin said. "You were saying something?"

"I was offering to leave you to rest. Why?" she asked sharply. "What were you going to say?"

Corbin knew what he *should* say, which was *good night.*

Instead, he said, "Do you want to sit for a while?"

Lady Io looked bemused by the offer and Corbin couldn't blame her. He was more than a little bemused by the offer, himself.

She sat and he gladly lowered his still weak body into the chair beside her.

They stared up at the stars.

And stared.

And stared.

Corbin opened his mouth.

"My brother said you have only worked for him for half a year. What did you do before?" she asked.

Corbin was not eager to travel down this road, but he could hardly ignore her question. "I operated a construction company with my father."

"Did you work for him long?"

"Twenty-one years. I started when I was sixteen. I only worked on holidays from school until I finished university." He hesitated and then added, "And then there was the War, of course."

"Why did you quit working for him?"

"He died last year."

"Oh, I'm so sorry," she said, sounding as if she meant it rather than merely uttering a social platitude.

Perhaps it was that sympathy which made him do something he *never* did and tell the truth, at least part of what had happened. "I did not quit working at the company voluntarily," he admitted. "My younger brother gained control on my father's death and he did not wish to associate with me." He paused and then said the words that still made him feel ill, even after all these years. "I am my father's natural son." He steeled himself for her reaction—for the way she would hastily excuse herself. And how she would look at him from now on: as if being near an illegitimate man would taint her by association.

Corbin should have known by now that Lady Io Hale never reacted the way he expected.

Instead of scorning him or leaving, she turned her entire body toward him the way he had noticed her do with her siblings when she was completely interested in something they were saying. It was charming, although Miss Barrymore was correct in pointing out that it was not a mannerism for sophisticated society.

"You never had another job all that time?" she asked.

"Other than soldiering in the war, no."

Her eyebrows drew down into a V over the bridge of her nose, the fierce expression making him think about Valkyries, for some reason.

"How long had your brother worked for him?"

"Richard never worked there." His younger brother was a gambler and a playboy, but there was no use sharing that information.

Her eyes widened. "And yet *you* had to leave?"

"Yes."

"But—but *why?*"

"Because my brother inherited everything." At her stunned, uncomprehending gaze, Corbin felt compelled to add an explanation, although he had only ever discussed this matter with Hastings. "My father amended his will years ago but failed to have it witnessed. It was sitting in his desk, where he'd evidently forgotten it. As a result, the entirety of his fortune, including the company, passed to his legal heir."

She made a noise rather like an angry goose—yet another sound that would not be acceptable in society. And yet Corbin could not help liking her for it.

"How preposterous!" she declared. "Is there no remedy under the law?"

Her outrage on his behalf warmed him. "It is unlikely that I would prevail, even though there are arguments to be made. For example, we made a gentleman's agreement years before. But there was nothing on paper. In any case, I do not have the money to pursue a legal action."

"Would Zeus not help you?"

Corbin knew that her question was not meant to embarrass him, and yet he felt as if he had suddenly wandered into the middle of a cocktail party at Lady Astor's house, wearing only his smalls. How could he possibly tell her that to accept the duke's offer of help would jeopardize one of the two things of value left in his life—which was his friendship with Hastings—without sounding weak and pathetic in the process?

"I'm sorry," she said, her voice making Corbin look up.

Lady Io gave him a sheepish smile—the first one of its kind he had seen on her lovely face. "That was a very personal question. My twin says I tend to come at people like a herd of stampeding cattle."

Corbin thought that an apt description.

Instead of agreeing with her, however, he changed the subject, "What about you?"

"What about me?"

"What did you do to occupy yourself at, er, Canoga?" Why the hell was he blushing?

You know why. Because you were thinking of Lady Io and her many lovers…

"Are you asking because you are genuinely interested? Or because you'd like an opportunity to ridicule our way of life?"

Ah, combativeness. This was something Corbin could contend with and far better than her sympathy.

"Forgive me," Corbin said coolly. "I thought we were having a civil conversation. Is it time to commence fighting like street brawlers?"

Io: The Shrew

Her eyes opened, and then, astonishingly, she laughed. "Fair enough—that was rude of me."

An apology from Lady Io Hale? Corbin was too flummoxed for words.

"I had my chores—everyone does—helping in the kitchen or the laundry. Our meals are communal, you know, so everyone takes a turn and learns how to cook, male or female."

Corbin thought that part of Canoga was quite wise. He'd had to learn how to do for himself in a hurry when he had been in the army. Knowing how to cook would have been helpful.

"We all joined in during the harvesting, and so forth. But what I did as a *job*—although we didn't really call them that—was teach the older children." She hesitated, and then said, "In addition to the radical pamphlets I help produce"—she smirked at him and emphasized the word *radical*— "I also write books."

"What sort of books?"

"Children's books."

There was something the investigator hadn't uncovered. Corbin wondered if Zeus knew about this. "What are the books about?"

"They are about a barnyard and all the animals who occupy it. I only write them," she said. "Another woman does the illustrations. At first, we wrote them for just the children at Canoga, but somehow word got out and soon so many people wanted them that we had them printed and a man would sell them to the various bookstores in the area. About four years ago, a man named Mr. Putnam approached us and now we—"

"Good Lord! Are you talking about *George* Putnam?"

"Yes, that is his name," she agreed. "He has produced the last five and we are working on number six. Even though I am going to Britain, I have—"

"The *last* five? How many are there? And what are these books called?"

"They are the *Take Charge* series. First, there was—"

"*Arnold Takes Charge*," Corbin finished for her, utterly flabbergasted.

She looked pleased. "You've heard of them?"

Corbin gave a disbelieving huff. "Have I heard of them? Why, they are the most popular books for children in New York City. Perhaps the entire

75

state, as far as I know. My—my friend's daughter is wild for them and I went to six bookshops to hunt down a copy of *Lizzy Takes Charge* for her."

It was her turn to look startled. "Indeed! You must like this little girl a great deal."

"Er, yes. Her family is very close." Corbin said vaguely, eager to move on. "I have read all of them. Half-a-hundred times each, I wager," he added wryly. He stared at her, trying to fit this new piece of Io Hale into what was an increasingly complex puzzle. "They are delightful books."

"Oh, well…thank you. You are very kind. I enjoy writing them a great deal."

Corbin had never seen her at a loss for words. It was dark, but he would swear that she was blushing.

"Can you tell me how many more there might be? Lizzy—er that is the little girl's name, hence the reason I hunted for that particular volume so persistently—is wild for them."

"We are contracted for three more." The look she gave him was curious.

"So, you will continue writing even though you are not at Canoga?" he asked, wanting to get as far away from the subject of Lizzy as he could. "Won't that be difficult with you in England?"

"No, not at all. You see, we have always done our parts independently."

"Tell me how this process works. Is it difficult to write a book with *two* authors?"

"Are you really interested?" she asked, a faint notch between her huge eyes.

"Who wouldn't be?" Corbin asked in all seriousness.

For the next half hour, they talked about writing and the relatively recent increase in demand for children's books.

While part of Corbin's mind was listening in fascination, another part was marveling at this new facet of Lady Io Hale.

Who could have guessed that a woman so opposed to marriage would write children's books?

Chapter 7

The Following Night

Io was the first one to arrive at the deck chairs the next night and for a moment she wondered if Mr. Masterson would come. Perhaps he had only spent time out here when he'd been too ill to—

"Good evening, my lady," his familiar voice said from behind her.

Io smothered her likely fatuous smile before turning. "Did you get caught in Mrs. Jordan's clutches again, Mr. Masterson?"

He gave her that faint smile that she had somehow begun to view as charming, rather than superior and irritating, and lowered himself into the deckchair Io now thought of as his.

"It is no great hardship to dance with Miss Jordan. She is a sweet girl."

Io's hackles rose. "She is eighteen, Mr. Masterson, hardly a *girl*. And I suspect her *sweetness* is another word for ignorance."

"What are you saying?"

"I'm saying that if her mother has her way, Miss Jordan will be married and swelling with her first child this time next year."

His handsome features rearranged themselves into a chiding expression. "That seems an unnecessarily harsh pronouncement, not to mention vulgar and not the sort of comment you'd want to make in company."

Io shrugged off his annoying chastisement, unwilling to be distracted from her point. "But it is true all the same, is it not?"

"Have you paused to consider that it isn't just Mrs. Jordan who would like to see her daughter married? Perhaps *Miss* Jordan would like a husband and children as well."

Io snorted. "That is what she *thinks* she wants because she has been told that is all she is good for her entire life." Masterson opened his mouth, but she did not give him an opportunity to speak. "Miss Jordan has the self-will of a veal calf and Mama Jordan is no different from a broker of cattle who wants their stock fat and sleek for the auction block, hoping for the wealthiest buyer. Not until her wedding night will poor Miss Jordan understand just whose blood will be spilled—and likely with as much compassion and tenderness as that which transpires in an abattoir."

Although Masterson's expression was as fixed and stern as ever, she could feel disproval rolling off him in waves. "Do you never think before you speak?"

Io bristled. "Do you?"

His lips pressed into a straight line. "If you think to shock me with vulgar references to fornication, you are doomed to disappointment, my lady. Just because I comport myself with decency and decorum"—his emphasis on those words left no doubt in Io's mind that he believed her bereft of both qualities— "does not mean I am some chicken-hearted namby-pamby to be unmanned by the crass utterances of a rebellious female bent on exhibiting all the worst characteristics of an adolescent stable lad."

Io laughed, delighted. "My, my, Mr. Masterson, it appears you have not been tamed, neutered, and domesticated just like a lady's lapdog, after all."

The look he gave her was withering. "Do not push me too far, or you will find out just how *undomesticated* I am, madam."

"Is that so? I believe I will take that as a challenge to arms, Mr. Masterson."

His eyes narrowed. "Tell me, Lady Io, do you think yourself so much better than other women that you revile all those who desire marriage and a family?"

She blinked at his sudden change in subject. "I do not revile them. And I do not think myself *better* than other women." Io felt a twinge of guilt at the claim but shoved it aside. She turned on her deck chair so she could face him directly. "You said that Miss Jordan was a *pretty girl*."

"I did. And I stand by my observation."

"In one way at least, you are right."

Io: The Shrew

"Why do I think I will regret asking what you mean by that?" Masterson said dryly.

"She *is* still a girl when it comes to what to expect on her wedding night."

His expression shifted subtly, exposing the censure she had known he felt toward her all along. "Yet again you are bringing up what goes on in someone else's bedchamber. What point do you hope to make?" His frown deepened. "Unless you are only harping on this subject in the hopes of outraging me? If so, you have sorely failed, my lady. All you have done is give me a disgust of your sordid interest."

Io absolutely *adored* this side of the erstwhile starchy man!

"My point is that Miss Jordan—just like those cows in my earlier analogy—is marching to the slaughter completely innocent of her fate. Like those cows, she has been deliberately kept ignorant of what awaits her. Nobody will tell her what to expect or how her body will never again belong to her once she is married. How her husband may impregnate her or beat her or lock her away if he wishes. How he may take mistresses and bring home diseases and—"

"What has happened to make you this way?" he asked, a glimmer of morbid fascination in his gray eyes.

"What way?"

"So bitter and disillusioned about men and women and the institution of marriage?"

Io gave a bitter laugh. "Now there is a question that only a man would ask." She got to her feet. "No, do not get up. I am leaving. I am too angry to discuss this rationally with you," she admitted, wanting to get away from him before she was reduced to slinging insults. "I bid you goodnight, sir."

Only when Io made it to the inner stairwell did she realize the thudding she heard wasn't coming from inside her head, but footsteps beside her.

She stopped and turned. "What are you doing?"

"I am escorting you back to your cabin," Masterson said.

"Why?"

"Because it is a gentleman's duty to—"

"Bullshit." To say the vulgar word was satisfying. To watch its effect on Masterson—who appeared to be carved from stone—was even more pleasurable.

Io enjoyed his reaction until he began to gather his scattered wits.

"I insist you allow me to accompany you," he said stiffly.

"You didn't walk me back to my room every other night. Why now?"

He looked pained. "I was hardly in any condition to—"

"Oh, just go away! I don't need you. I've survived the last few nights without you, not to mention the first twenty-five years of my life." She turned and strode off without another word, aware of his presence just slightly behind her.

Io ignored him. Or at least she tried to.

The truth was, she couldn't ignore Corbin Masterson even when she tried her hardest.

And that scared her more than her foolish journey to Five Points unattended had done.

***

Corbin was confused.

One moment, he and Lady Io had been pleasantly conversing almost like friends.

The next, she'd launched on a tirade about young women and marriage and cattle and it had been as if a cyclone had suddenly risen up in front of him. Her anger had turned into barely restrained rage in the blink of an eye.

It had been more than a little disturbing.

When they reached her cabin, she fumbled with her key and dropped it.

Corbin bent and picked it up. "Allow me," he murmured, relieved when she didn't argue.

He unlocked the door, opened it, waiting for her to enter before saying. "Good ni—" that was as far as he got when hot, soft lips molded to his mouth.

Io: The Shrew

The excuse that Corbin would cling to when he thought about his behavior later, was that he was still not up to snuff after his illness.

Because instead of stepping back like a *gentleman* would, Corbin wrapped his arms around her lush body with a groan and walked her backward into the room, hooking his foot on the door and kicking it shut behind him.

Io Hale was every bit as savage and passionate as Corbin had imagined, her mouth impossibly sweet, her uncorsetted, unbustled, and uncaged body nothing but soft, full curves.

Corbin had never before kissed a woman who attempted to *consume* him, but he should have expected it from her.

While they jousted with their tongues, he allowed himself to do something he had been fantasizing about for weeks—from the moment he had met her, if he was honest with himself—and slid his hands from her waist down to the feminine flare of her hips, his fingers stretching to grip her lush bottom.

Rather than earn him a slap—which part of him expected—she gave an approving groan and thrust herself against him, her hands firmly stroking his body until she grabbed the globes of his ass with both hands and squeezed. Hard.

Arousal tinged with amusement flared inside of him at her obvious aping of his own action. In response, he caressed his way back up to the uncorsetted nip of her waist, over her small ribcage, and came to rest on the sides of her body, his fingers scant, torturous inches from her magnificent breasts.

Yet again, Lady Io did not respond as he expected.

While her hands slid around his body and under his coat, they moved south instead of north. Her fingers digging into the sensitive muscles of his stomach while she ground her hips against him, her mound rubbing against his raging erection until he was slick with pre-ejaculate.

Corbin knew that together they were making a mortifying wet stain on his trousers but could not bring himself to care.

Christ! Her hands felt good.

He thrust his dick against her and thumbed the peaked tips of her breasts.

She let out a low, animal groan and plucked at his waistcoat and shirt before pulling away from his lips, panting hard. "Take off your clothes. I want you inside me."

The effect of her words was unlike anything he had ever experienced. He was simultaneously molten inside while his skin prickled as if somebody had just thrown icy water on him.

You are groping your best friend's sister. The woman Hastings asked you to protect.

"What is it, Masterson?" She demanded when he froze.

He looked down into her eyes. The lust that had been blazing in them dimming even as he watched, like a dark cloud passing over a brilliant sky.

Corbin stepped back. Or at least he tried to, but his hands were so happy on her breasts that they had other ideas.

Release her, he barked, thankfully only in his mind.

Io literally took the matters out of his hands by stepping back.

Once they were no longer touching, he gathered his wits enough to say, "I am deeply sorry."

She crossed her arms over her chest and, Lord, how he envied her forearms. "Sorry for what?"

Corbin's brows lowered. "For behaving so inappropriately."

"I am the one who kissed you, Masterson? Or have you forgotten? Should I apologize, too?"

He gritted his jaws to keep something sharp and thoughtless from flying out of his mouth. "That is different."

"Why?"

"You *know* why."

"Because I am a woman," she said, her voice flat.

It was not a question, so Corbin didn't answer. Instead, he said, "I will speak to His Grace and explain—"

She closed the distance with a step, her body pressing against his—not in lust this time—her eyes as hard as granite. "If you say so much as one word to my brother about the minor, insignificant tussle we have just engaged in, I will—"

"Insignificant?"

Damn it! Why did he say that? And why did he sound so much like an injured schoolgirl?

"Yes, insignificant," she said, cutting him a nasty smile. "At least it was to me."

And then, to Corbin's regret, she stepped away from his body, strode to the door, and flung it open. "Get out."

Corbin hesitated, trying to think of something to say that might make this end differently—less…contentiously.

Her face was like a beautiful statue, but Corbin knew that she viewed his actions—putting a stop to their trysting—not as an attempt to save her reputation, but as a rejection of *her.*

As much as it pained him, he said nothing to change her mind. If she hated him, the less likely he was to forget who she was ever again.

Or, perhaps more importantly, he might not forget who *he* was.

John Hale's best friend and employee.

And also a man who had nothing to offer to any woman except an illegitimate name and empty pockets.

Chapter 8

England
Hastings Park
A Few Weeks Later

Io had known that her brother had inherited a castle. But there was knowing something, and then there was *seeing*.

Hastings Park, the ducal seat, was enormous. In fact, it was a small city. The entire community of Canoga could fit into one wing of it with room to spare.

And yet it still was not large enough to keep Io away from her brother's fiancée.

"The clothing you are wearing," Edith said, sweeping Io with a scathing look, "is barely adequate for the country. You need to learn to dress appropriately."

The three of them—Edith, Io, and Eva—were sitting in one of the dozens of common rooms in the castle. The first week had passed in a blur as Io found her bearings in this strange, extravagant new world in which she and her siblings were aristocrats and everyone around them bowed and scraped.

Io now had a personal servant—a young woman named Moira. When she had resisted engaging one, Edith had threatened to find one for her. When Io had continued to refuse, she'd been summoned to the duke's study. Again.

"You must have a maid," Zeus had said, his tone weary but firm. "You will not be able to launder and mend and do the hundred other small tasks that will be necessary."

"I did them all at Canoga."

"But you are no longer at Canoga," he had explained with exaggerated patience. "And if you will recall, *you* were the one who agreed to come to England." His eyelids lowered over his gemlike eyes. "*When in Rome, Io…*"

Io: The Shrew

Io had smiled tightly, biting the inside of her cheek to keep from lashing out. He was right; she had agreed.

And so she now had a maid.

On the subject of her clothing, however, she would stand firm.

"I will purchase more when we move to London for the Season," she said to Edith. "And everything I buy will conform to my own principles. My clothing is not negotiable. And I'm sure you recall Zeus agreeing with me on this matter."

Edith opened her mouth.

"I read that the Countess of Fenhurst is an adherent of Dress Reform," Eva piped up.

Io bit back a smirk. Her sister had become an expert at defanging Edith by bringing up the name of some lord or lady to back up her arguments.

Edith did not answer, but she did move on to another subject. "We have been in residence for ten days and many people have left their cards. Eva and I will return calls beginning tomorrow. You will accompany us and we will—"

"I will *not* accompany you on morning calls."

"I am sure His Grace will have something to say about that."

"Probably," Io agreed. "But I already have plans for my day."

"And those are?"

"I am meeting the village schoolteacher, Miss Amelia Temple, and we are discussing how I might volunteer my time."

"*Teaching?*" Edith all but shrieked.

One would have thought that Io had suggested whoring her way through the male servants the way the other woman repeated the word.

"Yes."

"That is most inappropriate. His Grace will—"

Io smiled. "Let us go and see my brother now, shall we? But first, let me ring for Mrs. Dryden."

***

85

"Yes, it is true the former duchess volunteered at the village school," Mrs. Dryden said, visibly bewildered to be summoned to the duke's study to confirm such a simple fact.

Io smirked at Edith, who fumed and glared at the ethereally lovely housekeeper.

"Thank you, Mrs. Dryden. That will be all for now," Zeus said, gently dismissing the poor woman, who looked like she wanted to sink through the floorboards.

Io felt a pang of guilt at putting her in the middle—it was already clear that Edith didn't care for the beautiful servant—but the fact was that Mrs. Dryden had a cool dignity that lent credibility and Io needed that credibility to put a stop to Edith's attempted control of her entire life.

Teaching was a noble profession, and Zeus obviously felt the same.

"Io will cause no harm teaching a few days a week. Indeed, she will likely do a great deal of good," Zeus said to his fiancée, looking as if he would rather be anywhere else than in the middle of yet another argument.

Io felt the exact same way.

Edith stared at Zeus for a long moment, as if she could, by sheer force of will, make him change his mind.

But Io's reserved brother could sometimes be as immovable as a block of granite.

"I will leave you," Io said, eager to get away from the odd atmosphere between the two.

The meeting had convinced Io of what she had suspected since New York: she could not live in a house with Edith. She would go mad. She could not pull up stakes and move into other lodgings here in the country, but when they all went to London at the end of the year, Io was going to have her own place to live.

On that matter *she* was unshakable.

***

Over the next few weeks, Io combed the newspapers Zeus had delivered to the castle every morning. She took them to her chambers after everyone else had already read them. That way, she could make notes directly on them, circling lodging possibilities.

The allowance Zeus gave each of them was exceedingly generous and more than enough to hire five large houses with a dozen servants each. But that was the last thing Io wanted.

She would have liked to live on her own, but that would never be allowed. Besides, with the current demands on her time, she would need somebody to cook and clean. And, of course, she could not live on her own without a *male* to protect her. She grudgingly conceded that fact. At least until she became accustomed to her new environment.

She did not want to live in a castle large enough to house a village. Larger, actually.

And she did not want to live anywhere near Edith.

Volunteering at the village school had been the first thing to happen that gave Io hope for her new life since leaving Canoga.

Amelia Temple, the teacher at the tiny schoolhouse, had been delighted to have her help.

"We have twenty-two students between the ages of seven and sixteen, my lady. I've been teaching them in two groups, but it has been difficult to give the older students the grounding they require in mathematics and English."

Miss Temple was obviously uneasy to be talking to a *lady*. Io had wanted to ask her to call her by her Christian name, but she knew such a gesture would only make Miss Temple more nervous.

Instead, she had said, "Would you like me to take the older children three days a week?"

Miss Temple's eyes had widened. "I thought you could only come two days?"

I could come five days, she'd wanted to say, but she suspected that Zeus would not support that much work, which would come dangerously close to sounding like a *job*, something the sister of a duke was not allowed to have.

"Yes, I can do three," she'd said, smiling at the other woman.

And so Io was now teaching the nine older children—from twelve to sixteen—three days a week.

And she loved it.

But even with teaching, she still had too much time on her hands.

Io was just coming home from her sixth day of teaching, and considering asking Balthazar if there was some way she could help with the harvest—she knew that Bal, Ares, and Pol had been volunteering at the various tenant farms—when she encountered Mr. Masterson.

Io had avoided even looking at him since their last encounter onboard the ship, but as he was going up the stairs, and so was she, she could scarcely ignore him *now*.

Especially not after he said, "Good afternoon, my lady."

Io grunted, decided that was too rude, and said, "Good afternoon, Mr. Masterson."

"How is your teaching progressing?" he asked blandly, his slate gray eyes as opaque and unreadable as ever. He looked healthy and virile, his illness on board the ship clearly something he had put behind him.

Io examined his face for signs of disapproval—he was, after all, Edith's creature—but saw nothing to confirm her suspicion. "It is going well, thank you."

When they reached the second-floor landing, he turned right, which was the same direction she was going.

Io bit back a sigh of irritation.

"His Grace mentioned that you took Tuesday's *London Times*," Masterson said. "I wondered if you still had it?"

"I do. Why?"

"There was an article in it that I wanted to show him. Might I borrow it? I will return it after he has read it."

Io wanted to say *no*, just because she didn't want to prolong their exchange, but even she knew that would be unacceptably churlish.

"Of course," she said. "Shall I bring it down to—"

"I have time to come and fetch it right now. If you are returning to your chambers, that is?"

Io sighed. "Of course."

They walked the rest of the way in uncomfortable silence, at least on Io's side. She could not stop remembering that she had all but thrown herself into this man's arms the last time they'd spoken.

And he had rejected her.

Masterson reached for the door handle to her chambers and opened it. Io considered pointing out that she was capable of opening doors herself, but the sooner he got what he came for, the sooner he would leave.

She went to her desk and rooted through the various copies, which were not in order, looking for the one he wanted.

"Are you saving all those newspapers for a purpose?"

Masterson's voice came from right behind her and Io jumped.

She ignored his question and finished sifting through the pile. "Here it is." She turned and handed him the folded newspaper. "Please do bring it back when you are finished with it." Not that she really needed it. The same listings tended to appear every day.

His gray gaze went from the newspaper in his hand to the ones on her desk. Io could see he wanted to repeat his question.

"If you will excuse me, Mr. Masterson—"

He tucked the paper under his arm. "Of course. I am sorry to keep you from…whatever."

Io ignored his sly dig and waited until he'd left before letting out the breath she'd been holding. Honestly. She could never decide whether she wanted to hit the man or kiss him.

Neither action was appropriate.

The less time she spent around Corbin Masterson, the better.

***

"Where did you find the newspaper?" His Grace asked Corbin. "Somebody appears to be searching for a house to lease."

Corbin stared at his employer and scrambled to come up with an answer that would not implicate Lady Io, who already hated him.

"I believe it went through several hands before Lady Io ended up with it." That was not a lie.

Hastings's brow furrowed as he examined the notations.

Corbin recognized her handwriting because he had stolen that note she had written to him. To his shame and discomfort, he had stared at the brief missive more than a few times. It was the least ladylike handwriting he had ever seen and something about that fascinated him.

Liar. She *fascinates you.*

Based on the stack of newspapers he had seen on her desk, Corbin knew exactly who had circled all those listings and why. Lady Io Hale was planning to jump ship when the family moved to London.

That could not be allowed to happen. Corbin could just imagine the chaos an utterly unrestrained Io Hale could generate.

Still, Corbin was not eager to *tattle* on her, as she liked to accuse him of doing.

After a moment the duke appeared to put aside the matter of the notations and turned his attention to the bank merger story in the foreign section.

While His Grace read the article, Corbin thought about Lady Io. Did she really believe her brother would allow her to take separate lodgings in London? And why would she want to? What sort of activities was she planning that required her own establishment?

Corbin's mouth tightened. Nothing good, he would wager. Based on her antics in New York, the woman had no qualms about exposing herself to all sorts of danger.

Based on her antics with you aboard the Petrel *you should know exactly what she has planned.*

He grimaced. He did not want to think about Lady Io seeking sensual satisfaction in some man's arms.

Not unless the arms are yours.

Corbin brushed aside the voice and considered Lady Io's plans to rent her own lodgings. He would need to tell the duke—eventually—but first, he would try speaking to the woman herself and reasoning with her.

Io: The Shrew

Because that is something you've been so successful at in the past.

Corbin would talk to her tonight after dinner.

Dinner.

He scowled at the thought of the evening meal, which had become grimmer by the day as Miss Barrymore and the duke's siblings' clashes grew both in regularity and acrimony.

It wasn't only Lady Io who argued with Miss Barrymore. Some of the worst disputes occurred between the duke's fiancée and the younger twins. Or at least they were disputes on Miss Barrymore's side.

Lords Ares and Apollo were less likely to openly rebel against Miss Barrymore's strictures, but also less inclined to go along with them—even less than Lady Io—instead passively resisting her commands.

It was a state of affairs that did not make for a happy household or a comfortable meal.

That night at dinner the twins were once again absent.

And Corbin was not the only one to notice.

"Does anyone know if Ares or Apollo plan to come to dinner tonight? This is the third time this week they have failed to appear," the duke said in a tight voice, his gaze drifting over his younger siblings.

"Oh, dear! I am so terribly sorry, Zeus," Lady Eva said. "I'm afraid I got so caught up in my work that I forgot to pass along the message Ares asked me to give you. The twins went to a horse auction."

"Where?" the duke asked.

Lady Eva's forehead furrowed. "Goodness! They told me the name of the town earlier today, but it has slipped my mind."

Zeus eyed her with mild skepticism but seemed willing to accept her excuse.

Miss Barrymore, unfortunately, decided to challenge the issue. "You may think you are helping your brothers by offering excuses for them, Eva, but you are merely encouraging their mischief, my dear."

Lady Eva's lovely face seemed to harden, even though her smile remained. "Dear Edith, I hope you do not think the twins are doing snooks."

Miss Barrymore's eyebrows descended. Before she could speak, the duke intervened.

"*Doing snooks?* Is that an ancient phrase from your lexicon, Eva?" Hastings asked, an amused glint in his normally frosty eyes. Corbin had noticed that Eva was always able to melt the ice around her oldest brother's heart. He was delighted the duke was friends with at least one of his siblings. And Corbin had to admit that Lady Eva really was a darling.

"It is actually a brand-new term. Jeremy, one of the new grooms, is from Manchester and he shared it with me. It means to do this"—Lady Eva put her thumb against the tip of her pert little nose and then wiggled her fingers.

A grin flashed across the duke's face—the first Corbin had seen in ages. "I daresay that will come in very…*handy.*"

Lady Eva's eyes widened and she gave a gurgle of laughter. "*Very* good, Zeus. I adore puns."

The duke's other siblings chuckled.

Corbin breathed a quiet sigh of relief that the youngest Hale had deescalated what could have become an ugly scene.

But then Miss Barrymore cleared her throat and Corbin wanted to lower his head in his hands and groan.

"This sort of behavior is bad enough in the country with only the family at dinner. But when we go to London and move in elevated society—"

"What sort of behavior?" Lady Io interjected. "My brothers have gone to a horse auction. It is my understanding that horse auctions are something aristocratic men spend a disproportionate amount of their time attending. It seems to me that Ares and Pol should fit right in when we move in *elevated society.*"

"What you think hardly matters," Miss Barrymore retorted.

Lady Io's eyes widened, and she laughed. "I see. But what *you* think does?"

Miss Barrymore opened her mouth.

Io: The Shrew

"Please leave us," the duke said, his frigid gaze on the line of footmen listening with ears that were practically on stalks.

Once the door shut behind the last servant, Hastings looked around the table, his gaze lingering longest on his sister and betrothed. "I would prefer not to air our family differences in front of the servants."

Miss Barrymore's pale cheeks turned a dull red at what was obviously chiding, no matter how gently spoken.

Hastings fixed his fiancée with a stern look. "If my sister says the twins are at a horse auction, that is an end to the subject."

Miss Barrymore wisely nodded and said, "Yes, Your Grace."

Lady Io was smirking when her brother turned to her. "I would like to see you in my study after dinner."

His sister's face fell. "Of course, Zeus."

Miss Barrymore did some subtle smirking of her own, not willing to miss *her* opportunity to gloat.

Corbin could not wait for the meal to be over.

***

Io tarried more than an hour after dinner before dragging herself to Zeus's study to face whatever judgment awaited her.

"Please have a seat," Zeus said when Io entered.

Rather than sit behind his desk, Zeus took a chair beside her and crossed one long leg over the other, regarding her steadily for a moment before speaking. "It has come to my attention that you are seeking another house in London."

It wasn't a question, but Io nodded. "Yes. I have been looking for a property to lease." She hesitated and then boldly added, "Your allowance is so generous that engaging lodgings of my own is feasible."

He tilted his head slightly. "You must know that I cannot allow you to live on your own in London, Io."

She opened her mouth to say something foolish and antagonistic, but he was not finished.

"If you are so unhappy here, then I will send you home to your commune if you wish. But you will not use your allowance to rent separate lodgings in London.

"So what you are saying is that the allowance you give me is mine, but not to spend as I wish?"

His eyes narrowed slightly at her combative tone. "In this instance, yes. That is exactly what I am saying."

Io opened her mouth, preparing to rail against this stranger who now controlled her life.

But when she looked into his eyes, her anger faltered. For the first time since she had met him, Io did not see the reserved but benevolent face of a brother.

Instead, she saw the pragmatic, implacable man of business who had amassed a fortune equal to the likes of Stanford and Morgan.

She saw the officer who had won the Medal of Honor for charging directly into enemy fire to rescue one of his men.

She saw the Duke of Hastings.

And she knew that he would not be moved by harsh words, recriminations, or threats.

Io could not recall feeling quite as powerless as she did at that moment. Never in her life had her choices been taken away from her so blatantly and utterly.

That's not true. Have you forgotten about Lamar? Or the baby? Zeus is merely holding you to a promise you made. The elders at Canoga took away more than he ever has.

As it always did when any memory of that time in her life arose, her mind skittered away from it like a startled spider.

When she looked up, it was to find that the man across from her was no longer terrifying and stern, but once again Zeus, her brother.

He was regarding her with a notch of concern between his eyes. "What can I do to make your life in my house more pleasant, Sister?"

You could start by jilting your fiancée.

"I cannot think of anything right now," Io lied. And then she stood. "If you will excuse me," she said, before she opened her mouth and made an already tense situation worse.

Io might not be free to lash out at the Duke of Hastings, but that was not true for his tattletale, Corbin Masterson.

***

Corbin was sitting in the library looking over the furniture and drapery inventories that Mrs. Dryden had drawn up. It was his job to approve her recommendations and then contact the various vendors to set up accounts so she could take care of the actual purchasing.

More than anyone except Hastings himself, Corbin knew how rich the new duke was.

But as wealthy as his friend was, bringing a behemoth like Hastings Park up to snuff was going to cost a fortune—perhaps even two.

It boggled Corbin's mind to contemplate how much money would need to be spent over the next few years to make even basic repairs to the vast, rambling structure. And that would only be the beginning. Hastings would have to maintain the castle for the rest of his life. Honestly, Corbin was not sure it was worth it. But then his friend didn't really have a choice. The property belonged to the dukedom. Hastings could not sell it, even though that would be the wisest action.

He sighed and turned back to the stack of papers on the desk.

When he finished with Mrs. Dryden's lists, he turned to the roof estimate, wincing at the price of lead, which was—

Corbin jolted when the library door suddenly flew open and slammed against the wall.

Lady Io whirled into the room like a velvet tornado. "Just who do you think you are?" she shouted, coming to a halt in front of his desk.

Her scent—something clean and citrusy and far too appealing—had a deleterious effect on both his hearing and comprehension.

"I beg your pardon?" Corbin said stupidly.

She thrust her index finger at him, coming so close that she almost touched the tip of his nose. "Don't act the fool with me, Mr. Masterson!"

Corbin's temperature spiked at having a finger shoved in his face. "Evidently I really *am* a fool, because I have no clue what you are in such a twist about."

"You told Zeus that I was looking for lodgings in London."

Corbin opened his mouth to tell her that—against his better judgment—he had done no such thing. But she was not interested in hearing from him. Judging by the sparks flying from her eyes and her heaving bosom, Lady Io was on a full-blown tear.

"Don't even try to deny it!" she said in a ringing voice.

Corbin made no such effort.

Instead, he leaned against the desk and crossed his arms over his chest. He might as well be comfortable while he endured what would doubtless be an extended rant.

"You, sir, have *thrust* yourself into my business since the first day we met."

Corbin blinked.

"Why you believe that you possess the right to have any say at all in my affairs, I cannot guess. How would you like it if I decided to root through your life like a pig through a pile of scraps?"

Corbin opened his mouth but then paused, taken by that graphic image.

"I'll tell you how you would react," she raged on. "You would be furious and tell me where I could put my nosy curiosity. You would—"

"My interest in your activities is not nosy curiosity, it is part of my job," he said coolly. "A job as defined by my employer, who just happens to be your brother. If you don't care to have me *thrusting* and *rooting* around in your pile of scraps then you should be railing at His Grace right now rather than me. Trust me, I would be ecstatic if you could convince him to award the task of keeping you out of trouble to some other unfortunate soul."

Her jaw dropped.

Io: The Shrew

Somehow, they had ended up almost nose to nose. Or chin to nose, rather, Lady Io glaring daggers and breathing heavily while Corbin kept his seething on the inside.

"I have a theory, Mr. Masterson."

How did she manage to make Corbin's surname sound so… naughty?

"Do you know what I think?" she asked.

"I suspect you are about to tell me."

"I think you cannot keep your nose out of my business because you have no life of your own—at least nothing of any interest."

Corbin bristled. "I could say the same thing about you." *Damnit! Why do I allow her to goad me into incivility?*

"What are you talking about? I have never once meddled in your affairs."

"I am talking about the fact that you are constantly seeking out conflict, strife, and danger to give *your* life meaning."

Corbin immediately wished he could take the words back. Not only was it unprofessional of him to squabble with his employer's relatives, but something like pain flickered in her expressive eyes.

But she was the indomitable Lady Io Hale and rallied quickly. "I suppose you would suggest a husband and a half dozen children to make my life more meaningful?"

He shrugged. "That would certainly be a more productive, safe, and less contentious way of spending your time."

Yet again Corbin cursed his tongue. Being illegitimate, he had learned early on that he had to be twice as wary as any of his peers, always weighing his words and making damned sure they were the correct ones before he opened his mouth.

He *never* spoke thoughtlessly—or he never had before—and yet this woman had him striking out like a startled snake, over and over again.

She shook her head in disbelief. "You really are amazing."

Why did Corbin think that wasn't meant as a compliment?

"You needn't worry about reporting anymore to Zeus about my London plans. He has effectively quashed them by threatening to take away my allowance if I disobey him."

"Are you really surprised by that?"

"I thought you were the one who said he never went back on his word?"

Corbin sighed. "Surely you can see that a lady of your station could not live alone without attracting speculation?"

"What sort of speculation?"

"Are you being willfully obtuse?"

"No, I am *not*."

Corbin was not sure he believed her, but he explained anyhow. "You are a young unattached female who is, thanks to His Grace's financial endowment, wealthy. That makes you a target for unscrupulous men, who would have a far easier time compromising you if you lived without the protection of a male relative. Living alone at your age shows a lamentable independence that will mark you as a woman of questionable virtue in *ton* circles, which will make finding a suitable husband far more difficult." Corbin bit his tongue hard enough to draw blood, but the prudish words were already out.

"You sound exactly like a male version of Edith," she said, shaking her head in amazement and eyeing him with revulsion.

He could not deny the accusation; he really *did* sound like a moralizing, pompous prig.

But no matter how Corbin's words mortified him, that did not diminish the truth of them.

Strangely, Io didn't hurl the marble paperweight on the desk at his head. Instead, her eyelids lowered, making her appear even more sensual than she normally looked. And then she stepped closer, not stopping until they were almost touching.

Corbin uncrossed his arms and opened his mouth to ask what she was doing, but she stroked a finger across his lower lip and the question died an instant death.

Io: The Shrew

"Just look at you, Mr. Masterson." Her voice was low and sultry.

Step away—no run away, a voice shouted inside his head.

Corbin told himself that the reason he didn't back away was because he refused to allow her to push him around.

But that was a lie.

"What about me, my lady?" he asked in a gruff voice.

Her nostrils flared slightly, as if she were scenting her prey, her heavy-lidded gaze on his mouth. "You are an exceptionally attractive, masculine, and virile man Corbin."

Her audacious words, along with the sound of his Christian name on her tongue, sent a thrill up his spine.

And another directly to his cock.

She leaned even closer, until he could feel the heat of her body. "Have you ever considered that instead of dancing attendance on my brother's virago of a fiancée you might be better served finding a female of your own to please?" She paused and then added, "Someone who would give you pleasure in return."

Get the hell away from her! A voice like a klaxon blared in his head.

But Corbin could not have moved if she'd struck a match and set fire to him.

Her finger dragged down his lip, over his chin, and then down and down to his chest, where she splayed a hand over his heart. The entire time, their eyes were locked.

"Mr. Masterson your heart is *racing*," she said in a tone of mock surprise.

That was no exaggeration; his heart was pounding like a bloody war drum.

After a moment, her hand continued its southerly journey.

Corbin's eyes bulged. *She wouldn't. No… She could not be so—*

He hissed through clenched teeth when Lady Io's palm stopped on top of his erect cock.

By some miracle, he rediscovered his ability to speak. "What do you think you are do—"

"*Shhhh.*" She squeezed him lightly and he gasped.

Io leaned close enough that her breath was hot on his chin. And then she began to firmly stroke his aching rod. "You are tumescent, Mr. Masterson. Magnificently so if I may be so bold."

Corbin's brain was trapped between utter incredulity and arousal so fierce that he was a hair's breadth from ejaculating in his trousers.

"Here I am, an unmarried gentlewoman—in my brother's library—and the man in front of me—my brother's own secretary—has an erect penis pressing against my palm." Her lips brushed his chin. "My reputation, once so sterling, is now surely tarnished beyond repair. Isn't it?"

You are a disgrace, Corbin Masterson, a disgusted voice in his head shouted.

He *was* a disgrace; he could not deny it.

Nor could he step away from her hand.

"Are you going to report this little interlude to His Grace, I wonder? Tell him how unsafe my virtue is under his very own roof."

Her words—and his own shame—were, thankfully, *finally,* enough to break her spell.

Corbin closed his hand around her wrist and gently, firmly, and reluctantly lifted her palm off his cock.

And then he stepped away.

She was smirking up at him. "It seems to me that young ladies of gentle birth can find themselves compromised just about anywhere, Mr. Masterson. I don't even need to rent my own house." Still smiling, she brushed past him and sauntered to the door.

Rather than leave, she paused and turned to him. "But I discovered that I was wrong about one thing tonight."

"What?" he asked despite his better judgment.

"I once accused you of being a neutered, domesticated lapdog." Her catlike eyes dropped to his tented trousers. 'I was decidedly wrong about at least part of that."

Corbin was so addled that he didn't even think of opening the door for her until she was already closing it behind her.

Io: The Shrew

He sank into his desk chair with a groan of disbelief at what had just happened. At what he had *allowed* to happen without even a token act of resistance.

The woman was a bloody menace and it was time for him to admit that he had no backbone where she was concerned. The best thing to do— for everyone—was to give Hastings his two weeks' notice and run as fast as he could away from Io Hale.

Liar. You want to run toward *her.*

He ignored the taunt.

Unfortunately, Corbin also had to ignore the urge to run.

He had given the duke his word that he would stay for a year.

Io Hale might be able to drive Corbin's temperature up—and cause his body to respond in ways he could not control—but he would be damned if he'd let her outrageous taunts and lascivious needling cause him to behave like anything less than a gentleman ever again.

Today was the last time he would allow the woman to get under his skin.

Ever.

Chapter 9

A Week or so Later

I f you want a masquerade party for your birthday then you should have one, Eva," Io said.

"But Edith said—"

Io flung up her hands. "Good Lord! If I hear the words *Edith* and *said* together one more time, I will—"

"I'm sorry, Yoyo," Eva hastily said. "I didn't mean to upset you, it's just—well, there is so much arguing and strife in the house right now that the last thing I want to do is insist on a party that will only cause more trouble."

Io looked into her beloved sister's shadowed eyes and felt like a horrible, selfish shrew. "Oh, darling!" She wrapped her arms around Eva's slender shoulders and squeezed her tightly. "I am so sorry for ripping up at you. The rest of us are terribly guilty for leaving you to bear the brunt of Edith's incessant nagging and infernal demands. But never fear, love. I will see about getting you the birthday celebration you deserve."

Eva's eyes were glassy with unshed tears. "But I don't want to have a masquerade if it really *is* vulgar and tasteless, Yoyo."

"Of course, you don't, dearest," Io soothed, although why her sister cared what anyone thought, she really did not comprehend. But that was beside the point. "You let me take care of this, Eva. I will talk to Zeus about it."

"But…erm, you have been so angry with him. Are you sure?"

Furious would have been a better word. Io had scarcely spoken to her brother since the night he'd called her on the carpet about her house hunting.

"Are you *sure*, Yoyo?" Eva asked again. "Perhaps it might be better to have Bal approach him and—"

"Don't worry. I'll see that you get your party. You just start planning your costume."

Io: The Shrew

"Thank you," Eva said, looking as if she might cry.

"I will go and take care of it right now, darling." Io kissed Eva on the cheek and then left her sister, making her way not toward Zeus's study, but to find her twin.

Eva had been right about the tension between her and their oldest sibling. Io was the first to admit that diplomacy was not her strongest suit. She would likely say something thoughtless and rude to Zeus and that would be the end of the masquerade party.

Balthazar, however, had far more tact than Io did.

She smiled as she imagined pigeonholing her brother and making Bal do her dirty work.

What were twins for, after all?

***

"That is so kind of you, Mr. Masterson," Miss Barclay said, her blue eyes enormous behind her spectacles. "Miss Barrymore wants a style that is"—she paused, as if hunting for the perfect word. "One that is classic," she said. "I'm afraid I have not found one that pleases her.

"It is no problem at all," Corbin assured her—not entirely the truth, but he felt sorry for the little mouse. "I will have to remember where I saw them, but there is an entire trunk full of old invitations. Surely something a duchess sent in the past qualifies as classic?"

Miss Barclay nodded eagerly. "Indeed, it should. Please summon me at any time and I will come to wherever the trunk might be." She swallowed. "Even if it is in the attic."

Corbin bit back a smile. "Miss Barclay, have you been listening to rumors about ghosts?"

She laughed and her thin face blushed rosily, making her look almost pretty. "Yes, I am afraid I might let my imagination get the better of me. There is an especially dreadful tale about a—well, never mind. I daresay the servants are enjoying teasing the gullible Americans."

"Yes, I'm sure they are finding us an endless source of entertainment. In any case, if the invitations are in the attic, I will have them delivered to you."

"Oh, that is very—"

A rap on the door cut off her words.

"Come in," Corbin called out, and then wished he hadn't when he saw it was Mademoiselle Laveau, Miss Barrymore's supercilious dresser.

"Excuse me for interrupting," she said imperiously, cutting Corbin a dismissive glance before turning her sharp gaze on the other woman. "Miss Barrymore has been looking all over for you, Miss Barclay. She wishes to dictate the letter to the drapers. Now."

"Oh!" Miss Barclay popped up, reminding Corbin yet again of a startled mouse. "I thought that—but never mind." She turned to Corbin. "Thank you so much, Mr. Masterson."

"My pleasure, Miss Barclay."

She hurried from the room and Corbin turned back to the ledger he'd been working on when Miss Barrymore's cousin had knocked on his door.

He had barely finished three lines when there was another knock.

"Yes?"

This time, it was one of the footmen, Charles. "His Grace would like to see you if you have a moment, Mr. Masterson."

"He is in his study?"

"Yes, sir."

Corbin nodded and then made a mark to save his place before going to see what Hastings needed.

When he entered the duke's study a few moments later, it was to find his friend looking grim. These days that meant Hastings had probably had yet another argument with either his siblings or his betrothed. Or both.

"Thank you for coming so quickly. Sit," Hastings ordered and then stood and went to the table that held several decanters.

Corbin's eyebrows rose. It was barely four o'clock.

"Would you like one?" Hastings asked, lifting the whiskey decanter.

Corbin didn't really want one, but the other man obviously did not wish to indulge alone.

"Yes, please."

The duke returned with two glasses and handed him one.

"Thank you," Corbin said.

Instead of going back to his desk chair, Hastings dropped into the chair next to him and sighed before tossing back the entire shot.

Corbin merely sipped his and waited for Hastings to speak.

"They hate each other," the duke finally said.

"You will need to be more specific."

Hastings's head whipped around, his eyes wide. And then, to Corbin's relief, the other man laughed. True, it was more of a bitter bark, but at least it was a laugh.

"All of them hate Edith and the feeling, I'm afraid, is mutual. The only exception might be Eva, and it is possible that she is just better at hiding her dislike than the others."

Corbin suspected it was the latter. "What happened now?"

"Eva would like a masquerade ball for her twenty-first birthday at the end of next month."

Corbin nodded and waited for the problem.

"I can see by your expression you do not think this is a problem."

Corbin shrugged. "It sounds tedious, but I have attended them before in New York. I know you have, too, because we both went to the one at Astor's house. What is the problem?"

"Edith believes it is a vulgar way to announce our arrival here. It would be our first large function, after all."

"I find it hard to believe that *the* Mrs. Astor would have such a ball if it were vulgar."

"You make an excellent point. In any case, Balthazar came on Eva's behalf to argue for the party. He roped in Mrs. Dryden—the woman has, after all, been here for years—and she agreed with him. And you." He smiled tiredly. "*And* Mrs. Astor. So, there will be a masquerade ball at the end of the month. I hate to pile more work on you when you already—"

"I am more than glad to help plan the party," Corbin said, lying for the second time in an hour.

"I am relieved to hear it. Balthazar said he and Io would handle the arrangements—with some direction from Mrs. Dryden—but I suspect my younger brother and sister know as much about entertaining on a large scale as I do about farming."

Corbin took a sip of whiskey. He personally thought that Balthazar was far more interested in Mrs. Dryden than he was in a masquerade ball. As for Lady Io? Corbin could hardly think of a woman less interested in a frivolous activity like party planning.

"What do you know about this harvest festival that is fast approaching?" the duke asked, changing the subject.

"It is the high point of the fall so everyone for miles around will come. There will be booths with food, handicrafts, that sort of thing. There will also be a dance and feast at the end of the day."

"The vicar asked me this last Sunday if I would make an appearance. Of course, I said *yes*. He told me he would speak to you and let you know what is required of me."

"Yes, Reverend Thomas came to see me earlier this week with a schedule of sorts. There is a squash or pumpkin judging event—although they evidently call them *marrows* here—and you get that honor. I understand it can be quite contentious," Corbin teased.

The duke chuckled. "Well, that's something I've certainly become more accustomed to of late."

"He also asked if you would open the dance and stay for a few sets before you inconspicuously fade into the night."

"That sounds painless enough."

Corbin wondered if Miss Barrymore would feel the same. While he admired the duke's fiancée in many ways, she was not the most genial person. Still, he imagined most dukes and duchesses were not exactly warm when it came to socializing with commoners. Hastings, on the other hand, had experience leading men and knew how to speak to people from any social or economic class.

"How are my siblings fitting into the neighborhood?" Hastings asked.

"Your brothers are already quite beloved for helping with the harvesting."

Hastings smiled and it was the first genuine smile that Corbin had seen in a few days. "I am very pleased to hear that." His smile dimmed. "And what about my brothers' relations with the local female population?"

"You can breathe a sigh of relief on that score. None of the three are the sort to debauch virgins. Lord Apollo seems more interested in raising horses than chasing women. Lord Ares is smitten with the innkeeper, Mrs. Fletcher, who is well able to handle his attentions. And Lord Balthazar is—"

"Interested in my housekeeper," the duke finished, once again grim.

"He is. But nothing inappropriate has happened. And I don't think your brother is the sort to importune a woman."

"No, of course not." Hastings lifted his glass to his mouth, realized it was empty, and lowered it.

"And Io?" he asked with obvious reluctance.

"She spends most of her time either teaching or socializing with the village teacher, hatmaker, and modiste."

"And her political pursuits?"

"I've seen no sign that she is distributing radical literature or, er, condoms."

Hastings nodded. "I know it is not your job, Corbin, but if you could continue to keep an eye on her? I trust you more than anyone else to keep her out of trouble—or lend a hand if she needs it."

Corbin's face heated at the unfortunate wording and he said, "I will keep an eye on things, Your Grace."

Why don't you tell him about his sister's hand *and how it was on your cock a mere week ago?*

It was true that he'd kept that exchange from his employer, but the last thing Hastings needed right now was more to worry about.

What a humanitarian you are.

Corbin gritted his teeth and swallowed the rest of his whiskey.

He and the duke sat in silence for a moment.

"Do you think I've been foolish trying to become acquainted with my siblings at such a time?" Hastings asked.

"You mean in addition to learning how to be a duke, moving house, moving countries, and becoming engaged?"

Hastings sighed. "Point taken. But I have dragged them all away from their home so it is too late to do it any differently now." He reached out and put a hand on Corbin's shoulder, giving it a firm squeeze. "Thank God you are here. When everything else is in chaos, at least I know that I can always trust you, Corbin."

Corbin smiled weakly. "Thank you for your faith in me."

***

The Harvest Fair

Corbin sidled up to Lady Io and hissed, "What on earth are you *doing*, my lady?"

She ignored his question and handed a pamphlet—with a condom tucked inside—to a careworn woman dressed like a farmer's wife. "Here you are, Mrs. James."

Mrs. James swiveled around anxiously before she snatched what was proffered, hastily tucked it into a pocket in her gown, and muttered, "Thank you, my lady."

"You may always come to me if you have any questions," Io said.

The other woman dropped a hasty curtsey, cut Corbin a terrified look, and then scuttled away from the table without answering.

Io turned to Corbin. "You should not stand here. Your stern, puritanical glare will make women too terrified to approach."

"Answer my question, my lady."

"What does it look like I'm doing, Masterson?" she asked, using the curt, challenging tone that she seemed to reserve just for Corbin.

"It looks like you are giving His Grace's people radical literature and *prophylactics* right under his nose."

"Actually, they serve more of a contraceptive function for most of these women."

Io: The Shrew

"What do you think that woman's husband will say when he discovers she has a condom in her possession—and that the duke's sister gave them to her?

Rather than answer him, she abruptly turned to Miss Temple—who was doing a brisk business handing out more pamphlets and johnnies—and murmured something in her ear.

"Of course, my lady," the schoolteacher said, blushing when she caught Corbin glaring at her.

Lady Io leapt to her feet. "Come with me," she barked at Corbin, not waiting for a response before striding away from the bustle of the crowd.

Corbin trotted after her like a faithful hound, catching up to her with several long strides. "Where are we going?"

She ignored him and kept walking.

He was about to stop her when he realized they were approaching the small schoolhouse where she came to teach a few days a week. She took a key from a pocket in the plain, almost severe, navy gown she wore and opened the door before gesturing him inside.

Corbin paused, wondering where this was going.

She sneered at his hesitation. "Are you afraid to be alone with me, Mr. Masterson?"

He clenched his jaw and stepped inside.

There was a box of lucifers on a small table and she struck one of them and lit the candle beside it before shutting the door on the moonlit night and whirling on him. "How *dare* you?"

Corbin actually jolted, shocked by the volume of her voice, and more than a little relieved that she had led him so far away from the others.

Lady Io, it seemed, was going to give him yet another tongue-lashing.

Corbin suppressed the inappropriate flare of excitement that blazed in his chest and set his fisted hands on his hips. "How dare I what? Insist that you exercise decorum on His Grace's property? That I—"

"Do you know how many children Mrs. James has, Masterson?"

Corbin shook his head at this bizarre segue. "I'm sorry, who?"

"The woman you just *caught* me giving a condom to."

"Of course, I don't know how many children she has. I never saw her in my life before tonight."

"But you feel confident about judging her because she is a *woman*, don't you?" Before he could respond, she went on. "She has nine children. *Nine*. She had her first at sixteen. She is now twenty-nine."

Corbin was startled. He'd thought the woman was in her forties.

Lady Io nodded, as if he'd spoken. "Her body is worn out and she is not even thirty. And guess what, Mr. Masterson?"

Corbin found that he did not want to guess.

"She is pregnant. *Again*."

He felt vaguely nauseated by that information but rallied. "That may be unfortunate," he admitted, ignoring her huff at his choice of words. "But how many children the Jameses have is a matter for Mrs. James and her husband, not—"

"*She* has no say in the matter!" Lady Io shouted. "She is chattel, Mr. Masterson. If her husband wants to breed her to death so he can have more farmhands to work his fields it is his legal right to do so."

Corbin gritted his teeth. "As it happens, my lady, I agree that such incessant childbirth seems…inhumane. But I do not agree with your methods."

She flung up her hands. "How else can a woman like her get help? She works all day, every day. This harvest festival is her first night away from her life of drudgery since the *last* one. And tonight, when she gets home, there will still be chores to do. More chores and more children until she is dead from it."

The room echoed with her horrible but likely true words.

"Tell me, Mr. Masterson!" she demanded relentlessly. "Tell me what choices she has?"

"She could abstain." Corbin wanted to bite off his own tongue at the stupid suggestion—especially coming from a man with *his* past—and hastily said, "I just mean—"

"Abstain?" Her eyes threatened to bulge out of her head as she stared at his no doubt reddening face. "Do you have any idea of the range of entertainment available to country farmers with huge families that need to be fed? Do you think they should host a dinner party? Go to a ball? Attend the theater?" she asked, the words dripping sarcasm. "Sexual intercourse is the *only* entertainment available to people like the Jamses, Mr. Masterson.

He flinched at the word *sexual* on her tongue. "I do not doubt that what you say is true, my lady. But none of that is *your* concern. Mrs. James needs to speak to her husband about the matter." Some part of Corbin's brain was aware that he was essentially digging his hole deeper, but he could not seem to shut his mouth. "She needs to convince him that he must curb his desires, that—"

"What about *her* desires?"

Corbin blinked. "Er, what?"

"Or do women not have any sexual needs?" She took a step toward him. "Is that what you think, Masterson? That women don't like orgasms just as much as men do?"

Corbin was fairly certain that he had never heard the word *orgasm* spoken aloud. And he was positive that he had never heard a woman say it. He opened his mouth to advise her against using such an inflammatory word in the future, but her next words stopped him dead.

"What you know about female sexuality could barely fill a thimble, Masterson. If I were you, I would not be so eager to advertise my ignorance."

Corbin opened his mouth to protest, but then realized that she was likely right.

"I've seen the way you look at me."

His eyes bulged at this sudden change in tack. "And how is that?" he asked in a pompous voice that made him hate himself.

She stepped closer and Corbin jolted when her hand landed on his chest.

Oh God. She was doing it *again.*

Back away Corbin. Back. Away.

He stood immobile, barely breathing as her hand slid from his chest to his belly down to his erection.

His eyelids fluttered and he gave vent to a mortifying animal grunt when strong fingers closed around him.

"You look at me like you want to consume me whole," she whispered, giving his length a firm stroke. "Like you want to sink this remarkably fine weapon you are concealing in your trousers into my body and launch an assault."

How are you allowing this to happen again? Tell her to stop!

Corbin leaned into her stroking, held captive by both her hand and her black gaze.

"You look at me like you want to *fuck* me into submission."

He groaned, sounding like a cow in agony. Corbin knew he should be embarrassed about uttering such an unmanning sound. But—

Her second hand closed around his scrotum. His balls, already as hard as steel bearings, drew up tight to his body.

"I deserve a good fucking, don't I, Corbin?"

He could not have uttered a word if the President of the United States, the Queen of England, and the Lord Almighty had all demanded it of him.

But he could nod. She *did* deserve it.

"And I will get it," she whispered with a stroke that brought him to the brink of climax.

And then her hand disappeared and she stepped back. "But it won't be you who gives it to me."

For the second time in less than a month, she whirled and left him staring, mouth open, cock hard and wanting.

As battles of wits and wills went, what had just occurred was a savage, utter routing. The sensual equivalent of Gettysburg, with Corbin Lee to Lady Io's Grant.

She had thrashed and humiliated him *again*. Soundly.

But instead of being ashamed by his ignominious defeat at her hands, all Corbin felt was a crushing regret that she was gone.

Chapter 10

A Week or so Later

Are you sure you don't want me to accompany you to Northampton today, my lady?" Io's maid, Moira asked for at least the fifth time, her hands shaking slightly as she twisted Io's hair into a clever arrangement that made it appear as if it was longer than it was.

She met the younger woman's eyes in the mirror. "Moira, I told you to take today off and yet here you are working. Not only have you turned down a free day, but you have asked me over and over about accompanying me. Tell me what has happened."

Moira made a small squeaking sound. "Nothing, my lady. I promise you."

"Who told you that you needed to accompany me? Come. You can tell me. I will not be angry with you, I promise."

Moira chewed the inside of her cheek, her chest moving rapidly, just like a rabbit's.

"Was it Miss Barrymore?"

"No, my lady. Not her."

Io smiled and suspected it was not a pleasant expression when the younger woman winced. "Was it Mr. Masterson?"

Moira opened her mouth, but then closed it, and nodded.

"You do not need to do anything he says, Moira. *I* am your employer."

"Oh, my lady!" she wailed. "He is so stern and forbidding! When he looks at me with those cold eyes of his I feel as if he is seeing right into my soul an' taking note of all my sins."

Io was familiar with the expression; it had a similar effect on her.

Moira hurried on, "I don't want to make him angry—nor His Grace, either." She paused and then blinked. "And Mr. Masterson is quite right. You should not go about unattended," she said, her sudden flare of righteous indignation impressing Io.

"I won't be alone," she said, not entirely telling the truth. "I'm going to Northampton with my brother, Mrs. Dryden, Miss Barrymore, *and* Miss Barclay. That means four other people will accompany me. I assure you, Moira, both my person and my virtue will be well-protected."

The maid nodded, but reluctantly.

"But I would like to make one matter clear to you."

Moira's shoulders tensed again. "Yes, my lady?"

"In the future, if anyone tells you how to behave in my employ, I want you to tell me immediately."

"Even His Grace?"

"Yes, even the duke."

Moira swallowed hard, but then nodded. "Yes, my lady."

Io smiled. "Good. Now, you can finish my hair."

***

Corbin had just shrugged into his coat when there was a knock on the door and Harold, one of the footmen, entered his chambers. "Sorry to disturb you, sir, but I'm to tell you that Miss Barrymore will not be able to accompany your party to Northampton."

Corbin picked up his hat and gloves. "Why not?"

"She has sprained her ankle and Miss Barclay is staying to wait on her."

Lucky Miss Barclay, he thought. Aloud, he said, "I hope it is not bad?"

"She says not, sir." Harold held out a sheaf of papers. "I am to give you these."

Corbin was unsurprised to see they were lists written in Miss Barclay's neat handwriting.

He nodded and tucked the papers into his satchel, which already contained many other lists. "You can assure her that I will take care of these."

114

"Thank you, sir."

As Corbin made his way toward the stairs he hated to admit it, but he was glad Miss Barrymore wasn't accompanying them. While he got on with the woman just fine, there was no denying that she set the hackles up on every Hale except the duke. And, some days, Corbin wasn't so sure of that.

He was pulling his gloves on when he saw the group waiting in the foyer.

All eyes turned toward him as he descended the stairs. "Miss Barrymore has suffered a mishap and sprained her ankle. I have her list of warehouses and shall bring samples back for her."

Corbin almost laughed at the various expressions that greeted his pronouncement.

Lord Balthazar looked elated.

Mrs. Dryden looked concerned.

And Lady Io looked furious.

Corbin suspected that last expression was due to his presence rather than Miss Barrymore's absence.

"I hope the injury is not severe," Mrs. Dryden said.

"No, not severe," he said, amused that such a question never occurred to the other two.

Lady Io gave him a long, hard look, but then turned on her heel and marched out of the foyer.

A short time later the four of them were in the ducal coach and heading to the train station when Lady Io launched her first strike.

"So, you add interior décor to your formidable repertoire of skills, Mr. Masterson," she said before they'd even left the driveway.

"Do I have a *formidable repertoire?*" Corbin asked. "I wasn't aware that I did. I am flattered that you have such a high opinion of me, my lady."

Lady Io snorted.

They rode in silence for a few moments.

Once again it was Lady Io who broke it. "Were you born and raised in these parts, Mrs. Dryden?"

"No, I'm from Plymouth."

"You'll have to excuse my ignorance, but I'm afraid I'm not yet familiar with all the cities. Where is Plymouth?"

"It is in Devonshire. On the coast," Corbin said. And then turned to Mrs. Dryden. "One of the original counties listed in Doomsday Book, I believe."

Mrs. Dryden gave him an approving smile. "Yes, that is correct. You've been studying our country, I see."

"My brother tests Masterson weekly," Lady Io retorted before Corbin could respond, her eyes taunting as they settled on him. "For every question he gets wrong, Zeus bends him over the desk and gives him a swat with a ruler."

Mrs. Dryden looked stunned and even Lord Balthazar's jaw sagged at his twin's outrageous comment.

Corbin was the only one who was not rendered speechless by her audacity. After all, compared to having his cock grabbed—twice—this was a mild assault, and only a verbal one at that.

He smiled faintly and said, "Only three swats this past week—much better than the four I received the week before."

Lady Io merely snorted and turned away from him, looking out the window.

"Er, may I see the list of what we are shopping for today, Mrs. Dryden?" Lord Balthazar asked in a forced tone.

The rest of the carriage ride—indeed, the train ride as well—was uneventful. Corbin brought a book with him but could not have said what he'd read as his eyes insisted on drifting toward Lady Io, who was also reading. Or pretending to, at least, while her brother and the housekeeper chattered about the scenery or other innocuous matters.

It was not until they disembarked in Northampton that Lady Io once again primed her cannons.

"What time shall we meet back here?" she asked her brother.

"Before six-thirty, which is when the last train leaves."

Lady Io nodded and turned to leave.

Io: The Shrew

"I will accompany you, my lady," Corbin said.

She whirled on him so speedily that he thought she must have anticipated his offer. "I do not require a minder, Mr. Masterson." Corbin opened his mouth, but she wasn't finished. "Bal, please inform Mr. Masterson that I do not need a nursemaid."

Lord Balthazar regarded Corbin with amusement. "It's true, Masterson; my sister no longer requires a nursemaid."

Lady Io made a face at her brother's jocular tone.

"Duly noted, my lord," Corbin said. "I shall not attempt to feed her or change her nappy." He added blandly, "His Grace would be most displeased with me if I were to allow your sister to gallivant around Northampton unaccompanied."

"*Gallivant?*" Lady Io shrieked.

Corbin had to bite his cheek to keep from laughing. Lady Io could always be counted on to snap at any hook he dangled before her, regardless of the bait.

"What sort of shops did you have planned for today, my lady? I would be happy to escort you to any you desire," he could not resist goading.

"Believe it or not, Masterson, women do have interests other than shopping," she retorted.

"Oh, such as what?" Corbin asked, diverted when Lord Balthazar and the housekeeper exchanged a quick, speaking look, and then scurried away, leaving the two of them to their bickering.

"What I have planned is none of your business," she snapped and then stormed down the street.

Corbin easily fell into step beside her.

"Why are you following me? I thought you were Edith's errand boy," she said after they'd walked in silence for a few moments.

"It is true that I have many errands planned."

"You won't get them done following me around."

"No, probably not," he agreed mildly.

"Edith will be very displeased with you if you fail to measure up to the mark, Mr. Masterson. I daresay you will feel the brunt of that displeasure."

"Fortunately, Miss Barrymore does not spank me nearly as hard as the duke does."

Lady Io stopped, turned to him, and gawked up at him.

It was damned difficult to remain expressionless, but Corbin achieved it. "Yes, my lady?"

She resumed walking, muttering something under her breath.

Corbin took advantage of her distraction to enjoy a quick grin. *You are not the only one who can say shocking things, Io Hale.*

They walked for perhaps a minute before she stopped and whirled on him. "Why are you doing this?"

"Because gently bred young ladies don't go about town unaccompanied," Corbin explained—not for the first time—allowing his annoyance to show. "Why didn't you bring your maid if you did not want my company?"

She raised a hand and, for a moment, Corbin thought she might hit him. Instead, she poked him in the chest with her forefinger. "That reminds me. Don't *ever* talk to my servant behind my back again," she hissed, her eyes more green than brown today.

Corbin shook off the bizarre observation and said, "Very well."

Lady Io blinked at his easy acquiescence, her chest rising and falling in a way that tempted Corbin to lower his gaze—she had a magnificent bosom—but he exerted his will and resisted the urge.

"I am going to meet with some people called Mr. and Mrs. Taylor," she said, surprising him with her confidence. "They are part of an organization that maintains connections with the Ladies Aid Association. They invited me to talk with them about our New York City office and how we manage various campaigns and issues. I will probably be there for several hours. There will be no place for you to wait for me as it is their house. So, you might as well go off on your errands now and not waste precious time."

"I will escort you to their establishment. And—if you give me your word that you will wait for me to return for you—I will let you have your meeting without lingering around their door."

Corbin could almost hear her teeth grinding.

"Fine," she snapped. "I estimate our work will take three hours. But if it takes longer, you will just have to wait."

Corbin nodded. "Understood."

She continued her forthright striding, not speaking another word to him.

And when they reached the Taylors' house she strode up the walk without a backward glance.

Corbin watched as the Taylors' servant closed the door behind her before taking out his watch and sighing.

He had at least eight shops to visit, and barely three hours to get it all done.

***

Even though Io had spent the prior four hours working, she felt invigorated and revivified by the end of her meeting with the Taylors. Her brain, which had gathered cobwebs since leaving New York, was suddenly clear and functioning again.

And then she bid the Taylors goodbye, stepped out onto the stoop, and saw Corbin Masterson waiting for her across the street and all her goodwill fled.

"Where are all your parcels?" she asked in a catty voice as he trotted across the street and easily matched her stride.

"Everything I purchased will be delivered," he said, not looking at all perturbed that Io had—purposely, at least for the last half hour—kept him waiting on the street.

"Did you finish all your errands?"

"No."

"Edith will not be pleased, but I am beginning to believe you enjoy *her* spankings."

"You seem obsessed with the subject of me and spankings, my lady."

For some reason, his words reminded her of those two evenings—one in the library and one at the schoolhouse—when she had behaved extremely badly. She hated to admit it, but she had woken up more than once in the intervening nights recalling how his erection had felt in her hand.

119

"Are you hungry?" he asked, the question thankfully pulling her from yet more contemplation of his penis.

"The Taylors fed me." After a moment, basic manners made her ask, "Have you eaten?"

"No. But I am not hungry. Where are we going next?"

"You are going to insist on accompanying me," she said.

"Yes," he said, although it hadn't been a question.

"Fine. I am looking for a bookstore. I wish to purchase some books for the school."

"I passed one earlier today. It is not far."

Io grunted.

"How was your meeting?" he asked.

Io cut him a sideways glance. "Are you really interested, or just making conversation."

"Can't it be both?"

She considered saying something scathing, but decided she was still in too good a mood, and the day was far too pretty to argue.

***

Corbin was surprised when she answered him. "It was an excellent meeting. The Taylors were grateful for the information I brought from our physicians and we worked together to adapt our pamphlet to their needs. They also shared some interesting findings regarding early childhood nutrition." Her lips flexed into a dispirited moue. "It is only the two of them in the area, most of the larger organizations are in the urban centers. Their work has made them targets for rural ruffians, men who are opposed to women gaining some degree of bodily autonomy."

Corbin could imagine.

"It is unfortunate that the Taylors do not have a physician allied to their group just now as their last one died and none of the new doctors in the area—most of them young—are willing to risk their positions to help."

Corbin could imagine that, too.

She paused and then added, "If Zeus would agree to throw his name and influence behind our cause, I daresay doctors would be falling over themselves to help the Taylors."

"Probably," Corbin agreed.

"But he won't, will he?"

She sounded glum, rather than combative, and—for some reason—that gave him a pang. He realized with some surprise that he did not like to see her spirit dimmed.

"I think His Grace will not openly champion such a matter, but that does not mean he might not help in more subtle ways." *As you should be thinking of doing*, Corbin wanted to add, but—for once—did not.

She stopped and set a hand on his arm to bring him to a halt, as if this conversation was too important to carry out while walking. "Really? Such as?"

"He is not unsympathetic to the hardships that women—especially poor women—face, my lady. He might be persuaded to donate money, if not influence." Corbin tried to soften the blow. "At least not at this point. His Grace has not even taken his seat in Parliament. There are people—powerful ones—who would be displeased if he were to commence dabbling in politics before he is formally inducted. In any case, he must find his way before he can commit himself."

Rather than rail at him, Lady Io nodded thoughtfully, and they resumed walking. "I will have to wait until he is no longer angry with me."

"He is not angry with you."

"Oh, yes he is. He was furious about my plans to lease a house."

"He might have been unhappy at the time, but I've known your brother for most of my life. He is not the sort of man who remains angry for long. Nor does he hold a grudge."

She made a noncommittal noise.

"All His Grace truly wants is to get to know the five of you."

"Perhaps he should have gone about that without releasing Edith into our lives. Or using money to control us."

"Perhaps."

Her eyebrows shot up. "I cannot believe that you agree with that."

"I don't agree—or disagree." She rolled her eyes and Corbin explained, "There are no *only* right or *only* wrong approaches, my lady. Who am I to say what he should do? I think he is finding his way in a new and complex situation, just as the rest of you are. He has been forced to face a great many changes in a short period of time. There was the discovery that he is a peer who is responsible for hundreds of people an ocean away and then there was meeting five siblings for the first time at the age of thirty-seven. It is likely that not all his decisions will be the best ones, but his motivations are honorable.

"I agree he has a great deal to contend with, but so do the five of us. We might have accepted the various strictures he has imposed with more grace if not for the addition of Edith, and her strictures, as well. Why involve another person in such a situation?"

"Because Miss Barrymore will be his wife and an integral part of his life. It is only natural that he wants her to meet his siblings," Corbin said, unwilling to engage in tearing down his best friend's chosen mate.

"Come, Masterson. You cannot honestly tell me that you want him to marry her? I know you find her admirably *ladylike*, but does that make up for her brutal treatment of her subordinates? Like her cousin, for example. Do you have no sympathy for poor Miss Barclay?"

Miss Barrymore's treatment of her cousin was a raw spot that just became more inflamed the longer he was forced to watch. But it felt too disloyal to Hastings to admit as much, and so he said, "Miss Barclay is an adult woman, is she not?"

"I know what you are getting at, and I agree that part of the blame is hers for staying with Edith and enduring such abuse. However, I do not know Miss Barclay's circumstances. Perhaps she cannot leave easily? Perhaps there is nowhere else for her to go? In any case, Miss Barclay's refusal to simply leave her position does not excuse Edith's behavior."

Corbin glanced at a sign just ahead of them and grasped at it as if it were a lifeline. "I know we are headed to the bookstore. But might we stop here—briefly? It is a silversmith's shop that your brother wished me to visit for him. Perhaps you might assist me in matching this pattern, my lady?"

She stared at him for a moment before snorting. "Fine—but next is the bookstore." Io paused and then added. "Since you waited so patiently for me at the Taylors' house, I will accompany you on a few of your errands. But only until five o'clock, Mr. Masterson. And then I would like to see a bit of the town."

Corbin nodded. "We have a bargain."

***

Io hated to admit it, but she had rarely enjoyed an afternoon shopping as much as she had today. Watching Mr. Masterson in action was rather like watching a virtuoso musician or athlete. His lists were organized and sensible. He was efficient and quick without ever being rude to any of the shopkeepers he dealt with. And, best of all, he *never* dithered about his purchases.

They'd just left the stationer's shop when Masterson pointed to a tiny coffee shop next door. "Would you like to stop for a cup?"

"Yes, please," Io said.

The shop was mostly empty so late in the day, so their waitress quickly brought their pastries and coffee.

Io watched with amusement as Masterson spooned a copious amount of sugar into his coffee, added a generous dollop of milk, and then took a sip and sighed in contentment—*almost* smiling.

When he saw Io watching him, faint slashes of color streaked his cheeks and he said, "Coffee is one of my vices."

"Sugar, too, apparently."

The stern Mr. Masterson looked almost sheepish at her accusation.

"As vices go, neither are especially bad," Io teased, taking a sip of her own coffee, which she drank black. "Did you notice that the plaque on the door said this business has been in continuous operation since 1668?"

Masterson nodded. "The seventeenth century was something of a heyday for coffee shops." He glanced around at the timbered ceiling and ancient wood floor, which was deeply worn from the tread of untold feet. "It is easy to see why Europeans view Americans as barely leaving our infancy as a nation."

"There are people in our country who have far deeper roots than any English aristocrat," Io pointed out.

He blinked at that, and then said, "You are right, of course. While the indigenous population of the Americas left far subtler footprints than we Europeans, their ancient history is indisputable."

"I am impressed that you recognize their contribution," Io said, not lying. "It is unusual."

"You mean it is unusual in a man of business," he said, his lips twisting faintly. Before Io could respond, he said, "I spent nine months traveling from the coast to the interior of the Canadian Territory, and then returning to New York by river."

"Just to explore?" she asked, pleasantly surprised.

"My father sent me to formalize a timber agreement, but I extended my trip to do some exploring." He paused, his gray eyes going vague and his stern features softening slightly. "It is a magnificent, awe-inspiring landscape that is still home to people who have been living the same way for a thousand years."

Io thought he looked like a different man. Almost tranquil.

But then he noticed her staring and shook himself, taking a sip of his coffee before saying, in his usual proper manner, "It was most educational."

But Io wasn't ready yet to let that other, less formal, man escape quite so easily.

She propped her chin on her hand and looked him in the eyes. "Tell me what you saw, Masterson. Tell me about the things that amazed you."

To her astonishment, he did. And for the next quarter of an hour, Mr. Masterson lost his rigid mask of reserve and came alive. His love for the wilderness and the people he'd encountered was obvious. It was a side of him Io would never have imagined existed.

By the time they left the coffee shop and headed back into the shopping fray, Io was more in charity with him than she had ever imagined possible.

She should have known it would never last.

Chapter 11

Lady Io glanced at the watch pinned to her bodice. "It is almost five o'clock. Which means that it is well past the time for us to stop shopping and explore the area, Mr. Masterson."

Corbin glanced down at the various lists he'd been tasked with. There were still several items he would need to see to, but at least he'd taken care of all Miss Barrymore's requests.

He closed the small leather journal he used to structure his days, dropped it into his satchel, and then turned to her. "Very well. Do you have a list of where you want to go?"

"List?" She gave him an exasperated look. "We are going to wander."

"Wander?"

"Yes. There is no set agenda, no plan, no itinerary—just going where our feet lead us."

Corbin grunted at that. "Well, lead on, then."

She took an immediate left and Corbin spied a hint of the river directly ahead.

They walked in silence, but it felt companionable, rather than hostile as it had that morning. Was it possible to have normal relations with this woman? Corbin had to admit he was feeling hopeful.

"I was surprised to hear you say that Zeus might donate money to people like the Taylors," she said a moment later, her words dashing his optimism.

He made a noncommittal noise. "Why do your siblings call you *Yoyo*?" he asked, hoping to derail a potentially dangerous conversation before it could even begin.

She frowned slightly at the change in topics, but then said, "Eva could not say my name when she was little and pronounced it *Yoyo*. The twins thought that was very amusing, so it has stuck."

"Ah."

They walked for a bit without speaking.

Corbin was just beginning to think he had averted disaster when she spoke. "If somebody of Zeus's status were to support the Taylors, then many others would follow," she said, obviously not willing to be distracted from the issue.

Her words prodded at his conscience, reminding him of all the things he had left *unsaid* earlier that day; practical, pragmatic, and stringent requirements. Such as the guarantees the duke would inevitably require. Legally binding assurances—with contractual repercussions—that any money he donated did not make its way into either criminal or morally objectionable causes.

And then there was the fact that Hastings would demand a detailed prospectus on where, when, and how such money would be spent. The duke was, after all, a banker to his very marrow. No matter how much he might want to please his sister, he would never just throw money away.

Corbin knew that to say any of that right now would sour the newfound harmony between them.

But to hold his tongue and allow Lady Io to believe there were no obstacles to securing her brother's benevolence was no better than a lie, wasn't it?

Unwilling to fracture their fragile peace just yet, Corbin opted to avoid either continued obfuscation or harsh reality. Instead, he forged a middle path: one of evasion.

"You were surprised?" he said. "And why is that?"

They approached a narrower walkway that ran along the sleepy-looking river and Lady Io turned onto it.

"Yes, very surprised. I knew he would contribute to charities, of course, but I had not considered that he would be amenable to championing one which is so, er, untraditional," she said after a few moments of contemplation. She cut him an uncertain look, her forehead furrowed. "And even if he did agree, I would have thought that you would counsel him against extending support if he asked your opinion."

Her words, unfortunately, left Corbin no choice but to answer honestly. "Yes. It is likely that I would advises him against such involvement."

She stopped in the middle of the walking path and turned on him. "Why would you say such a thing?"

Corbin opened his mouth, and then paused, meeting her angry gaze.

"The least you can do is be honest with me, Masterson," she snapped, reading the source of his hesitation correctly.

"Very well. I would advise him to wait until you had given him several assurances."

"Such as?" she prodded when he did not go on.

Corbin sighed. She was going to force him to say it all. "I would advise him to require that you stop associating with people like the Taylors. That you quit personally distributing pamphlets and, er, paraphernalia. That you agree to a less prominent role in your organization—or at least a less conspicuous one. That you stop hurling yourself into dangerous situations—not just dangerous to your person, but to your reputation. That you—" he broke off at her outraged expression. "I can see that you take my meaning."

"Oh yes, I take your meaning. You would actually counsel my brother to withhold money from impoverished, vulnerable women."

When she put it like that…

"It would be within *your* power to make sure that money was not withheld, my lady."

"You mean by giving up everything that makes my life worth living," she said grimly.

Corbin met her furious, appalled gaze and gentled his tone, "Is it not possible that there are a plethora of other activities and pursuits that might yield an equal–or perhaps even greater—amount of pleasure and fulfillment with considerably fewer drawbacks?"

She crossed her arms. "Please enlighten me, sir. What sort of activities?"

"For a start, you might actually give *tonish* society a fair chance—as your sister is doing—rather than purposely sabotaging your reputation and relegating yourself to the fringes."

She stared at him without speaking for a long moment, and then quietly said, "You are a vile man."

Corbin recoiled at the loathing in her voice. "I am sorry you feel that way," he said stiffly.

"It is not a feeling. It is a statement of fact, sir. You hate that I am passionate about a cause because you despise anything that distracts a woman from her true purpose, which is motherhood and family. You will not be satisfied until I am some man's chattel."

In truth, Corbin's mind revolted at the thought of her belonging to some stranger.

That is because you want to possess her, yourself.

He blinked, uneasy at the accusation. "I am not saying you should abandon your causes," Corbin said, his protestations sounding lame to his own ears.

"Then what are you saying?"

"I am suggesting that you learn to compromise."

"Compromise?" She gave a bitter laugh. "Your notion of compromise is me collared, kept on a very short leash—a leash held by my husband's hand—my belly swelling with his child, and my mouth shut like an obedient little woman."

Her words evoked a shockingly potent and arousing image—one that Corbin could easily picture in his mind's eye. In his version, however, her body was lush and rounded with *his* child.

As for the part about having her collared, leashed, and obedient to his every whim?

Bloody. Hell. Corbin's cock almost ripped its way out of his trousers.

He was appalled by his primitive reaction.

"Have you nothing to say for yourself?" she demanded, thankfully unaware of Corbin's graphic and licentious fantasizing.

He cleared his throat and gathered up what remained of his wits before saying, "Life is nothing but a series of compromises, my lady. Only a child believes otherwise. If you truly are as passionate as you say about your cause, then you must give something in return."

"Give *up* something, you mean." Her eyes suddenly narrowed. "And did you just call me a child?"

"You certainly exhibit some child-like tendencies`."

"Such as?" she shot back.

"Do you really want an answer to that?"

"Yes, I *really* do."

Corbin sighed and held up a hand. "You are terrifyingly naïve about the way the world functions." He ticked off one finger. "You capriciously follow your whims, heedless of the outcome." He ticked off another finger. "You are frequently willful to the point of folly." He ticked off a third finger. "You are—"

She spun around on her heel and stormed off the path and through the high grasses, heading in the general direction from which they had just come.

Corbin stared after her for a moment and then pulled out his watch. It was just as well she was striding off in a huff as it was getting near the time they should be making their way back to the train station.

He slipped his watch into his pocket and set off after her, easily closing the distance between them.

"Get away from me," she snarled when he fell into step beside her.

"I will escort you back to the train station."

"If you dare accompany me after I've told you not to, then I will scream."

His patience, already frayed, snapped. "You *are* a child, because this is how children behave when a discussion is not yielding the outcome they desire; they storm off in a huff. No doubt your behavior is due to where you were raised and—"

"Don't you *even*—"

Corbin raised his voice to be heard over hers. "You are a child who never received the proper discipline when you were young, so now you—

"*Discipline?*"

He winced at her increased volume. "Yes. Discipline. When I was a brat, my father would turn me over his knee and give me a spanking. I daresay if your father had done the same it would have worked wonders."

"You *would* be the sort of barbaric swine who believed in corporal punishment."

"If you insist on misbehaving, then—"

"Perhaps it is *you* who needs a firm hand, Mr. Masterson. Have you ever considered that? Perhaps I should turn you over *my* knee and spank your bottom!"

Corbin opened his mouth to invite her to try it, but she wasn't finished.

"I suppose you are going to run and tattle to my brother about my meeting with the Taylors when we get home." She threw the words at him, all but sprinting now.

He lengthened his stride. "Run and tattle?" He gave a harsh laugh and pointed to the path ahead of them. "Do you see that bench, my lady?"

Her brow furrowed. "What of it?"

"Why don't we stop a moment and see which one of us gets the other over their knee first, *hmm?*"

"I would like to see you try that!"

"And I would be delighted to oblige you," he retorted. "Then *you* could run and tattle to your brother and tell him that his barbaric *servant* finally did what should have been done twenty years ago."

"If you lay so much as a finger on me you will be the sorriest man in England."

"Why is it so easy for me to imagine being that man right now, I wonder?" he asked with heavy sarcasm.

A pair of older ladies came around a curve in the path, their round-eyed stares telling Corbin that one or both of their voices must have carried.

He tipped his hat at the women as they passed.

Io: The Shrew

After that, they walked in silence, Lady Io Hale's too-desirable body rigid with anger.

Their brief truce from earlier was over and Corbin had been the one to destroy it. He told himself that was for the best.

Only if she hated him was Corbin safe from succumbing to the emotions that were already churning inside him. Emotions that were becoming harder and harder to suppress.

That all-too-brief oasis at the coffee shop had proven to him that enmity was the only acceptable state of affairs when it came to this woman.

Corbin only hoped it was enough to keep him from making a mistake that would be impossible to fix.

Chapter 12

A Few Weeks Later

Until Wednesday, then," Io said to Miss Amelia Temple.

"I look forward to it, my lady, er, *Io*," the village schoolteacher amended at Io's chiding look.

Io smiled. "Better."

Amelia glanced around at the moonless night. "You really should not be walking alone so late. Perhaps I should accompany you."

"Then I would need to walk *you* back. Don't worry. I'm going to the King's Quarrel. My brothers all but live there. One of them can walk me home."

Her new friend looked faintly distressed at the mention of the local pub. It was acceptable for women to go there during the day—in pairs—but not at night. And certainly not alone.

Truly, women were often more eager to build their own cages than men were.

"Good night, Amelia," Io said firmly, and then turned before the other woman could come up with any other suggestions.

The walk to the pub was less than five minutes. Instead of thinking about the book club discussion at Amelia's cottage, her mind went to the vicious argument she'd had with Edith earlier that day.

Io felt like she was always bickering with the woman, but a new level of hatred had entered their clash today because Edith had learned what Io and her small cadre of friends had distributed the night of the Harvest Fair.

"What, precisely, did Masterson tell you we were distributing?" Io had asked Edith, hoping to force the other woman to say the word *condom*.

Io: The Shrew

Edith had not denied that Masterson was her informant. "Do not trifle with me. You know exactly what you were doing."

"That is true. I do know. And you can do nothing to stop me." She had smirked in a way that drove her twin mad and worked a similar effect on Edith, if her heightened color was anything to go by.

"You are determined to drag His Grace's name through the mud—to shame him and the rest of us with your abhorrent behavior." Her voice had risen to unladylike levels by the time she'd finished and Io had taken vengeful pleasure in witnessing Edith's mask of civility slip.

"It may surprise you to discover that I do not consider offering aid to impoverished women *abhorrent*, Edith."

"You might not care about your own reception here, but your sister does," Edith had retorted, ignoring Io's words as if she'd never spoken.

"Eva would not want me to suppress my beliefs regardless of what society thinks."

It was Edith's turn to smirk and Io had to admit the woman had the hateful expression down to an art form. "That is what she would tell *you*, of course."

"What are you driving at?"

"As you refuse to pay calls on the local gentry with us you will not have witnessed the cool reception Eva has received. None of the mothers in the area will allow their daughters to associate with her. Not because of *Eva* herself, but because they fear your pernicious influence."

As much as she had wanted to scorn the accusation, Io had heard the truth in the hateful harpy's words and had stood mute with fury and shame while Edith had sailed from the room, her chin high in triumph.

The other woman's criticism had rankled all day and even during the book club, an activity she normally savored. Was what Edith said true? Could Io really be ruining Eva's standing in their community?

The sound of loud male laughter shook Io from her thoughts, and she was startled to see that she had reached the inn while she'd been fuming. Noise and light poured from the windows of the King's Quarrel and Io hoped at least one of her brothers was inside. Not because she needed an escort home, but because she desperately wanted a pleasurable distraction from her unhappy thoughts.

She pulled open the ancient wooden door and smiled with relief when she saw the twins—although not *her* twin—sitting around a table with an enormous man all the villagers called Small Jim.

Ares saw her first and waved a hand in greeting, grinning widely. Judging by his rosy cheeks, the pint in front of him was not his first.

"Look who the cat dragged in," Ares said loudly enough for the surrounding tables to hear every word.

Io slanted a look at Apollo. "How long has he been here?"

"Ever since Mrs. Fletcher rejected him," Pol said, a glint of amusement in his mixed-color eyes.

"Thanks very much, Pol." Ares gave his twin a sour moue.

"I don't know why you look so stricken," Io chided her wild, willful younger brother, who really looked nothing like his twin. It always amazed her how their faces could be identical and yet so very different.

"I'm *stricken* because some of us possess the finer emotions," Ares shot back.

Io laughed. "Well, you'd best toughen up, hadn't you? I never thought you were stupid, but if—" she broke off to smile at the serving woman who came to their table. "Good evening, Suzy."

"My lady," the young woman said, blushing and dropping a curtsey, as if Io were something special rather than just another female a few years older than her. But she had already given up on trying to change people's awe of her ducal connection. Instead, she said, "Another round of whatever these three fools are having—my treat—and a pint of homebrew for me as well," she added, not caring if it raised eyebrows that she was drinking in the main room rather than the parlor or snug or whatever it was called, or that she was consuming ale rather than a more ladylike shandy.

Suzy left and Io turned back to Ares to continue her harangue. "As I was saying, I never thought you were stupid. You should have known Mrs. Fowler would tire of a pup like you once she nailed your tail to her trophy wall." She rolled her eyes at the other two men, who were howling with mirth, and raised her voice to be heard over their laughter. "Even an idiot could see it was Bal she wanted all along," Io continued, amused at the red stain and sudden sobriety on Ares's handsome face. "Every single time the two are in proximity the woman all but humps poor Bal's leg."

Io: The Shrew

Io shook her head as Small Jim and Pol fell off their chairs laughing. Idiots.

She had no issue with women taking what they wanted, but Jo Fletcher had hounded Bal relentlessly, putting him in the uncomfortable position of having to reject her advances, again and again.

Just because Io's family had grown up in Canoga everyone assumed they were sex crazed maniacs. It was annoying.

Io looked up when the barmaid speedily returned with their drinks. "Thank you, Suzi."

Ares nodded absently at Suzi—evidently not noticing the worshipful look on the young woman's face—and then glared at his still-chuckling friend and twin before turning back to Io. "Did you just come in here to insult me? Or do you want to play darts?"

"Do I have to choose? Why can't I do both?" She sipped her drink and surveyed the small taproom, which was lively and crowded. Her eyes screeched to a halt and then retraced their steps, landing on a familiar, unwanted face.

It was Masterson and he was sitting alone with a pint in front of him. And he was looking at *her*.

"What is *he* doing here?" Io said, not bothering to lower her voice.

Pol followed her gaze to the secretary and gave one of his slight smiles. "I believe he is here to make sure we behave."

"Zeus sent him?"

"Edith," Ares said, making the word sound like a multilegged insect that had crawled up his trouser leg and bitten him someplace sensitive.

Io scowled as she once again recalled what Edith had told her earlier. She was disgusted and disappointed but not at all surprised that Masterson had tattled to Edith about the Harvest Fair.

"I trust you have been giving him plenty to report back to his mistress?" Io asked, needing to exert far too much effort to wrench her gaze from Masterson, whom she'd not exchanged a word with since their explosive argument in Northampton when—yet again, she had behaved in a way that shamed her, screaming at him like an enraged toddler and losing control of her emotions, allowing him to goad her into acting like a spoiled child.

Io grimaced at the memory and turned back to her brother Pol, who was studying her with a far too knowing look. "What?" she demanded, hoping that his sharp eyes didn't notice the heat that flooded her face. "

But he only said, "Ares does his best to give Masterson plenty to report back."

"And what about you, Pol? What have *you* been doing?"

Io hadn't meant the question to sound quite as arch as it did—she'd just wanted to move his attention away from her—but her brother blushed and she felt a twinge of guilt.

"I did not mean it that way," she said in a low voice.

"I know."

Io and Pol had always been close and it was no surprise to her that her brother had confided his secret several years back. A secret she would never breathe a word of to anyone else, not even her twin.

"Do you hate it here?" she asked when he didn't offer anything else.

"Surprisingly, no. How about a game of darts?" he asked, obviously wanting to change the subject just as much as she had.

Io took a gulp of ale and wiped the foam off her mouth with the back of her hand. "Very well. I'll give you a game. As long as you don't cry and carry on when I thrash you."

Pol snorted. "I shall try to restrain myself."

***

Corbin knew he should stop staring at the woman currently making a spectacle of herself in front of the entire population of the village. Well, the male half, at least. Although he admitted grudgingly that Lady Io wasn't the only female in the lively pub. But the other two women were demurely sitting with their husbands or sweethearts in the part of the building designated for women, while Lady Io was boldly playing one game of darts after another, drinking beer, and winning every game, while a crowd of eager, admiring males followed her every move.

She was a disgrace to her brother's name.

She was also so bloody beautiful that it hurt to look at her. Her hair, while still short, had grown out since New York, and the dark curls were wild as they danced around her perfect face. Her cheeks were flushed, and her catlike eyes sparkled with good humor—an expression they never held when looking at Corbin.

Just now she was laughing with exasperation as her twin brothers *mooed* at her, of all things. Corbin had heard them do that before. Just what the hell did it mean?

He pushed the perplexing thought aside and his mind immediately cleaved to its normal path: his obsession with Lady Io.

Right now, he was more than a little concerned with the hard-on he was desperately trying to conceal beneath the pub table. He told himself that was why he'd not got up and dragged Lady Io out of the place and home to the duke an hour ago. But the truth was that he had never enjoyed watching anyone so much in his life.

Corbin could not get her out of his mind. Even when she wasn't in front of him, he saw her.

Now that he'd experienced her touch—albeit mostly over his clothing—Corbin *felt* her all the time.

Especially on his dick and balls.

Of course, it was really his own hand—which had been as busy as a cock in a henhouse—that he'd been feeling. If Corbin had possessed any shame at all he would be mortified at how often he masturbated.

But he was rapidly learning that he had no shame where Lady Io Hale was concerned.

None at all.

***

Io could feel Masterson's eyes on her as she made her way back to the castle.

"He is following us," she muttered to Pol, who'd wanted to walk back with her while Ares went and made a fool of himself with Mrs. Fletcher.

"He is following *you*," Pol amended.

Io didn't argue.

"What are you going to do about it?" he asked quietly.

"What am I going to do? Nothing!" She chewed her lip and then said, "What in the world *could* I do?"

Pol snorted softly, a smirk on his handsome profile. "The sexual tension between the two of you is enough to power a steamship, Yoyo."

She groaned. "Is it that obvious?"

Pol laughed outright this time.

"You are suggesting I work him out of my system."

Pol merely shrugged.

"*We* might have been raised to believe that sexual relations are merely another human need like breathing or food, but a man who once trained to become a Presbyterian minister certainly would not," Io said.

"But he is *not* a minister, is he, Yoyo?"

Io opened her mouth, and then closed it. Pol had a point.

"Besides, when have you ever let a small matter like unpalatable opinions stop you?" Pol goaded.

"I cannot believe you are encouraging me in this."

Again, Pol shrugged. "They have dragged us into their world. It only seems fair to give them a taste of ours."

Io was still thinking about her brother's words an hour later, when she was in bed. She was unable to sleep, even though it was late, and the house slumbered all around her.

While Pol's suggestion that she work Masterson out of her system had some appeal, she knew all too well what a moralizing prude the man was. It didn't matter that he looked like a Viking god come to life, he still possessed the worldview of a country parson.

She glared at the opposite wall, which held a tapestry Mrs. Dryden told her was five hundred years old.

"It was made by your ancestresses," the older woman had said, her beautiful features placid, as they always were. Except when Io's twin Balthazar was anywhere in the vicinity.

Io liked Mrs. Dryden a great deal. She also pitied her because Edith had taken a rabid dislike to her the very first day and picked on her at every opportunity. The only person Edith harried more than the housekeeper was her little mouse of a cousin, Susan Barclay. A woman Io pitied more than anyone she had *ever* met, including the street urchins thronging the streets in New York City.

Those children might be hungry and homeless, but at least some of them had still held a spark of life or resistance in their tired eyes.

Susan Barclay looked like somebody who'd been hollowed out by Edith's oppression, and then refilled with abject misery and fear.

Io was starting to like her brother Zeus—although she was still furious at him for putting a stop to her plan to lease her own house—and she could not comprehend why he was betrothed to a bombastic, small-minded, cruel harpy like Edith Barrymore. It hurt her to think about their eventual marriage. She had never seen any true sign of affection pass between the two. But Zeus was excessively reserved—even more than his best friend and secretary—and hard to read, so it was possible that he might care for Edith.

But to her mind, Edith viewed Zeus as a status symbol and nothing more.

Io huffed a sigh, bored with thinking about Edith. She pulled her gaze from the exquisite tapestry that so many women had slaved over and looked at the clock. Four minutes had passed since the last time.

She growled, swung her legs out of bed, and rammed her feet into slippers before pulling on her favorite dressing gown, which was made from silk that looked like a peacock's tail. It was the only feminine and colorful article of clothing she owned. For her daily wear, she preferred garments that were plain to the point of ugly. Because if a woman emphasized her appearance, then that was all the men around her would see: the pretty shell.

Right now, she thought as she tied her sash and tidied her hair in the mirror, she wanted to be a pretty shell.

"Are you sure you know what you are doing, my girl?" she asked her reflection.

The woman in the mirror just stared.

Io hissed and snatched up a candlestick before striding out of her chambers.

She made her way through the ancient corridors toward the rooms she knew Masterson occupied, a suite that was not far from Zeus's.

When she reached his door she knocked immediately, not giving herself time to change her mind.

The door jerked open before she'd even lowered her hand and she yelped.

Corbin Masterson stood in the doorway.

Io's mouth, which had been dry, flooded with moisture at the sight of him. He was wearing only the deliciously worn leather riding breeches he'd had on earlier—she always noticed what he was wearing—and a shirt that was open down the front, exposing his magnificently muscular chest, which was surely an endorsement for pugilism.

While Io gawked at his body, he poked his head outside the room, looked left and right—as if to see who else was in the hallway with her—grabbed her arm and ungently pulled her into his room, shutting the door without a sound before turning on her.

"What are you *doing* here?" he demanded, an actual expression—disbelief—on his face for a change. "Are you not aware that His Grace's rooms are just down the hall?"

"So what?" she asked, refusing to whisper and earning a wince and a scowl from him. "Do you think Zeus is interested in your nocturnal activities? If so, perhaps you might tell him why you were mooning over me all night at the King's Quarrel and then stalked me home, even though I did not require your protection—and I use that word with reservations."

Guilt flashed in his gray eyes, but it was only there for a second before he had himself sternly under control. "What do you mean by *reservations?*" he retorted, his voice so arrogantly, smugly, annoying aloof that Io *had* to shake his calm.

She absolutely *had* to.

"I mean that the only one I need protection from is you, Masterson. And we both know it."

He opened his mouth.

And then Io sank to her knees in front of him and reached for the placket of his leather breeches.

Chapter 13

orbin had to admit that when he'd seen Io outside his door, he had immediately prepared himself for another cock-grabbing session.

But he had *not* prepared himself for this.

His jaw dropped as Lady Io gracefully lowered to her knees in front of him, her huge eyes dark as she stared up at him, her slender but strong hand opening his tented leathers with a few deft flicks.

This cannot be happening.

Corbin could not look away as she yanked down his drawers and freed his hard, leaking cock.

He opened his mouth to order her to get up—to *command* her to stop immediately—but then she made the most astonishing noise in the back of her throat—a low, earthy grunt of approval that communicated sensual hunger better than a thousand words could have done—and Corbin's words froze in his throat.

The look on her face as she lowered her gaze to his erection was pure carnality. And when her hand closed around his iron-hard shaft, Corbin knew he was lost.

***

Io had not been mocking Masterson when she'd commented on the size of his penis. He was, as the saying went, truly blessed in that department.

It had been a very long time—years—since she'd taken a man into her mouth so perhaps she had simply forgotten how much she enjoyed it.

Or perhaps she had never before wanted it as much as she did the moment her palm closed around him and a shudder rocked his big body, his eyelids drooping and jaw going slack as he stared down her, his expression a mixture of profound befuddlement and bottomless hunger.

Finally, the man was exhibiting some emotion.

It was hard to know where to look—at the lovely appendage in her fist or the beautiful man attached to it. Io pulled her gaze away from his lustful eyes only long enough to give him a few firm strokes, coaxing pre-ejaculate from his slit and then licking it off.

Masterson made a noise the likes of which she had never heard before. At least not from a human being.

Io smirked, parted her lips wide enough to make her jaws ache, and took his thick red crown into her mouth.

It was her turn to groan, both at his earthy male scent and the unmistakable taste of masculine arousal on her tongue.

"Oh, God," he muttered, sounding so enslaved by his own need that she almost felt sorry for him.

Almost.

But then she recalled what a sanctimonious, hectoring prig he was and reined in her sympathy. Instead, she proceeded to take him apart—slowly and piece-by-piece—determined to show him that he was no better than any other man and—when his behavior was contrasted to his stated intentions—a great deal worse.

***

Lady Io Hale worked Corbin's erection with more skill than any woman he'd ever encountered, and that included both those he had paid to service him as well as lovers.

Gratitude, arousal, and desire warred with jealousy as he tried to ignore how Io would have learned to wreck a man the way she was currently destroying him.

If he lived to be a hundred years old, he would never forget how she looked kneeling in front of him, her full lips stretched taut, her eyes heavy and hot as she swallowed him deeply, taking more of him with each stroke.

Corbin had been hard for her all damn night. He had just stripped off his coat, boots, and waistcoat and was preparing to give himself a much-needed fisting when the object of his lustful imaginings had materialized on his doorstep like an apparition made flesh.

For a fraction of a second, Corbin had believed he was either dreaming or had died and gone to Heaven.

Lady Io suddenly groaned and the low, sensual growl rolled up his shaft and settled in his balls.

Io: The Shrew

Corbin grabbed a handful of her silky black hair and tried to lift her off his cock. "My lady, I am going to—"

She slapped away his hand and worked him more vigorously, her cheeks hollowing with her erotic efforts.

Corbin not only lost the battle to be a gentleman; he turned into a beast. This time, when he fisted her hair, it was not to spare her, but to drive himself deep.

Rather than try to get away, Lady Io grasped his buttocks with both hands and held him close as he flooded her with his release.

***

Watching Masterson come undone was one of the more erotic sights Io had ever seen. His usually stern features went slack, his expression one of raw, mindless sensuality as he lost his battle with self-control.

Unfortunately, his annoying composure came back as quickly as it had fled.

He lightly but firmly took her face in both hands to remove her from his cock before she was finished with him. "Up," he murmured, helping her to her feet with strong, gentle hands.

He was still breathing heavily and his lips were parted slightly as he stared down at her, tucking himself back into his breeches without taking his gaze from her face.

Io could practically *hear* him thinking and knew what he would say the moment he opened his mouth.

She had to forestall that at any cost, and so she marshaled her features into a superior smile, patted his cheek, and said, "Please spare me your proposal, Masterson. What I just did doesn't mean we're betrothed. It was just an orgasm; not an invitation to pledge your troth to me. I merely thought I'd give you something interesting to report back to your mistress for a change. I imagine Edith will find your account…eye-opening."

He flinched back, heat suffusing his face, and something that looked like pain flickered briefly in his gray eyes.

Guilt stabbed at her at his all-too-human reaction but Io brutally turned her back on both the unwanted emotion and the man who'd elicited it and strode toward the door.

She had barely gone two steps before a hand as hard as an iron manacle closed around her upper arm and stopped her.

When Io looked up, Masterson's chill gray eyes were as beautiful and distant as the moon.

I did that to him, she realized. *I made him retreat into himself.* Io eyes felt odd and itchy in a way that was so foreign she almost didn't recognize it for a moment.

Masterson sneered faintly at whatever he saw on her face. "Don't worry, my lady. I'm not going to break down and weep at your callous behavior. Nor am I going to importune you with unwanted offers." The nostrils of his aquiline nose flared as his gaze flickered dismissively over her. "You will wait here while I make sure there is nobody about."

Io didn't trust her voice, so she made a mocking *please, be my guest,* gesture with her hand.

Once Masterson was satisfied that neither her brother Zeus nor Edith's spies were lurking outside his chambers, he opened the door wider.

Neither of them said a word as she left.

Chapter 14

The Night of the Masquerade Ball

Io stared at her reflection in the mirror and for a moment she did not recognize herself.

Rather than the neatly tailored day dresses and luxurious velvet and silk evening gowns of the last few months, she was back in the plain cotton clothing she had worn all her life.

The woman who looked back at her had freshly cropped short black hair and wore bloomers beneath skirts that scarcely reached her calves.

The garments were as familiar as the back of her hand. And yet they no longer fit right.

Oh, the size was fine—she had neither lost nor gained any weight—but Io was no longer that same woman. Somehow, without realizing it, this new life had left its mark on her. Had changed her.

She accepted, for the first time, that there was no going back to the life she'd left behind.

"Are you sure you don't wish for any jewels, my lady? Or even a flower or ribbon in your hair?" Moira said in a plaintive voice.

Io shook off her odd mood and turned to her maid, who was visibly anguished that her mistress had rejected her offer of hairdressing.

"This will do just fine, Moira," she assured the younger woman. "Why don't you go and change into your own costume now? I won't need you again tonight. I will undress myself when I come to bed," she added, when the maid looked ready to argue.

Moira nodded sadly, as if she were being sent to face a firing squad rather than attend a fancy dress party.

It had been Eva's idea, naturally, that the servants could do their jobs every bit as well in costume as they could in their uniforms, and so they would all get a chance to enjoy Eva's birthday ball.

Which was more than Io could say for herself. The fight she'd had with Edith about her 'costume' tonight had sapped her of any enthusiasm she'd had for the event. Granted, that had not been much to begin with. Parties and balls and frivolity wore on her like a lathe shaving a block of wood. She found them far more exhausting than standing on a frigid street corner, passing out literature to scowling strangers for hours on end.

As Io left her chambers and made her way down to the main drawing room, where the specially chosen dinner guests were to assemble before the meal, she briefly wondered if it was too late to claim sickness and skip the dinner.

But that would crush Eva, and so she continued to trudge toward the social crucible awaiting her. For some reason, she recollected a conversation with Susan Barclay from several weeks ago—not long after she had gone to Masterson's room and behaved so very recklessly. Again.

Io had gone to the library to fetch a book and had discovered Miss Barclay seated at the secretaire desk, her small hands smudged with ink and her hair less tidy than usual.

"What are you up to?" Io asked, smiling at the tiny woman.

Miss Barclay's pale, heart-shaped face blushed—as it always did when anyone spoke to her—and she gestured to the sheaf of parchment. "I'm writing out the invitations for Lady Eva's party."

Io had felt a twinge that Edith's already overworked companion had been saddled with even more work.

"May I help you?"

"Oh, that is kind. But I am almost finished.

"How many guests?"

"Three hundred."

Io's jaw sagged. *"Three hundred people?"*

Miss Barclay chuckled, making Io realize that she'd never heard the other woman laugh before. "Yes, that is correct."

"May I see the guest list?"

Miss Barclay handed her several sheets of paper.

Io glanced down the list, recognizing some of the names from the guests who had already attended dinners at Hastings Park. Most of the others had titles next to them.

Io: The Shrew

"Where are all these people coming from?" she asked, glancing up.

"From all over. When my cousin expressed disbelief that people would make such a long journey for just one night, Mrs. Dryden assured her there was nobody in Britain who would not make the time and effort to attend the new Duke of Hastings's first ball."

Io turned back to the list. "I would like to add some names."

Susan chewed her lower lip. "Er, Miss Barrymore has already instructed the stationer to print these, my lady. If there are more—"

"Don't worry. I shall see to it," Io said. "I can't help noticing that all these guests appear to be aristocrats."

"For the most part."

"What a dull affair it will be."

Miss Barclay's eyes bulged. "I beg your pardon?"

"No writers? No actors? No philosophers, poets, thinkers of any sort?" Io shook her head. "What nonsense! I shall have more than a few additions."

"And do you wish me to tell Miss Barrymore so that adjustments can be made to the food and drink and dinner seating?"

Io had met the other woman's anxious gaze and had immediately guessed who would bear the brunt of such changes.

A struggle had raged inside her, the desire to force Edith to accept people *Io* wanted to socialize with warring with the realization that she would be heaping more work onto this poor woman.

She had forced a smile and handed her back the list. "I have changed my mind. I will give you my list for the next party. I understand there is to be one when we are at Hastings House in London?"

Miss Barclay's shoulders had sagged with relief. "Thank you, my lady."

Mrs. Dryden's prediction had been startlingly correct and all but a handful of the invitations had been accepted.

And so Io would spend the evening engaging in vapid chatter with three hundred people whose lives were so barren and bereft of value that they would travel half-way across the country to attend a costume ball.

When she reached the drawing room door she saw that Charles, one of her favorite footmen, was stationed outside.

Her smile was genuine when she saw that he was garbed as a Viking warrior.

"Good evening, my lady," he said, giving her a grin that would have sent Edith into paroxysms.

"You are looking fierce tonight, Charles. I daresay there are a few dozen ladies who would not be averse to a bit of ransacking at your hands."

His fair skin turned scarlet. "Ah, Lady Io, you're a one you are. If you don't mind me saying."

"Not at all. I like being a *one*, Charles." Io was still smiling like a fool when she stepped into the drawing room.

Her smile curdled like sour milk when the first person she saw was Edith headed toward her, her face pinched and eyes blazing as she took in Io's *costume*.

"You are late, my lady," Edith said, managing to speak the words without disturbing the frosty smile on her face. "I see you've followed through on your threat and have shown up garbed in such a way as to shame all of us."

"How kind of you to say so." Io cocked her head and gave the other woman a quizzical look. "What costume are you wearing, Edith? I can't decide if you are dressed as a nagging scold or a grasping tufthunter?"

Edith's eyes narrowed as she leaned closer and hissed, "If you leave right now and change your clothing you will miss dinner but can still return in time for the ball."

Io just laughed and glanced around the room, looking for her sister.

She grinned when she saw Eva, who made a spectacular Marie Antoinette. "If you will excuse me, Edith," she said, leaving without waiting for an answer.

Eva was surrounded by a clutch of young male dinner guests, so Io veered toward Bal, instead.

Her twin was staring moodily at nothing in particular but shook himself and smiled when she approached. "You looked delightful, Yoyo."

Io snorted. "You've seen me dressed like this all my life."

"True, but not since we've all…metamorphosed."

"Hmph." Io studied his worn clothing and the bits of straw jutting out of his sleeves, neck, and pockets. "This scarecrow costume is an appropriate look for you."

"They are called *hay men* here."

"Ah. But you are missing something."

"I'm afraid to ask."

"You should have some straw spilling from your ears, shouldn't you?"

Bal laughed, his eyes dancing. "Thank you, twin. Thank you also for this idea."

"You only like the costume because it did not cost you anything."

"Well, that's true." His gaze slid to where Ares stood, garbed as a Cavalier. "He'll be miserable in that heavy velvet doublet after a few hours," he predicted.

"Forget about the doublet. What about that *hair?*"

They laughed at the brown curly wig that draped over their youngest brother's shoulders and fell almost to his waist.

Ares chose that moment to look at them, his eyes narrowing as if he knew he was the object of their mirth.

"Where is the Roundhead?" Io asked, glancing around.

"I haven't seen Pol tonight."

"Do you think we will?"

"I'm hoping he stays away, even though it might hurt Eva's feelings. Edith seems to have a special dislike for him—even more than she does for you—and she will likely carp at him if he does make an appearance."

"I just wish Pol would snap back at her."

"He cannot do that, Yoyo. Gentlemen do not attack ladies—not even verbally and no matter how much they might deserve it."

"Oh, I know, I know." She smirked. "I will try to make up for his inability to lash out."

Bal laughed. "You already do an excellent job." His eyes widened slightly and Io turned to see what he was looking at.

It was Masterson and he was dressed like a Pilgrim—or at least like all the paintings of male Pilgrims Io had ever seen. He wore dark knee-breeches with thick white stockings and black buckled shoes. A tall capotain hat completed the costume.

His black and white apparel was striking against his blond good looks. And his calves, she couldn't help noticing, were muscular and well-formed. Io had not paid attention to his legs when she'd shown up in his bedroom that night almost three weeks ago, the last time they'd spoken to one another, although they'd exchanged plenty of looks—amused sneers on her side and haughty sneers on his—in the interim.

Somehow Masterson, with his trenchant, cool mien, managed to make the ridiculous black hat, high white collar, and buckled shoes look adorable. A reluctant smile curved her lips.

And then Edith stepped close to Masterson and laid a hand on his forearm and whispered something in his ear.

And Masterson *smiled* at her. True, it was not the huge dimple-exposing grin he'd shown Io that one time when he was ill onboard the *Petrel*, but it was a genuine smile all the same.

"Yoyo? *Yoyo.*"

Io wrenched her gaze from the happily chatting pair and turned to find her twin regarding her with concerned amusement.

"What?" she barked.

"You were, um, looking at poor Masterson as if you wanted to carve him up like a side of beef."

"The notion is not without some appeal."

Balthazar laughed. "I can't help noticing that your interest in him seems to have—"

"I have no interest in Masterson."

Bal blinked at her sharp tone. "Ah."

"Other than to expose his hypocrisy to the world," she amended. "To show that his scrupulously proper façade is just that: a façade. To prove that he has feet of clay, just like any other man. To—" Io stopped when she saw the knowing look in Bal's eyes.

She turned away from her twin abruptly, irked by the heat creeping up her neck, and forced herself to look at anyone *but* Masterson.

Her gaze was snagged by her oldest brother. Zeus was dressed like a Roman senator, his toga short enough to show off muscular legs and sandals that laced up to his knees. His shoulders looked even broader than they did sheathed in a suit.

On his head was a circlet of olives leaves.

He looked very…senatorial. Io was stunned that her reserved sibling had donned such a revealing costume. She wondered, with a smirk, what Edith made of his attire.

The man beside him was almost as handsome as Zeus, although his haughty expression made him far less attractive, in Io's opinion. There was quite a crowd in the room and yet the two of them seemed to have a buffer of empty space between them and all the other guests.

"Who is that man talking to Zeus?"

"That is the Duke of Axbridge."

Io raised an eyebrow at her twin's rather sour tone. "Is he as proud and disagreeable as he looks?"

"Even more so."

"Why is Zeus talking to him?"

Bal shrugged. "Because he is a duke, I suppose."

"Are they forming some sort of duke club?"

Bal laughed. "I think you should go over and ask them."

Io slanted a look at Masterson to make sure he could see her before she nodded at her twin. "Perhaps I will."

***

Corbin desperately wished that Miss Barrymore would go stand next to somebody else so that he could gawk his fill at Lady Io.

He had seen her in her *traditional* clothing before, but he'd forgotten how appealing she made the unusual garments look. Of course, she would make even an oversized burlap sack look attractive.

151

Just listen to you! Smitten. It is pathetic.

Corbin ignored the scolding voice—he'd had plenty of practice lately—and tried to concentrate on Miss Barrymore's conversation.

"—and I believe he will not make an appearance tonight. You should see if you can find him. Otherwise, the table will be unbalanced."

Corbin's mind scrambled to recall who she might be talking about.

"I daresay he will be in the stables, as he always is," she added with venom in her tone, answering his unasked question.

"I saw Lord Apollo earlier," Corbin lied, not wanting to pour kerosene on an already incendiary situation. "I will go look for him, Miss Barrymore."

"You should make haste as there is not much time before we go into the dining room," she said crisply, and then turned at the sound of somebody saying her name.

Corbin's shoulders sagged with relief when she was gone. He was bloody exhausted from trying to keep the Hales and Miss Barrymore from each other's throats.

Especially when all you really want to do is grab Lady Io Hale and whisk her up to your chambers.

He could not deny it.

The object of his obsession suddenly broke away from her twin's side and strode across the huge room, her confident, loose-limbed walk attracting the eyes of every man in the room.

His nostrils flared when he saw where she was headed: right toward the Duke of Axbridge.

Corbin did not dislike many people on sight, but Axbridge was one of them. The man was arrogant to the bone, not to mention judgmental and opinionated. For whatever reason, Hastings seemed determined to tolerate him. Corbin wondered if it was just a relief for his old friend to have another duke to talk to. The status of a duke was so rare that he knew Hastings must feel isolated, and so Corbin tried to tolerate Axbridge for his sake. But the proud, supercilious Englishman was hard to palate.

Io: The Shrew

Lady Io came to a halt in front of the two dark-haired men. Although she was tall, they both towered over her.

Even from this distance Corbin could see the change in Axbridge's expression. He didn't smile, but he warmed up by several degrees when Hastings introduced the two.

Corbin watched in fascinated fury as Lady Io worked her unique brand of charm on the aloof peer. Right before his eyes he witnessed the remarkable change in Axbridge, until he was all but eating out of her hand. Hastings looked on with approval while the other two chattered with increasing animation. Was his best friend hoping to marry off his sister to Axbridge?

Corbin heard a low rumble and realized that it had come from him. He was growling like a dog in the manger.

"Good evening, Mr. Masterson."

His head whipped around and then down to the voice's owner. "Good evening, Miss Barclay," he said, and then gently teased, "But where is your costume?"

She blushed as she gestured to her drab gray dress, which was the dowdiest evening gown that Corbin had ever seen. "I am in solidarity with my cousin," she said, referring to the fact that Miss Barrymore was still in mourning, and also not in costume tonight.

"Does that mean that you won't be at the ball?"

"I will take a peek, but no, I will not be participating in the festivities."

He thought he heard some regret in her voice.

She cleared her throat and cut him an uncomfortable look.

"Is something wrong, Miss Barclay?"

"Miss Barrymore wondered if you had gone to fetch Lord Apollo yet?"

Damnation! "No, I haven't." He darted a look at Lady Io and her new swain. It galled him to leave them to their flirtation, but what else could he do? He turned back to the tiny blonde woman and forced a pleasant expression. "I will do that right now."

***

Io could not believe it when Masterson simply left the room. She had seen him gawking as she'd outrageously flirted with Axbridge. She had felt his anger burning a hole through her from across the room.

And then he had simply left.

No doubt to run some errand for his mistress.

"Your brother tells me that you are an authoress," Axbridge said, pulling Io from her thoughts.

She looked up at the duke—not a hardship as the man was gorgeous—and smiled. "I wasn't aware Zeus knew that."

"I didn't," Zeus chimed in. "Axbridge meant that Balthazar told him. And then he told me," he added with a slightly aggrieved look. Was that pain she saw in his pale blue gaze?

"Ah," was all Io could think to say.

"I would like to read one of your books," Axbridge said.

Io laughed. "I'm afraid you aren't the intended audience, Your Grace. Did Bal not tell you they are for children?"

"He told me. I have several nieces and nephews who are of an age to enjoy your stories," he said, surprising her with his tenacity.

"I have several copies and would be delighted to give you one."

"You are generous as well as lovely."

As always, a sneer wanted to jump to Io's mouth at such hollow flattery—what did her looks have to do with giving him a book, after all? Shouldn't he be complimenting her brain?

But a glance at Zeus made her curb her tongue and say, "You are too kind, Your Grace."

There. She could play the game just as well as Edith.

"Hastings tells me that you will be joining him in London next month," Axbridge said.

"Yes, along with my sister and brothers. Have you met them all?"

Axbridge's dark brown eyes narrowed slightly and when they slid across the room Io couldn't help noticing they stopped where Eva held court. "I have met everyone except the elusive Lord Apollo. It appears he is not here tonight."

Io cut a glance at Zeus to see how he received that information, but he had a slight frown on his face as he regarded Edith, who was standing with her cousin. Based on the way Miss Barclay was cringing, Edith was berating her for something or other.

Axbridge lightly cleared his throat, reminding her that he was waiting for an answer.

"Apollo is here, Your Grace. He is just elusive," Io said, smiling. *Oh, Pol. Where are you?*

***

Corbin backed away from the large corner stall as quietly as he was able, wincing when he stepped on an especially loud plank. Not until he was out in the open air did he release the breath he'd been holding.

He inhaled deeply and hurried back toward the castle, his mind in chaos at what he'd just seen. Belatedly, he realized that he should be composing an excuse for Apollo's absence that would, if not satisfy, at least temporarily appease Miss Barrymore.

But when he slipped into the dining room a short time later, he discovered that every chair was taken, so she must have had the servants subtly adjust the seating.

Corbin was relieved that he'd not needed to lie to his employer's fiancée, not that he would have hesitated to do so.

With what he'd discovered in the stables still at the forefront of his mind, the meal sped past like a blur.

Did Lord Apollo's siblings know?

Did *Hastings* know?

Those thoughts consumed him and Corbin was sure the women on either side of him thought him the worst sort of tongue-tied dunce.

Even the sight of Lady Io shamelessly flirting with Axbridge could not penetrate his preoccupation and he fled the dining room with unseemly haste the moment the meal was over, giving Hastings a vague excuse of needing to tend to a ball-related matter to escape the masculine postprandial ritual of port and cigars.

Corbin was on his way to the ballroom, wanting to at least make good on his lie by ensuring that all was ready for the masses of guests who were about to descend on the castle, when a quiet voice stopped him.

"Masterson."

Corbin jolted and swung around, encountering the miss-matched gaze of the subject of his recent musings.

"Lord Apollo," he said, sounding stiff and stilted to his own ears.

"I know you saw me—us," the younger man said, dispensing with any attempt at subterfuge.

"I did," Corbin admitted. "And I have not told anyone. Nor will I."

Relief flickered across Apollo's face. "Thank you." Without another word, Lord Apollo strode in the opposite direction from the ballroom.

Corbin watched him until he disappeared. Only when the other man turned the corner did it occur to him that they were dressed similarly. Lord Apollo's stark Roundhead garb was oddly suitable for the morose, introverted young man.

He was relieved they'd spoken—as brief as it had been. It had felt wrong to scurry away from the stables like a fleeing rodent, but it would have been worse to stay. Or at least a hundred times more awkward.

Now Corbin could turn his thoughts back to another Hale, this one far less accommodating than her reclusive brother.

Chapter 15

That Same Evening, Several Hours Later

Even Io knew that three dances with the same partner was beyond the pale behavior.

But Axbridge was a duke and he did not seem bothered by the sly looks and tittering they were attracting, so she wasn't, either. Especially not when she saw the expression on Edith's face.

Although the sour woman claimed she would not attend the ball, Io saw her sitting at a prominent table, like a specter at a feast, surrounded by similarly sour-faced women whom Io suspected were chaperones and the like.

Infuriating Edith had not been even half as rewarding as causing the veins in Masterson's temples to bulge more fiercely with every dance.

"I know you are using me."

Io's head whipped up at the duke's voice. While Axbridge was not smiling—she wasn't sure he knew *how*—there was an amused glint in his dark brown gaze.

Why lie? she thought.

"Yes, I am," she admitted, sneaking another look at Masterson before turning her attention to the handsome man currently leading her around the massive dance floor in a waltz. "Why do I think you might be using me a little, too, Your Grace?"

He gave her a sardonic look. "*Using* is such a harsh word."

"I'll remind you it was *your* choice."

"So it was," he agreed mildly. "To be fair, I'm not sure how I could have politely rejected your requests for the second and third dance."

Io laughed. "No, I daresay I put you in an uncomfortable position."

Axbridge shrugged slightly. "I could have simply left the ballroom if I had truly wanted to avoid you."

Io was amused by his cool, unchivalrous retort. Here was a man more reserved than Zeus and more rigid and judgmental even than Masterson. She could tell by his faint, supercilious sneer that he did not approve of her in the least—he probably did not even like her—and yet he could have left the dance to avoid her attention, so Io must have been providing him with at least a little diversion.

"Have you ever been asked by a woman to dance before?"

"No," he said. And then Io swore he *almost* smiled.

"I have been unforgivably forward and vulgar, Your Grace."

"Forward, perhaps, but not vulgar."

"My brother's fiancée would say they are the same thing."

His dark eyes flickered toward Edith and he blinked slowly before turning back to Io. "Miss Barrymore seems a very proper sort of young woman."

"Unlike me, you mean?"

"I would never suggest such a thing." This time he *did* smile and the expression made his already handsome face stunning.

Io laughed. "Of course not. So, Your Grace, we both know why I'm doing what I'm doing," she said, relieved to have the truth—or at least part of it—out in the open. "But why are you shattering convention by dancing three times with me? Other than because you are a gentleman."

"My answer will sound arrogant."

"Who cares how it sounds if it is the truth?"

"I find your attitude refreshing. Unfortunately, few among our circle will share it."

"So my brother's fiancée tells me. Daily. But don't try to deflect my question. Tell me why you are dancing with me. I don't think it was only because you are too gentlemanly to reject my offers. I noticed that you had not danced a single set until you asked me for that first dance. Why not? There are at least a hundred women all gazing at you with stars in their eyes while their mothers are all but throwing daggers at *me*."

"*That* is the reason."

"Ah, I see. You are tired of being hunted."

"Just so."

"How do you know I'm not hunting you?" He lifted one eyebrow and Io laughed. "Am I really that obvious?"

"Not as obvious as the target of your interest. No. Do not turn and look at him just now—he is glaring at you—and me—and wearing a most un-Pilgrimish expression of jealous fury."

"Now I really want to turn and look. Masterson is usually the epitome of cool disinterest."

"Ah, but not if you know what to look for," he countered in a blandly disinterested tone that made Io laugh.

"We have a saying for that in America."

"Oh?"

"*It takes one to know one.*"

"How quaint. No—" he said when she would have turned to look at Masterson. "You must restrain your curiosity, my lady. Take my word for it that you are driving him to distraction."

Io laughed yet again. "You are not making this easy, Your Grace."

"Things that are not easy are often the most rewarding. Besides, I do not believe he will be able to restrain himself much longer." He lowered his voice. "Ah, you see—I am right. Here he comes now," the duke added as the dance ended.

Io was not even off the dance floor before Masterson's hand closed around her arm. "I will escort Lady Io to her brother's side," he snarled at the duke.

Axbridge merely raised an eyebrow—a gesture that was so infuriating Io vowed then and there to learn how to do it—and then bowed slightly to Io and drifted off without speaking a word.

"Annoying, arrogant jackass," Masterson bit out before all but dragging her across the room.

"What are you doing?" Io asked laughingly, enjoying his jealous devolution into primitive man far too much.

"We are going to have a discussion."

"Mm, about what, I wonder?"

He ignored her taunting as he blatantly frog-marched her from the room. Or at least it felt blatant, although a quick look around told her that nobody seemed to be paying them much mind.

"I hope this does not take long as I'm committed for the next set of dances," she said as he picked up speed once they were out in the corridor.

"To Axbridge, of course."

"Who else? Why do you look so angry, Masterson? Have I done something amiss?" Io winked at Charles, the footman, who was staring at them with a very un-Viking-like look of surprise.

He ignored her taunt and flung open a door, dragging Io into a small sitting room.

She glanced around. "I don't believe I have ever been in this room before."

"Shut up," he snarled, and then slammed the door and threw the lock before turning to her.

"Why, Mr. Masterson, you seem almost—"

"Just what are you up to dancing with that—that—"

"Duke?" she suggested.

His gray eyes narrowed. "Is that what you are after? His title?"

"What business is it of yours if I am?"

Masterson's cold gaze suddenly flared to life.

And when he grabbed her, Io wondered if she had finally pushed him too far.

***

"What the hell is wrong with you?" Corbin raged between clenched teeth as he yet again dragged her, this time toward a settee.

"Quit fighting it, Masterson."

"Fighting what, you—you merciless *jade?*"

"Merciless jade?" She laughed and her eyes became liquid heat, her full lips slack and lush. "You know you want me," she taunted, her gaze dropping to his mouth. "Kiss me, Corbin."

Io: The Shrew

This is a dreadful idea! Dreadful! Dreadful! Voices screamed in his head.

Corbin ignored them and slammed his mouth over hers.

And then yelped and jerked back when her sharp teeth sank into his lower lip.

She stared up at him with blood—his blood—on her white teeth and plump lips, her pupils huge.

Corbin wiped his mouth with the back of his hand and glanced at the blood before looking up. "You vicious bitch!"

Lady Io smiled taunting up at him, temptation in female form.

***

"You vicious bitch," the unflappable Corbin Masterson roared.

Finally. *Finally,* Io had done something that got through his ironclad reserve.

Io smiled.

You are taunting the beast, a niggling voice whispered.

But the pulse of desire emanating from between her thighs was so loud it drowned out the voice of reason.

And then Io's world spun—literally—and she shrieked as Masterson's hard thighs pressed against her abdomen, the elegant Aubusson carpet scant inches away from her nose.

"What do you think you are doing?" she demanded shrilly.

"Who is the domesticated *lap*dog now, my lady?"

"Have you gone *insane*, Masterson?"

"I think I am sane for the first time since meeting you," he muttered under his breath.

"Let me up immediately!"

You could at least struggle a bit to make that sound convincing, a sly voice suggested.

"I told you in Northampton what you deserved—what a *brat* needed—and now you are going to get it."

Io's body stiffened in shock, and something deeper and more unnerving, as his hand, large and strong slid down her back to her buttocks.

"You would not dare." She had meant to come across dismissive and mocking. Instead, she sounded breathless and excited.

And needy, the same voice whispered.

"Wouldn't I?" Masterson retorted, his voice a darkly amused purr.

"If you so much as—*Ow!*" Io yelped as her bottom suddenly combusted.

"That's one," her tormentor said, his hand resting on the still-stinging flesh. "How many do you deserve, *hmm?*"

"If you strike me one more time, I will—*ow!*"

"Two." The hand on her back flexed when she tried to get away. "Be a good girl and quit squirming—or I will just add more."

To Io's horror, his words caused her sex to flood with heat.

Above her, Masterson made an approving humming sound when her body went limp. "Yes, that is much better."

"You *vile bast—*"

The hand that had been gently, and distractingly, rubbing her bottom, suddenly clamped over her mouth. "I don't want to hear that sort of language out of your mouth, my lady."

"*Go sod yourself!*" she shrieked. Or at least that is what Io *tried* to yell. Unfortunately, all that came out was. "*Uff uff uff uffff!*"

"*Tsk, tsk.* I understood the gist of that." Masterson's big body suddenly folded over hers, the action bringing his mouth near her ear. "One more outburst like that and I will gag and bind you."

A mortifyingly needy groan escaped before she could stop it, making Io hate herself even more than she hated *him* at that moment.

He gave a low, evil chuckle. "I think you would like that, wouldn't you? Collared, kneeling, and obedient—wasn't that what you said? With *my* hand holding your leash."

Io inhaled deeply to tell him what he could do with his collar, leash, *and* hand.

Io: The Shrew

"Shhhh," he whispered before she could utter a sound. "I am going to take my hand off your mouth and you are going to behave like a good girl. You won't get another warning. The next time you curse or yell I will strip off my belt and bind you hand to foot. If that is what you want, then disobey me again." He paused. "Nod if you understand me."

Io gritted her teeth against the raw lust invading every fiber of her being, her heart pounding so hard that her ribs ached, her thighs so slick that evidence of her arousal would soon be visible.

She groaned at the mortifying thought.

"Hmm? What was that?" Masterson asked.

You had better nod, or else he will learn the true depth of your desire for what he is offering, a wryly amused voice cautioned.

Io jerked her head.

"Good girl." His big warm palm slid away from her mouth and returned to her bottom.

Say something! What is wrong with you? her pride shouted.

Io opened her mouth. And then abruptly shut it again when he began to lightly caress her buttocks, although not quickly enough to stifle a grunt of arousal that slipped between her lips.

"That's better. See how nice I can be when you please me?"

Io caught her lower lip with her teeth to keep from retorting.

Or groaning again.

He continued his caressing, but she refused to be lulled, her body taut as she waited for the next blow.

"It will hurt less if you relax. Trust me," he murmured in a low, disturbingly sensual voice she never would have imagined him possessing.

It took effort, but she forced her muscles to unclench.

And then his hand disappeared, and Io squeezed her eyes shut. *"Ow!"* she shouted before she could catch the cry. "Sorry," she blurted, and was immediately furious at herself for apologizing.

"You don't need to apologize. I like hearing you whimper."

She gritted her teeth at his gloating tone, imagining what she was going to do to him once she got free and—

"*Ow!*" she yelped, although it sounded distressingly like a moan to her ears.

She could only hope that Masterson didn't notice her body's reaction and had no idea what this was doing to her.

"Four," he said calmly, gently rubbing her now flaming buttocks. "You're doing so well."

She preened at his praise.

And the next time his hand came down, Io didn't even try to hide her moan.

***

"Ten," Corbin said, his voice hoarse with lust. He knew a man couldn't die from a painfully hard cock, but it seemed possible at that moment.

You once swore to her that she could never manipulate you with her adolescent antics. Now look at yourself, all but unhinged!

Corbin sometimes felt like he had been suppressing his urges all his life. Always painstakingly careful to never allow his passion to gain the upper hand as it had once before, all those years ago, when he had discovered just how easy it was to carelessly destroy somebody else's life.

But suddenly, Corbin simply could not bring himself to care about anything.

At least not about anything other than slaking the seemingly unquenchable thirst this woman had created within him.

He palmed her soft, full buttocks, wondering if Lady Io could feel the way his hand shook. After the fourth swat, her body had gone limp. After the fifth her cries had undeniably turned into moans.

He was not the only one aroused. Not by a long shot.

Don't say it, Corbin. Do. Not. Say. It!

"Are you wet for me, Io?"

She jolted and made a noise that sounded like, "*Whryrgh.*"

"I think you are. Should I check?"

Her breathing quickened and Corbin waited for her to reel in his insanity and tell him *no.*

Io: The Shrew

Stop me now, he silently pleaded.

Instead, she spread her knees an inch, the invitation unmistakable.

Corbin did not hesitate, pulling up the short cotton skirt and plain petticoat with shaking fingers and exposing those blasted bloomers that so incited him.

When his hand brushed against the damp split, he bit his lip, not caring that he reopened the cut she'd made earlier. "My God," he groaned, sliding a finger through her drenched, swollen folds.

"I hate you, Masterson," she moaned. And then she spread wider for his touch, canting her plump bottom and offering herself up to him.

"Shut up and take it," Corbin muttered, and then slid a finger into tight, wet heaven of her body.

His eyelids fluttered shut as he pumped her with slow, lazy strokes. How long had he wanted this? From the moment that he'd first seen the evil, hazel-eyed bitch in Hastings's drawing room all those weeks ago? Maybe even before he'd met her?

Corbin had always enjoyed his lovers and their bodies. But never before had he felt a physical, unstoppable compulsion to wreck his life and throw away friendships and everything he'd worked for just to be with someone.

Io Hale would be the end of him.

And Corbin would go down without a fight.

***

Io didn't just hate Masterson—she hated how much she wanted him even more.

She hated how badly she wanted to feel his thick erection—which was currently pressing against her hip—inside her, stretching and filling her until it hurt.

That's what she wanted, what she craved.

But she'd happily settle for his fingers, which were astonishingly skilled for a man who'd once considered a career as a Presbyterian minister.

"You are a naughty, filthy girl, aren't you, my lady?"

Oh, God. Io's hips gave an involuntary buck. If there was one thing she loved more than a confident, masterful lover, it was a confident, masterful lover with a dirty mouth.

"Aren't you?" he whispered in her ear, his finger missing her clitoris in a way that had to be intentional given his dexterity up to that point.

He suddenly stopped stroking her altogether. "Answer me."

She opened one eye and glared at the carpet. "You cannot be seriou—"

His finger began to withdraw.

"Yes!"

"*Yes,* what?"

She growled. "Yes, I'm naughty!"

"And filthy?" he prodded, both with his words and his divine finger.

"Yes, yes, yes," she chanted in time with each thrust. "I am a naughty, filthy girl."

His smug laughter vibrated from his chest through her body. "Good. Now you will come hard for me."

God help her, Io did exactly what he told her.

***

Corbin's balls ached—so did his prick. But he deserved to suffer pain and frustration for the idiocy of what he had just done.

He must be losing his mind, there was no other explanation for his unprecedented behavior. Not only had he never raised his hand to a woman before, but he'd certainly never spoken words like those that had just flowed out of his mouth.

The body draped across his thighs shifted lazily, reminding him that he'd not yet paid the piper for his recent foolishness.

He needed to apologize for spanking her—it didn't matter that she'd obviously enjoyed it. What he'd done had been reckless and *wrong*. Deeply wrong.

It had also elicited one of the most erotic reactions he'd ever received from a lover.

But that was beside the point.

Io grunted softly and tried, but failed, to turn.

Corbin slid his hands beneath her and rolled her into his arms, until she was cradled against his chest and staring up at him, slit-eyed, flushed, and sated.

He almost spent in his trousers just looking at her.

Her lips curved slowly. "You must be a naughty, filthy boy yourself to have such exquisite skills, Masterson."

Corbin snorted and shook his head. Trust Io Hale to come out of a debauched encounter without an ounce of shame.

She squirmed, rubbing her lush bottom against his throbbing erection.

Corbin hissed in a breath.

Her smirk told him the action was intentional. "I'd offer to see to that for you, but you wouldn't want to take advantage of an unmarried maiden, would you?" She reached up and caressed his cheek.

Instead of pulling away as he ought to have done, Corbin pressed against her palm, all but purring at this unprecedented show of affection.

And then she scratched him.

He cursed and shoved her away.

She laughed and scrambled inelegantly to her feet.

"What on earth is wrong with you?" Corbin demanded, rubbing a palm over the already rising ridges on his cheek.

"Poor Masterson," she cooed mockingly. "You were expecting wide-eyed wonder and gratitude because you know how to give a woman an orgasm?"

The urge to grab and spank her again was almost overwhelming. But then he remembered how much she enjoyed it.

You were going to apologize, remember?

Not bloody likely!

Corbin stood and straightened his coat, the irony of his costume—after what he'd just done—not escaping him. He scowled down at his tented Pilgrim trousers, evidence that while his brain might loathe Io Hale, his body was infatuated.

When he looked up, it was to find her staring at his groin. "You might want to take a few minutes to deal with that before you go back out there."

And then she sailed from the room, leaving Corbin erect, furious, and more besotted than ever.

Chapter 16

London
Hastings House
Several Weeks Later

I o's eyelids felt as if they were made of lead when she lifted them that day—her seventeenth in London.

She winced at the sunlight that was shining between a gap in the drapes and knew before she even glanced at the clock that it would be late.

Even so, her heart sank when she saw it was half past one o'clock. In the afternoon.

At this time of year, the sun went down before five o'clock. And Io had spent most of the day abed.

On the heels of her shame came a sharp pang of sorrow. As it did every day, it took Io a moment before she could identify the cause: Balthazar had not accompanied the rest of them to London.

Her twin had married a month ago at Hastings Park. Immediately afterward, he had moved with his new wife and stepson to a house of their own. Never again would Io, Bal, and their other siblings all live together as a family.

Io sighed softly. Although nobody could have been more pleased than Io when her brother fell in love and married Mrs. Dryden, she missed Bal horribly.

She did not begrudge her twin his new life, but she felt as if a part of her was missing.

Of course, she was still furious at Bal for keeping the truth of their grandfather's will from her and their other siblings. She could not believe that Bal had needed to marry an *acceptable* woman before he could inherit. He could very well have ended up with a woman like Edith if Zeus had rigidly adhered to their deceased grandfather's idea of what constituted *acceptable*.

Fortunately, Zeus—the executor of the will—had given his enthusiastic stamp of approval to Victoria Dryden, even though she was a servant. Io suspected that Horace Sinclair would not have been pleased.

According to the last letter she had received from her twin, Bal was still furious with Io and their younger siblings for refusing to accept a share of the four million dollars he had inherited.

He had not been willing to take *no* for an answer and had divided the money five ways and created trusts for each of them. Whether she wanted it or not, Io was almost a millionaire.

"All is well that ends well," she muttered, her voice dry and croaky from all the pointless chatter she had engaged in the night before.

And the night before that.

And the night before that.

"This torment ends today," she said. And then ruined her firm declaration with a jaw-cracking yawn.

Rather than ring for Moira, whom she knew would not intrude until Io summoned her, she washed with cold water and dressed herself. Her hair was still short enough from its last sheering to require nothing more than a vigorous brushing.

When she was finished, she examined herself in the mirror. For the first time in three weeks, Io recognized the woman who looked back at her. Instead of the rich velvets and silks she'd worn since arriving in London she was garbed in a navy gabardine that was cut in the clean, severe style she favored.

Garbed in her armor of choice, she left her chambers and went searching for Zeus, locating him easily as two footmen always stood sentry outside any chamber the duke occupied.

"Is he alone?" she asked the footman, Nathan, she thought he was called, a haughty London-born man whom she did not like nearly as much as the servants they'd brought with them from the country.

"His Grace has asked not to be disturbed," Nathan said in a lofty tone.

"He won't mind seeing his sister." Io reached for the door handle but the footman's white-gloved hand got there first. She looked up at him and for a moment there was a silent battle of wills.

Io: The Shrew

Io wondered what she would do if the footman refused her entry.

As it turned out, that didn't become an issue because Nathan opened the door and announced, "Lady Io to see you, Your Grace."

Io pushed past the stuffy servant. Zeus was not sitting at his desk, but standing in front of the fire and seemed to be staring at it before he turned to Io, his expression…odd.

"Is something wrong?" she asked.

His vague gaze sharpened and he nodded at the footman, whom Io only then realized had not shut the door, waiting for his master's approval before leaving him alone with his own sibling.

Io reined in her irritation as the door shut almost soundlessly, reminding herself that she had not invaded Zeus's sanctum to argue and fight about the obsequious habits of servants, but to request a favor of sorts.

Zeus gestured to a chair nearest the fire. "Nothing is wrong," he said, seating himself across from her once she'd settled.

Only when they were sitting face-to-face did Io notice that her brother had dark smudges beneath his arresting sapphire eyes.

"You look tired," she said with her usual candor—or what Bal would term her usual lack of tact.

"You look fresh and rested," he countered.

She snorted. "That's because I only left my bed"—she glanced at the clock on the mantle, a gold monstrosity that evidently had once belonged to the Duke of Wellington—"three-quarters-of-an-hour ago. I daresay you were up early even though we all came home together last night." She cocked her head. "Does one still refer to it as *last night* when it was after four in the morning?"

Zeus gave her a look that wasn't quite a smile but toed the boundary line. "Did you enjoy yourself at the Winchester ball?" he asked, obviously not interested in discussing semantics.

"You didn't go to bed at all, did you?" she asked, taking a leaf from his book and ignoring his question.

"Did you come here to inquire into my sleeping habits, Sister?"

She snorted. "Lack of them, I should say. But no. That is not why I am here."

He suddenly stood. "I believe I will have some fortification before I hear this," he said, crossing the room to a walnut drinks table that had a cunning cover in the shape of a globe.

Io was more than a little surprised that he would indulge in spirits so early in the day. While not abstemious, Zeus normally drank very little.

"May I get you something?" he asked, pouring what looked to be whiskey.

"I'll have what you are having."

He turned to her and lifted an eyebrow. "It is whisky."

"Yes, I know."

He stared a moment longer, then sighed and poured a second glass.

Io couldn't help noticing that the tumbler he handed her held half the liquid of his own.

Her temper spiked at his obviously patronizing gesture, and Io forced herself to take a deep breath and just sip from the glass, rather than tossing the entire amount back just to antagonize him.

"What can I do for you?" he asked.

"I cannot continue on the way I have these past weeks, Zeus."

He stared, expressionless. After a moment, he said, "What are you saying? Do you wish to go back to New York?"

Io couldn't help noticing that he no longer called it *home*.

"Are those my only options, Zeus? To frantically drink and eat and dance and gossip until four o'clock every morning of the week or go home?"

"What do you have in mind?" he asked, eyeing her levelly.

"Fewer engagements, for one thing. For another, I'd like to have the right to choose some of my own evening entertainments."

"Suffragette marches down Bond Street? Condom distribution in Trafalgar Square?" he suggested with very un-Zeuslike sarcasm.

Io: The Shrew

Her hand tightened on the glass.

"I'm sorry," he said before she could decide which of the five retorts—all of them uncivil—she would deal him. "That was unnecessary."

"I was thinking more of intellectual gatherings," she said with admirable coolness. "Although I only write children's books, I would still like to spend some of my time meeting other authors. Also painters, philosophers. In short, anyone who does something other than spend all their time attending parties, routs, and balls."

"And how many nights a week do you need for that?"

"Seven would be nice."

Faint amusement glimmered in his eyes. "How about two?"

"I could get by with three."

He swirled the liquid in his glass before lifting the drink and downing it in one gulp. When he met her gaze, his face was once again impassive. "You will accompany your sister or Edith—or both—four nights a week to various *ton* functions. The other three nights you may attend literary and artistic events, provided none of them lead to arrest and incarceration."

Io bristled at his commanding tone, but quickly stuffed down her annoyance. Instead, she smiled and opened her mouth to say *thank you*.

But then Zeus had to go and ruin the goodwill she was feeling.

"I will want to know where you are going in advance and you will take one of our brothers or a suitable chaperone with you to all acceptable functions," he said. "And you will allow Edith to help you decide to which functions you will accompany her and Eva as she will know which are of more importance." His eyes, which usually resembled pale blue gems, were suddenly paler, their hue more closely resembling the highly polished steel of the regimental sword that hung beside the fireplace. Io knew the weapon belonged to Zeus from his time with the 5th Cavalry Regiment. It was one of the few personal items her brother had added to the décor in the massive London house.

Her nostrils flared as she tried to suck in enough air for all the retorts that exploded inside her. Zeus rarely exerted himself to establish authority over Io and her siblings, but when he did, he could be as hard and inflexible as the razor-sharp blade.

"This is non-negotiable," he said before she could get even one word out of her mouth.

Io set her glass down on the marble-topped end table with a loud *crack*.

"So be it," she said.

He stared at her for a long moment, as if searching for some subterfuge behind her acquiescence. But then he nodded, set his glass down a good deal more quietly, and said with no trace of irony, "I am glad we could come to an agreement."

***

That same evening…

Corbin sensed conflict beneath the politely brittle conversation taking place around him at the dinner table, and he knew it was coming from at least two sources—Lady Io and Miss Barrymore—but, oddly, he also felt it emanating from his friend and employer.

It was a rare dinner at home with all the family—except Lord Balthazar, of course, who had not come to London—in attendance. He was surprised to see Lords Apollo and Ares, who had scarcely spent a night at Hastings House since the family's arrival in London three weeks before.

The twins, along with Zeus, had been speedily welcomed into Brooks's gentlemen's club and, like every other aristocratic young buck in London, Ares and Apollo spent a great deal of time there.

Corbin knew the duke had been relieved to discover that neither of his younger brothers cared for gambling or any of the blood sports that seemed to attract so many young males.

During the day they both seemed to have their own pursuits, Lord Ares had struck up a friendship with Nigel Carey, one of the foremost furniture makers in Britain, and Lord Apollo haunted Tattersalls and a half-dozen other auction houses and stud farms with an almost feverish intensity.

But as much as they lived their own lives, they still showed their faces at numerous *ton* engagements to please their oldest brother.

Lady Io, Corbin had been stunned to see, had attended each and every social event with Lady Eva. Miss Barrymore usually accompanied them, unless she deemed a function too festive for half-mourning, in which case she sent Miss Barclay in her stead.

Corbin knew little of women's clothing or fashion, but even he could see that Miss Barclay wore the same gray silk gown to almost every affair. Why Miss Barrymore treated her cousin with such wanton neglect, Corbin did not know.

But then he no longer regarded Miss Barrymore as highly as he had done in years past.

Just like the duke, Corbin had been shocked and deeply unsettled by the way Miss Barrymore had meddled in Lord Balthazar's secret romance with Mrs. Dryden.

Although Corbin did not know the full extent of her interference, he knew enough to realize that she had been responsible for the brief schism between the couple, who were very obviously in love.

Hastings would never admit it, but Corbin suspected the duke was experiencing crippling doubts about marrying a woman who appeared to not only dislike his siblings but was willing to go out of her way to do them harm.

Corbin knew there had been some sort of promise between Hastings and Kelvin Barrymore—Miss Barrymore's deceased older brother—and he believed that promise was the reason that his friend had become engaged to Miss Barrymore. He had known John Hale a long, long time and suspected the other man had very little affection, or even regard, for his fiancée after her awful behavior these past months.

The duke had a difficult choice ahead of him and Corbin did not envy him one bit. He only hoped the man chose what was best for *him*—the man—rather than the duke, friend, brother, or well-respected member of society.

In any event, Lord Balthazar had gone off to his new estate with his new wife and new stepson, leaving his wild twin to her own devices.

Since reaching London Lady Io had been suspiciously compliant. Of course she had also proceeded to gain a name for herself among the *ton* as an Original. She wasn't the only woman who wore artistic dress—the Pre-Raphaelites had, after all, brought the medieval-like style into fashion some years back—but she was easily the most outspoken person, male or female, at almost every gathering.

Regardless of Lady Io's compliance, His Grace's London home was filled with increasing rancor between Io and Miss Barrymore.

For the most part, Corbin had managed to keep out of the middle of their battles.

Indeed, since the night of Lady Eva's birthday ball, when Corbin had behaved like a despicable lust-mad ravisher—he'd avoided being alone in the same room with Io.

But he had watched her plenty.

Just like he was doing right now, as she was chattering away with Axbridge, who, to Corbin's displeasure, spent almost as much time at Hastings House as he did at his own house, which was—unfortunately— just across the square from them.

Not only had Axbridge and Hastings become fast friends, but the insufferable peer seemed to seek out the company of Lady Io and the two could often be seen sitting off to the side together at any number of functions, bickering. Or at least Io bickered while Axbridge just smirked haughtily.

The only positive thing Corbin could see in their odd association was that it appeared to be platonic. Indeed, if he were to hazard a guess, he would have said that Lady Io latched on to Axbridge to placate her older brother and make him believe that she was, finally, falling into line.

If Hastings believed that his sister was interested in any sort of relationship with Axbridge then his old friend was barking up the wrong tree.

Lady Io already *had* a new lover and Corbin knew that because he'd followed her to their trysting place at the Boynton Hotel.

Corbin saw that he was holding his fork hard enough to cut ridges into his palm and loosened his grip.

It had been bad enough to control her headlong behavior in the country, but at least there she'd had the *somewhat* mellowing influence of her twin.

Corbin had quickly discovered that Lord Balthazar was not the villain the press had painted him. Indeed, the young lord was, in reality, a thoughtful and steadfast man.

Io: The Shrew

Lady Io, on the other hand, seemed bent on destroying her reputation—and that of her family—with alarming celerity.

Corbin had been tempted to tell Hastings of his sister's liaisons with Everard Gordon, the younger son of an earl who had pretensions to being a painter but was merely a lazy dabbler—not just in art, but also in various social issues.

Gordon and Lady Io had met four times—that Corbin knew of—at Boynton's, an expensive, exclusive hotel that was worryingly near Mayfair. Neither of them had bothered to do a thing to hide their assignations.

He suspected Miss Barrymore was aware of the meetings, although—after her cruelty toward Lord Balthazar and Mrs. Dryden—he was no longer in her confidence as he had politely but firmly made it clear to her that he was not an ally in her cause, which appeared to be discrediting all the Hales except Hastings. Indeed, it shamed Corbin to recall that he had ever agreed with the woman.

But his loyalty to Hastings was unshakable. As little as he wanted to justify Lady Io's accusations of *tattling,* Corbin feared he might just have to do exactly that if her relationship with Gordon was not brought to a halt.

Her hatred for him now would be nothing to how she would feel about him if he did such a thing.

Why did the thought of an irreparable breach between himself and Lady Io not make Corbin feel relief, but deep, grinding remorse?

Chapter 17

Later That Same Night

Io was in her dressing gown and had already sent Moira to bed by ten o'clock. She was looking forward to an early night for a change, when the door to her bedchamber flew open and Edith blazed into her room, garbed in finery for the Merrivale ball, which is where everyone except Io was going after dinner.

"By all means, come in, Edith," Io said with heavy irony, striding to close the door the other woman had left hanging open. For some reason, she suspected this conversation was not one she would want the servants to hear.

Edith whirled on her. "I have just come from Hastings's study, where he told me about the bargain he struck with you."

"Would you like to have a seat?" Io asked sweetly, gesturing to the seating area in front of the cozy fire.

Edith closed the distance between them. They were very close in height and Io found herself staring into the eyes of a woman who honestly looked maddened to the point of insanity.

Concern flooded her at the other woman's obvious distress. "Edith, perhaps you should—"

"You are a slut."

Io's jaw dropped—not so much because Edith would call her that, but because she was flabbergasted that the moralizing prude even knew the word.

She couldn't help laughing. "Coming from you, that is not exactly an insult."

It was Edith's turn to stare open-mouthed. But she regained her wits with admirable speed. "I know about you and Everard Gordon—I daresay fully half of London knows what you two have been getting up to."

Io seriously doubted that. But she felt no compunction to set the other woman straight about her connection with Mr. Gordon. "Is that what you've come here to say? What a waste of your time. Why don't you go and tell Zeus?"

"His Grace already knows and has done for weeks."

That surprised her. "So, if Zeus has not said anything to me, then what objection should you have to my friendship?"

"*Friendship,*" Edith sneered, her beautiful face ugly at that moment. "Is that what you are calling it? You must know that Gordon has been investigated and is under suspicion for seditious activities."

"That is in the past and he was cleared of all those charges. Or didn't your sterling sources bother to mention that part?"

"Where there is smoke, there is fire."

"That is very pithy, Edith. Did you just coin it?"

"The truth is that you choose to cavort with traitors and society's outcasts and your brother is so enthralled by the illusion of family that he has let his better judgment slip and allows you to drag his name and honor through the mud by indulging your treasonous leanings."

"Why do I have a hard time imagining you saying those same words to Zeus?"

Edith's flush told her it had been a killing hit.

But again, the other woman rallied.

Io recalled reading somewhere that you could judge a person by their enemies. If that were truly the case then Io was fearsome indeed to have attracted a foe like Edith Barrymore.

"His Grace may be distracted right now, but Mr. Masterson, I assure you, is not," Edith retorted with a malicious smirk. "He has a low tolerance for consorting with scum like Gordon."

Any amusement Io had been feeling was gone in a blink. "Oh. I see— he is your source on my liaison, is he?"

"There are still men you cannot corrupt."

Io wondered what Edith would say if she'd been a fly on the wall during her exhilarating last exchange with Masterson on the night of Eva's birthday ball, when reserved, proper Corbin Masterson had demonstrated his taste—at least sexually—aligned better with Io's than any man she had ever met.

Indeed, they aligned so perfectly that Io had made a concerted effort to never be alone in a room with Masterson ever again. Not because she feared what he would do to her body, but because she feared what she might do to *his*. Io knew she wouldn't just let him do whatever he wanted to her. She would *beg* him to have his way.

Of course she kept all that to herself but couldn't help taunting, "Oh, and I suppose you believe Mr. Masterson is one of those incorruptible men, do you?"

"No doubt you think to tempt Mr. Masterson off his path of righteousness with your crude, common appeal, but you will fail. He has fallen once, but it has been many years. And a woman like *you* is hardly likely—"

"What are you talking about?" Io asked, even though she feared she would regret it.

The hateful sparkle in Edith's gaze confirmed that fear. "Mr. Masterson was in seminary when he got a young woman of loose morals and no family connections pregnant. He did not marry the female of course—nor did he accept the woman's claim that her daughter was his spawn. Although Mr. Masterson is illegitimate, his family name on his father's side is an ancient and well-respected one. He was forced to leave seminary, but it was fortunate for him that his father overlooked his lapse and paid for him to go to Harvard. Thanks to his friendship with Hastings, Mr. Masterson had a second chance. To my knowledge, he has not had such a lapse in judgment again."

Io reeled at this information, utterly off balance. "What happened to the woman and her daughter?"

Edith sneered. "You *would* care about such creatures, being one of them yourself."

With Io still in shock, the other woman pivoted on her heel and left after getting the last word, and a painful one at that.

Io: The Shrew

Io despised many things about Corbin Masterson—his allegiance to Edith, for a start—but she had never believed that he would be so hypocritical as to impregnate a woman and then shirk responsibility for his child. Especially given his own background!

She paced her room, profoundly disappointed to have discovered this new, and repulsive, facet of his character.

But her shock quickly turned to anger. And then to vengeful fury.

How *dare* he try and make Io feel like a whore when he was far, far worse?

Io shoved her feet into slippers and flung on her favorite old wool shawl before storming from her chambers.

Just as they'd been at Hastings Park, Masterson's rooms were not far from Zeus's, both of which were at the opposite end of the house from Io.

She saw no servants on her way to his chambers and wouldn't have cared if she had.

She rapped loudly on his door. When he did not immediately open it, she wondered if he'd accompanied Eva and Edith to the Merrivale ball, something he did far too frequently for Io's liking since they'd come to London.

Liar. You love having his gaze on you as you flirt your way through London ballrooms.

Well, that was true.

Io was just about to knock again when the door opened and Masterson appeared, garbed in everything except his tailcoat.

His jaw dropped and his nostrils flared in anger. "Are you mad to be coming to me *again?*"

And then, unbelievably, he began to shut his door.

Io shoved her foot in the gap and leaned her body against the solid slab of wood. "Open up and let me in or I shall make an ungodly racket, Masterson."

For a moment she thought he would opt for crushing her foot rather than allowing her into his chambers.

But then he made a noise of furious exasperation and flung open the door.

Io smirked in triumph and strolled into his room at her leisure.

He quietly shut the door, crossed his arms over his chest, and leaned back against it. "I won't offer you a seat because this—whatever *this* is—will be brief. Now. What do you need so desperately that you would come here at this time of night? Miss Barrymore and your siblings are gone, but the duke is in his library with Axbridge as we speak."

"I have long believed you to be an insufferable prude, Masterson. But not until today did I think you were a hypocrite and a despoiler."

His frown deepened. "What do you mean?"

"I think you know."

His gray eyes narrowed. "Indulge me."

"The woman who holds your leash told me about your ejection from seminary and the reason for it."

If she had believed him chilly before, he was now a wall of ice.

"What, exactly did Miss Barrymore say?" he asked quietly.

Io hated that he didn't deny his relationship with Edith, but his reaction was not the anger and masculine bluster she had expected.

A whisp of worry snaked its way into her belly. Something told her that he deserved to know exactly what Edith had said, and without any derision or embellishment this time.

"She said you got a woman pregnant and were kicked out of seminary. She said you refused to marry the woman and left her and your child to their fates."

His jaw flexed and his eyelids lowered, but not before she saw a flare of hot rage behind the ice. "And you believe her."

It was not a question. But…

"I don't want to believe her, Masterson. But is she wrong?"

"Why are you asking? Do you need another weapon to wield against me? Proof—other than what I have already given you—that I have feet of clay?"

"Damn it! Tell me. Is. She. Wrong."

He stared at her with such brooding hostility that she thought he would kick her out of his room.

But then, he said, "Only partially."

***

After the way Miss Barrymore had behaved toward Lord Balthazar and Mrs. Dryden, Corbin was not surprised that she had disseminated such information about him. But he *was* deeply disappointed. He'd not believed her to be a cruel woman. But then perhaps she had hoped to destroy the attraction that blazed between him and Lady Io. Corbin was no idiot—well, not usually—he knew that Hastings, and probably everyone else in their small circle, was also aware of the attraction.

Or whatever it was.

Corbin had never wanted to talk to anyone about Emma before. But, for some reason, he did now.

"I did get a woman pregnant," he confessed, wincing at how bald the words sounded out loud. "But Miss Barrymore has the story the other way around. I did not refuse to marry her, nor did I abandon her. The woman in question was not free to marry *me."*

He was vaguely amused by the astonishment on her face.

"No, it is not what you are thinking. The self-righteous seminary student did not commit adultery with a woman who was living with her husband in holy matrimony. But there is a grain of truth to it. Although I did not know it at the time, I committed adultery with a woman who had been abandoned by her husband."

He'd not thought about his relationship with Emma in years. But now that he was forced to mention her, he felt the same regret he always did.

"I did not abandon Emma or my son."

"A son? But Edith said you had a daughter."

"No. I had a son and both died in childbed."

Io's jaw dropped, and then her face crumpled so suddenly it was shocking to watch. "Oh, Corbin. I am so sorry."

His body's reaction to hearing his Christian name on her tongue was inconvenient, not to mention inappropriate, especially given the somber subject matter. But Corbin had long been convinced that he could spring an erection in the middle of a funeral as long as Io Hale was there.

"Why would Edith say that you had a daughter?" she asked.

"I suspect she has her information muddled. The little girl Miss Barrymore was talking about is Lizzy and she is not my daughter."

"She is the one you gave the book to—my book?"

"Yes." Corbin allowed his chagrin to show. "I must admit I'm not pleased that anyone knows of my contact with Lizzy because I have taken pains to keep our association private."

"Why? Who is she?"

Corbin cut her an exasperated look. "Please. Don't hold back."

To her credit, she blushed. "I'm sorry. I should not be—"

"Lizzy is the natural daughter of my half-brother, Richard."

Furrows marred her smooth brow. "The same one who has your business?"

He had to admit the words *your business* warmed him. "That is the only brother I have. At least that I know of," he amended dryly. His father had liked women; it wouldn't surprise him to one day discover more siblings.

"But…" She broke off, her teeth sinking into that plush lower lip that tormented him in his dreams.

"You want to know why I am caring for my brother's child and taking pains to hide it?" he guessed.

She nodded.

"I'd like to say I'm doing it because I am a decent, moral man who tries to do what is right. But I'm sure a large part of my motivation is guilt—guilt that I wasn't able to save my own child and his mother. In any case, it is little enough money and Lizzy is well worth the amount and more." He only wished he had more to give her. "Her mother died four years ago and since that time she has been living with an elderly couple. They are kind, but they are only looking after her for the money I send. As to why I try to keep my connection with Lizzy a secret," he sighed. "That is because my brother would likely take her away and make sure I never saw her again if he knew I was caring for her. Not because he loves her, but because he hates me."

Her eyes grew glassy with unshed tears. "I am so sorry for believing the worst of you."

Corbin blinked, bewildered by her emotion. "Er, thank you."

"I should have known you were not the sort of man who could do such a thing."

Corbin tried to find words to respond, but all he could think about was her current involvement with Everard Gordon, a man suspected of spreading sedition. And also the man who was her lover.

The second of which you consider the far greater crime, is that not true?

To his shame, it *was* true.

Ask her if it is true, you fool! Now is your chance.

If he asked her, he knew her expression would change instantaneously.

If he asked her, she would go back to openly loathing him, while the look she was giving him now was almost…tender.

You are a coward.

When it came to Io Hale, he was.

"Good night, Masterson," she said, robbing him of his chance to wreck the tenuous truce between them. "Don't worry, I will make sure nobody is about before I go," she said, her smile weary rather than sarcastic or combative.

Corbin roused himself to get to the door first and open it for her, watching mutely as she slipped out of his room and disappeared, leaving nothing but an ache in his chest and the faint smell of lavender in his nostrils.

And if Corbin's chest felt as if it had just been kicked in as he watched her leave? Well, he would get over it.

He always did.

Chapter 18

London
The Boynton Hotel
Eleven Days Later

orbin glanced out the big picture window at the end of the long hotel corridor. The storm that everyone had been expecting had finally arrived. Trees were whipping back and forth in the wind in the small park below and there were snow flurries. It made him shiver just looking.

A door opened at the far end of the hallway and Corbin quickly stepped back inside the linen closet, not fully closing the door behind him. He felt not only like a pervert, but also like the biggest fool in London as he watched through the gap. A couple—not Lady Io and Everard Gordon—left their hotel room and walked toward the stairs, laughing and chatting like normal people. Not like a desperate man who hid in linen closets for hours on end and spied on a woman he coveted.

Once the pair had gone, Corbin slipped out of his hiding place, which he'd bribed a servant to use, and leaned against the closet door, his gaze yet again turning toward the window and the snowstorm.

It was yet another day he had wasted shadowing Lady Io Hale and her lover.

It might be cold, but at least you have your jealousy and fury to keep you warm.

Corbin scowled but could not deny it.

He was yanked from his brooding by the sight of Lady Io's hotel room door opening and Everard Gordon—social scourge and infamous provocateur—stepping out. He was immediately joined by Lady Io *in her dressing* gown.

Corbin ground his teeth at the sight and watched with growing rage as neither of them made any effort at all to disguise the fact that Io—an unmarried lady—was alone in a hotel room with a scoundrel.

In her dressing gown.

Io: The Shrew

When she stood on her toes to kiss Gordon's cheek Corbin's vision went black and for one irrational moment, he thought his head might actually explode.

When his vision cleared, he realized, belatedly, that he had not ducked back into his hidey-hole.

And Lady Io was leaning against her doorframe, arms crossed, smirk visible from even this distance.

Corbin was torn. Storm directly to Io and throttle her? Or follow Gordon and beat him to death. Slowly.

He chose the former. After all, he knew where Gordon lived and it would be far better to commit battery at the man's lair rather than in the corridor of one of London's most exclusive hotels.

As he strode toward her, her dark eyebrows arched and she gave him a look of unholy glee. "Fancy seeing *you* here."

"What the hell do you think you are doing?" he retorted, too furious to lower his voice.

She winced and glanced up and down the empty hallway.

"Oh, *now* you are worried about attracting attention," he raged.

She grabbed his arm and yanked him into her room, slamming the door behind him.

Corbin could not hold his anger in check for another second. "I know you have no care for your reputation, but a gentleman should make every effort not to cast shame on a woman. At least not one he respects or admires. By being with you in a hotel—alone—Gordon has irreparably damaged your reputation, my lady. And if—"

"*You* are alone with me in my hotel room, Masterson."

Corbin's jaw sagged.

"That is—that is *different*," he sputtered.

"Yes, it is. But not for the reasons you think."

"Why? Because I am not your *lover* but merely your brother's employee?" he lashed out, closing the distance between them and not stopping until his body was pressed against hers, his hands like manacles around her upper arms.

"No. Because *he* isn't."

Corbin goggled. "He isn't *what?*"

"My lover."

He remained riveted in place.

Lady Io shrugged and he realized he must be hurting her.

When he released her, she tugged on her sash and removed her robe.

Corbin gaped; she was fully dressed beneath the dressing gown. That seemed…odd.

He looked up from her staid navy wool walking costume and met her mocking gaze. He cleared his throat, scrambling for his outrage, finding only scraps remaining. Still, he pressed on. "If he is not your lover, then what was he doing in this room?"

"Two things. One, we were talking about the article I'm writing for his magazine. And two—as you have been so devoted to stalking me—I decided that I should use the opportunity to make you jealous."

"*Jealous,*" he roared. "Oh, you only wish that were true. For your inf—"

"I know it is, Corbin."

His mouth hung open as his eyes followed her fingers, which were unbuttoning her bodice.

"What are you doing?" he demanded sternly, although to be truthful it sounded more like an asthmatic wheeze.

"What does it look like I'm doing?"

He swallowed as she exposed the hint of a very plain chemise.

Corbin yanked his gaze back up, his eyes narrowing. "You are *torturing me,*" he hissed and then stepped closer and put both hands around her slender throat. "You are *always* torturing me." His fingers flexed. "It would be *so* easy to choke the life out of you."

"Do it," she taunted, tilting her chin back and baring her throat for his hands. "I know you want to."

His hands tightened and her breathing roughened, her gaze as provoking and defiant as ever. "I should," he muttered. And then words he had never intended to speak spilled out of his mouth. "I should fuck you—get you out of my system—and then throttle you."

Her eyes blazed and her body went pliant at his crude words. Before he could open his mouth to beg her pardon for his unforgivable crude lapse, she gave a mocking laugh and said, "I suppose that is better than throttling me and *then* fucking me."

Had he been thinking about apologizing?

"But tell me, sir, do you think one *fuck* will be enough to exorcise me?"

Oh, her wicked, wicked mouth and the words that came out of it!

And what those words did to his cock.

You are a man, not a beast.

Corbin gritted his jaw hard enough to crack his teeth and reluctantly released her throat. "You are the very devil herself."

As she had done twice before, she laid her hand on his chest. But the expression was far different than those other times—not sly and challenging, but almost…yearning. "You must know that I want you."

"Damnation, woman," he said, his voice thick with desire.

She smiled, and it was a wry expression. "I think you want me, too."

"With the heat of a thousand suns," he blurted.

She laughed. And then she turned on her heel. "Then shut up, come to bed, and take me."

***

Io genuinely did not think Masterson would follow her. Indeed, she'd been far more certain that he would strangle her as he'd looked like a man demented and nothing like the cool, implacable, moral pillar of society she had met all those weeks ago.

She unbuttoned her gown enough that she could shimmy out of it as she walked from the suite's entryway to the bedchamber, pausing long enough to step out of the dress, leaving it on the floor behind her.

When she reached the bed, she wore only her shift, hose, and garters.

Io turned around, not sure of what she would find.

Masterson was only a foot away, his gray eyes so hot they were all but smoking.

Io watched the man in front of her war with himself. Morality clubbed desire over the head, but desire fought dirty and kicked the legs right out from under morality.

"You witch," he snarled, and then moved like a blur.

When his arms closed around her and his mouth crushed hers, Io melted into his embrace.

He was hard beneath her, the heat of him searing her through her thin chemise. His large hand slid over her body as if becoming reacquainted after an absence of years.

Io surrendered to his kisses, allowing him to set the pace. He plundered her with a deep, passionate desire that his normally cool, controlled façade belied. She had long known a man lived beneath the layers of proper suiting and stern convention, but she'd never dared to hope that she would one day hold him in her arms.

He pulled away, breathing heavily, and plucked at her chemise. "I want this off."

She shivered at his heated, hungry tone. "And I want *you* naked," she said, lifting her chemise over her head.

The noise he made as his eyes swept up and down her body turned her already weak knees to jelly.

"You are exquisite," he said gruffly, raising ink-black eyes to hers.

Io was not shy about her body and knew she was attractive enough, but his consuming gaze made her feel like a goddess.

As much as she liked his admiration, she wanted to do some gawking herself. She jerked her chin at him, "Now it is your turn," she said, sounding far cooler than she felt. "Let me help you." She stepped close enough to work the buttons on his cuffs.

He paused at her order, but only briefly, his deft, elegant fingers tossing his hat onto a chair, his hand flying over the buttons of his overcoat, coat, and waistcoat and shrugging them all off as if they were one garment.

Io laughed at his haste and he startled for a moment, but then his lips twitched slightly as he saw the humor in the situation. She finished with his cuffs and quickly moved to the row of buttons down his chest while he toed off his boots.

When the last button on his shirt was unfastened, he shrugged his shoulders, the movement causing a fascinating cascade of muscles beneath his pale skin.

She allowed herself to gorge on him, drinking in the thick, chiseled slabs of his pectoral muscles before meandering down to the tight ridges of his abdomen, her sex clenching at the line of fine blond down that disappeared beneath the black trousers currently being unfastened.

And then his drawers and trousers hit the floor and the erection she had been fantasizing about sprang free.

"Hello there," she murmured, instinctively reaching for his thick ruddy shaft.

Masterson caught her wrist and she looked up to find him giving her a pained look.

"What is it?" she asked.

"If you touch me, I will humiliate myself."

Io laughed, both flattered and amused at his declaration. "Hmmm, I see. Well, then fetch a condom and we can make this first time quick." Her eyelids lowered. "And the next one more leisurely."

He frowned. "Condom?"

Her good humor fled. "Have you never heard of them?" she asked sweetly.

He flushed. "I have no diseases."

"They are not only prophylactics, Masterson. They are also for my protection. Against pregnancy."

His jaw flexed and he stared at her.

"Oh," Io said, taking a step away from him. "*I* see. If we were to fuck, then marriage would speedily follow." She cocked her head and asked with mock innocence. "Or are we already betrothed because you've seen my bare breasts and sex and I've had your penis in my mouth? And if we are engaged then it naturally follows that I will immediately wish to be plowed and seeded by you."

His face turned a dull brick red and he reached down and yanked the drawers and trousers he'd just dropped a scant moment before.

When he stood, his expression was as cold as a winter wind coming off the Great Lakes. "I. Apologize," he said, enunciating each word because he knew that she *hated* such masculine chivalry.

He made short work of buttoning his trousers and ruthlessly shoved his feet back into his shoes.

Here you go again, subverting your own desires with that razor-sharp tongue of yours.

The words were like a splash of icy water—both waking her up and cooling her sudden burst of temper.

"Oh, no you don't," she said when Masterson snatched up his shirt and began to shrug into it. She stepped up to him and claimed his hard, frowning mouth, wrapping her arms around his neck and pulling him lower.

For one horrible second that seemed to last a lifetime he did not move—not to push her away, but also not to return her kiss.

And then he growled—a savage noise she would never have thought he was capable of making—and seized her in a crushing embrace.

Io released his neck and shoved her hands between their bodies, her fingers fumbling on the buttons of his trousers.

He groaned and grabbed her, leaving the undressing to her as he worshipped her body with his hands.

Only when she'd unbuttoned his trousers and shoved them down with his drawers did she break away and mutter, "Shoes."

Once again, he toed off his polished shoes, which had likely been ruined by today's cruel treatment. When he was naked, she held him at arm's length, holding firm to his bulging biceps when he tried to get to her. "Stand still, Corbin. I want to see you."

One moment she was staring at him and the next she was flying through the air. Io gave an undignified shriek as she landed on the bed.

"You will issue no more orders today, my lady. At least none that I will obey," he added darkly.

"But I—"

"I've had all I am going to take from you. On your back. *Now*," he snarled as he stalked toward the bed.

Io shivered at the raw domination in his voice and decided she liked it too much to defy him. Even so, she took her time obeying him. Just because.

Only when she was positioned the way he wanted did she look up and meet his crazed eyes as he loomed over her, his chest rising and falling far faster than was usual for the tightly laced Mr. Masterson. "Spread your thighs," he barked.

Her lips parted in shock.

"If I have to repeat myself, I will—"

Io quickly complied, curious and excited to see what would happen next.

Corbin yanked the low bench from the dressing table over, sat down, and then lowered his head between her thighs.

Any worry she'd had that he might not know what he was about fled at the first touch of his tongue.

Io was beyond stunned. She would have wagered a year's allowance that Corbin Masterson had never even heard of any sexual act beyond that involving a penis and vagina.

Sometimes, she thought, arching her back and moaning, it was nice to be proven wrong.

***

It had been ages since Corbin had wanted to engage in such an intimate act with a woman. But he'd been starving for Io Hale for what felt like years.

Part of him knew he'd be shocked by his coarse behavior later, when he wasn't consumed by lust, but his actions and tone had been just what she wanted.

Besides, he wouldn't have been able to temper himself if he'd tried.

And he was going to make this proud, arrogant woman beg him to make her scream his name.

She was so wet for him—so eager—that it knocked any vestiges of sense from his head.

Corbin teased her little nub just enough to make her shudder and murmur and then he drifted away, exploring the rest of her, licking and nibbling her outer and then inner lips before settling over her tight entrance, probing her in a manner that was suggestive of what he was going to do to her next.

Her hands slid into his hair. "Masterson… please."

He smirked, closed his lips around her pearl, and sucked.

"Yessss," she hissed, thrusting herself against his mouth while her hand pushed him lower.

Corbin released her, amused by her groan of disappointment and the way she tried to chase his tongue as he resumed exploring the rest of her.

Not until she growled, sounding just like an enraged mink he'd once heard while he'd been in the far north, did he look up and meet her furious gaze.

"Corbin," she said, making his name a quiet threat.

"Hmm?" he hummed, lightly licking.

"I am not amused."

He burst out laughing, earning a scowl. "I'm terribly sorry," he lied. "Am I doing something wrong? Why don't you instruct me?"

"You know what I want!"

"Tell me anyway," he taunted, using the very tip of his tongue to rub a part of her he knew would loosen her resolve and demolish her pride.

Her eyelids fluttered and she groaned. "My God. Just give me a damned orgasm."

He raised his eyebrows.

"Please," she snarled.

Corbin sucked the scowl right off her face, easily working her responsive body toward a climax. When she was lifting her hips off the bed and he could feel the contractions building for release deep inside her, he again pulled back.

Her eyes popped open, her look one of utter disbelief.

Corbin smiled. "Now, ask me again. Sweetly, this time. Like a good girl would."

*****

Io was not nearly as surprised by Corbin's silky command as she was by her body's reaction to it.

Judging by the smug look on his face—which was twice as attractive as usual with his red, slick lips—he'd felt her body gathering for release and had purposely pulled away to deprive her.

The *demon*.

"Like a *good girl?* I suppose you will be wanting me to call you *sir*, next?"

His eyelids, already drooping, lowered even more. "*Masterson* will do nicely until I come up with something better."

Io had experience with men—more than most women her age and probably more than most men—but this, as the sailors on her brother's ocean liner might have said, was uncharted territory.

Who could have guessed that staid, conservative Corbin Masterson should have been marked by a warning sign: *Here be monsters*.

What a delightful surprise.

Io's body softened before her resolve. Long before. But neither took too long.

"Please…Masterson… won't you suck my clitoris and let me come?

His stunned expression was as satisfying as the feel of his hot, skilled mouth lowering over her sex.

Well, almost.

*****

Corbin reveled at the shudders that shook Io's lush body, a feeling of achievement flooding him at having given this clever, taunting, demanding woman not just one, but two consecutive climaxes.

Now that she was sated, Corbin could please himself and take his time, slowly licking all evidence of her passion from her flushed body, carefully avoiding her sensitive bundle of nerves.

Clitoris was a word he'd always thought of as too clinical and sterile to describe the charming little bead of flesh. But then he had never heard it spoken by Io Hale before, either.

Please…Masterson… won't you suck my clitoris and let me come?

Corbin's eyes almost rolled out of his head just thinking the words. Words that surely deserved to be immortalized in stone.

He explored her silky petals until he reached a place he desperately wished to be, gently spearing her opening with his tongue, groaning at the rich taste of her.

When she did not stop him, Corbin settled into a steady rhythm, probing her a little deeper each time, his brain—normally an uninteresting, prosaic place to be—crowding with all the erotic, and even deviant, thoughts of everything he would do to her.

Corbin didn't recognize himself. He felt like a stranger in his own mind.

And he liked it.

He also liked *this*. He could stay between her thighs all day long.

Corbin had almost laughed hysterically when willful, wayward Io Hale had obeyed his command to spread her legs, opening herself without hesitation.

Who would have believed it?

And then later, when she'd begged him so sweetly…

He growled at the memory of it. Corbin had been called Masterson all his life—through boarding school, college, the war, and his career. It wasn't his father's name—men did not give their bastards their surnames—but his mother's. He'd never been ashamed of it, but neither had he been particularly glad of it. Always in the past it had been a badge of otherness proclaiming that he was not his father's real son. Not a real member of the group he was part of. Not the sort of man that any decent woman would want to marry.

But the way Io had said it? It had sounded like the most sensual word in the world.

Listen to yourself! a voice inside him scoffed. *You are smitten.*

Corbin had no problem ignoring the voice for once. Instead, he slid deeper, seeing how much he could get away with, tonguing her deeply, until his nose was nestled at the base of her clitoris.

She shifted, slowly pushing up on her elbows. Rather than look shy after screaming out her climax—*climaxes,* he mentally amended—her eyes were hooded and she was smiling even more wickedly than usual. Which was saying something.

"Are you going to stay down there all day?" she teased.

"I will if I please," he retorted.

She crooked a finger at him. "I like this—but we can come back to it later. Right now, I want to feel that thick cock of yours inside me."

Corbin choked on his own spit and had to sit up, wheezing as she laughed.

She grinned, unabashed. "I'm sorry. Was that vulgar?"

He could only shake his head, his eyes blurring with tears from his hacking.

She reached down and took his hand, drawing him up on the bed, and rubbing his chest soothingly while he caught his breath.

Corbin kept expecting her to claw or bite or insult him, but she merely stroked him almost…lovingly.

He was almost sorry when he stopped coughing like an idiot and no longer required her soothing patting.

But then she slid her hand down to his achingly hard shaft and he forgot all about gentle soothing.

"*Mmm,*" she hummed, manipulating his shaft every bit as expertly as he did.

Just what did they teach these women at Canoga?

Corbin didn't want to think of that now. Instead, he gave himself up to the pleasure of her hot hand, his hips gently thrusting.

"You are beautiful."

His eyes, which had drifted shut, snapped open like Roman shades. *"Beautiful?"* he scoffed. "Men aren't beautiful."

"You are. Your chiseled handsome face, your hard, masculine body, and *this* magnificent thing."

Corbin gulped loudly.

She grinned at the mortifying sound and then squeezed his shaft so hard that it was almost painful.

Just the way he liked.

In fact, it was too much the way he liked it.

"I need to be inside of you," he said gruffly. "Before I give you yet another reason to mock me."

She laughed and laid back. "Put a condom on and fuck me, Masterson. There is one in my satchel," she added when he hesitated.

Corbin opened his mouth to ask what in the hell she was doing traveling around with johnnies in her bag but decided to leave it for later.

He found them tucked inside the folded pamphlets she always gave away—no matter the place or time—and heaved a sigh of relief, grateful that she did not seem to have brought them for Gordon.

He tore it open and was about to put it on when she called out, "Come here and do it. I want to watch."

Corbin bit back a groan. He would never make it through the next five minutes without ejaculating and embarrassing himself.

As things turned out, he embarrassed himself a lot sooner than that.

He took the *rubber* out of its packet and perhaps he gripped it too hard or pulled it too tightly. Whatever the reason, it tore.

Io's mesmerizing eyes narrowed as she stared up at him, comprehension dawning. "You've never used one of those before, have you?"

Corbin wanted to lie—to keep the sparkle in her gaze—but he could not bring himself to do it. "No."

She looked genuinely shocked. "Never?"

He ground his teeth. *"No."*

Io: The Shrew

"Corbin Masterson," she said, making his name sound like an especially vulgar epithet. "You are such a typical, selfish, thoughtless man. If not for your own protection, you should always wear one for your lover."

He sighed and absorbed her abuse rather than take umbrage and storm from the room as one or both of them had done far too many times in the past.

"Are you finished mocking me yet?" he asked with exaggerated patience.

She ignored his question. "The only way you will *ever* put your tallywag into my nettle bed is with it covered in rubber."

Rather than lose his erection at her carping, not to mention her crude cant for human reproductive organs, Corbin got harder than ever and something else happened as he absorbed her abuse—something visceral and *shocking*.

He briefly closed his eyes, appalled as he put a name to the emotion that had been tormenting him for weeks—nay, months. Corbin had gone and done the most foolish thing in his life.

He didn't just want Io Hale. He'd fallen in love with the beautiful shrew.

Fortunately, Io didn't appear to notice the way the world had suddenly shifted on its axis.

"Get another rubber, Masterson," she barked. "This time I'll put it on you."

***

Masterson had looked so chastened, so guilty, about the condom that Io hadn't the heart to keep haranguing him—a fact that would have amazed her siblings, who wouldn't believe that she could be anything less than militant about contraception and prophylaxis.

He obediently returned to the bed with another condom. "Come closer, Masterson. Your trouser serpent is impressively long—it is my arms that are too short to reach you," she teased.

He gave a startled laugh, but came closer, a blush creeping up his truly splendid chest to the strong column of his throat. "Trouser serpent?"

"My sister is working on compiling the world's greatest lexicon of cant. I have learned a few things along the way."

"Most of them naughty, I'll wager."

"You would probably make money off that bet," she admitted absently, surprised and pleased that he was still as hard as he'd been before this lesson in responsible coitus. "Umm, what a delicious love wand you have, sir." Io smirked as he gasped—whether at the ridiculous term or her firm stroke, she didn't know.

His thick shaft jerked in her hand and the copious amount of pre-ejaculate flowing from the lovely fat crown told her that poor Mr. Masterson was on the edge, so Io had mercy on him and quickly pulled the thin rubber sheath over his length.

She had not been exaggerating when she'd complimented his size: he was stretching the device to the limit. The manufacturer needed to make more sizes, that much was clear.

When she looked up, she saw that he was staring at his cock, his teeth snagging his lower lip, his brow furrowed.

He looked... *adorable.*

Adorable?

I must be going soft in the head.

When he raised his dark gaze to meet hers a powerful bolt of desire shot to her core at the raw need she saw in his eyes. "How do you want me?" she asked in a husky voice.

***

Corbin was a bit dizzy from the emotions that had battered him over the past ten minutes.

Arousal, shame, embarrassment, more shame, continued arousal— against all logical odds—deeper shame, and, finally, so much desire he was surprised he hadn't already lost control.

How did he want her?

Good God.

"Are you trying to kill me?" he muttered climbing onto the bed and facing her. "I suppose it doesn't surprise you that I would choose the most mundane position."

She grinned. "*Nothing* is mundane with me, Masterson."

Hell. Was he now going to spring an erection whenever anyone said his name?

She slid her hands around his neck, her gaze suddenly softening. "I want you inside me, Corbin."

He took his shaft in hand and slid it through her flatteringly wet sex. It felt different—muffled—to have something between the most sensitive part of his body and the object of his desire.

Her legs spread wider in invitation and Corbin took her message to heart, lining himself up with heaven and then pushing slowly.

"*Mmm*," she hummed, tipping her pelvis toward him.

"You are so *tight*," he muttered without thinking, and then met her gaze.

Rather than be offended by his crude pronouncement, she looked sensually expectant. As if she liked what he'd said and wanted more.

Corbin had felt deeply for Emma, but their sexual relations—or at least his seventeen-year-old memory of them—had been nothing like this.

He did not stop until he'd filled her and his balls were resting against her hot, wet skin.

She tightened her arms and held him—not that he wanted to go—and whispered, "Stay a moment. The stretch is delicious, and this feels lovely."

It was beyond lovely. It was an epiphany.

Corbin felt a stab of guilt using a word typically reserved for religious experiences. But then…this was life-altering. Not just the physical sensation—which was, admittedly, amazing—but the act of bedding a woman as an equal. Of *being* bedded, himself.

Her arms went slack, and Corbin began to move.

Chapter 19

Several Hours Later

The sun was going down when Corbin woke with a start, confusion flooding him as he looked around him.

The first thing he noticed was Lady Io Hale. Completely dressed, sitting in a chair, watching him.

He sat bolt upright, saw he was naked, and yanked a sheet over his groin. "I cannot believe I fell so deeply asleep," he said, more to himself.

"You were exhausted after all that exertion," she said her teasing tone making him blush like a schoolgirl.

"Why didn't you wake me?"

"Because I was thinking."

Why did her words give him chills?

"I greatly enjoyed this afternoon, Masterson. I want to do it again."

Corbin's jaw dropped at her words, which were the last he'd ever expected to hear. "Then you agree to—"

"Meet you once a week. Here. Until we can work this…whatever it is between us, out of our systems."

The joy he'd been feeling was instantly snuffed. "That was not what I had in mind," he said when it was obvious she wanted an answer.

Her eyes narrowed. "Please tell me you weren't thinking along other, more boring and predictable lines.

"As I'm naturally so *boring* and *predictable* you will have to define that more clearly for me," he said icily, flinging away the sheet and swinging his feet off the bed.

He glanced around for his clothing, which he vaguely recalled throwing to the four winds, and spotted all his garments draped neatly across the back of a chair. Corbin knew he had her to thank for it, which only, irrationally, made him angrier.

As did her eyes on him as he crossed the room. A woman of virtue would have looked away from his nudity. Not so Io Hale.

"You know what I mean," she said as he jerked on his drawers first. "Marriage. Babies. Family. Me as your legal chattel. That sort of boringness."

Corbin did not turn until he'd pulled on both his trousers and shirt and had buttoned up the former. It was a good decision because his molten fury had turned to cold, cutting sarcasm by the time he finally faced her.

"Ah. I see," he said, fastening his cuffs, an action that brought to mind, painfully, who had *un*fastened them.

"Do you?" she asked, squinting at him, as if genuinely interested. "Can you comprehend the sheer terror of giving your person, your *freedom*, and your very life into another's keeping? Tell me, Masterson. What would you do if the law said that when you married me, you became *my* possession? I could beat you, breed you, starve and lock you up, take away your children and your money, and control every facet of your life. Would you be so eager to be my husband?"

Her words hit him like a pallet of lumber dropped onto his chest.

Corbin wanted to say something flippant like, *not bloody likely*, but she deserved a genuine answer from him. And it was a simple one for him to formulate.

"No. I would not marry you, or anyone else," Corbin admitted, even though the words were bitter on his tongue.

Her lips parted and he watched as her righteous anger bled away. "Thank you for answering me honestly."

He did not want her gratitude. He wanted *her*, goddammit. Rather than admit that mortifying fact, he slipped on his waistcoat and said, "So then, what did you have in mind?"

"We meet here at the Boynton—or somewhere else you choose—once a week until we work each other from our systems."

Corbin was tempted to tell her that would be *never* for him. But half a loaf was better than none at all, wasn't it?

Except Lady Io Hale is not a loaf of bread. And you will likely feel pain equal to losing a limb when she tires of you.

He suspected that was true. He also suspected he would miss her until the end of his days.

And yet Corbin opened his mouth and said, "I agree. We will meet here. Every Wednesday."

Chapter 20

One Week Later

Io was so excited that she could not concentrate on the article about Canoga that she was finishing up for Everard Gordon's magazine.

Instead of working, she was fussing with her satchel, to which she had just added a few toiletries, in anticipation of her first Wednesday liaison. Or rather, the first she and Masterson had agreed-upon, rather than last week's *accidental* meeting.

Io allowed herself a brief smirk at how clever she'd been to get Masterson into that hotel room last week.

Knowing that she could see him on Wednesday—could cross verbal swords with him and feed her sensual hunger—had made the week's vapid activities far less unbearable. Indeed, she had gracefully capitulated to Eva's entreaties to attend a truly tedious ball and spent an extra evening socializing outside of the four she had promised Zeus.

But her waiting was almost over.

At three o'clock today she would slip from the house to allegedly attend a suffragette meeting and then an evening lecture on botany directly afterward. Moira would accompany her, although her maid would really be spending time with her own swain at a supper club and music hall. The two of them would meet up later at an agreed upon place and return to Hastings House together.

It was a great deal of subterfuge to endure just to engage in sex. At Canoga, nobody needed to sneak and hide. Her relationship with Lamar had taken place openly and was publicly acknowledged by everyone.

The dissolution of your relationship was equally public if you will remember…

Io gritted her teeth against the memory. *Of course I remember.*

She jolted at the sound of somebody rapping on her door. "Yes," she called, shaking off her odd, contemplative mood.

The door opened and one of the maids, Jilly, popped her head in. "His Grace asks that you join him in his study, my lady."

"Thank you," Io said, smiling at the servant, and then losing the expression immediately once the door had closed.

What in the world did her brother want *now*? And why did any summons from him always lead to conflict?

Io glanced at the clock and then sighed when she saw it was only a little after one-thirty. There was still plenty of time before she needed to leave.

When she arrived at her brother's study one of his snotty footmen opened the door without grilling her for a change.

With a sense of foreboding, she entered the large room.

The first thing she saw was Zeus rising from behind his desk.

The second was the man she was going to meet later that day.

And then she saw Zeus's fiancée and stopped short a few feet into the room. "Am I getting called onto the carpet?"

Her brother's pained look answered her question.

Io pointed at Edith. "If she stays then I go."

Zeus inhaled deeply, his almost colorless eyes fixed on Io for several seconds before he said, "Please excuse us, Edith."

Io wasn't the only one who was stunned. Edith's expression of shock was priceless. "But, John—"

Edith's poisonous cake hole shut with a snap when Zeus turned to face her. She nodded, obviously stung. "Very well," she said, her bearing stiffly regal as she stood. "I will leave you to your discussion." And then she sailed from the room, head held high.

Io's malevolent gaze turned to Masterson.

"Do not glare at Corbin," the duke said. "He is not the one who reported what you are doing."

Irrationally, that disclosure only made her glare harder at her lover before wrenching her gaze away and facing her brother. "If this is about Mr. Gordon you should know we are not, and have never been, lovers. I am only writing an article for Mr. Gordon's magazine. I am *not* financing any of his endeavors."

"This is not about Everard Gordon."

Io flung up her hands. "Then what else have I done now? Failed to speak to the correct people at yesterday's wretched tea party at the Countess of Morland's house? Or did I not give the correct curtsey to the Dowager Duchess of Sale?"

"I know how you have been spending your allowance."

It was not what she'd been expecting. "And?"

"And this money is for *you*, Io."

She shrugged. "Yes, I know. I *am* spending it."

"Why are you doing this?" Zeus asked, wearily.

"Are you really saying you don't agree with me donating money?"

"Putting aside the nature of the charities you have chosen to sponsor"—he glanced down at something on his desk and said—"organizations such as the, er, the Bluestocking Brigade, Society of Sappho, and the Ladies National Association for the Repeal of the Contagious Diseases Acts, to name but a few"—he looked up, "your allowance was intended for you to spend on yourself—for personal items and such."

"These expenditures *are* personal."

He sighed. "Do you want me to curtail your allowance?"

"Do what you feel you must," she retorted.

His nostrils pinched and his jaw tightened in a way that told her he was reining in his temper. That was unusual. Just like his best friend Masterson, Zeus normally exhibited as much emotion as a block of wood. Io wondered what was making him so tense of late.

Perhaps you are, a wry voice suggested.

Zeus massaged his temple with one hand. "If I offered to donate the same amount of money to similar charities on your behalf, would you spend your allowance on yourself from now on?"

"What could I possibly need? What could *any* of us need?" She gestured around at his study, which would not look out of place in Versailles. "Thanks to Edith's nagging, my dressing room is stuffed to overflowing and I have enough clothing for at least a hundred people."

"You don't need to buy gowns. What about books? Jaunts to the theater or a museum? Is there nothing that gives you pleasure?"

Io could not keep her eyes from sliding to Masterson. "There are a few things," she admitted. "But the sort of things that give me *pleasure*" she emphasized the word, amused by the hot color that infused her lover's face— "do not require money, Zeus."

Her older brother had long ago stopped flinching at his given name. When Io had learned he'd repudiated his real name and gone by *John* all his life, she had been determined to make him accept who he was: another son of Bates Hale, Jr., the same man who'd spawned the rest of them, but had only raised five of his children, discarding his eldest.

Her siblings thought Io's insistence on using Zeus's real name was merely to annoy the dignified man who sat before her—every inch a duke, in Io's opinion—but the truth was that only if a person owned a ridiculous name like *Zeus* or *Io*, did they truly understand what it meant to be one of the Hale siblings of Canoga.

"I am displeased that you will not spend such a trifling amount on yourself," Zeus said, pulling Io from her thoughts. "And I am also concerned that some of the organizations you've chosen—such as the Bluestocking Brigade—have funded violent clashes with authorities—"

"I never intended my donation to be used in such a way," Io interrupted. "I have told the women in charge that I will not be giving them more money." Indeed, Io had been furious when the Bluestocking Brigade had essentially funded a collection of brutes to go on a looting, burning, smashing rampage.

Zeus regarded her steadily before continuing. "Despite my reservations, I cannot feel right punishing you for giving your money to charity. It is your money; do as you like with it." His expression hardened. "Just be prepared to accept the consequences if any of that money should find its way into the wrong hands."

Io's conscience twinged at his generosity. Not only was he generous with her allowance, which was *not* trifling in the least, but he was generous in his treatment of her. Io was no fool. She might be over the age of twenty-one and legally an adult, but she knew the courts in England would not hesitate to throw their weight behind a man like Zeus if he ever took it into his head to truly curb her independence. And there was no judge in this country or New York who would find Io's behavior acceptable.

Axbridge, a man she'd begun to like despite his high-handed, haughty nature, had not scrupled to warn Io of the fine line she skated.

"No other aristocratic man would allow his female dependent as much liberty as Hastings does you," he'd said a few nights earlier when they'd been passing the time arguing at yet another tedious ball. He'd given her his dismissive, ducal sneer. "I certainly wouldn't tolerate your behavior for a moment and most of my peers would have you locked up by now; an action which is well within your brother's power as the head of your family."

Axbridge's warning tempered her behavior now, and Io nodded at Zeus. "Thank you… Brother. I will endeavor to select the charities I support with more care."

It was the first time she had called Zeus *brother* without sarcasm or mockery, and the faint pink stain that spread over his sharp cheekbones told her that he was not unaffected by the term of affection.

Io gave Corbin a dismissive look as she strode from the room. He might not have tattled on her, but she had seen the judgment in his gaze. He had not defended her, either. She briefly considered marching to Edith's chambers to crow about her victory, but decided it was not worth the strife it would cause. It was obvious that Zeus and Edith were having problems. Hopefully, their betrothal would crumble on its own.

Io opened the door to her chambers and stopped when she saw her little sister sitting at her dressing table, frowning.

Eva leapt up. "Ah, you are back sooner than I hoped." She pulled a face. "I knew why you'd been summoned. Edith mentioned it earlier."

"I see. So, why were you frowning at my dressing table?" she asked, taking her sister's hand and pulling her down beside her on the settee nearest the fire.

"There is nothing on it—no scent, lotions, jewelry, or…anything."

Io laughed. "Moira is very tidy."

"I suspect it is more a case of you not having anything for her to *keep* tidy."

That was the truth but Io did not admit it. "To what do I owe the honor of this visit?"

"Oh, Yoyo, I wish I were *good* like you," Eva said, laying her head on Io's shoulder.

"Good?" Io laughed, gazing fondly at her little sister. "Hardly that."

"I just mean that you dress in moderation, you do not want jewels, you do not care if you wear the same gown to every ball, whereas I…"

Io squeezed her adorable little sister tightly and kissed the top of her head. "Don't ever wish away who you are, Eva. You are pure joy in human form. There is no shame in enjoying pretty things, dearest. As for me being *good,* what you fail to understand is that it is not a sacrifice for me to forgo jewels and clothing because I do not want them. In fact, I find it a burden to think about clothing. That is one of the things I miss from Canoga: a simple wardrobe that took none of my mental power."

"But you are so beautiful. You could wear gowns that made you the toast of London and have every eligible bachelor in the *ton* at your feet."

Io shivered, and it was only partly in jest. "That sounds like a nightmare to me."

And there is only one man I want at my feet.

"You miss Bal, don't you?" Eva asked.

"Yes, I do." They had been separated before, of course, when Bal went off to Princeton. But he had come home often, missing her company as much as she'd pined for his.

Now, he was blissfully happy with Victoria, his wife, and her son. And Io really was happy for him. He wrote to her often, his letters full to bursting with things to share.

Io wrote back to him every week, her letters scant and empty, because of everything she had to conceal.

"I miss him, but I am delighted that he is happy," she said.

"It must be nice to have a twin," Eva said wistfully, not for the first time.

Io felt sorry for her sister in that regard. The closeness that existed between her and Bal and Ares and Apollo was indeed a special sort of intimacy.

"Fortunately for you, my dear, you are all our favorite sibling," Io said. And that was not a lie.

Eva laughed. "You are so kind." She paused and then said, "I notice you are very friendly with Axbridge."

"Mmm," Io said, her mind on three o'clock. While it would be tempting to give Masterson a piece of her mind about the meeting with Zeus, she did not want to waste precious moments arguing. After all, they could do that any time. Although they had scarcely exchanged a word—hostile or otherwise—since last Wednesday.

"—is it that you find to talk about all the time? I think he is a dreadfully haughty and unfriendly man."

"What's that, love?" Io asked.

"Axbridge," Eva said with some asperity. "I was asking why you are friends with him?"

"Friends?" Io mused and then laughed. "I would call us acquaintances who like to argue."

"But *why*?" Eva persisted, not diverted.

Io shrugged. "The same reason I am friends with anyone—because I enjoy his company."

Eva pulled a face. "You *do*? But why? He is so stern and disapproving and—and—I don't know. Unpleasant."

"Is he?" Io asked, laughing at her sister's uncharacteristically sour expression. "I confess that I hadn't noticed. I like him because he never pays me flowery annoying compliments and always says what he is thinking."

"He certainly does," Eva muttered darkly.

The clock on the mantle struck the quarter hour and Io sat up. "Oh, look at the time," she said in a voice that sounded false and overly excited to her own ears.

"Are you leaving?" Eva asked. "I thought we might go to the Park later today."

There was only one *park* worthy of the name in her sister's opinion: Hyde Park, which was Io's idea of hell at any time, but especially when all the *ton* was on the strut.

"I can't today, darling. But I will go with you tomorrow. I promise."

Io tried to ignore the excitement pounding in her chest and failed.

"Where are you going?" Eva asked.

"A suffragette meeting and then a talk. Just my usual *little causes*," she said, adopting Edith's tone on the last two words.

"Oh. Perhaps I might come with you sometime?"

Fear struck Io's heart, causing it to stutter.

"Although I cannot today," Eva added, sighing as she pushed up off the settee. "I am going to get measured for my court gown."

"Oh, good! I mean—er, aren't you glad about that?" Io scrambled at her sister's odd look.

"I would be if not for—" Eva stopped abruptly and smiled. "I am enjoying it greatly."

Io knew she should delve into this subject, but not today.

Today she could only think of one person.

***

Corbin paced the luxurious hotel room, castigating himself, which is what he'd been doing since *last* Wednesday.

He should not have come. He was a terrible friend to Hastings, not to mention a traitor to his own principles.

And yet wild horses could not have kept him away.

Corbin stopped his frenetic pacing, slumped against the wall, and then lightly—so lightly—coasted a palm over the fabric tented by his dick, which had been hard for days, no matter how many times he'd fisted himself dry.

He glanced at the clock: there was still twenty minutes until they were meant to meet. Like the eager, horny fool that he was, he'd arrived at the hotel a full hour early. He knew she was angry with him and had hoped she might arrive early, as well, so that they might get the arguing out of the way first.

But here he was all alone, mooning like a schoolboy with a hard prick.

It would be wise to take the edge off, wouldn't it? Corbin was tired of embarrassing himself in front of the woman. If she *did* show—which was not at all guaranteed after the look of loathing she'd given him in Hastings's study—the last thing he wanted to do was go off like a Roman candle.

He glanced at the clock. It was fifteen seconds later than the last time he looked.

There was plenty of time.

Corbin closed his eyes, deftly working the buttons of his fly with only one hand. He groaned when his hot shaft hit his cool palm, squeezing himself until he'd pumped out enough slick to ease his stroking.

His hand felt nothing like Io's. It was the difference between gold and dross.

You aren't doing this to fall in love with your fist, fool, you are doing this so you don't humiliate yourself. Again.

Fair enough.

Corbin stroked and imagined her body laid out before him like a feast, his tongue laving and caressing, her taut thighs flexing, soft breaths quickening—

Something—a faint sound or disturbance in the air—made him open his eyes.

Io was leaning against a wall, arms crossed, smiling at him. "Please. Do not stop on my account. I am entranced."

Chapter 21

Io deeply regretted it when Masterson opened his eyes and found her watching. She was unsurprised by his reaction—horror—and the immediate cessation of an activity that had, quite frankly, been one of the most erotic sights she had ever seen. Severe, reserved, gorgeously masculine Corbin Masterson stroking himself.

Io suspected the image would be branded into her brain for a long, long time.

Predictably, Masterson stood up straight and dropped his cock as if it were a burning coal, his face turning brick red.

"Lady Io." The words were a frigid contrast to the rest of him.

She didn't want to grin, but…

His jaw tightened and eyes narrowed. "Come here."

The words were all the more menacing—and exciting—for how quiet they were.

Io took one step, and then recalled the resolution she'd made before coming here today. If he wanted her, he would have to come prepared.

"I did not bring any—"

"We don't need a condom for what you are going to do."

The bolt of lust that struck her sex at his stern words almost drove her to her knees. Io scrambled to hide her arousal at this cool, commanding facet of his nature. She had already shown him the last time—and far too eagerly—how much she liked it.

Instead, she fluttered her eyelashes and adopted a vapid look. "Why, whatever do you mean, gentle sir?"

He ignored her attempt at levity. "Strip."

Io had been so entranced by the sight of him that she'd forgotten she was still completely dressed, her satchel slung over her shoulder.

Io: The Shrew

She let the bag slide to the floor with a *thunk* and then pulled off her gloves, finger by finger.

His eyelids drooped and his nostrils flared as he watched her without speaking, without moving—like a predator cornering its prey, ready to pounce.

Io tossed her hat onto a nearby chair, her cloak joining it.

His eyes roamed down her body. For once, Io wondered what he thought about her adherence to dress reform—not that she would change anything to please him, but she was curious.

Liar. You wore this gown today just for him.

That was true, but she had not rushed out and bought a new gown; she'd already owned the teal velvet. It was an unusual, softer choice for her, far different from her usual grays or navy blues—and while it was cut along more romantic lines, it was still imminently practical.

If it hadn't been, she could not have stripped herself as quickly as she was doing—certainly not if she'd been garbed in one of the tightly laced, monstrously bustled gowns that were fashionable.

The rich velvet slid to the floor without a sound.

Beneath it, she wore only a single silk petticoat and a whisper-thin chemise without a corset.

Corbin's dark eyes lowered to her breasts and his chest swelled.

Io glanced down to see what he was staring at as she pulled the tape on her petticoat.

Her hard nipples were thrusting against the white silk chemise— luxurious undergarments were Io's one weakness when it came to clothing.

Once she'd dropped the petticoat, she stepped out of it, and kept walking until she'd closed the distance between them.

His jaw flexed, his eyes rampaging over her body. And then he reached out without a word and nudged one, and then the other strap off her shoulder, causing it to float to the floor.

He took his time inspecting her as she stood naked before him, his gaze a tangible caress as it stroked over her breasts, belly, and mound and then made its leisurely way back up.

Io's own jaw clenched at the tightly leashed desire she saw in his eyes.

215

He took a pillow off the chair and tossed it to the carpet at his feet. "On your knees."

***

A man would never be entirely sure where he stood with Lady Io Hale.

When Corbin ordered her to her knees, he would not have been surprised if she'd told him to go to Hell, laughed, or ordered him to *his* knees, first.

Her reaction—immediate compliance—was the one reaction that *did* surprise him.

Her full lips slackened and he *felt* the desire that ripped through her at his cold command.

Despite her loud protestations to the contrary, his lady liked this dominant side of him—a side Corbin had always kept firmly in check—and she responded to it as if she had been specially created just for *him*.

She sank to her knees with an eagerness that gutted him. His urge to master her—which had flared to life when he'd opened his eyes and found her watching him take his private pleasure—softened at her willingness to yield to him.

His prick, however, only became harder.

Corbin was in the same boat he'd been in when he'd decided to masturbate—worse, even—because there was no way he could acquit himself with Io kneeling at his feet and looking up at him with such sweet submission, waiting for his next command.

He reached for her face, turned up toward him like a flower, and a low groan slipped from his clenched jaws when she rubbed her satiny cheek against his palm, her ridiculously lush eyelashes like two black fans against her flushed pink skin.

Corbin slid his fingers into her short dusky curls and exerted the slightest of pressure. "Take me in your mouth, Io."

She shivered slightly, her eyes never leaving his as she parted her lush lips and took him only as deeply as his crown, sending waves of erotic shock through his body—waves that grew even stronger when her low moan of pleasure vibrated up his shaft to his tortured balls.

Io: The Shrew

"Io," he whispered, his burning lungs reminding him to breathe.

Her lips curled slightly as she took him deeper, the smile lines at the corners of her eyes letting Corbin know that just because she was the one on her knees, did not mean he was the one in control.

Io Hale reveled in the power she had over him.

And Corbin would not have her any other way.

***

Io had always enjoyed pleasuring a man with her mouth, but never more than just then—when Corbin's mask of control began to crack, pieces of it falling away faster and faster as she used every weapon in her arsenal.

Unlike the last time she had done this, she was not trying to exert her will and manipulate him.

This time, she wanted only to please him.

His jaw was like stone as he stared down at her, the intensity in his gaze as arousing as the way his hips jerked even as he visibly struggled to control them.

Io doubted he was aware of the way his hands were guiding her to take him deeper, something that the rational, proper, controlled Corbin Masterson would never do to a *lady*.

He would castigate himself later for his behavior—for exhibiting his raw need—but right now… Right now, he was a creature of desire and she was the one thing in his world that mattered.

Io held him pinioned with her gaze as she took him deeper, her eyes watering at the length of him, her jaws all but unhinging.

But it was worth any discomfort when she swallowed around him.

He shouted something incomprehensible, hips thrusting hard as his spine arched sharply and his head dropped back.

Even as the first drop hit the back of her tongue, she felt his body jerk in awareness and begin to withdraw, to spare her.

Io sank her fingers into the tight weave of his muscular ass and pulled him closer, swallowing everything he gave her.

Only when he began to pull away, too sensitive for her touch to be pleasurable, did Io release him.

When she looked up, she wondered how long it would take for his Puritan guilt to begin assaulting him.

***

Corbin felt reality invade even though he tried to keep it at bay.

The events of the last moments replayed in his head like one of the flip-books Lizzy loved so much. The shame he felt at using a woman—a lady—so roughly spread through him like the rush of an incoming tide.

He forced himself to look down at Lady Io, who still knelt at his feet.

Naturally, she was waiting for him. "Please tell me you are not going to suffer a fit of the male vapors."

Her gibe and smirk forced a disbelieving huff from him. Corbin shook his head, at a loss for words, and extended his hand, grateful when she took it and allowed him to lift her to her feet.

Instead of stepping away, as he'd thought, she stepped closer, sliding her arms around his neck and pressing the length of her body against his, her hot naked skin and the springy curls of her sex reminding him that his softening cock was hanging out of his trousers like a surrendering soldier.

She pressed her face close to his, standing on her toes, forcing him to meet her gaze. "Are you?" she asked, and then lightly and with uncharacteristic tenderness, kissed him on the mouth before pulling back and waiting for his answer.

Corbin tasted himself on her tongue, a flavor he'd not experienced since he'd been a young, curious boy exploring the thrill of masturbation. He'd thought the taste would repulse him, but it only made him remember how tenderly and hungrily she had just serviced his need.

"No, I will not suffer a fit of the male vapors." It was only partially a lie. He ran his palms down her back until he cupped a soft buttock in each hand. "I hope you will give me an opportunity to acquit myself—in a short while," he added, kissing her as softly as she'd done him.

She chuckled wickedly. "I look forward to it."

Corbin reluctantly released her and gestured to the table in the adjacent sitting room. "I took the liberty of having champagne and some sustenance delivered before your arrival."

Her eyes brightened. "Oh, yes please. I'm peckish as I had no tea earlier."

Corbin was about to pull the counterpane from the bed to wrap her up against the cold when she said, "I brought my dressing gown with me."

He goggled and she laughed.

She gestured to her satchel, which she was never without, and pulled it open, extracting a whisp of silk.

Once she was garbed in a wrapper that resembled a peacock's tail—and after he'd tucked himself away—Corbin fed the fire with more coal and they sat on the settee near the small feast set out on the low table.

He opened the bottle with a soft pop and poured them both glasses of champagne.

"Mmm," she said, after taking her first sip. "I love the bubbles."

"Yes, I've noticed."

"You have?"

"Axbridge always brings you champagne," he said before he could stop himself.

"Have you been spying on me, Masterson?"

He snorted, refusing to indulge her teasing about a matter that made him so jealous he'd all but ground his teeth to stumps.

"I was very angry at you earlier today—in Zeus's office," she said after a moment.

"I could tell."

"Don't worry, I don't wish to argue about it."

"Good. Because I only learned about what you were doing with your allowance five minutes before you came in, when Miss Barrymore interrupted us to tell Hastings." He did not admit that he had wanted to strangle the duke's fiancée for causing more strife.

She lifted an eyebrow.

"It is the truth," he said.

"Hmmph."

"Just out of curiosity, when were you going to tell me that Gordon was never your lover?"

"I thought I already had?"

"Not in so many words."

She shrugged. "You never asked."

Corbin tucked his annoyance away. Already the precious minutes were ticking past and he did not want to waste them bickering.

"By the way, the article I am writing for his magazine is about the various movements pursuing the expansion of the voting franchise back home," she said, her smile slight. "Nothing too inflammatory."

Again, Corbin might have disagreed, but he merely nodded.

She turned to face him fully, which brought her knee against his thigh. Even through two layers of clothing excitement arced from her touch. "Most of what I know about you has been collected second-hand." Her full lips flexed into a frown. "A great deal of it seems to have been promulgated by Edith. Will you tell me about your time in seminary?"

Corbin took a sip of his champagne to mask his surprise. "What do you want to know?" he asked warily.

"What made you go?"

His lips twitched.

"What? Why are you smiling like that?"

"How am I smiling?"

"Just tell me!"

"I was smiling because I was thinking about what a sanctimonious, humorless, and self-righteous prig I was at seventeen."

"*Was?*" she taunted.

Corbin rolled his eyes. "Very well, perhaps I am still a bit priggish."

"*A bit?*"

"You are relentless. Has anyone ever told you that?" he retorted, exasperated but amused.

"Everyone I have ever met," she admitted, looking proud rather than remorseful. "Why do you think you were so—"

"Devout?" he suggested wryly. "I suspect it had to do with the fact that I was conceived out of wedlock. My mother was a maid in my father's boyhood home," he said before she could ask.

Io's beautiful face hardened. "And did he—"

"My father did not force himself on her," Corbin assured her. "Although the outcome was no different. He was already betrothed at the time—to a woman from a very powerful and wealthy family—so there was never any possibility of him marrying my mother."

"You mean that *he* did not consider the possibility."

"No, nor did his mother and father," Corbin agreed. "In any event, my father married whom his parents wanted and spent the rest of his life with a woman who despised him."

"Did she despise him because she knew about your mother?" she asked.

"That was only the first of many reasons."

"Your father was a philanderer?"

Corbin could not help being amused at her direct question. "I am sure that his wife had a great deal to tolerate," he said, sidestepping her question.

"And what about your grandparents?"

"What about them?"

"Did they reconcile themselves to your existence?"

"To a degree. I never met them, but they paid for my upkeep and schooling. To be fair, they gave my mother enough money that she never needed to work again for the rest of her life, so they were generous."

"With their money," she said tartly.

"Yes. With their money," he agreed.

"And you met Zeus at boarding school?"

Corbin smiled fondly. "Yes. He came upon me fighting off four boys and flew to my assistance without a word. Even back then he was a figure of respect and his friendship spared me a great deal of misery. He told the boys they were fools to care about whether or not my parents were married. He said there were far better reasons to want to thrash somebody."

"That is wise for one so young."

"He has always been practical and deeply empathic."

"An admirable combination. So, tell me, then—why is he betrothed to that vindictive bitch? A woman who treats her own flesh and blood like a slave?"

Corbin met her fierce gaze. "If you want an answer to that question then you should ask His Grace. It is not my place to speculate." Even though he did so plenty in the privacy of his own mind.

"Fair enough," she said, surprising him with her mild acquiescence.

"You asked about seminary," he said, deciding to answer her question. "The truth is that even before I met Emma, I knew it was not the right place for me. I would have left after that first year. My departure was merely…hastened."

"How did you meet her?"

He cocked his head. "You really want to know?"

"What? Do you think I cannot talk about your former lover without becoming jealous?"

Corbin knew he could not talk about *her* former lovers without wanting to track them all down and hurt them, but he doubted she wanted to hear that.

He had never spoken of Emma to anyone before, not even Hastings. And yet now he found himself almost eager to share. "She was the daughter of a publican in the nearby town, his tavern was a place where seminary students congregated. She told me that she'd moved back to live with her parents because her husband had died. I did not find out until after I asked her father's permission to marry her that her husband was still very much alive."

Io's eyes bulged. "*She* did not tell you that?"

Corbin felt embarrassed for his dead lover, a reaction that was ridiculous. He tried to explain. "Emma was…a daydreamer." That was the kindest way to put it. He forced himself to hold Io's gaze. "She was also extremely lovely." He was not surprised when understanding dawned in her eyes, which were more brown than green today.

"You were only seventeen," she said after a moment, her words kinder than he deserved for falling in love with a woman who had a pretty face and very little substance.

He had been so proud when Emma—who had drawn the attention of every young man in the area—had settled on him as a suitor. He'd never seen such a beautiful woman, and at four-and-twenty—a whole seven years his senior—she had seemed worldly and sophisticated.

"I was a young fool," he said. "And Emma knew that. Of all the men chasing her, she picked me. Not because I was the most handsome or because she loved me, but because she believed she could convince an illegitimate man to marry her."

"Even though she *was* still married?"

He nodded. "She had hoped that we would run off and marry. When I approached her father for his permission, it was unbeknownst to her."

"So, he is the one who thrust a spoke in her wheel?"

"Yes. I set about finding her husband once I discovered Emma was with child. He was not hiding and it is possible I could have forced him to agree to a divorce, but then…"

"She died in childbed," Io finished for him, the sympathy in her gaze harder to take than scorn would have been. "That is a great deal of pain for a youth of seventeen to bear."

"I was an idiot."

"You were young. We've all done stupid things at one point or another."

Corbin wondered if she was referring to her *mentor* lover Lamar Jacobsen. He had no intention of inquiring. Indeed, he could not think of a subject he was less interested in knowing about. Or any of her other lovers, either.

She reached out to take a berry and dipped it in devon cream "You must have paid a fortune for these at this time of year."

He had, but he'd noticed how she liked them at breakfast this past autumn and thought the expense well worth it if it gave her pleasure.

She brought the cream-swathed berry not to her mouth, but his.

"They are for you," he said.

"I know. But I want to share with you. Take it…Corbin."

***

The only other man Io had met who could cloak his emotions so effectively was her brother Zeus. Perhaps that was part of their training at their expensive boarding school.

Only the slight flexing of his jaw told her how the use of his Christian name affected him.

When he opened his mouth, Io deliberately smeared some of the cream on his fuller bottom lip before setting it on his tongue.

He closed his mouth and began to chew, his smoky gaze never leaving her.

Io stood and then lowered onto the settee, putting one knee on either side of his hips. She was taller than him and enjoyed the rare opportunity to look at him from above before slowly lowering until her buttocks rested on his thighs. "Let me get this for you," she murmured, and then licked the bit of cream from his lip.

His nostrils flared as he swallowed, his hands closing around her waist.

Rather than pull her closer, he held her with one hand and then reached for the sash of her robe with the other, pulling it loose with a tug before pushing the thin silk from her shoulders.

His eyes were almost black as they swept over her breasts. He slid his hands behind her back to hold her cradled as he lowered his mouth over one peaked nipple.

Io moaned when he nipped her, her back arching when lips as soft as flower petals gently sucked the same spot. She surrendered to pure sensation as he alternated breasts, biting and soothing and laving.

"I need you inside me, Masterson," she said when she could take the teasing no longer.

He nipped her one last time and then looked up, his eyelids heavy. "Are you sure?"

Io gave an unladylike snort. "I think I should know my own body."

"Still, I should check to make sure that I have prepared you properly," he said, and then stroked a finger between her swollen lower lips, the warm pad circling her clitoris in a way that made her grit her teeth to stop a lustful growl. "No," he said, shaking his head, his expression thoughtful. "Not quite ready, I fear."

"Masterson!"

"*Tsk, tsk*. So hasty. I need to make sure you are nice and wet for me before I take you."

He was trying to kill her.

The next five minutes proved her suspicion as he teased her toward the brink of orgasm and then stopped just as her body began to shake and come apart.

When he started down the same road a third time, she grabbed a thick handful of blond hair.

"Ow!" He tried to flinch away, but Io held him in place.

"If you do that one more time, Masterson, I will take my revenge on you in a most diabolical way."

He appeared to consider that threat for a moment before saying, "Perhaps you are *almost* read—"

"I. Am. Ready." She released his hair. "If you check my satchel, you will find—"

"I don't need one of your condoms," Before she could tell him that he most certainly *did* need one, he said. "I brought my own today." He gave her a smug, haughty look. "In fact, I brought several."

And then her serious, stern lover winked.

Io laughed, delighted by both his preparedness and his playfulness. "Then what are we waiting for? Take me to bed, Mr. Masterson."

Chapter 22

The Following Wednesday

Io tugged on the silky hair of the man between her thighs. "No more—please, Masterson. I cannot."

His wicked tongue and lips paused their erotic labors and she felt him press a closed mouth kiss against her mound before prowling up her body beneath the blankets.

When his head emerged, his blond hair was an amusing mess. Who knew the painstakingly neat and tidy Corbin Masterson could look so disheveled?

And who would have guessed that such a fastidious man enjoyed orally pleasuring her so much?

"What are you smirking about?" he asked as he rolled onto his side and propped his head on his hand.

She reached out and smoothed down his wild locks. "You look as if chickens have been nesting on your head."

"I wonder whose fault that is?" His lips twitched into that slight smirk that always made her belly tighten. The fact that his barely smiling lips were swollen and reddened from pleasuring her just made the sensation more intense.

But Io needed time to recover from the pleasure he'd just forced from her body before she commenced their next round of bed sport.

And so she purposely changed the subject to one that was not in the least erotic.

"Pol said you went with him to Tattersall's yesterday."

Corbin blinked at her question. "Er, yes. I did."

"He said you helped him with the documents he needed to sign. That was kind of you."

Masterson's cheeks flushed at her praise. "It was nothing. Besides, I was there to look for new bloodstock for His Grace." He paused and then asked, "Er, has Lord Apollo always had difficulty reading?"

"I think you can just call him *Apollo* when we are alone together. Indeed, I'm sure my brothers and sister would all appreciate you dropping the rather empty titles."

"I will continue to do as I have been doing, my lady. Regardless of where I put my lips."

Io laughed. "Naughty humor from stern Mr. Masterson. Who would have guessed it was possible?"

"I am not stern."

She rolled her eyes. "You are the sternest person I know—next to Zeus. And the most unreadable."

"You can't read *my* expression?"

"See," she said, pointing at him. "This is an excellent example of what I mean. You sound slightly disbelieving, but your handsome face merely looks bored."

He gave a bark of laughter. "Nonsense."

"It is true. Of course now that we are lovers, I get to see more than your Extremely Disapproving Mr. Masterson expression."

His eyelids lowered. "You do like to say my name that way, don't you?"

"What way do you mean, sir?"

"You know damned well what I mean."

She grinned. "I *do* like saying your name with that particular emphasis…Mr. *Master*son. And you like to think of yourself as my master, don't you?"

"In bed, I do," he said, his big warm hand sliding over her hip and settling on her belly. "When it comes to mastering this magnificent body, I do."

They locked eyes and Io felt the heat began to build.

"I have something for you," he said gruffly, and then thrust his erection against her thigh.

Io hissed and he pumped his hips again. And then again, his lips parting, a slack, sensual look on his face as he rhythmically stroked.

Io chuckled and then reached down to close her hand around his length. "Are you humping my thigh, Masterson?"

Amusement joined lust in his dark gray gaze. "You are the most *astonishing* woman. I never know what you are going to say next."

Io did not think she flattered herself that he sounded more than a little admiring.

***

And yet another Wednesday…

"Did you follow me yesterday?" Io demanded the minute she walked into Room 320.

Masterson looked up from the bottle of wine he was opening, his eyebrows raised in that haughty, pretension-suppressing way he had. "Hello to you, too, my lady."

Io flung down her satchel and stripped off her gloves. "I am not in a mood to be toyed with. What I want to know, is—"

"Yes, I followed you yesterday," he said, pouring two glasses of ruby-colored wine.

"Damnit, Masterson!" Io flung her gloves at the console table, missing it completely.

"If you don't want me to follow you then you should bring your maid," he said coolly, bending over to pick up her gloves and then setting them on the table beside his own before turning to her. "You *know* I work for your brother. And after what happened this last Saturday, he yet again tasked me with—"

She lifted a hand. "Please. I have heard it before."

"Then you should be accustomed to it and not harangue me on the subject," he retorted, and then handed her the wine.

Io: The Shrew

Io snatched the glass from him and the liquid almost sloshed over the side. She hated that Zeus asked Masterson to follow her and, for once, her brother had a very good reason to doubt her common sense.

Last Saturday had been a disaster. She had gone to meet Gordon and several of his cohorts at a coffee shop in a part of town that was, granted, less than sterling. Moira had wanted to see her swain and it was her usual half-day, so Io had gone without a maid.

And had been caught in the middle of a riot.

Only the fact that Masterson had been in a handsome cab behind Io's had saved her from a very nasty afternoon. The crowd, ironically whipped up by Gordon and his cronies, had quickly turned into an unstoppable mob that had attacked friend and foe alike.

When a handful of protesters-turned-ruffians had begun to rock her cab—after the driver had fled—only Masterson and his pistol had stopped the men.

He'd not spoken a word to her on the way home. When they'd reached the foyer, he'd only uttered a few terse words. "You should change your clothing immediately. Your skirt is badly torn in the back." And then he'd pivoted on his heel, heading back out the front door.

"Are you going to tell Zeus?" she'd called after him.

Masterson had opened his mouth, but it had been Edith's voice that had filled the foyer.

"If he does not, then I will."

Io had looked up to find Edith standing on the second-floor landing, smiling nastily.

And so that had been that.

The rest of the day had been wretched, at least an hour of it spent with Zeus—thankfully alone—explaining what had happened. Strangely enough, her brother had believed that it had not been her fault. Although he'd rightfully been annoyed that she'd not taken one of his carriages, he'd at least understood why she'd not wanted to ride in such a conspicuous vehicle.

When Zeus had finished with her then Eva, Ares, and Pol had had *their* angry say. Io had truly been in everyone's black book.

That had been the disaster on Saturday. But yesterday was *Tuesday*, so—

"Io?"

She looked up from her thoughts and scowled at him. "What?" she demanded rudely.

"I know you are not angry about yesterday. What is the real reason you are so furious today?" Masterson asked, only lowering himself into a chair after she did.

Io wanted to argue, but she was too weary and he was, after all, right. She heaved an irritable sigh. "Why do you think?"

"Did you tangle with Miss Barrymore again?"

"*Me* tangle with *her?*" Io's eyes threatened to bulge out of her head. "*She* tangled with me. What is *wrong* with that woman? And that was a rhetorical question before you tell me what a lady she is."

He sipped his wine, his expression unreadable.

Io hated how the only time she could tell what he was thinking was when they were engaging in sex. At any other time, he was more sphinxlike than the Sphinx.

"Edith will not be happy until all of us have gone back to New York—or, better yet, died on a sinking ship while headed back," Io said, gulping half her glass in one swig.

This time, she *did* see an emotion on Masterson's face before he schooled his expression. "Miss Barrymore is very…rigid, but she does not hate you, Io."

Io snorted. "You only see what you want to see, Corbin. If you opened your eyes—and your ears—you would realize that she spends all her time thinking of ways to drive a wedge between the five of us and Zeus." She tossed back the rest of her wine and stood. "No, you sit—I can fill my own glass." She could see he wanted to argue, but he stayed where he was while she slopped wine into her glass, her hand still shaking from how angry Edith had made her.

"What did she say, Io?" he asked when she returned to her chair and dropped gracelessly into it.

Io: The Shrew

"She was harping on Apollo again. We were at breakfast and you know he hardly comes around these days."

His eyebrows arched with surprise. "Miss Barrymore came to breakfast? I thought she usually ate in her room."

"She does. All I can think is that she came down especially to take digs at him." Io turned the glass in her hand, seeing her brother's face instead of the rich red liquid. "I was so happy to see him and we were talking about going riding in the park when she came in and started making sly comments about all the riding Pol did."

Io was terrified that Edith knew about Pol—terrified that she would use who he was as a weapon against him.

Why else would the woman hound her brother so relentlessly?

She hoped it was merely Edith's inclination to pick on people who did not fight back—like her cousin Susan because she couldn't stand up for herself and like quiet introverted Pol who *wouldn't* stand up to her—but she was afraid the woman knew the truth.

Io slanted Corbin a look. Sometimes she thought the canny man might have guessed her brother's secret. But she could never be the one to say anything first. What if he was as awful and self-righteous as Edith on the subject? She didn't want to think of her lover that way, but there was no denying that Masterson was a pious man. Or at least he had been before these Wednesdays.

Io slanted a look at Masterson, but for once he wasn't looking at her. Instead, he was gazing down at his glass. Judging by the slump of his broad shoulders the subject of Edith and her squabbles with the younger Hales was one that made him miserable, as well.

Here they were in this room for only a few hours—the best hours of her week—and she was wasting it talking about her brother's fiancée!

Io set down her glass, stood, and began to unbutton the wrists on her long-sleeved navy wool walking dress.

When Masterson looked up and saw she was on her feet he began to get up.

"No. Stay where you are," Io said, smiling to soften her words.

He sank back in his chair and stared up at her with heated eyes.

***

Corbin wasn't surprised by the argument they'd just had. It had been a mistake to let things fester without exchanging a word since Saturday.

It had not been Io's fault that the idiots Gordon had been riling up had erupted and run amok.

But the woman needed to start taking the family carriage—regardless of what attention it garnered—and bringing along the big footmen her brother employed.

Corbin shuddered to think what might have happened if he'd not been there. Certainly, the cab driver had not stayed to help. As for Gordon, he might have come to Io's aid if he'd not been all but trampled by his own supporters.

In any event, he wouldn't have said anything to Hastings about it. He'd already decided he would take care of Io in his own way. To hell with his loyalty to his friend. Wasn't he already destroying that every week by fucking the man's sister?

Suddenly, Io stood.

Corbin began to get to his feet, the action reflexive.

"No. Stay where you are," she said, her hands going to the button closures on her simple but flattering blue gown.

And then she began to undress.

His cock, which had wilted when they'd begun bickering, was instantly interested in this change in plans.

Her eyelids lowered and her moves were languid, sensuous. She unfastened first one tight sleeve from wrist to elbow, and then the other.

Corbin swallowed when she switched to the front of her gown and he spread his thighs a little to give his cramped erection a bit of room.

Her dress was one of the artistic sort—or perhaps it was dress reform, he wasn't sure of the terminology—and the fabric was of a quality that only a wealthy woman could afford, but it was designed for a woman to put on and remove without the services of a maid.

Io: The Shrew

It had buttons all the way down the front—from the prim white collar to the hem of the full, sweeping skirt—but her hands stopped once she'd unfastened the button just above her mound.

Corbin realized he was still holding his wine glass—squeezing it—because his hand hurt and he tossed back the rest of the wine and set the empty glass on the end table without looking, fortunate that he didn't drop the damned thing onto the floor.

When she shrugged the loosened gown off her shoulders Corbin sucked in a breath at what she wore beneath.

His eyes darted upward to meet hers. "A corset?" he said in a raspy voice.

She nodded slowly and stepped out of the puddled gown.

"I thought you didn't believe in them?"

"I don't for everyday wear." Her smile was slow and wicked. "But Wednesdays are special. I wore this for you, Masterson." She paused and held her arms out to the side, encouraging him to look his fill.

Corbin didn't hesitate, his greedy gaze flickering over the straps of the whisper-thin pale pink chemise and the black and pink striped corset that ran from her hips over a ridiculously small waist and thrust up Io's full breasts.

He was on his feet before he'd even thought it, hands reaching to feel her.

Io was a tall woman—easily five foot six—without her heeled ankle boots she was a good six inches shorter than Corbin. Although she had a personality big enough for a three hundred pound, six-foot five stevedore.

"What are you smirking about?" she asked, her neck craned to look up at him while he stroked from the full curve of her hips over her tiny waist up to those delectable breasts.

"Was I?" he murmured absently, dragging a finger over the spot where the lace of her chemise met the unspeakably soft skin of her breasts.

"You were," she retorted, but she sounded almost as distracted as he felt.

Corbin slid his hands back down to her waist and spread them out, her waist feeling even smaller than it looked.

He met her heavy-lidded gaze. "You look very attractive in these garments," he said.

"That was the idea."

"But you never need to dress any way other than how you want, Io. Not for me."

"I know. That's why I did it."

He barked a laugh. "Contrarian."

Her hands settled on Corbin's hips and her fingers dug into the wool suiting and his buttocks beneath. "I want to crawl into bed with you and not get out again until we have to leave." Her eyes lowered—something she had never done—and Corbin noticed the tension in her jaw as she gazed at the floor, her body suddenly feeling small and vulnerable in his hands.

Corbin nudged her chin with his knuckle until she looked up at him. "We can do whatever you want, sweetheart."

He had believed that Io didn't like him to be tender—that she only wanted his spankings and the sharp edge of his tongue—but she melted into his arms and he caught her up and held her against his chest, carrying her to the bed.

She might like to call what they did *having sex* or *fucking*. But today Corbin was going to do what he wanted.

He was going to make love to her.

***

When Corbin's arms swept her up Io had the oddest urge to cry. She had no idea what had come over her—why she was surrendering herself so utterly and completely—but suddenly she needed to be held by strong arms. Not because she couldn't take care of herself. Not because she *needed* a man.

But because she wanted one. And not just any man. Only the one currently laying her out on the bed with such tenderness.

She was suddenly so very tired.

Io watched from beneath heavy-lidded eyes as he dimmed the gaslight until it was barely a glow, pulled the heavy drapes shut, and then stripped off his clothing quickly and efficiently.

Io: The Shrew

He was such a beautiful man—not just his exterior, but the person who inhabited the strong, masculine body. He was gentle and caring and protective.

She knew he wanted to be all those things for her.

And, for today, Io would let him.

Surely that wasn't so bad? To rely on Corbin's seemingly endless reserves of strength for a few hours? Was it a crime to not always be strong?

Just for a while. Tomorrow she would pick up her weapons and fight the good fight.

Tomorrow…

The mattress dipped and Io woke with a start. "Oh! I must have fallen asleep for a few seconds. I'm so sorry, Masterson. I don't know what—"

"*Shhh*," Corbin murmured into her hair before kissing her temple and wrapping his arms around her body, pulling her close so that her head was resting on his biceps. "You need to rest for a little while."

"But—"

"Rest," he murmured.

And that was the last thing Io heard.

Chapter 23

A Tuesday

The weeks that followed were, without a doubt, the best of Corbin's entire life.

But they were not without difficulties.

The most notable being his shame every time he looked the duke in the eyes and pretended that he was not debauching his best friend's sister in a hotel room every Wednesday.

Actually, the debauching was entirely mutual. Lady Io was no blushing maiden, but a woman who demanded what she wanted.

Together they had engaged in every carnal activity known to man.

Even a few that were new to Corbin.

While his guilt was the main thing distracting him from fully enjoying what should have been weeks of pure pleasure, there were other matters that caused him some anguish. Not the least of which was the question of where this *thing* with Io was going. And how would it end?

Most pressing: *When* would it end?

Given her former reactions to any suggestion of a more permanent relationship between them, Corbin would rather bite off his own tongue than suggest marriage again.

Was he avoiding raising the issue out of fear that she would simply put an end to things *now*?

Yes, absolutely.

Was that cowardly of him?

Yes.

Did he care?

No.

Well, maybe a little. But he cared more about not disturbing the delicate balance between them.

And so he locked his concerns in the same mental cell where he kept his shame and betrayal toward the duke.

He also avoided Io from every Thursday to Tuesday, fearing that he could not hide how he felt from those who lived in such close proximity with them.

Well…he avoided her as much as he could.

But not today, because His Grace had asked Corbin to accompany him and his siblings on an outing to the National Portrait Gallery.

Miss Barrymore, for a change, would not be going. She alone had been invited to tea at the Duchess of Malverton's—evidently a great honor.

Corbin had needed to rise early and take care of a few matters so he could have the afternoon free to go on the junket. As a result, he was later than usual to breakfast, which he normally ate either alone or with Hastings, who was also an early riser.

Today when he opened the door to the breakfast room, he saw Io, Miss Barclay, and Apollo at one end of the long table, engaged in conversation.

At least the two Hales were talking. Miss Barclay was as quiet as ever, but for once she did not have the hunted expression she always wore in her cousin's presence.

After greeting the three of them with a nod and a curt *good morning,* and avoiding meeting his lover's eyes, Corbin turned to the buffet to fill his plate, listening to their chatter.

"Oh, I'm afraid I could not go with you," Miss Barclay said in her soft voice. "I have far too much to—"

"You must accompany us, Miss Barclay," Io said in her firm voice. "It will only be a few hours and this is a special exhibit which will change shortly and you will lose your chance."

"But Miss Barrymore wanted the invitations finished today and I am only—"

"I will help you write them," Io said.

Corbin was glad his back was turned so he could hide both his shock at the offer and his amusement at Miss Barclay's polite, but firm, response.

"It is so kind of you to offer, my lady," Miss Barclay hastily said, doing an admirable job of lying. Io Hale had the worst penmanship of anyone Corbin knew—man or woman. "But Miss Barrymore specifically asked me to write them out."

He heard Lord Apollo bark a laugh and then attempt to disguise it as a cough.

"What is so amusing, Pol?" Io asked her brother in a frosty voice.

"Nothing," Lord Apollo wisely answered.

Miss Barclay suddenly said in a musing tone, "I suppose I could finish them this evening, after dinner."

"Then you will go with us?" Io asked. "Even Ares is accompanying us, and getting him to look at anything other than furniture or wood is all but impossible. You *must* join us."

There was a pause and then, "Yes. I will go."

"Excellent!" Io said.

When Corbin turned, he sneaked a look at Io and saw that she was smiling, genuinely pleased that Miss Barclay was coming along for what was surely a rare day of pleasure.

It embarrassed Corbin to admit that he forgot that Miss Barrymore's rather colorless cousin and companion was even in the room most of the time. Susan Barclay was one of the meekest women he had ever met. Objectively, he supposed she was pretty in a delicate, fairylike sort of way, although such slight women had never been his preference. However, it wasn't her physical appearance that he found so underwhelming, but her very diffidence. Io Hale's almost constant defiance of anything she did not agree with could be infuriating, not to mention exhausting, but at least she had blazing light shining from her eyes.

Miss Barclay, by contrast, looked as though somebody had snuffed out the flame inside her long ago.

As if speaking the youngest male Hale's name had summoned him, the door opened and Lord Ares entered the breakfast room, murmuring a very quiet *good morning* before slumping into a chair and nodding to the hovering footman who was offering him coffee.

Corbin recognized the look on the younger man's face as being one he'd had often, although not in many years.

Evidently, so did his sister. "Are you feeling a bit delicate this morning, Ares?" she asked in a strident voice that had to be deliberate.

Lord Ares winced. "Must you shout, Yoyo?"

"Yes, I must."

He groaned and pushed to his feet. "I'm going back to bed."

"You most certainly are *not*. Today we are all going to the National Portrait Gallery and you are coming along."

"I don't recall agreeing to that."

"You are agreeing to it right now."

He huffed a sigh and then winced again. "Can't I go another day?"

"Of course you may go another day," she said.

Lord Ares began to smile.

"But you will still be going with your family *today*."

Lord Ares slid a look to his twin, who gave a slight shrug.

Finding no support in that quarter, Ares said, "Fine." And then he turned to the footman, Charles. "Would you please bring me a tankard of ale and two raw eggs?"

"Of course, my lord," Charles said, his lips curved into the faintest of smiles as he went to do Ares's bidding.

Satisfied that she had sufficiently badgered her brother, Lady Io turned to Corbin just as he swallowed a scalding mouthful of coffee and said, "And you will be accompanying us, as well, Mr. Masterson?"

"Yes, my lady. The duke has invited me to enjoy the day."

"I don't believe I have ever seen you take time to yourself before," the vixen prodded, smirking. She turned to Miss Barclay. "Have you seen Mr. Masterson have a free day, Miss Barclay?"

Miss Barclay fixed Corbin with a startled look, her eyes magnified by her spectacles and looking large enough to swallow her small, heart-shaped face. "Er—"

"All work and no play makes Jack a dull boy," Io went on blithely, not waiting for an answer to continue her torment. She smirked, her eyes fixed on Corbin as she asked her brother, "Is that not the case, Pol?"

Corbin met the mismatched gaze of the most reserved Hale sibling, who merely regarded him quietly for a moment before saying, with humor glinting in both the pale blue and dark brown eye. "I have certainly found that to be the case, Yoyo."

"And I'm sure Ares agrees, don't you?"

"Yes," her youngest brother croaked so speedily that Corbin suspected he didn't even know what he was agreeing to.

Io lifted her brows. "Well. There you have it, Mr. Masterson."

"I would hate to be accused of being *dull*, my lady." Corbin did not bother to hide his sarcasm and the two younger Hales sniggered.

Lady Io's eyes glittered. "Oh, rest assured, Mr. *Master*son, we Hales will never allow that to happen."

Yes, she was definitely emphasizing the *master* in his name. Corbin resolved to make her pay for her taunting tomorrow afternoon, which seemed frustratingly far away.

***

Io knew it was bad of her, but she couldn't help shadowing Masterson as he perused the portraits.

After leaving Pol with Miss Barclay and Zeus, she strolled with Ares for a few moments. But her woodworker brother was more interested in the floor and joinery than the portraits and she easily left him behind, finding her quarry standing at an odd angle from a very strange painting.

"What are you looking at?" she asked as she came up beside him.

"*Shhh.*" He turned to look down at her, a slight frown of disapproval on his brow. Io *loved* that expression almost more than any other he displayed—except the one of utter surrender when he reached his climax— and cocked a challenging eyebrow at him.

Io: The Shrew

"What are you looking at?" she repeated in an exaggerated whisper.

He compressed his sensual lips into a prim line and said, "It is an anamorphic portrait of Edward VI by Scrots."

"Scrots?" Io laughed, drawing another disapproving stare from a nearby couple—their expressions not nearly so charming as Masterson's. "What is a Scrot?" she said in a marginally quieter voice. "And what is ana—what did you say?"

"William Scrots was the painter. Anamorphic means you must study the painting at a certain angle to see it." He hesitated, and then lifted his hands, and said, "May I?"

Io nodded, curious.

Masterson took her shoulders and gently moved her into position. "There. Now look."

Io stared for a moment, still only seeing smears. "I don't unders—Oh, wait! I see it!"

"Once you do, it's hard to believe you ever missed it, isn't it?"

"Yes, it is."

They stared at the odd painting for a few moments and then, without verbal agreement, the two of them fell into step together, spending the next quarter of an hour in companionable silence until they came to a halt in front of the photograph of Victoria and Albert that dominated a series of images of the royals.

This one had been taken shortly before Albert's death. He was standing beside his famous wife's chair, the difference in their sizes—more than a foot—made obvious.

Io knew the Queen was still mourning his passage, but she thought Albert looked… tedious. As for the Queen herself? Victoria looked much like you'd expect a woman to look when she controlled most of the globe and was prepared to go to any lengths to hold on to it.

"What do you think?" Masterson asked.

"I think Prince Albert dressed to the left," she said, smirking while she waited for his frown of disapproval.

When he instead gave a low chuckle, Io gawked.

Masterson leaned close and murmured, "You devil." His breath was hot on her temple, the feel of it going immediately to her sex.

"I don't want to wait for tomorrow," she impulsively whispered back, feeling his body jolt beside her.

Io expected a stern, chiding rejection—which she would have enjoyed, too—but was happier when he said, "Me neither. Today—five o'clock, instead of three."

Chapter 24

The Boynton Hotel
Five-Thirty-Three That Same Day

Corbin and his lover lay side by side, sweaty and panting.

"That was…" Io began, and then apparently lost interest in finding a word to describe the two orgasms she had just experienced.

Corbin chuckled, out of breath but happy. "Magnificent."

"Yes. That is exactly the word I was searching for." Io rolled onto her side as sinuously as a cat and then rose up onto her knees. She yawned and extended her arms over her head.

Corbin made no bones about enjoying the spectacular sight of her stretching her truly glorious body.

"Thank you for accommodating my request to meet today," she said, looking almost shy—for her. "I hope we will meet tomorrow, too?"

He had been wondering the same thing. "Yes," he said firmly. "We will."

Her face softened. "I am glad."

They stared at each other for a long moment before she glanced away and said, her tone brisker, "I enjoyed the afternoon. It was lovely to be with all my siblings. Well, except Bal, of course."

"What is it like to have a twin?" Corbin asked.

She wrinkled her nose. "People always ask that, but it's impossible to answer because I don't know what life is like without one. All I can say is that I miss him dreadfully."

"I've seen the letters on the salver and know he writes you often."

"He does. And that helps, but it still feels empty without him sometimes. As if something cannot really have happened if Bal was not there to witness it with me." She shrugged. "But I am happy for him."

"Did you ever expect that he would marry?"

She laughed. "Lord no. Of all of us, he was the happiest at Canoga. His skill when it came to farming and his mechanical innovations were both things that brought a great deal of money into our community. As a result, he was given what he needed to pursue his interests. Not like poor Ares and Apollo, who were both constantly stymied. Ares because the Council at Canoga decided it would be better if he focused his skills on mass production of furniture, rather than the one-of-a-kind pieces that he lives to make. As for Apollo, the Council saw no reason to pursue thoroughbred breeding. They changed their minds somewhat when the sale of several of his horses brought in a great deal of money. And Eva"—she huffed out a breath. "Let's just say that she never would have agreed to communal child-rearing. I suspect her time at Canoga was limited regardless of this sojourn to Britain. And of course, she has always been a mad Anglophile, so the chance to come to England was her dream."

"What about you?" Corbin asked.

"What about me?"

"Were you happy at Canoga? What was your dream?"

She inhaled deeply and then sighed. "I realize now that I was, like my younger siblings, rather stymied. Not just when it came to my *little causes*," she said the last two words in a voice that sounded remarkably like Miss Barrymore, "But also when it came to my life." She slid a glance at him. "I am sure you've heard of the Canoga policy of sexual mentorship—I know the journalists love to harp on that, as if it is the only important part of the Canoga credo."

"I have heard of it," Corbin said carefully, having to impose all his will to keep from allowing any judgment to seep into his words.

Even so, her eyes narrowed slightly before she said, "I suppose you believe that people should remain chaste until marriage?"

"I would be the worst kind of hypocrite if I did, wouldn't I?"

She smiled at that. "So then it is only women who should not take lovers?"

"You must admit that the consequences are certainly higher for women."

"Oh yes. Especially if men deliberately keep them ignorant about things like condoms. But tell me truthfully, Masterson, is the possibility of pregnancy the only reason you believe women should wait until marriage to engage in sex?"

Corbin ground his teeth. Infuriated at her for putting such a question to him and angry at himself for what his answer needed to be if he was going to tell the truth. "No," he bit out. "But it is the main one."

"I appreciate your honesty. And I won't put you on the spot and ask if you think I am a woman of low morals for being here with yo—"

"I do not."

"Thank you," she said quietly.

Corbin felt compelled to try and explain himself. "I do not know why I feel so differently about men and women having intimate relations before marriage. It shames me to admit that I have never examined my thoughts on the matter until I met you. I suppose my attitude is simply one I was conditioned to have.

"I am pleased that you are considering the issue rather than simply dismissing my point of view out of hand. In any case, I strongly believe that young men and women—those above eighteen and especially older than twenty-one—should not be kept ignorant about their sexuality *or* their partner's." An emotion Corbin could not identify slid across her face. "Whether sexual mentorship is the way to do that…I am not so sure. The relationship between me and my own mentor—Lamar Jacobsen—was not as straightforward as I was always led to believe. It was neither brief nor without repercussions. Indeed, it lasted for a long time, which was frowned upon and—"

"Frowned upon?" Corbin could not help asking. "By whom?"

"By most of the members of the community and the Council." She inhaled deeply and looked as though she were searching for the right words. "People are dissuaded from viewing others as their possessions. It is one of the main tenets of Canoga." She pulled a wry face. "And there is nothing more possessive than monogamy."

A snort of disbelief slipped out of him.

She raised her eyebrows, her expression cool. "You find that amusing?"

"You are serious," he said, realizing she had not been making one of her irreverent quips.

"Yes, Masterson. I am serious."

It was too difficult for Corbin's brain to comprehend such a bizarre view of emotional intimacy, not to mention marriage.

But then something struck him. "You said people were *dissuaded.* Dissuaded how?"

"It is called being *sticky* when a person pursues an exclusive relationship. The Council usually steps in and talks to one or both partners if somebody becomes…sticky. In my case, they spoke to Lamar and he was the one who severed the relationship."

What sort of madness was this?

"And he just…*left* you just because they told him to?" Corbin asked, not caring that he sounded disbelieving and affronted.

She shrugged. "He probably would have done it once he realized I was pregnant, but yes, their intervention was the impetus for his decision."

"*What?*" he thundered.

She looked at him with cool eyes. "Yes, Masterson. At Canoga, people do not propose when a woman is pregnant."

His mouth worked, no doubt making him look like a landed fish. The expression on her face told him this discussion was headed toward an argument. And this time, it would be his fault for starting it.

But Corbin found that he could not leave the subject alone. "And didn't it bother you when Jacobsen…ended your relationship?"

Her lips twisted into an expression that Corbin could not identify. "Rejection is never pleasant, Masterson."

Corbin stared at her, hoping for more. But her gaze was vague, as if she were staring at something else entirely.

***

How in the world had Io ended up talking about Lamar and that mess?

246

Io: The Shrew

She looked at Masterson, unsurprised when his expression was one of profound incomprehension leavened with a dash of disbelief and a pinch of revulsion. It was a look she had seen many times before on people's faces.

Just what would he think if she told him the rest of her sad little tale?

He told you his story. Are you too proud to share your own?

"I became pregnant with Lamar's child," Io blurted, as if she could not *wait* to see the loathing blossom in his eyes. "And I lost the baby."

There was no disdain in his expression, only the sympathy of a man who had suffered a similar loss. "I am sorry, Io."

She ignored his apology; she did not deserve it. "The miscarriage was my fault."

He frowned. "How do you mean?"

Io looked down at her hands for a moment, and then made herself look up again. "I was such a brokenhearted little ninny that I did not take care of my own health. I lost the baby."

"That is hardly your fault!"

"It is nice of you to take up the cudgels on my behalf, but there is no use in—"

"You did nothing wrong," he said firmly, his arms sliding around her body. "What did you tell me about the mess I made with Emma? You said I was young," he answered before she could rouse herself. "So were you, Io. Young and brokenhearted. Nothing that happened was your fault."

Io held herself rigid for a few seconds, but then sagged against him.

"I cannot believe Lord Balthazar did not thrash Jacobsen to within an inch of his life."

The words were an angry rumble that vibrated through Io's body and made her smile.

"Trust me, I worried about that, too. Not to mention Pol and Ares. I told Lamar to let it be known that I was the one who ended our arrangement."

His arms loosened around her and he pulled back until they could see each other's faces. "I'm sorry that happened to you."

"I know you are." Io slid a hand down his bare side. "I do not want to be sad today."

"What can I do to make you happy?" he asked without hesitation.

"You can lie down on your back."

His eyebrows arched, but he immediately rolled over.

Io grabbed a handful of blankets, but then paused to ask, "Are you cold?"

He shook his head, his dark gaze fixed on her, quiet anticipation lurking in the twin pools of his inky black pupils.

"I want to see you," she said.

"Have you not seen me?"

"Not as closely as I want. I'm usually in such a rush to *touch* you that I don't get to fully enjoy the looking."

His lips quirked into a faint smile. "By all means."

Io pulled back the bedding, savoring him the way one would a fine wine, slowly and thoroughly.

And he *was* fine. His shoulders were broad and elegantly capped with muscle, his bulging biceps those of a man who'd engaged in his share of physical labor in his life—not to mention the boxing sessions he engaged in with Zeus at least twice a week.

Hard, slabbed pectorals led to a tight muscular abdomen that narrowed into a V at his slim hips. His cock was half-hard and lying on his thigh like a lazily resting predator, filling out more even as she looked at him.

The dark blond trail of hair that grew down the center of his chiseled belly spread into a curly nest at the base of his cock.

Io's breathing was labored as she jerked her chin at his groin. "Spread your thighs for me."

His body jolted and his thick shaft hardened the rest of the way, but he did not obey her.

When she lifted her gaze to meet his she saw that his jaw was like iron. His mind, she suspected, rebelled at being viewed as a sexual object, but his body liked it a great deal.

Io: The Shrew

And then he spread his legs for her.

***

Never in his life had Corbin been the recipient of such a thorough—and sensual—visual inspection.

That Io liked what she saw was undeniable as her eyes became darker the longer she stared at him.

His own arousal was bobbing and leaking on his belly even before she'd commanded him to spread for her.

Her hand, cool and smooth, slid over his thigh and he grunted when she cupped his sac, every muscle and nerve in his body tightening at her touch.

"Very nice," she murmured, and then used her other hand to caress the muscles of his belly.

Corbin's eyes wanted to close so he could sink deeply into this experience, but he wanted to see her face even more.

Her fingers dug into his abdomen while her other hand slid off his balls and up over his erection—which was doing plenty of silent begging—cruelly moving on before finally settling on his chest.

"Ah, *God!*" he shouted when she pinched his nipple. *Hard.* His hand shot out and closed around her wrist.

She gave him an exaggeratedly innocent look. "Oh, did that hurt? Let me kiss it better."

"If you bite me, Io, I will—" he warned, but the feel of silky heat around his stinging nipple forced a moan from him.

"*Mmm,*" she hummed, moving to his other nipple while she rubbed his abdomen in circles, brushing against the throbbing head of his prick with every pass, until his body was so damned primed he thought he'd explode from sheer need.

And still, she teased and teased and teased.

"Enough!" he finally roared, easily flipping her onto her back beneath him.

Her body shook with laughter as he pinned her wrists above her head.

"You are a sadistic witch," he hissed, and then commenced tormenting her far larger nipples with equally punishing nips and kisses, until she bucked beneath him.

"Masterson," she murmured, trying to grind her mound against him.

Corbin sucked the nipple he'd been teasing one last time before releasing it. "What?" he demanded rudely, still holding her wrists with one hand while he contorted himself to reach between her thighs. "Ah, nice and wet." He fingered her sensitive bud until she was writhing beneath him, never giving her quite enough to reach her peak.

"Please," she begged, body writhing.

"Please what?"

"Please give me an orgasm."

He barked a cruel laugh and gave her clitoris a pinch that made her cry out.

"Please give me an orgasm…" he trailed off.

She growled. "What are you—"

"You like to torment me when we are around others," he said. "Now you can pay the price. Beg me. And do it properly. Tell me who is the master here, now?"

She glared when he took his hand away completely. "You will suffer for this."

"I have no doubt of that."

"Please give me an orgasm, *master*."

He grinned, his finger already in motion. "There's a good girl—see, that wasn't so hard."

"I need you inside me," she gasped, her body beginning to shake.

Corbin glanced around for his coat—which is where the condoms were. "Hold on, just let me—"

"You don't need to put one on."

He gaped. "But—"

"Trust me."

Some part of him suggested this was a bad idea, but his little head was already throbbing with joy.

"As you wish," he murmured, and then positioned himself at her entrance and filled her with one long, hard thrust.

She shattered even before he'd begun moving with her, her body clenching him so damned hard that he almost came himself.

Instead, he sank deep inside her and kept her filled as her climax washed through her, her tight inner walls exquisite torture on his aching shaft.

Only after the last contraction had wrung her out did he withdraw all the way.

Her heavy eyes lifted. "What? Why are you—"

"*Shhh*, darling." He gave her a lingering kiss and then—clenching his jaws to keep from moaning—laid down beside her. "We still have another hour," he explained. "Plenty of time for me to fetch a condom and take my pleasure in a way that will not leave you wondering and worrying."

Her eyes widened, suddenly glassy.

"Don't get all sentimental on me," he teased. "The only weeping I want you to do in bed is when I spank you."

She gave a watery gurgle. "I never cry."

"I know you don't," he lied. "Oh, there was something I've been wanting to ask you for months."

"*Months?*"

"Yes. Why do your brothers *moo* at you?"

She laughed again. "Because they are idiots, it is their way of expressing affection. You know the Roman myth about Io, don't you?"

Corbin wracked his memory. "I was obsessed with both Greek and Roman mythology when I was a boy, but I don't recall Io's tale—other than she was one of Jupiter's lovers."

"But then, who wasn't?" She pulled a face. "As for the myth, the story goes that Jupiter's long-suffering wife was furiously searching for her husband's current lover and so the endlessly priapic king of the gods decided to turn poor Io into a heifer."

"Oh, *now* I remember."

"Hmm, well so do those two fools. When Ares and Pol were little, they would follow me around, driving me mad." She snorted, looking more amused than annoyed. "It didn't matter how often I boxed their ears, they would beg, *Moo, Yoyo. Please, just once.*"

"And did you?" Corbin asked.

She made an irritable noise. "Sometimes—but just to shut them up." Her green eyes narrowed at him. "Don't even *think* about mooing at me, Masterson."

"I would never," Corbin lied.

She laughed. "Oh, I just bet you wouldn't."

Chapter 25

January 17, 1872
Last Wednesday

Corbin's jaw sagged as he watched Io disappear into a scrofulous shack two streets away from the waterfront, a structure that even he would hesitate to enter alone.

Very few things or people in life rendered Corbin speechless, but Lady Io Hale was one of those people who did it without even trying.

Last Tuesday, after she had confided her painful past to him, Corbin had hoped their relationship was heading in a new, more emotionally intimate, direction.

That hope had been bolstered when Io had shown up the following day—their Wednesday—and they had fallen into bed and made love and talked and made love again and then talked some more. By the time they had left room 320, Corbin had been more optimistic than he'd felt in ages.

They had not spoken during the week, of course, but whenever Corbin had stolen glances at her at dinner or breakfast, he'd caught her peeking back at him.

Everything appeared to be going so well.

And then today, *this* happened.

Io had not done anything this reckless for weeks. But suddenly, an hour ago, she had sneaked out the side entrance of Hastings House and only by chance had one of the footmen—Nathan, an uppity Londoner Corbin did not care for—come directly to Corbin as Hastings was tied up with Parliamentary duties.

Corbin had been damned fortunate that he'd been able to catch up to her before she disappeared.

He'd been furious and terrified when his cab had followed her down to the docks just in time to see her stroll—just as careless and heedless as ever—into a nasty-looking building.

"Wot next, guv?" the London cabbie asked, interrupting his roiling thoughts.

"Do you know what sort of business is in that building?" he asked.

The driver shrugged. "Jes some shippin' 'ouse."

Shipping? What was she—Corbin groaned. Condoms. That must be what she was about.

He chewed the inside of his cheek; should he march in there and drag her out?

He winced at the thought of the scene she would cause.

Corbin glanced around them. There was nowhere unobtrusive to wait, and he could hardly ask the man to keep his horse standing in such frigid weather. "I want to keep an eye on that building. Just drive back and forth, keeping it in sight, until that lady comes back out."

***

Io glowered at the man across from her, deeply displeased. "Mr. Gordon said you would handle all legal requirements. The crates my associates were offered when they came to retrieve them this morning had *no* customs stamps. These people traveled a long way and at great expense to collect the promised shipment. Now they will need to make another journey. Not only that, but I suspect that you have implicated me in criminal activity by avoiding paying the proper duties, Mr. Branson."

Branson, a skinny, pockmarked weasel of a man, just smirked and shrugged. "It ain't up to me, is it?"

"That is not what you said when we made this agreement," she retorted sharply. "Now, I am here to arrange for yet another delivery date—this time with the proper customs stamps."

Again he shrugged. "Too late. I already sold that batch."

"What? You had them this morning!"

"I did *then*. But now they be *gone*. You want the next shipment comin', or not?"

Io ground her teeth to keep from giving him the sharp edge of her tongue. Although it nearly killed her, she politely said, rather than yelled, "Of course, I want them. As long as they go through the proper channels."

He stared for a long moment and then said. "Fine. But that will cost extra."

"How much extra?"

"The same again."

"*Double?*"

"Aye."

"That is *outrageous!*"

"You needn't buy 'em."

Io dearly wanted to turn around and walk out of this odious swine's office, but that would only mean more delays.

And so she forced herself to ask, "When will you have them?"

"I dunno, 'zackly. I'll send word to Gordon when they come in—jes like last time." He chuckled. "But *after* they've gone through the *proper channels,*" he said, doing a fair job of mocking her accent.

"See that you do." Io reached into her bag and took out the money she'd counted out at home—money that *should* have bought a second batch of condoms—and tossed the packet onto his cluttered desk. "It's all there. But feel free to count it," she added when his none-too-clean hand reached for the money.

He halted at her snide words, his eyes narrowing in a way that suddenly reminded her she was alone in his office. "Naw, a *lady* like you would never cheat such a man as me, eh?"

She snorted, sliding her hand unobtrusively into her satchel and closing her fingers around the handle of the pistol she had pilfered from her brother's gunroom, just in case she had need of it. "When can I expect the shipment? A day? A week? A month?" she demanded, keeping her hand in the bag.

Branson lolled in his seat, leering up at her in a way that sorely tempted her to shoot him. "Next week sometime. You tell 'em I'll only make the delivery at night the next time."

"At night," she repeated flatly, not liking the thought of anyone coming to this slimy office to meet this slimy man at any time, most certainly at night.

"Aye. At night," he repeated with more iron in his voice. "Your sort showin' up 'ere in broad daylight ain't the type o' attention I need."

Of course, he would say that. "Fine," Io snapped, eager to get away from. Also eager to get to her Wednesday rendezvous. She would already be late as it was. And Corbin would grill her, no doubt.

Io slammed the door behind her and then looked up the street for the cabbie she'd told to return in a quarter of an hour, pleased when it came rolling up just as she stepped away from the house.

Io was squinting up at the driver; he did not look the same.

The cab door flew open, and a hand shot out and clamped around her upper arm.

"Get in!" Corbin hissed at her, yanking her inside none too gently. He pushed her into the seat across from him before slamming the door.

"What in the name of *hell* are you doing down here, Io? I thought we came to an understanding weeks ago about you leaving without taking—"

"I don't recall any such understanding!" Io lashed back, her heart still pounding from the shock he'd just given her. But that shock quickly turned to fury. "And just what are you doing following me *again*, Masterson? Because I thought we'd come to an understanding about *that*."

"Answer me, dammit."

Io flinched back from the anger in his tone. "Who do you think—"

He grabbed her upper arms, his fingers biting into her flesh. "Do you not recall what almost happened to you in the Five Points? This part of London is every bit as bad."

Io jerked away from him—or tried to, but he held her for a moment, making her feel his greater strength before allowing her to slip free.

"What I *want* to do is manage my affairs without anyone interfering. I refuse to live in fear of what some man might do. And that includes you, Corbin."

A vein pulsed in his temple and he glared for a long moment, chewing the inside of his cheek, doubtless to keep from losing his temper.

Io had never seen him quite so…unhinged.

Io: The Shrew

"What was it you went to do inside that building?" he asked in a firm but cool voice after a long, unpleasant silence, his expression stern and unrelenting.

Io ignored him and crossed her arms, turning away to stare out the window at the slate-gray afternoon. There had been no new snow for weeks, but the weather had been brutally cold and the nasty grayish-black crust that seemed to cover every surface refused to melt.

"Are you going to answer me, Io?"

"What I was doing in there is none of your concern."

Oh, Io. Why not just tell him?

"I beg to differ." Something that looked almost like desperation flickered across his severe features, but it was gone before she could be sure.

But the one emotion that she did recognize was his obvious effort to rein in his temper.

"Right now is a delicate time for your brother. He is—" Masterson broke off, his jaw flexing. "He is forming associations that will make a great deal of difference for him in the years ahead."

"You mean he is forming alliances in Parliament so that his banks may receive the most beneficial treatment."

His face hardened. "That is not the only issue of interest to him."

"Oh? Tell me one single matter that interests my brother that doesn't involve making money?"

"If you want an answer to that you can ask him yourself and I am sure he will gladly tell you. But all that is beside the point."

"What is your point? That I should stop pursuing my goals—stop fulfilling promises I've made to people in New York and here—and instead pursue a flirtation with one of the fools I am forced to see and speak with at every *ton* function? Perhaps Lord Danvers? He has shown a marked interest in me. I daresay he could be persuaded to offer marriage with very little effort on my part. Is that the sort of activity you would prefer I pursue?"

"Danvers is a fool and—"

"Ah, but he is a *marquess* and can trace his family tree back to the Conquest. Probably back to the Bible. Not as far as Adam and Eve, perhaps, but—"

"Neither I nor your brother are saying you should marry," Masterson seethed.

"Danvers is said to be one of the catches of the Season," Io went on.

"All I am saying," Masterson continued grimly, "is that for the first year, if you could comport yourself more as a—"

"If you say *lady,* I shall scream."

He clamped his jaws shut and glared.

Io could not take his censure one moment longer. "For your information, I might have gone to that scoundrel's office alone today, but the money I gave him came from none other than Viscountess Kendrick and the Duchess of Malverton"—Io nodded at his look of disbelief. "Yes, *Malverton.* While the paragon of the *ton* is drinking tea with *ladylike* Edith, she is slipping me donations under the table. *Unsolicited* donations, by the way."

Masterson's shock was like a fine wine and Io savored it.

"Does this have to do with—"

"Contraception and prophylactics," she finished for him. "Yes."

"But…the Duke of Malverton has—"

"Supported legislation that would make the sale or distribution of contraceptive devices if not illegal, then certainly close to impossible for most women to access," she finished. "Especially poor, powerless ones." Her eyes narrowed. "I must admit the duchess's motives are not entirely altruistic."

"What do you mean?"

She scoffed. "Oh, come now. Despite His Grace's disgusting taste for virgins the man still keeps two mistresses mounted, visits brothels, and has managed to infect his wife with syphilis—along with a great many other women, I should imagine."

Masterson's jaw shifted from side to side as he masticated on the matter. "That is a subject—"

"Which subject? Whores? Syphilis? His Grace's myriad mistresses? Or purchasing virgins?" Io goaded, not letting him answer before adding, "Let me guess: you were going to say they are *all* subjects that are unfit for ladies?"

"As it turns out," he said acidly, "you do not yet know *everything* I am thinking. It will surprise you to learn that what I was about to say before you interrupted me was that the Duke of Malverton's unsavory engagement in the virgin trade is a subject your brother and like-minded men in Parliament are determined to bring an end to."

"I *am* surprised to hear that," Io wasn't ashamed to admit. "It is yet one more reason I am increasingly fond of my oldest sibling. It also makes it all the more curious as to why you disapprove of what I am doing so fiercely."

"It is your *methods* I disapprove of." He regarded her steadily before adding. "As I think you well know, as much as you seem to derive amusement from accusing me of possessing the social opinions of a cave dweller."

Io snorted at the image of proper Corbin Masterson living in a cave with his tidy three-piece suits and meticulous ledgers.

"What is so amusing?"

"Nothing," she lied. "As for the other matters you mentioned—brothels, mistresses, and disease—I daresay my brother will not be addressing any of *those* matters with his like-minded Parliamentarians. No, those are all jealously guarded privileges of males of all classes, but most especially the wealthiest ones." She paused and amended. "Well, not the diseases, but the unfettered access to female bodies."

"And do you count me among that number, my lady?"

"I don't know, Masterson. Have you visited a brothel? Employed a mistress?" She snorted at the color that darkened his cheeks and directed her disappointed gaze back to the window. "Never mind. Don't answer that," she said.

"Ah, I see."

She turned at the sound of his bitter words. "And what do you see?"

"You have already sat as judge, jury, and executioner on my character."

She crossed her arms. "Are you telling me you have not treated women as commodities you can purchase—like a pound of nails from a mercantile or a loaf of bread from a baker?"

"Aren't you the woman who said—and I quote—*men are only good for one thing and most of them are not even good for that?*"

"You know I said it because I said it to your face, Masterson. What of it?"

"Men are all the same to you. Different faces and bodies but the person inside them is interchangeable." He suddenly leaned forward, his mask of cool civility sliding off to reveal molten intensity. "Isn't it treating men as commodities—*things* that are only good for a *fuck*—to espouse an opinion like that?"

Io jolted at the crude word. Masterson almost never cursed, which made it all the more startling.

"Tell me, Io," he said, his voice so low she had to lean forward to hear him over the sound of the hansom wheels. "How would you have reacted if I'd said that women were only good for sex?"

Shame, as sharp as a slap, caused Io to flinch back.

He gave a slight nod and then turned to look out the window, leaving her to her unwanted thoughts.

If he had said something like that you would have clawed his eyes out.

That was true; she would have.

"I told the driver to take us to the hotel," Masterson said. "If you'd rather go home to Hastings House, speak now and I will tell him to change direction."

When she did not immediately answer, he turned to her.

Io studied his expression, searching for clues as to his thoughts. After a moment, she gave up looking. "I do not wish to go home. But neither do I want to be harangued about what I was doing today."

His jaw flexed and he nodded. "Very well. No haranguing."

Tell him why you went alone today! Tell him!

Io clamped her jaws shut. She did not owe him, or anyone else, excuses for what she did.

You will regret not telling him…

"The reason I didn't bring Moira today is because she had already left on her half-day when I received the message to go to the docks. As for why I didn't bring a footman—or take one of my brother's carriages?" She snorted. "Well, I should think that would be obvious, Masterson. It would be damned difficult to explain to one of my brother's servants why I was headed to Boynton Hotel, wouldn't it? Or," she added, "I suppose there is a third option: I could have just missed our meeting this week. In any event, that is why I behaved recklessly and chose to take a cab."

He regarded her levelly but did not respond.

Io turned away from him with a huff and stared out the window.

Not another word was exchanged between them until they reached Room 320.

Chapter 26

Three-Quarters of an Hour Later

Waves of raw lust rolled through Io's body as she leaned over the settee, her muscles quivering and her hips canted for more of Masterson's cruel palm.

The moment they had reached the hotel room—still without speaking—he had swiftly stripped off her hat and cloak and bent her over the back of the settee.

"I promised not to harangue you about your behavior today," he hissed hotly in her ear. "But I made no such promise about not punishing you."

And then he commenced to deliver a spanking that would doubtless leave bruises on her bottom.

He spanked her like he *needed* it. As if he craved it every bit as much as Io did.

His big warm palm smoothed away the hurt he'd just inflicted on her flaming buttocks.

Io shivered at the odd, addictive blend of pleasure and pain this aloof man had discovered she needed. All her anger at him—at the world and life and the injustice of it all—bled away, swamped under waves of pure satisfaction.

He slid a finger between her lower lips, his confident, proprietary stroking adding more layers to what was already a blissful experience.

And then he did something unexpected. Something…shocking, coming from him…

He used her arousal to wet her back hole, a part of her he had never touched before.

Io thrust her hips higher. "*Mmm*, Masterson… that's so *naughty*."

"I am going to take you back here next time."

His cool and—yes—masterful tone made her inner walls clench to be filled. Lord. If he ever learned just how fiercely he affected her and with so little effort on his part, she would never live it down.

Io grabbed the reins of her rapidly spiraling desire and yanked hard. She forced herself to utter an insouciant laugh and then say, "Of course you may do that."

Her reward for such self-control was the slightest jolt of his hand.

"You would allow it?"

Io bristled at his tone, which sounded almost…bored. Damn the man! Was there nothing she could do to get under his thick hide? Well, nothing *inside* the bedchamber, at any rate.

"*Mmm-hmm*," she hummed, striving for the same degree of boredom in her own voice. "Right after I do it to you."

Her words struck their target and she felt incredulity roll through his body.

"I can almost see your face, Masterson." This time she didn't have to force her amusement.

"Fortunately for me, you are not adequately equipped to carry through with your threat, my lady."

His smug, superior words surprised a bark of laughter out of her. "Are you really unaware of how a woman can do such a thing? Oh, Masterson! How I look forward to giving you *that* lesson." Io reveled in regaining the upper hand.

"I am hard-pressed to imagine a less likely scenario," he retorted, somewhat lamely she thought.

"You really are an innocent, aren't you, darling?"

His hand struck her cheek with a loud *crack*. "Shut up, you obstreperous jade."

Io laughed.

She immediately stopped laughing when she felt the hard, hot silk of his shaft stroking her folds, his skilled caresses driving her quickly toward the brink of an orgasm.

Io pushed her ass up as much as she could, not caring how desperate she sounded or looked, and forced herself to say, "Put on a condom and fuck me, *now.*"

She bit back a groan when his body moved away to comply with her demand. She'd been reckless with him once before—engaging in sex without a condom for the first time since she had become pregnant—and had been fortunate that he had kept his wits and not spent inside her.

Io had been ashamed of her weakness and would not place that burden on him again. Corbin, for all his rigid morality, had accepted her demand for protection far more readily and willingly than Lamar had ever done. The irony of that did not escape her: a Council member from Canoga had begged her to engage in intercourse without a condom while a Presbyterian ex-seminary student had never once questioned her wishes.

You were the one who made the decision to do without a condom. It is almost as if you wanted to fall pregnant and trap the man…

Io violently thrust the unwanted thought away and twisted around, desperate not to be left alone with her thoughts. "What are you doing back there, Masterson?" she called out. "Composing a sermon?"

He grabbed a fistful of her hair and yanked her head back *hard.* "Stay put and don't speak unless I tell you or I will gag you, my lady."

Io's body responded to his threat in a way that shocked her. For a moment, she thought she might actually climax as she met his fierce, hard gaze.

As it was, she could barely manage to utter the few words that her addled brain came up with. "*Please…sir.*"

Masterson's nostrils flared and then he uttered an animalistic snarl and drove himself deeply into her body.

"*Yes,*" Io hissed, her eyes threatening to roll back in her head.

"My God," Masterson said in a voice that almost sounded…broken.

And then he commenced to ride her as if the hounds of hell were on his heels.

The orgasm, when it came, was shattering and Io was so caught up in its grasp that she didn't even notice Masterson removing her gown and carrying her to the bed afterward.

Io: The Shrew

When she could force her eyes open, she saw that he had collapsed alongside her, still completely dressed, his lips parted, eyes closed, breathing deep and even.

Io smiled at the sight and then promptly drifted off herself.

***

Corbin woke up with a start, disoriented. There was a deliciously soft warmth along one side and he saw that Io was still sleeping soundly beside him.

It all came back to him then.

He had carried her to the bed after their torrid session, stripped her, and then—amazingly—fallen into a deep, dreamless sleep.

Corbin took his watch from his pocket and winced. They had less than an hour remaining. He was furious with himself. How could he fall asleep when they only had a few hours together?

He could only think they had both been exhausted by the emotional ride from the wharf to the hotel.

Not to mention the physical ride you gave her once you got to the hotel.

Corbin shook his head at the snide mental voice. He quietly slipped off the bed and retired to the bathroom to salvage what he could of his appearance. Although he'd removed her gown and draped it over the clothes horse, his own garments were horribly wrinkled from sleeping in them.

There wasn't much he could do other than fix his mop of hair—he desperately needed a haircut—wash his face and iron the worst of the wrinkles from his clothing with the palms of his hands.

It would have to do.

Corbin opened the bathroom door and was startled to see that Io was lounging—nude—on the settee in front of the fireplace.

"You're awake," he said stupidly.

She merely grunted, not looking up as she flipped through the small journal she carried with her in the ugly satchel she was never without.

Corbin snatched unobtrusive glances at her as he pretended to gather up his gloves, coat, and hat, which he'd scattered around the room in his haste to have her.

"I see you looking," she muttered,

So much for being *unobtrusive*.

"Are you not getting dressed to go?" he asked, irritated by his inability to concentrate when she was unclothed. Or clothed. Or in the same damned room, for that matter.

"Does my nudity bother you?" She lifted her head and fixed him with the coolly mocking look that always made him feel as if she could see every perverted, debased desire he'd hidden in the dark recesses of his mind for decades.

Until *she* dragged them into the light.

"I don't care what you wear or don't wear," he lied. "Suit yourself—or not, as the case may be," he added with forced lightness. He turned his back on her and pretended to straighten his four-in-hand, not wanting her to notice that he was half-hard just from looking at her.

"You are tumescent, Masterson, aren't you?"

Corbin squeezed his eyes shut and prayed for patience. So much for hiding his condition. He ignored her comment, hoping she would drop the subject if he did not engage her.

"Modern medical science suggests that it is healthier for a man your age to ejaculate more than one day a week," she went on. "Perhaps you need an additional lover to—"

Corbin swung around to face her. "I am not planning to have sex with another woman," he seethed.

She arched one of her elegant black eyebrows, the action infuriating. "Whyever not? Is it because of your Puritanical—"

"It is because I am not an animal in rut, unable to control my own base impulses."

Her sly smile warned him of what she was about to say.

"Except when it comes to *you*, evidently," he said before she could speak.

"Hmm. Well, if you won't find a woman to relieve your needs then please tell me you masturbate regularly."

Io: The Shrew

Corbin could only give a disbelieving huff before turning his back again and slipping on his overcoat.

"Or are you too Puritanical to touch yourself? Do you believe in the sins of Onan? Or perhaps you don't know how to masturbate? Oh, wait—of course you do! I recall that time when I interrupted you in the midst of—"

Corbin whipped around. "I will not discuss my masturbatory schedule with you."

She raised both eyebrows this time. "So you *do* have one, then?"

He inhaled deeply and then exhaled slowly. "Where are you going with this, Io?"

"I just told you, medical research—"

"Not that. *This*"—he made a gesture that encompassed them and the room around them. "Where do you think this is leading?" The words were out before he could stop them.

Her amusement slowly drained away. "I thought we came here to sate our carnal desires on one another." She cocked her head. "Why? Where do you think this is leading?" Before he could answer—not that he had one—she gave a mocking laugh. "Please tell me you are not so misguided as to believe we are headed toward love and marriage, Masterson?"

Corbin swallowed down the bile that rose within him at her sneer. "No. I'm not so misguided as that," he admitted grimly.

"What are you trying to say, Masterson? That you want to end this?" she asked, cutting him a mildly curious look, as if she did not care one way or another how he answered.

Corbin desperately wished that he'd just kept his mouth shut. But he hadn't. And now it sounded as if she was ready to call an end to things right *now*.

Say yes *and save yourself further pain*, self-preservation urged.

That was exactly what he should do. But he simply could not force himself to say the word.

Instead, he said, "When we agreed on this arrangement, we both said either of us could stop it at any time. If neither of us shows up next week, we will know where the other stands on the matter." The words were like acid on his tongue, but at least he had not been the one to call an end to things.

She slipped her journal back into her bag. "Fine," she said, her careless shrug making it painfully obvious that she had no interest in any future that included the two of them together in any meaningful way.

Corbin's lungs felt as if they were on fire and he realized he'd stopped breathing some time ago. He needed to get out now, before there was nothing left of himself to rescue. He pulled on his gloves, snatched up his hat, and strode toward the door, pausing only after he opened it, but not turning around.

"Fine," he said, his word a harsh echo of hers.

***

Io began to dress immediately after the door closed behind Masterson. She liked to remain naked in his presence because it always wrong-footed him so badly. And because he was the most articulate, cleverest, and quickest man she had ever known and Io needed every advantage in their skirmishes.

Skirmishes she greatly enjoyed.

Skirmishes that were evidently over.

Thanks to her.

Io stared blankly at the hands holding her chemise, infuriated to see they were shaking.

Fine? You said fine? *You should have said something else—*anything *else. He is a proud man. After the way you just behaved, he will not be here next week.*

She flung the garment away and dropped onto the settee, not sprawling as she'd done earlier with Masterson—like a seductress in one of the dreadful naughty novels her younger brother Ares read and which he thought nobody else knew about.

No, all that posturing had all been for Corbin's benefit, because it was so easy and so enjoyable to assail his prudish sense of decorum.

But Corbin wasn't there. And chances were, thanks to her rash behavior and *fine*, he wouldn't be there next week, or ever again.

Io drew her knees up to her chest and wrapped her arms around them.

Io: The Shrew

The room was colder than it had been only moments earlier. Frigid.

These Wednesday afternoons with Corbin Masterson had been the most wonderful of her life, and not just sexually, although she had never admitted that to herself until that moment.

Io rolled onto her side, still clutching her knees, marveling at how she'd not even known Masterson a year ago at this same time and yet he seemed to have invaded every single corner of her life.

Or at least he had, until today.

But now these meetings—which had been the highlight of her week, although she would die before admitting that to Masterson—might be over.

And it is all due to your foolish pride and crippling fear.

The last time I set aside my foolish pride *for the sake of a man I not only lost my dignity; I also lost a child. What I have done today is neither foolish nor weak. It is wise.*

It is self-preservation.

Self-preservation. The words had been a mantra for over four years, ever since she'd thrown caution to the winds and followed her heart.

For some reason, the words had a hollow ring to them this time.

Chapter 27

This Wednesday

Io was avoiding him.

Although they rarely spoke during the days between their trysts, this past week had been even more barren. She had not teased or taunted Corbin at dinner when the opportunity had presented itself and they had not exchanged so much as one stolen glance since the week before.

Normally, he would have something to look forward to today—it was a Wednesday, after all—something to make life worthwhile.

But Corbin could not forget how he and Io had left things last Wednesday. The memory of their parting had eaten at him over the intervening days. And because he was a pathetic, besotted fool, he decided to go down to breakfast later than he usually ate that morning, timing his meal so that he might steal a few glances at Io and try to gauge whether he would show up to an empty room that afternoon.

If he was not such a coward, he would just bloody ask the woman.

But he was a coward.

And he was terrified of the answer he might receive.

Unfortunately, he and Io were not the only ones in the breakfast room. Indeed, *all* the Hales—even the duke—had gathered for the morning meal, an unusual occurrence.

"We are going to The Tower," Eva announced with a smile the moment Corbin sat down with a plate of food that he had no interest in eating.

"I thought you went to The Tower just after we arrived in London," he said, stirring a spoonful of sugar into his coffee.

"Eva loves the ravens," Ares said. "She would roost with them if they'd let her."

"I would," Eva agreed, unperturbed by her sibling's gentle ribbing. She cast a sly look at her older sister. "But I'm not as bad as Yoyo."

Io: The Shrew

Corbin looked from Eva to Io—everyone else was, so why shouldn't he?

Io gave her younger sister a pained look. "Please, not this story. Again."

"Yoyo insisted that she was a hen when she was little," Apollo explained, smirking from Corbin to his older sister.

"You were not even born yet, so it's not as if you remember," Io shot back.

"One night she was missing at bedtime and everyone was frantic," Apollo continued. "There was much rending of hair and tearing of clothing—"

"Not to mention a great deal of despair and wailing that she was lost," Ares said, picking up the story.

"Search parties were deployed," Apollo intoned in a deep melodramatic voice that made his twin hoot. "But no trace of her could be found…"

Io muttered something that sounded vaguely threatening, but her siblings were enjoying themselves too much.

Eva smirked at Corbin. "After hours of anguish and agony, she was discovered inside the chicken coop, asleep, sharing one of the nesting boxes with a hen."

"I was *not* sharing a nesting box with a hen. They are far too small, and you know that, Eva," Io said icily. She looked at Corbin, her expression as regal as a queen's. "It was my *own* nesting box."

"It's true," Ares said. "Even though she was barely five years old she'd built a nesting box with her very own hands." He gave his sister the respectful look of one woodworker to another.

"That's not the best part," Apollo said, nudging his twin in the ribs.

Ares grinned. "My father slipped an egg in beside her before they woke her up."

"She thought she'd laid it and insisted on brooding it for an entire *week*," Eva added gleefully.

"It was *not* a week," Io said, addressing her words to Corbin. "It wasn't even a day because I fell asleep while *brooding* and a rotten boy named Davy

Rollins stole the egg and took great pleasure in frying it and proving to me and all the other children that it was merely a regular hen egg."

The others chuckled at what was obviously a family favorite story. Zeus, he couldn't help noticing, was smirking along with the rest of them, looking happier than Corbin had seen him look in weeks—months, even.

"I can't think why my siblings enjoy that story so much," Io said. "There are far more entertaining Hale tales." An evil smile stole across her face. "Like the time Ares and Pol found bullfrogs and—"

"*Mooooo.*"

"*Moooooo.*"

The duke—who obviously knew the story behind the *mooing*—laughed when the twins' raucous noise drowned out whatever tale Io was threatening to tell.

The door opened just then and Miss Barrymore entered a room filled with *moos* and laughter.

Corbin swore the temperature in the room dropped.

He and the other three men stood and *good mornings* were murmured all around.

Lady Eva hurried to fill the awkward silence by badgering her brothers to accompany her ice skating later that day.

Miss Barrymore almost always had breakfast delivered to her chambers, so Corbin's antennae were twitching. He wondered if she was going to The Tower with the rest of the family, but somehow doubted it.

When she turned away from the buffet, he saw she had only one dry piece of toast on her plate.

"—but then Mick said the best skating is somewhere called Millpond and he would know as he was born and raised here," Eva said. "Will you ask him where it is, Pol?"

Apollo gave his younger sibling a wary look. "If Mick suggested it, I'm not sure it will be—"

"Mick?" Miss Barrymore interrupted, looking up from her meager meal. "Is that the boy who runs behind your carriage?" she asked, turning her cold gaze toward Apollo.

Io: The Shrew

Corbin had noticed the woman never said any of their names if she could help herself. And when she *did* address them, her expression was invariably pained or unpleasant.

Silence greeted her question.

"Yes, Mick is his name," Apollo finally said.

Corbin knew damned well that she was aware of who Mick was. Hell, most of London read of the flamboyant young tiger's exploits. To the amusement of Apollo's family and the many avid Hale-watchers both aristocratic and common, Mick had dogged the young lord relentlessly for the position of tiger, an antiquated role that Apollo most certainly had not been looking to fill. Anyone even slightly acquainted with Apollo knew that he'd hired the lad out of kindness, not to garner attention.

"Your behavior has become the topic of some rather unsavory speculation," Miss Barrymore said after a moment had passed.

Apollo finished chewing, took a drink of coffee, and wiped his mouth with his napkin before saying, "Is that so?"

Corbin's eyes slid to the duke, but Hastings seemed to be fascinated by the beefsteak on his plate.

Io, who had a forkful of egg lifted halfway to her mouth set it back down without taking a bite, her gaze sharp.

Even Lady Eva, normally the one to deflect any argument, had a notch of concern between her violet eyes.

Corbin's own gaze settled on Lord Ares and stayed there. The youngest of the brothers *seethed* as he stared at Miss Barrymore, who appeared unaware of the danger.

Corbin opened his mouth to say *anything* to stop the pot from boiling over but he wasn't fast enough.

"Indeed," Miss Barrymore continued in a cool, unpleasant tone. "The way you have been jaunting about with this… *boy* dressed like a doll and the—"

A fork clattered loudly and Miss Barrymore's eyebrows shot up as she turned to Ares, the source of the noise.

"Enough." The word was like the low rumble of a jungle cat and utterly unlike anything Corbin had ever before heard from the sunny natured Ares.

"I beg your pardon?" Miss Barrymore glared at Ares as if he had thrown his fork at her head—still a distinct possibility, in Corbin's opinion— rather than drop it on his plate.

"You heard exactly what I said," Ares shot back in a tone of unbridled loathing.

The duke finally looked up, and the exhaustion on his face stunned Corbin, especially when compared to his expression of only moments before when he had been laughing with his family.

Miss Barrymore swelled, like a hen fluffing her feathers. "Do not speak to me in that—"

"Your incessant insinuations, your nagging, your relentless belittling of my siblings stops *now*," Ares said, raising his voice to a low roar to be heard over Miss Barrymore's angry tone.

Miss Barrymore gasped and turned to the duke, "Hastings, I demand—"

"I will speak to you after breakfast." The duke's voice was all the more commanding for how quiet it was compared to his brother's or fiancé's.

Miss Barrymore smiled smugly and turned to Ares. "I will allow His Grace to settle the matter. I'm sure you will—"

"I did not mean Ares," the duke said, fixing his fiancée with eyes that were the pure, cold blue of arctic ice.

Corbin could not tell who was more shocked: Ares or Miss Barrymore.

When he risked a glance at Io, who had not joined in the argument for once, her eyes glittered with triumph as they slid from brother to brother, and something that looked like relief colored her face when her gaze settled on Apollo.

Miss Barrymore shot to her feet. "I will have that meeting *now*, Hastings," she said, her voice shaking with fury. And then she pivoted on her heel and sailed toward the door. One of the servants—three of whom were still in the room—sprinted to open it for her.

Once Miss Barrymore was gone, the duke turned to Lady Eva and said, "I'm afraid I won't be able to accompany you to The Tower." He stood and said to Corbin, "I am sorry to cut your breakfast short. But would you mind joining me in my study in ten minutes?"

"Of course," Corbin murmured.

The door shut behind the duke and—for once—none of the Hales said a word.

***

Six hours later...

The day had been one of the most awkward and miserable of Corbin's life—even including the years he'd spent fighting in the war.

As bad as the past hours had been for him, they'd been ten-fold worse for his employer, although Hastings remained as distant as the moon even through the worst of it.

Miss Barrymore made sure that the end of their betrothal was as painful as possible—not to mention awkward and expensive—for her fiancé.

Corbin was bloody exhausted just from observing.

At the same time, he felt as if a huge weight had been lifted off his chest.

The flash of rage in Ares's eyes as he'd stared at Miss Barrymore that morning had been extremely worrying. How had Corbin been so blind to the dislike—nay, hatred—swirling around him all these months?

Yet again Io's words came back to him clearly, "You only see what you want to see, Corbin."

It was true, he'd had his head in the sand for months—years, even.

His best friend had taken steps to set his life to rights today. Now it was Corbin's turn.

The question of how to approach Io about sharing their life—not just one day a week—consumed his thoughts as the hansom cab rolled toward the Boynton Hotel. And behind all those thoughts, pulsing like a raw wound, was his fear that she would not be there today.

That she was finished with him.

That—

"Oye! We're 'ere, guv," the driver said, shaking Corbin from his reverie.

He absently paid the cabbie and crossed the street toward the hotel, excitement speeding his steps as a painfully simple solution to their problem began to take root in his mind.

Of course! What a fool he had been, considering marriage the only viable choice because it was what *he* wanted and—

Corbin staggered to the side as a large black coach screeched to a stop, all but running him over. Two men in dark suits leapt out and lunged toward him while somebody behind him—two or three somebodies— grabbed his arms.

He jerked and twisted but the men holding him were strong. "What the bloody—"

"You are coming with us, Mr. Masterson," one of the men from the coach said.

"The hell I will!" he shouted and slammed his head back, catching somebody's nose with a dull *crunch*. A muffled scream was followed by two hands dropping away.

With one arm free Corbin managed to turn on his other captor and drew back his fist for what would have been a leveler.

But then his head exploded like the Fourth of July, pain and blinding white light driving him to his knees.

"I love you, Io." The words were gravelly and slurred and Corbin wasn't sure who'd spoken them.

The world, which had been so painfully bright only a moment earlier, faded to a murky gray.

"What did he say?" somebody asked.

"It doesn't matter! Get him into the coach," a distant voice ordered. "Quickly now!"

Those were the last words Corbin heard before the darkness pulled him under.

***

Io: The Shrew

It had been an agony to go to The Tower and pretend that all was normal. But, surprisingly, it had been Apollo who'd insisted they carry on with their plans.

"Zeus deserves to have the house to himself while he deals with Edith," he'd insisted.

Personally, Io had wanted to purchase box seats and settle in with opera glasses to watch, but her brother had a point. Besides, if allowing Zeus time meant that he would give Edith the boot, then Io could spend all day staring at ravens and jewels.

And so the four of them had gone on their jaunt.

The moment they returned home, Io had sped up to Zeus's office.

Nathan and Albert stood outside the duke's study door like a pair of handsome gargoyles dressed in livery.

"His Grace has asked not to be disturbed, Lady Io," Nathan said in his prim voice.

Io opened her mouth to argue but just then the door at the end of the corridor that concealed the servant stairway opened and Charles, her favorite footman came bounding out, a piece of paper in his gloved hand.

She hurried toward him. "Is Miss Barrymore *still* in the study with my brother?"

He glanced at the other two footmen, who were frowning at them, and then leaned close enough to whisper. "No, my lady, she is packing her things as we speak." He paused and then added in a dramatic voice. "Miss Barrymore is going back to America."

Io's heart almost exploded with joy. "Are you *sure*?"

"Aye, my lady. She is going to stay at the Clarendon for now but will take one of His Grace's own ships back."

"When does she leave?"

"In only two or three days, we were told."

Io's mind raced.

"Miss Barclay isn't going with her," Charles added with a scarcely suppressed grin.

"She isn't? What is she going to do?"

"She will stay on as Lady Eva's companion."

"She *will?*" How in the world had Eva worked so quickly when they'd just returned from their jaunt to The Tower?

"Mr. Masterson is going back with Miss Barrymore."

"*What?*"

The huge footman jumped at her shriek. "Aye. His Grace's man—Mr. Crombie—says Mr. Masterson is cutting his year short to escort Miss Barrymore home."

"His year?" Io repeated. "What year? I don't understand."

"Mr. Crombie says as how Mr. Masterson was only supposed to stay a year with His Grace before returning to America, but now that has changed."

Corbin had only agreed to come for a year?

"I don't understand. Why only a year? And what is he going back for?"

Charles shrugged. "I don't know, my lady."

Io refused to believe it. Surely Corbin would have told her if he was only here for a year?

She knew she shouldn't be gossiping with a servant—especially not in the middle of the corridor—but she had to ask, "Are you saying that Mr. Masterson is leaving His Grace's employ *permanently?*"

The footman opened his mouth, but then closed it, his brow furrowing. After a moment, he shrugged. "Mr. Crombie didn't say that Mr. Masterson was *not* coming back, now that I think about it. But he *did* say that His Grace wanted Miss Barrymore to have an escort."

"Is Mr. Masterson in his rooms?"

"Nay, my lady, he's gone out on his half day, just like he always does on Wednesday."

Io's heart leapt at the news. Corbin wasn't finished with her—at least not yet—and had gone early to the hotel to meet her!

"Thank you, Charles." She kissed the startled footman on the cheek and all but ran to her chambers to fetch her cloak and hat.

Io: The Shrew

Io flung open the door to her room, rushed inside, and gave a yelp of surprise when she almost collided with Edith.

"My, my. Don't *you* look pleased with yourself," Edith hissed like the snake she was, her eyes glittering with malice.

"What are *you* doing in my room?"

"I came here so you could gloat, *my lady*. I am leaving. Doesn't that make you happy?"

Io didn't bother to hide her grin as she held up her hand, her forefinger and thumb separated by a half-inch of air. "Just a little bit."

The other woman snorted. "You are pathetic."

"Says the woman whose fiancé just sent her packing."

"At least I *had* a fiancé. While you are just a cow giving away free milk every Wednesday."

Io's eyes narrowed. "What are you talking about?"

"Corbin told me all about your sordid little arrangement."

Io recoiled, her jaw sagging.

Edith's smirk grew at Io's obvious shock. "He will be accompanying me back home. You should have seen how grateful he was at the news, how happy that he can slip away before you get a chance to make a scene."

"I don't believe you."

"It's true. He's already gone to make our arrangements for the journey." She smiled nastily. "I'm afraid he won't be making your Wednesday meeting today."

"You're a liar! Corbin is only going with you because you are too useless to ride a ship home without some man pandering to your every whim."

Edith sneered. "You poor fool! Don't you know that you are everything he despises in a female? Haven't you figured out yet that he has only been using you? He was willing to stomach your incessant advances and vulgar ways because it was cheaper than paying a prostitute but—"

Even as Io's hand flew, she knew that sinking to violence was a despicable reaction. But the look of shock on Edith's face and the rewarding sting on Io's palm were both worth the temporary loss of principle.

Edith shrieked and raised her hand to her red cheek. "You *animal!*"

"Violence is not the answer and I should not have hit you," Io said, unable to make herself say *I'm sorry.*

"You have shown yourself for the common *whore* that you are."

Io bristled and took a step toward the other woman, who stepped back so quickly she stumbled over her own feet. "I should not have hit you," she repeated. "But I do not regret it. Now, get out of my room before I deal with you the same way I would with any other vermin." Io punctuated her threat by stalking after Edith, backing her out of the room until she was standing in the corridor.

And still, Edith lingered. "This last half year with your family has been the most lowering of my life. I will be grateful to see the last of you and all your wretched siblings—and that includes your oldest brother. And if you think—"

Io slammed the door in her face, cutting off whatever bile was coming next. She had to admit it felt even more satisfying than the slap had.

Even though Edith was gone, her awful words lingered like a foul smell.

How had the other woman known about their Wednesday meetings?

No matter what Edith claimed, Io could not bring herself to believe that Corbin had told the other woman about Room 320. Nor could she believe that he would have said such awful things about her.

Edith had lied to her before—or at least twisted the truth until it was unrecognizable—there was no reason to believe she was not doing the same again.

Still, that did not answer the question of how Edith knew about their meetings.

Could she really be so vindictive that she would have had somebody *following* her?

You know she could be that vindictive and more, a dry voice said.

Yes, that was true. The woman had proven she had no limits when it came to manipulation. Io hated to think what Edith had learned about Apollo. As far as she was concerned, the sooner Edith left the country, the better it would be for all of them.

The one thing Io *could* believe was that Corbin was accompanying her back to New York. That was exactly the sort of antiquated chivalry he would exhibit.

But she refused to believe that he was planning to stay there. He would have told her if that was the case. She was sure of it.

A quick glance at the clock showed her that eight precious minutes had passed while she'd dithered.

If Io did not hurry, she would be late to her Wednesday meeting.

Chapter 28

Several Long Hours Later

asterson is not coming; you might as well just go home.

Io ignored the voice. Just as she had been ignoring it for the last five hours.

Evidently at least part of what Edith had said was the truth: Corbin was not coming to room 320 today.

Even so, Io couldn't make herself go home.

Instead, she curled up on the bed and shivered, the tears that she *never, ever* allowed to fall flowing freely.

Corbin was going back to New York. With Edith.

The words twisted in her belly like so many knives.

"That means nothing," she whispered to the empty room, grabbing herself by the scruff of the neck—metaphorically speaking—she said the next words aloud, too, "Corbin does not love Edith. I'm not even sure that he likes her anymore. I saw the way he flinched at Edith's words just this morning."

Perhaps. But she is a wealthy, well-bred woman. She could give him what you never thought to offer: money to do what he does best, rather than serve as a secretary for your brother.

"Corbin would never take money from her! Or from me, for that matter."

He would take money from his wife.

Io moaned. "Shut up," she muttered and shoved her face into a pillow.

Marriage. The bogeyman all her life. Her twin had always said she was the most contrary person alive. It seemed Bal was right, because why else would Io fall in love—yes, *love*, why bother to keep denying it—with Corbin Masterson? A man who would settle for nothing less than total and complete legal subjugation from any woman he allowed into his life.

Io: The Shrew

It doesn't matter how contrary you are; you love him. Will you make yourself miserable because you are a coward? the irksome voice taunted.

Because being in love worked out so well for me the last time.

What you felt for Lamar was not love. It was the infatuation of a girl.

Io lowered the pillow and considered that possibility as she stared at the canopy of the bed where she'd had so much pleasure.

When she tried to summon Lamar's face, the image was an indistinct blur. It seemed odd that she could recall so little of him because he had continued to live at Canoga—and take many new lovers—right up until the day Io and her siblings had moved away.

And her memories of him were vague, as well. What had they talked about? Had she teased him as she did Masterson? Somehow, she thought not.

Only scant snippets came back to her of their time together, and nothing from the end when she had been emotional and brokenhearted.

Had she loved him?

What does any of that matter now? *Because you surely love Corbin.*

Io groaned, her head pounding and her eyes burning.

Leave me alone.

She closed her eyes as if that would somehow block her own thoughts.

Was this really the way it would end between them? Was he *really* going to escort Edith all the way back to America and stay there?

If you want him, then you will need to do something. Soon.

"Leave me alone," she muttered, sleep tugging at her weary mind. "Just leave me alone…"

And that was the last thing Io remembered until she woke up to chaos the following morning.

***

Corbin had never been in jail before.

Thus far, he had occupied two cells. This second one—which he'd been moved to right before Hastings paid him a visit—was far nicer than the first, which had been dank, filthy, and infested with vermin, of both the human and animal sort.

It pained him to know that his friend had likely expended political capital getting him moved to a cleaner cell that he didn't need to share.

Still, he was grateful that Hastings had made the effort, especially considering how angry the duke was at Corbin at the moment.

"You did *what?*" the duke demanded—no, shouted.

"I confessed to the smuggling charges, Your Grace."

The duke leveled a long forefinger at Corbin, almost close enough to touch the tip of his nose. "Don't you *dare* Your Grace me right now, Corbin."

Corbin sighed. "Fine...*Zeus.*" If he'd expected his friend to smile at Corbin's first-ever use of his outlandish Christian name, he was sorely mistaken. He took a deep breath and said, "Io has been importing condoms. Evidently the man she purchased them from ignored customs duties to line his pockets."

Zeus's eyebrows shot up in disbelief. "And they have thrown you in jail and summoned a duke because of unpaid duties on condoms?"

Corbin winced at that. "I'm sorry to drag you into this."

"My *sister* dragged me into this. Tell me the rest," he barked.

"It seems the man who Io was dealing with, Branson, used the condoms as a cover to smuggle weapons."

Zeus groaned and dropped his head in his hands. Corbin felt sorry for him, but then remembered his friend had recently liberated himself from Edith Barrymore, and then he did not feel so bad.

Corbin doubted that now would be the time to congratulate the other man on his narrow escape.

"They cannot believe you purchased weapons?" Zeus said.

"I don't think so. I think they are hoping I will provide them with solid evidence to flush out Branson and his cohorts."

"Can you?"

Io: The Shrew

"I know nothing about all of this. I wouldn't have even known the man's name if they'd not dropped it while interrogating me."

Zeus raised an eyebrow. "Interrogating?"

"Don't worry, they didn't get out the thumbscrews."

"Good. That means it will be all the more painful when I use them on you." His eyes narrowed. "Don't think I have forgotten what you have evidently been up to with my sister. For months. Under my very nose."

It was Corbin's turn to wince. He decided that the truth would be the best defense. "I love her."

Zeus inhaled deeply and when he exhaled, he seemed to expel all his anger along with the air. "I know you would not trifle with her." He snorted. "Indeed, I should probably be worried about *your* virtue."

Corbin smiled sadly. "You probably should, because she will never marry me, Zeus."

"Must you call me that, too?" His Grace of Hastings begged in a very unducal way.

"The name suits you," Corbin said. "*John* was never a big enough name for a man as impressive as you… Your Grace."

The duke blushed. "I will not forget this."

Corbin snorted as he glanced around the cell. "I doubt I will, either."

"I will have to bring Io in—she will need to give them her statement."

Corbin sat up straighter. "Absolutely not. I forbid it."

Zeus smirked at that. "I appreciate you trying to protect her, but they know she is involved. The only reason they did not take her, was out of courtesy to me."

"Damnit! I don't want her in a place like this, Zeus."

"Too bad," the duke shot back coolly. "So, where is she?"

Corbin frowned. "But I thought you knew about—"

"I know you've been meeting, but my *source* would not tell me where."

"Who is your source?"

"That is none of your concern," Zeus said icily.

Corbin sighed. "She is at Boynton's Hotel. Room 320."

Chapter 29

Thursday

*T*hud, thud, thud.

"What is it?" Io yelped as she bolted upright with a start and blinked groggily around her, more than a little disoriented.

Oh, she thought after a moment. *I'm still in room 320.*

And light was streaming between the gaps in the drapes.

She had fallen asleep.

Thud, thud, thud.

"Io, dammit! Open the door!" a muffled angry male voice shouted.

"Corbin?" Io scrambled from the bed, catching her foot in the counterpane in her haste and falling to the floor with a squawk. "I'm coming, Corbin!" she shouted, freeing her foot with some effort before limping across the room. She flung open the door. "I knew you'd—" Her face fell. "Oh. It's you."

"I am so sorry to disappoint you," Zeus said coolly.

"Er—"

"May I come inside, or must we have this conversation in the corridor, Io?" he asked, looking and sounding every inch the Duke of Hastings from the toes of his expensive black leather shoes to the top of his high-crowned beaver hat.

Io turned away and shuffled into the room without answering. Behind her, she heard a soft *snick* as the door shut.

"Why are you limping?" he asked.

"It's nothing," she muttered, and then dropped onto the settee.

Zeus removed his hat, set it aside, and then stripped off his gloves one finger at a time, his eyes glacial.

Io rolled her eyes. "Oh, please, Zeus. Must you? I already know I'm in trouble for not coming home."

He threw his gloves into his hat and came to stand over her, looming.

"You are hurting my neck. Just sit. Please," she added at the last moment. After all, he was a duke, a fact which had probably gone to his head.

An uncomfortable moment passed before he lowered his long body into the chair across from her.

"You are angry," she said.

"That is one word for it."

"I suppose Edith told you where I was. I'm just surprised it took her so long to tittle-tattle."

"Then you would suppose *wrong*."

She sat up straighter, hope leaping in her chest. "Corbin told you? Then where is—"

"An agent from British Customs told me."

Io's jaw sagged. She lowered her voice, "Is—is it against the law to have"—at the last moment she changed *sex* to something less offensive— "er, carnal relations outside wedlock?"

Zeus stared. If his eyes got any frostier it would start snowing inside the room. "Your illicit meetings with my friend are not why they have taken Corbin into custody," he said in a withering tone.

"Corbin is in jail?"

Zeus winced. "Please modulate your voice. It is still possible that not everyone in London knows my secretary has been arrested for smuggling."

"*What?*" she shrieked, not caring how hard her brother winced. "What in the world are you talking about?"

"Evidently," he said icily, "it is *you* they should have arrested."

Io's mind raced and it didn't take long to reach the finish line. "They threw him in jail for importing *condoms*? The last time I checked that was not illegal. As for the custom duties, that is the responsibility of—"

"Your associate, Mr. Branson," Zeus finished for her.

"Yes, exactly. If anyone is to blame, it is Branson."

Io: The Shrew

"You are correct about the duties. Unfortunately, that is not all Branson was dealing in, Io. He was using *your* shipment of condoms as a cover for far more nefarious business."

Io briefly squeezed her eyes shut before she forced herself to ask. "What?"

"Weapons."

"Oh, God."

"Indeed."

She forced herself to meet his gaze. "And you say he is in jail?"

"Correct."

She swallowed and then forced her face into a humble expression— not her forte by a long shot. "Can't you talk to them and convince them he is innocent, Zeus?"

"I have already spoken to the men holding him." A scowl settled on his handsome face. "Regrettably, Mr. Masterson had already muddied the waters so badly they have refused to let him go, regardless of my appeals."

"What do you mean he muddied the waters?"

"By *confessing*," Zeus hissed, anger finally flaring in his gaze, but melting none of the ice.

"Confessing? But *why*?"

"To protect you, Sister. Corbin is in jail and facing a very long jail sentence for *you*."

***

Io crossed her arms as she stared up at the man in the cheap, ill-fitting suit. "I won't answer another question without seeing Mr. Masterson.

The agent—Elder, his name was—looked at his partner, Carver. Whatever he saw on the other man's face made him nod. "Fine," he said, fixing Io with a hard look that was no doubt meant to terrify her. "You can have five minutes—"

"Fifteen minutes."

Elder looked as if he was going to fly across the scarred table that separated them and strangle her. Io was well-familiar with that look, having seen it on so many peoples' faces over the course of her life.

289

Behind her, Carver sighed heavily. "Fine. Fifteen," he said, strolling out from behind her chair, where he'd been standing since she'd taken her seat. She assumed it was meant to make her nervous so that she would break down sobbing and confess to anything they wanted.

Instead, it had irritated her and stiffened her resolve to give them nothing, her only words repeated demands to see Corbin.

Carver leaned a hand on the table and bent until his eyes met hers. "But once the fifteen minutes are over, you will tell us *everything* about Branson and agree to help us in an operation to bring down his smuggling operation."

Io brightened. "An operation? Yes, of course! I will be happy to do that. I already have a pistol in my satchel and—"

"No pistol!" they both said in unison.

Io glared at the men. "I was only trying to be helpful. So," she said after a few seconds passed and they said nothing. "Are you going to fetch Mr. Masterson now or are we going to engage in yet another contest of wills? Because I still recall how your last one with my brother ended."

Scowling, they turned and stormed from the room, slamming the door behind them.

Io grinned to herself as she relived the memory of Zeus and how masterful and ducal he'd been when they had arrived at the Customs Office.

"Out of courtesy and a desire to help, Lady Io has agreed to speak to you," he'd said in a quiet voice laced with menace. Then he had loomed over Carver. "If you harm a hair on her head you will discover that the retribution of an English dukedom will feel like the sting of a gnat when compared to the ire of an American brother. Additionally, I took the liberty of sending word to my dear friend the Duke of Axbridge before coming here. Should it be necessary, he stands ready to vouch for my character, that of my sister, *and* Mr. Masterson."

Carver's harsh craggy face had blanched at the name *Axbridge* and only a subtle nudge from Zeus had kept Io from laughing.

She had been so proud of her brother! He'd turned out so nicely. And to think a mere half a year ago she'd despaired of him ever becoming human.

Io: The Shrew

The door opened, interrupting her private celebration.

"Corbin!" She scrambled up from her chair and threw herself into his arms, which closed around her like iron bands.

"I am going to spank you so hard you won't be able to sit for a week," he growled in her ear.

Io laughed and reluctantly released him just enough to pull back and see his face. "Is that a promise…Mr. Masterson?"

Corbin snorted. "You can take that to the bank, you vixen."

Io gazed into his tired gray eyes, her humor dimming. "I am so terribly sorry to have dragged you into this, darling."

He pushed a lock of hair off her brow, his eyes consuming her, as if he'd not seen her for a month instead of just yesterday morning. "And I'm sorry I wasn't there to meet you last night. Zeus told me you did not come home."

"I kept hoping you would have a change of heart and show up, so I waited. And then I fell asleep," she sheepishly admitted.

"Poor darling." He cupped her cheek, his look so tender it squeezed her heart.

"I have told the men who arrested you that I will give them a statement and all the information I have on Branson, but only after I spoke to you." Io chewed her lip, debating mentioning the part about the secret operation, and deciding against it given how stuffy Corbin could get about such things.

He slid his knuckle under her chin and forced her to meet his gaze. "What are you keeping from me?"

"Er—"

"Io." He raised a dark blond brow.

Io sighed. "They also want me to help them bring Branson into custody."

"Absolutely not! That is out of the question."

"I will be utterly safe. You can even come along—I will make that a term of our agreement."

He eyed her steadily. "Is that *all* or is there more waiting to surprise me?"

"That is all. Once I write out my statement, we should be free to go." Io caressed his stubbly jaw with her palm. "Mmm, so virile," she murmured. She had never seen him so disheveled before. If not for his current predicament she would have enjoyed this more rugged version of her normally polished lover.

Corbin snorted and reached up to feel his other cheek, grimacing at the rasping sound his hand made. "I am eager to get home and wash off the stink of this place."

Io knew it was neither the time nor place, but she could contain herself no longer. "Edith said you were leaving with her and not coming back here. She said you'd only ever planned to stay a year in Zeus's employ." She bit her lip. "She said uglier things, too—about us."

Corbin gave her an exasperated look. "I cannot believe you would listen to a word Edith Barrymore said."

"So then it isn't true and you aren't going?"

"No, that part is true. I am going back to New York City."

"Can't Zeus send somebody else to act as nurserymaid to her? Does it have to be you?"

"I am not going because of Miss Barrymore—that is just a favor I am grateful I can do your brother. I am going because I promised Lizzy that I would return in a year. Although a year is not up, I have decided I don't want to wait any longer."

"So…you are not coming back, then?" Io felt like the lowest of creatures being jealous of a child.

He eyed her with sudden coolness. "Your life will be so busy that I doubt you will even miss me."

Io's jaw dropped. "*What?* Of course, I would miss you. How could you—" She stopped when a tiny smile tugged at his stern lips. "Corbin, are you *toying* with me?"

The faint smile turned into a distinct smirk. "Perhaps a little."

"You beast!" She struggled to get away from him, but he held her easily.

"Stop squirming," he murmured, his expression suddenly tender. "You must know I would never leave you, Io—not for long."

"So you *are* coming back?" She was so jumbled up inside that she was unable to keep a tear from falling.

"What is this?" Corbin asked, looking alarmed. "Tears? From *you*?"

"What? You didn't think I could cry?" she snapped.

"No. I thought only venom came out of your tear ducts, my darling viper."

Io gave a watery laugh. "Bal told you that, didn't he?"

Corbin laughed, the rare sound intoxicating. "It might have been your brother who mentioned it."

"Traitorous twin. So then what is your plan?"

"I will collect Lizzy and we will come back here. I have already told Hastings that she will be living with me and he kindly offered us a suite of rooms." He pulled an almost sheepish face. "It is not the first time your brother has tried to help me in such a way, but this time… well, this time I will put aside my pride and accept his generosity."

"What if I were to go with you?" Io blurted.

When he just stared, Io tried to inject some levity. "After all, you will need somebody to protect you from Edith's machinations."

Corbin hesitated only a second before saying, "I would like that, Io."

She could guess the reason for his reserve and decided it was her turn to toy with him a little. "I would not go as your lover, Corbin."

The pain that spasmed across his normally inscrutable features gutted her. "I shouldn't have teased on such a subject. What I meant is that I would go as your wife. If you want to marry me that is."

The hope in his eyes was almost as agonizing to behold as the pain had been, as if he didn't dare be happy. His lips parted. "Are you—I mean, marrying you is my dream come true. But is this really what you want? Are you sure?"

"I am sure about *you*, Corbin. As for the institution of marriage?" Io shrugged. "I will just have to trust you, won't I?"

He nodded somberly. "I wish I could change the laws for you, darling, but what you say is true. You *will* have to take my word that I will never control or inhibit your actions or beliefs. I swear to you right now."

"Even if I want to bring cases of condoms into the country and hand them out at tea parties?"

He smiled. "Even then." His expression became stern. "I have one condition that I would like your word on. It is one I will not budge on."

"What is it?" she asked warily.

"I insist that you bring me with you when you visit dangerous men in the worst parts of town—or jeopardize your safety in any way. I promise not to interfere in any way and I will stand by you when you venture out to spread your message. I might not hand out any pamphlets personally, but I will protect your right to do so. I swear that on everything that is sacred to me. I just do not want you hurt in the process."

"Of course, I can agree to that."

"Are you *sure*? It will mean me tagging along with you."

"I am sure." She frowned when she saw a shadow fall across his eyes. "What is it? There is something else?"

"I know you do not want children, but Lizzy is—"

"I never said I didn't want children."

He blinked. "Er—"

"I said I did not want to be some man's broodmare. As for Lizzy, I look forward to having her with us, Corbin. How could you think otherwise?" she asked, pained that he would believe such a thing.

"I'm sorry, love. I didn't mean to hurt you. I only meant that most people do not start off their marriages with a child—it is something that usually comes later."

"Bal married a woman who has a son," Io retorted.

"That is true," he soothed, and then suddenly smiled. "Lizzy will be over the moon when she learns the mind behind *Lizzy Takes Charge* is to be her new mama. I hope you are prepared to endure a great deal of hero—er, heroine—worship. Not to mention that you will have to tell her all your new stories before you launch them out into the world.”

“That sounds wonderful, Corbin. And she won’t just have the two of us—she will have all my brothers and my sister, too.”

“I know. Your family is so generous and loving it shames me how I misjudged you at first. Will you ever forgive me, darling?”

She tapped her chin consideringly. “Perhaps after I have made you grovel a bit more.”

He laughed.

Io pulled him down and kissed him. “I have already forgiven you, you maddeningly wonderful man.”

“I am relieved to hear it. As for going to New York, if you want to come with me—and I hope you will—we will have to have a small wedding and very soon, sweetheart. The ship leaves just three days from now. But we can have a celebration once we return. At Hastings Park, if you’d rather, so that Lord Balthazar can attend.

“That sounds perfect. I’ve never wanted a large ceremony.” She paused and gave him a considering look. “Normally I would not cavil, but as I am now embarking down a more traditional, conservative, virtuous path”—she ignored his bark of laughter— “I don’t recall ever hearing a proposal from you, Mr. Masterson.”

“No. Surely I proposed?”

“You did not.”

His eyelids drooped. “Will you marry me my clever, beautiful temptress vixen harpy—”

“Corbin!”

“—my wicked green-eyed virago—”

“What sort of a proposal is that?” she demanded.

“—the other half of my heart and the love of my life?”

Io stopped glowering and gawked up at him, lips parted. “Oh.”

“Is that a *yes*, sweetheart?”

She nodded dumbly.

Corbin swooped down and kissed her soundly, his lips as firm and satiny as ever, but his scratchy bristles startling a gasp out of her.

Corbin pulled away and set his forehead on hers. "You have made me a very happy…person."

Io snorted. "And I promise that I will be a faithful, loving, and *obedient* wife."

As she'd hoped, Corbin threw his head back and laughed.

And then, the adorable man *mooed* at her.

Epilogue

Although Io and Corbin officially pledged their troth on a cold day in January, they both considered their real wedding day to be March twentieth, or 3-20 by the American calendar, a date they both believed to be an excellent omen for future happiness—if two such practical people were to believe in foolish things like omens or fate.

And yes, it just so happened to be a Wednesday.

Even though it was the middle of the Season, the duke had insisted they all return to Hastings Park for the celebration. To Corbin's surprise, his friend had no plans to return the family to the London residence.

"We can return next year and stay the entire time. I know we could all use some time to relax," was all Hastings would say when Corbin had inquired as to his change of plans.

He suspected part of the reason for Hastings's desire to return to the country was that the sudden dissolution of his betrothal to Miss Edith Barrymore had made life awkward for his friend in London.

In any event, it was a merry group who converged on Hastings Park to celebrate Corbin and Io's union on that chilly, but sunny, day in March.

The house party included not just relations, but new friends and many country neighbors who were delighted to have the leading family back home during a time of year when life was generally quite dull in the country.

Surprisingly, several others—like the Duke of Axbridge—had taken time away from the social whirl to come to Hastings Park.

While it was true that the majority of the guests were acquaintances of either the duke or Eva—the most gregarious of the Hales—Corbin had seen more than a few of Eva's friends casting shyly admiring looks at Io.

He suspected that his wife would soon have an even larger following among the daughters of the aristocracy than she could already claim.

Io and Corbin were not taking a wedding journey as they'd already had one—at least the journey *back* from New York with Lizzy, not the one out, with Edith.

The journey home—and part of him would probably always think of New York as home—had naturally been tense. Courtesy was more or less bred into his bones, but Miss Barrymore had strained his manners to the breaking point. Often. She had not made the journey easy, especially not for Io.

"Fortunately, I will have my delightful husband to soothe my ruffled feathers every day," Io had teased before they'd begun the long sea voyage. "And I shall have his body to take out my aggressions on every night."

Io had done that and more.

As enjoyable as the nightly sensual abuse had been, the days had been filled with a brittle courtesy that had snapped often over the course of the nine-day trip and Corbin had been relieved to hand Miss Barrymore over to the care of her uncle and aunt.

From New York City they had journeyed to the small town where Lizzy lived with her elderly caretakers.

Corbin had expected Lizzy to fall in love with Io, but his new wife's obvious delight in the girl had made him love her even more, which Corbin had not believed possible.

While he had looked forward to their delayed wedding party—and had greatly enjoyed himself today—he was glad when it was time to bid everyone goodnight and retire to the part of the castle that His Grace had granted Corbin and his small family.

"I know it is too much to ask you to call me *John* or even Zeus," the duke had said. "But please accept the use of my house—it is big enough for ten families. And I would be honored to share it. Besides, it would be nice to have my sister nearby for a little longer."

What else could Corbin say to such an offer?

"Zeus is beginning to grow on me," was all his wife would say when Corbin asked if she was content to live at the castle.

The day would likely come when Corbin and Io would want a house of their own, but neither of them were in any hurry.

Io: The Shrew

"Are you tired?" Io asked Corbin, who was carrying a very exhausted Lizzy. They had just left the drawing room, where their wedding party was finally beginning to wind down.

"Not in the least," Corbin said. "Are you?"

"No."

"I'm not tired either, Papa!" Lizzy piped up even though she could barely keep her eyes open. "I want to go to the Quarreling King with Uncle Ares."

Io and Corbin exchanged an amused look. "Uncle Ares is going to take you riding tomorrow—along with Uncle Pol," Io reminded her. "But you need to get some sleep tonight so that you can keep up with them."

"And will you come, too, Yoyo?" Lizzy asked, smiling shyly as she spoke his wife's pet name.

"Of course, I will. So will your Papa."

Lizzy had asked Io about names while they'd been aboard the ship.

"What should I call you?"

"What do you want to call me?"

"Should I call you *mama*?" Lizzy had asked, not looking entirely happy at the thought. After all, she still remembered her own mother.

"Why not just Io?"

Lizzy had looked delighted at the opportunity to call an adult by their Christian name.

But when they had arrived at Hastings Park and she'd heard Io's siblings call her Yoyo, she had been entranced by the nickname.

The rooms they'd chosen to use as the nursery were up three flights of stairs and Lizzy's eyelids had almost drifted shut by the time Corbin set Lizzy down on her bed.

"Are you leaving?" Lizzy asked, blinking up at them.

"It's time to get some sleep, darling. Give me and Yoyo a kiss," Corbin said.

Lizzy yawned, stretched her arms around Io's neck, and gave her a peck before kissing Corbin's cheek.

"She's tired," Corbin whispered to Nanny Bedford, who'd come bustling toward them as soon as they entered the room.

The older woman, whom Victoria, Balthazar's wife, had recommended, smiled. "Aye, I'll take care of her. Good night, sir, my lady."

"Good night, Nanny."

Once they'd slipped out of the nursery Corbin turned to his wife. "Did you enjoy the party?"

"Very much," she said, and then pulled a wry face. "Although I must admit I was ready for it to be over a few hours ago." She stifled a yawn and leaned on his arm more heavily. "What did my twin say to you earlier, after dinner, when the two of you were talking so seriously?"

"He just wanted to welcome me into the family," Corbin said, leaving out that Balthazar had also threatened to beat Corbin to a pulp if he ever hurt Io in any way.

The younger man had also shared some unhappy details of Io's relationship with Lamar Jacobsen in the process.

"Jacobsen broke her heart. She was so ill that we feared she would die." Raw emotion had throbbed in Balthazar's voice. He'd cleared his throat and continued in a more level tone. "I never thought she would trust herself enough to fall in love again. And I certainly never expected that she would marry."

Neither had Corbin.

"You don't regret not going to the King's Quarrel with all the others?" Io asked. *The others* being her siblings and many other guests, mostly younger, who had not yet had enough reveling.

"Not in the least," Corbin assured her. "I have other plans."

She laughed. "Why, Mr. Masterson, what could those be?"

He smirked and opened the door to their chamber. "You will soon find out."

"Ah, a feast! Just what I need after stuffing myself all day," Io mockingly said, gesturing at the table groaning with food. "I daresay this is Zeus's doing."

Io: The Shrew

Corbin plucked a grape off the astounding array of food and offered it to her first, popping it into his own mouth when she shook her head.

"Ugh. I cannot believe you are still eating, Corbin."

"I would rather be eating something else, but—"

"Mr. Masterson! Are you being naughty?"

"If you have to ask then I am doing a dreadful job of it."

"Mmm," she hummed wrapping her arms around his waist and nuzzling his neck. "You will just have to do better."

He laughed. "And let me guess—you *might* have a few suggestions?"

***

Io ran her hands up and down her husband's hard body. "First off, you have too many clothes on."

"On that, we agree."

The next few minutes were filled with the sound of unsexual grunting, muttering, a bit of torn clothing, and at least one button bouncing its way off the carpet across the wood floor.

Io had trained Corbin well and no longer had to bark, *"Condom,"* at her husband.

Indeed, he was sheathed and lying on his back before she could shimmy out of her far too elaborate wedding gown.

"No fair," she muttered as she climbed up onto the bed and straddled him.

"It was your idea," Corbin reminded her, lifting her by the hips and notching himself against her entrance.

He was referring to Io's thoughtless comment about whoever made it to the bed first—naked—would get to choose the position.

"I might want to renegotiate that," she complained, and then hissed as she slowly took his hard length into her body.

"You're just angry because you have to do all the work." He smirked up at her, his palms behind his head as she finished seating herself.

"And you're just smug because you get to be laz—" Io yelped as the room spun and she landed on her back.

"You were saying, my princess?" he mocked, slowly pulling almost all the way out before slamming into her hard enough to drive her up the bed.

Io moaned at the pleasure of being so stretched and filled, enjoying it for a moment before muttering, "Don't call me that."

Corbin laughed, withdrawing and then pinning her to the bed with another punishing thrust. "Mmm, what should I call you then?" he asked in a gruff voice, swiveling his hips in a way that gave her just the perfect amount of friction, exactly where she needed it. "My queen?"

Io gasped and then choked out, "All Knowing and Powerful Supreme Being will be sufficient."

Again, her husband laughed, his hips pumping faster and harder. "Rather a mouthful to shout at the moment of climax, don't you think?"

Io opened her mouth.

Before she could answer, Corbin lowered his lips to one of her breasts while his hand slid between their hips.

For some reason, Io's clever retort slid completely out of her head.

"Say it," Corbin hissed as he worked her relentlessly toward the precipice.

"*It.*"

A very un-Corbin-like guffaw burst out of him.

Just for that adorable sound, Io decided to give him what he wanted. "I love you, Masterson."

"You'd better," he growled.

And then he gave her exactly what she needed.

Not The End...

Second Epilogue

The King's Quarrel
That Same Evening

Apollo winced as Balthazar's wife—Victoria—who was playing against Ares, threw a dart that narrowly missed the pub window, which was a good six feet away from the bullseye.

At the next board, two giggling friends of Eva were playing doubles against two young men whose names he could not remember.

It had stunned Apollo how many people had come all the way from London to attend his sister and brother-in-law's celebration.

He knew that Io had not made that many acquaintances, nor had Masterson, who spoke as little in company as Apollo did.

He could only assume that most of the guests who'd come to the wedding hoped to bask in his brother Zeus's reflected glory.

They were bound for disappointment as Zeus was even less inclined to engage in frivolous socialization these days than he usually was.

Zeus was the only Hale—well, other than Io, who was with her new husband—who hadn't accompanied the group to the King's Quarrel after the festivities

Instead, his oldest brother had retired to his study with his august, starchy peer—in every sense of the word—the Duke of Axbridge. The two dukes had refused politely, but firmly, Ares's invitation to join the rest of them at the King's Quarrel.

Apollo had noticed that his oldest brother had been even quieter and more reserved since his own betrothal had ended. The shadows in his pale blue eyes hinted at pain that none of them would have suspected. Had he really loved Edith Barrymore? Or was there some other reason for his obvious unhappiness?

"I don't understand," Jamie, Balthazar's stepson, broke into Apollo's thoughts and he looked up from his half-empty pint.

Those in their group not playing darts sat around several tables that had been pushed together.

"What don't you understand, son?" Bal asked, wincing when his wife threw her last dart, yet again missing the board and almost spearing an unsuspecting pub patron in the back of the head.

Ares, her opponent, threw back his head and laughed.

Really, Apollo thought, his twin could celebrate a win regardless of the merit required. Anyone could see that Victoria had all the skills of a kitten when it came to the game.

Hopefully, Bal would avenge his wife's honor.

"It is just…" Jamie broke off. "Well, Aunt Io and Uncle Corbin kept talking about three-twenty, as if that meant today. But today is twenty-*three*."

Eva, who'd been chatting quietly about something with Miss Barclay, suddenly chimed in. "Maybe here it is, Jamie, but in America, it is the other way around."

"That makes no sense," Jamie insisted.

Apollo only half listened to his little sister try to explain why the calendar was different—a thankless task, in his opinion, as the American method was ridiculous. He studied Miss Susan Barclay beneath his lashes.

The woman had been Edith Barrymore's dogsbody for most of the time Apollo had known her. Only for the past two months had she been free of the harridan.

While her huge blue eyes had lost some of the haunted expression they'd always held, she now put him in mind of a garment that had been packed tightly and cruelly into a box that was too small and would only slowly return to its normal size. Even when it did, there would always be creases and marks to indicate the harsh handling it had once received.

Objectively, Miss Barclay was pretty. But there was something repellant about the fear that rolled off her—even now. She was damaged, maybe even irreparably broken by her time under her cousin's brutal yoke.

Apollo knew a few things about fear.

And he knew about how easily things broke, too.

Io: The Shrew

A hand clamped on his shoulder and shook him and Apollo looked up into his own face.

"Are you asleep, twin?" Ares teased.

"Are you finished thrashing a person who has never thrown a dart in her life?" he countered.

Undaunted by his scathing look, Ares grinned. "Is that a challenge?"

***

Susan Barclay sipped her shandy and tried to stay invisible. But Lady Evadne—or *Eva* as she tried to make Suki call her—would not let her. Although the younger woman was well-intentioned, Suki was grateful when Lord Balthazar interrupted their conversation, which was about how she should accept an entire wardrobe from Eva, her new employer.

"May I borrow my sister from you, Miss Barclay?" the huge lord asked with a gentle smile, his face so handsome that it made her blush just to look at him.

"Of course, my lord," Suki murmured.

"We will resume this conversation later," Lady Eva warned with a look of mock severity.

Suki smiled and nodded, exhaling a breath of relief when she was alone. A quick glance around the table showed that only Lord Apollo still sat at the table, and he was consumed by his own thoughts and not paying her any mind.

The brooding lord had livened up briefly while he'd beaten his twin at the dartboard earlier, but he'd been silent since returning to the table, although he, too, had given her a kind, if vague, smile.

All the Hales were lovely to her.

But only because they did not know who—or what, rather—she was.

Or at least not all of them.

Only the duke knew her horrible secret. Edith had made sure of that before she'd left London, furious when Suki had refused to go with her.

"Stay if you like," Edith had said, frost on her words. "But do not think I will leave you here without telling Hastings the truth about you." Fury had twisted Edith's beautiful face when she'd mentioned the name of the man who'd made it impossible for Edith to remain in London.

Suki knew that Edith loved living in England. She'd especially loved the prestige of being betrothed to not just the handsomest man in England, but probably the wealthiest. And kindest.

And Edith had lost him.

Suki could not help but celebrate that fact.

Edith had jerked her cold gaze back to Suki, as if she'd heard her thoughts. "I will tell Hastings the truth about you and you will soon find yourself back on the streets, earning your money the way you were before I rescued you. And if you think Lady Eva will protect you…" Edith had laughed cruelly. "You are even stupider than I have always thought. Hastings will not want a creature such as you to come anywhere near his *beloved little sister.*" Her lips twisted as she spat the last three words, confirming what Suki had long suspected: Edith was jealous of the affection growing between the duke and Lady Eva, the most affectionate of the Hale offspring.

For more than three years Suki had watched as Edith—who possessed beauty, wealth, prestigious connections, and a fiancé whom every woman in New York City and London envied—had poisoned the very air around her. Nothing was ever good enough, no person ever perfect enough, or even adequate, for Edith Barrymore.

The Duke of Hastings had not seen his fiancée's true reaction to the news that he had a family he had never met and that he wanted them all to accompany him to England.

Back then Edith had been too clever to show Hastings what she had really felt about his new siblings—raw fury—but Suki had not only witnessed Edith's wild-eyed rage, she had borne the brunt of it.

She had borne all Edith's ill will for far too long.

While it might be foolish, Suki had decided to take the opportunity to say one thing to her cousin before she had walked out of her lushly appointed chambers at Hastings House for the last time two months ago.

"You are right that you rescued me, Edith. And I loved you for it. At first. But my love was never enough for you. Nobody's love is—not even a man like His Grace—and now you are alone. Just like I was. I pray that whoever rescues *you* does so with more kindness."

Io: The Shrew

And then she had left her cousin with her mouth hanging open, holding her head high for the first time since that snowy December morning three years ago.

And here she was, living among kind, loving people. Under false pretenses.

Suki sipped her drink, relishing the lemony tang in the beer, and glanced around at the Hale siblings, her mind on one who was not there.

Edith had been wrong about one thing, at least. His Grace had not banished Suki from his home or family when he'd found out about her past.

He had called her to his study once Edith had left in a cloud of recrimination. As always, he'd risen when she entered and bade her to sit, not keeping her standing as Edith always had.

"You must know why you are here," he had said, not unkindly, but not with his usual warmth, either.

"Yes, Your Grace. Edith has told you about my past."

"Is what she said true?"

"I—I don't know, Your Grace. What did she say?" Suki had hoped beyond foolishness that maybe Edith had reconsidered at the last moment.

"That she found you working in a brothel."

What had remained of her hope had died then as she'd met his steady unreadable gaze.

But for once she had not cowered. "It is true."

Something flickered in his icy eyes. Disappointment? Disgust? Suki didn't know what and it was there and gone too quickly to identify.

"I have already packed my things and can leave directly," she'd said, ignoring the bone-grinding weariness that swept through her as she got to her feet.

Naturally, the duke stood when she did. "Please, Miss Barclay—a few more minutes of your time, if you would."

She sighed, wavering.

"Please. Sit," he said, his voice almost gentle.

And so Suki had sat.

"I am not throwing you from my house, ma'am."

She had blinked.

"Everyone deserves a second chance, Miss Barclay. I have known you for three years—since you began working for Miss Barrymore—and your behavior has been exemplary. You are welcome to stay in my employ as a companion to my sister, who has begged me to persuade you." His riveting eyes lost some of their reserve. "I am sure you are aware of Eva's persuasive abilities."

"I am, Your Grace. And I gratefully accept. As long as, well, as long as staying does not offend your sense of decency?"

"No, Miss Barclay. It does not."

And so here Suki was, free of her cousin's control and living in the house of Edith's former fiancé, the Duke of Hastings.

A man Suki had been secretly in love with from almost the first moment she had met him.

It was heaven to live under his roof—especially without Edith constantly shaming her in his presence.

But it was hell to know that Suki could never, ever have him.

***

"You seem… anxious, Eva?" Balthazar said as he pulled the darts from the board and handed them to her.

Eva took her mark and threw all three darts before answering her brother's question. "I am a little restless, I suppose."

"Because the Season ended so abruptly?"

"Partly," Eva admitted.

"I'm sure you could have stayed—Zeus would have made arrangements for you."

"He already offered but I wanted to come back here with him. He is hurting, Bal, even though he doesn't show it. And I also wanted to come here for Susan's sake."

"Taking her as your companion was very kind, Eva." Bal's gaze slid to the table where Susan sat alone, staring at the pub around her as if it were the most magical place she had ever been. Eva had noticed that the other woman looked at every place that way now that she was out from under the iron fist of her cousin.

"I want her to accept some clothing from me—just a few things—but she refuses, Bal."

He shrugged and turned to the dartboard. "Perhaps all she has left is her pride, Eva."

Eva considered that.

Pride. The deadliest of the seven sins.

A different face popped up in her mind's eye when she thought of pride—that of the Duke of Axbridge, a man who was rapidly becoming one of Zeus's closest friends.

Axbridge's face should be in the dictionary under the definition of pride.

Perhaps Eva would put a drawing of Axbridge in the lexicon of cant that she was compiling. She could use his proud image to define some common, vulgar term—something that would horrify and infuriate him when her dictionary was finally published.

Indeed, she could make up an awful definition just to plague him. An Axbridge: a haughty, disagreeable individual that people went out of their way to avoid.

Eva snorted.

Yes, she could call that sort of person an *Axbridge* and perhaps the term would make its way into common usage. Years from now she might be at a party somewhere and overhear somebody say, *so-and-so is such an Axbridge!*

Eva grinned to herself.

But of course she would do no such a thing.

Because—no matter how beyond the pale Axbridge seemed to think she was—all her life Eva had always done the decent or proper thing. Unlike Io, Eva had no beliefs that were so important to her that she would risk everything and everyone's regard to fight for them.

While she dearly wanted to be like her sister, the truth was that Eva was a coward. Unlike Io, who spoke her mind freely regardless of what others thought, Eva was…wishy-washy.

Wishy-washy. An excellent term dating from the late seventeenth century.

And a perfect word to describe her. She wanted people to like her too much to risk offending anyone.

Even Axbridge, who looked at Eva as if she were an insubstantial piece of fluff, his dark eyes judging and dismissive whenever they landed on her.

Eva knew she was fortunate, that people tended to like her because she liked them. And she was aware that she was pretty, which meant that some things—like attention and praise—came easier to her. Perhaps all that adulation had spoiled her?

That was certainly what Axbridge seemed to believe.

Her face burned just thinking about the words she had overheard him speak at her own birthday ball! And before she'd even met the man. Cruel words that were forever emblazoned in her mind.

Eva had been standing beside the wall of potted palms that Victoria—then Mrs. Dryden—had cunningly arranged to divide one section of the massive ballroom from another. Although the plants had looked like a wall, they were no barrier to what was being said on the other side.

"That elder Hale sister is beautiful," an arrogant male had proclaimed, the sound of Eva's last name instantly garnering her attention.

"She's a diamond," another voice agreed. "Unfortunately, she looks like the sort who would eat a man after mating him."

The others had laughed, and Eva had frowned, opening her mouth to remind them that they were in her family's ballroom, and she could hear them.

But then hearing her own name had stopped her.

"The younger one is nothing like her—except a bit in looks," a new voice said.

"She is a real darling," said the first voice. "Genuine, fresh, and innocent. It is hard to credit they both came from that commune."

"I agree," said yet another, making her wonder just how many men were loitering. "I'm not ashamed to say I asked Hastings if I might call on her when they come to London. He told me that his sister was in no hurry to marry. He then said that it was his sister's choice who called on her and that I should apply directly to her."

Eva recognized the voice now—it was the Earl of Gaston, whom she'd just danced with. He'd come to her birthday ball with two of his friends and they'd dressed as the three musketeers.

"Poor Gaston!" somebody teased.

"Thwarted at the starting block!" another voice jeered.

"I *will* ask her!" Gaston said, sounding harried as his friends laughed and ribbed him.

"What say you about these sisters, Axbridge?" the first voice asked. "You've spent some time around Hastings, haven't you?"

The Duke of Axbridge.

Eva knew who he was, of course. Zeus had introduced her to him earlier. He was one of the few men who'd not bothered with a costume, as if such a thing was beneath his dignity.

He was a contemporary of. her brother's and notable for being a handsome, unmarried duke and therefore a marital catch. He'd also been the man who'd danced with Io a scandalous *three* times earlier that evening. Eva couldn't believe her sister's audacity sometimes.

"I know Hastings, although not well," Axbridge drawled in his cold, haughty voice.

"What is Lady Eva like?"

"Lovely to look at, as is her sister. Both are also petted and coddled and overindulged. Any man who took one of them to wife would need a disciplined hand, a will of iron, and many years of patience to undo the damage inflicted by their bohemian upbringing."

The men laughed.

"I say, Axbridge. That is rather… harsh," Gaston protested—although not with much force.

"It may be harsh, but that does not make it any less true," Axbridge replied coolly. "Neither of them is worth the bother, in my opinion."

"Here you go, Eva. I'm sorry it took such an age," Io said.

Eva jolted at the sound of her sister's voice and blindly reached out to take the proffered glass of lemonade, feeling dizzy.

Io frowned. "Is something wrong, Eva?"

Just then the men on the other side broke up and several of them came around the foliage.

Gaston, who must have heard Io, went pale when he saw Eva, and then scurried away.

The duke pinned Eva with a hard look that seemed to last a hundred years—although it couldn't have been more than a few seconds—his dark eyes almost black, his angular face aloof and cold.

And then he turned away, somehow managing to make even *that* seem dismissive and insulting.

They know that I heard them talk about me. And Axbridge, at least, is glad.

"Eva?" Io repeated, "Are you ill?"

"No. I am fine," she'd lied, sick at his words and scathing look.

"Was that Axbridge just then?" Io asked, sipping her drink and glancing around.

"Yes."

"I wonder what made him look at us so coldly," Io mused and then laughed. "Even more coldly than usual, I should say."

"You know him a little, don't you?" Eva had heard herself ask.

Io had snorted. "Know him? I wouldn't say that. I just danced with him three times." A shadow passed over her sister's beautiful hazel eyes and then she muttered, "I might just ask him again before the night is through. I wonder how he would like *that*," she said, speaking under her voice.

"What did you say?" Eva had asked.

"Oh, nothing. I said I just met him."

"Then why did you dance with him three times?"

Io eyelids had lowered and then she'd said, "Mostly to avoid dancing with any of these simpering fools. And also because we both share a dislike of society."

"And was he…kind to you?"

"Kind? Axbridge?" Io laughed. "Hardly. He has told me that if I were his sister, he would beat me and lock me in my chambers until I learned to behave properly."

As that was not such an unusual male response to Io, Eva had not been especially surprised.

But what had *Eva* done to have Axbridge judge her so harshly? She was polite, courteous, respectful, and ladylike.

"Doesn't it bother you that he is so…disapproving?" Eva had persisted.

"He's a peer of the realm—a duke, for pity's sake. He cannot help himself. Being disapproving of American upstarts is as natural to him as conquering the globe and riding to hounds." Io had chortled, but then frowned when Eva hadn't joined her. "What is it, darling? Please tell me you are not allowing these arrogant jackasses to get under your skin?"

"No…no, of course not," Eva had said.

But, for weeks, whenever she saw Axbridge—which wasn't just at functions but also at Hastings House as he and Zeus came to know each other—she had felt the same unease, no matter how she'd chastised herself. *Not everyone will like you, Eva. The same way you do not like everyone.*

True, but she didn't *loathe* anyone. Not even Edith. Well, at least she hadn't until the woman had gone after Apollo that day.

Eva had been startled when Axbridge had come to partake in Io and Corbin's celebration. She'd been even more flummoxed to see her sister laughing and chatting with the haughty duke earlier that day—as if they were dear friends. But then, Eva reasoned, Io *would* find such a stern, implacable man amusing considering that her new husband was nearly as severe and proper as Axbridge, although not even half so arrogant.

"Eva?"

She looked up at Bal's voice and realized she'd frozen, a dart in her hand.

"Is aught amiss, Eva?" he asked, concern evident on his handsome face.

She forced a smile and made it convincing. "Nothing at all," she said with a grin, and then turned to the board.

And if Eva imagined Axbridge's handsome, sneering face instead of a bullseye, who did it hurt?

The End

Dearest Reader:

Three books published in three months!! If I wasn't crazy going into it, I'm crazy now, lol.

This book…ah, this book was a roller coaster…

First, I thought I'd never finish it.

Second, I thought it should be a novella.

Third, I started writing it (as a novella) and it took over and made itself into a novel.

When I originally started the book several months ago it immediately grew into a historical romance novel that was very heavy on the *historical* part. The romance began to get lost as I got caught up in researching the history of reproductive rights.

I was sitting at about 65 pages and the romance had barely even begun.

So, then I decided I didn't have the time to either keep going with that approach nor scrap it and start over. I decided I'd just have to postpone the book.

As soon as I made the decision to postpone the book, it seemed to free up my brain and I came up with the novella concept.

I talked it out with author pal Jeffe Kennedy who really liked my idea—basically to keep the story very focused on the couple—and then I did something I've never done before and wrote an extremely detailed outline FOR EVERY CHAPTER OF IO! Yes, I really did. And it made me feel high, lol.

So then I started writing the "novella" but this story just did not want to stay small, even though I kept the focus super tight on Io and Corbin.

Anyhow, although I had to scrap everything I had and start over from scratch the story came out without hardly any effort, which was lovely, and it also hewed very closely to my outline (which was freaking amazing! Maybe I'll write another one some day??)

So, there is the long, twisted tale of *Io: The Shrew*.

There are hundreds of books on reproductive rights—mostly without romance, lol—so if you want to explore the 19th century life of the condom (and a great deal more), there is no shortage of reading material.

Next to the character Hyacinth (from my book HYACINTH) Io has been the easiest heroine I've written to date. And Corbin is the sort of hero that I just love—buttoned down on the outside, but a hot, passionate sexy alpha when you get to know him.

Sometimes it is difficult (for me) to get my characters to talk to each other, but Io and Corbin never had any shortage of things to say—or argue about. That made writing their story both fun and easy.

Like my **BELLAMY SISTERS** series, **THE HALE FAMILY SAGA** stories all overlap to a certain degree. This makes some of the storytelling tricky.

My husband, who is always my first reader, kept asking me to tell him more about certain parts of the story—like why the hell is Zeus engaged to Edith!?—and I had to keep telling him, "Sorry, honey, but that isn't something the reader gets to discover until Zeus's book."

In any case, after this book, the rest of the 4 Hale stories won't overlap timewise quite as much, although—especially in Zeus's case—I will need to dig into some backstory.

But that is for next year!

As you can tell from that Second Epilogue, I haven't decided who gets the next book. Who do you think should be next? All four of the Hales are clambering to tell their stories. The only character who I didn't give a POV in the Second Epilogue—Ares—is the one I've written the most on. The author brain is a messy, messy place.

As usual when I am writing like crazy and under deadline I have at least 2 new book ideas and this time was no different. I got the idea for another **VICTORIAN DECADENCE** story that I am DYING to write!! Unfortunately, I'm "booked up" for the next year, so it's unlikely there will be any deviations from my schedule (but you never know!)

A VERY BELLAMY CHRISTMAS is next on my schedule—in September—and I've already started on that and am really enjoying myself.

I've just sold the series to both a German publisher and an audiobook publisher, so there are officially 7 books in that series.

Anyhow, I hope you enjoyed **Io: The Shrew** and please do reach out and weigh in on which story you'd like to read next. I DO listen to requests.

I always love to receive reader emails: minerva@minervaspencer.com

Have a great summer my lovely readers!

Take care and happy reading.

Xo

SM/Minerva

Who are Minerva Spencer & S.M. LaViolette?

Minerva is S.M.'s pen name (that's short for Shantal Marie) S.M. has been a criminal prosecutor, college history teacher, B&B operator, dock worker, ice cream manufacturer, reader for the blind, motel maid, and bounty hunter. Okay, so the part about being a bounty hunter is a lie. S.M. does, however, know how to hypnotize a Dungeness crab, sew her own Regency Era clothing, knit a frog hat, juggle, rebuild a 1959 American Rambler, and gain control of Asia (and hold on to it) in the game of RISK.

Read more about S.M. at: www.MinervaSpencer.com

Follow 'us' on Bookbub:

Minerva's BookBub

S.M.'s Bookbub

On Goodreads

Minerva's OUTCASTS SERIES

DANGEROUS

BARBAROUS

SCANDALOUS

THE REBELS OF THE *TON:*

NOTORIOUS

OUTRAGEOUS

Io: The Shrew

<u>INFAMOUS</u>

<u>AUDACIOUS (NOVELLA)</u>

THE SEDUCERS:

<u>MELISSA AND THE VICAR</u>

<u>JOSS AND THE COUNTESS</u>

<u>HUGO AND THE MAIDEN</u>

VICTORIAN DECADENCE: (HISTORICAL EROTIC ROMANCE—
SUPER STEAMY!)

<u>HIS HARLOT</u>

<u>HIS VALET</u>

<u>HIS COUNTESS</u>

<u>HER BEAST</u>

<u>THEIR MASTER</u>

<u>HER VILLAIN</u>

THE ACADEMY OF LOVE:

<u>THE MUSIC OF LOVE</u>

<u>A FIGURE OF LOVE</u>

<u>A PORTRAIT OF LOVE</u>

<u>THE LANGUAGE OF LOVE</u>

<u>DANCING WITH LOVE</u>

<u>A STORY OF LOVE*</u>

Io: The Shrew
A SECOND CHANCE FOR LOVE (A NOVELLA)

ANTHOLOGIES:

THE ARRANGEMENT